T0038580

WARBOUND

Book III
of the Grimnoir Chronicles

BAEN BOOKS by LARRY CORREIA

NOIR ANTHOLOGIES (EDITED WITH KACEY EZELL)
Noir Fatale
No Game for Knights
Down These Mean Streets

THE MONSTER HUNTER INTERNATIONAL SERIES
Monster Hunter International
Monster Hunter Vendetta
Monster Hunter Alpha
The Monster Hunters (compilation)
Monster Hunter Legion
Monster Hunter Nemesis
Monster Hunter Siege
Monster Hunter Guardian (with Sarah A. Hoyt)
Monster Hunter Bloodlines

MONSTER HUNTER MEMOIRS
The Monster Hunter Files (anthology edited with Bryan Thomas Schmidt)
Monster Hunter Memoirs: Grunge (with John Ringo)
Monster Hunter Memoirs: Sinners (with John Ringo)
Monster Hunter Memoirs: Saints (with John Ringo)
Monster Hunter Memoirs: Fever (with Jason Cordova)

THE SAGA OF THE FORGOTTEN WARRIOR
Son of the Black Sword
House of Assassins
Destroyer of Worlds
Tower of Silence

THE GRIMNOIR CHRONICLES
Hard Magic
Spellbound
Warbound

DEAD SIX (WITH MIKE KUPARI)
Dead Six
Swords of Exodus
Alliance of Shadows
Invisible Wars (omnibus)

Gun Runner (with John D. Brown)
Target Rich Environment (short story collection)
Target Rich Environment, Vol. 2 (short story collection)
Servants of War (with Steve Diamond)

To purchase any of these titles in e-book form, please go to www.baen.com.

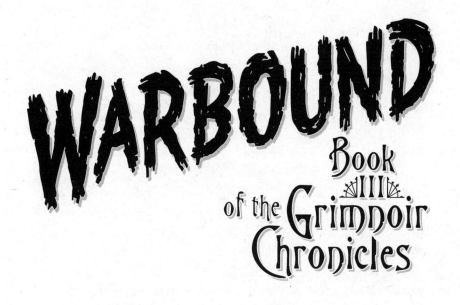

WARBOUND

Book III
of the Grimnoir
Chronicles

LARRY CORREIA

BAEN

WARBOUND: BOOK III OF THE GRIMNOIR CHRONICLES

This is a work of fiction. All the characters and events portrayed in this book are fictional, and any resemblance to real people or incidents is purely coincidental.

Copyright © 2013 by Larry Correia

All rights reserved, including the right to reproduce this book or portions thereof in any form.

A Baen Books Original

Baen Publishing Enterprises
P.O. Box 1403
Riverdale, NY 10471
www.baen.com

ISBN: 978-1-9821-9334-8

Cover art by Alan Pollack
Interior Art by Zachary Hill
Glossary Art by Justin Otis and Aura Farwell

First printing, August 2013
First mass market printing, May 2014
First trade paperback printing, April 2024

Distributed by Simon & Schuster
1230 Avenue of the Americas
New York, NY 10020

Library of Congress Control Number: 2013006715

Printed in the United States of America

10 9 8 7 6 5 4 3 2 1

To Joe

ᴁ Acknowlegements ᴁ

Thanks to Reader Force Alpha for the comments,
advice, and corrections; Mike Kupari for brainstorming
Grimnoir into existence; Justin Otis and Aura Farwell
for the glossary art; Zachary Hill for the interior artwork;
and the awesome staff of Baen Books for all that they do.

⚜ Prologue ⚜

I cannot accept your canon that we are to judge Wizard and Pope and King unlike other men, with a favourable presumption that they can do no wrong. If there is any presumption it is the other way, against the holders of power, increasing as the power increases. Power tends to corrupt, and absolute power corrupts absolutely. Great men are almost always bad men, even when they exercise influence and not authority, still more when you superadd the tendency or the certainty of corruption by authority. History shows the greatest names are coupled with the greatest crimes.

—Lord John Dalberg-Acton,
The Rambler, 1885

Xinjiang, China
1887

THE PATHFINDER was close.

Okubo could sense its unnatural presence lingering in the air. The gates of the fort lay broken open before him. Several of his scouts had gone inside to investigate, but he already knew what they would report. There would be no sign of survivors. The visible gatehouse told him a too-familiar story, no bodies, only drying puddles of blood, unidentifiable scraps of meat, and stained fabric whipping in the desert wind.

The horse beneath him shifted, protesting, not wanting to get any closer to the dangerous scent. Animals seemed to be able to sense the Enemy long before men could, but that difference no longer mattered. Even those without the slightest inkling or familiarity with magic could feel the wrongness in this place. The entire desert stunk of corruption.

1

It would not be long now. Their pursuit would end shortly, with what Okubo could only hope would be a battle worthy of legend.

The man astride the horse next to him spoke politely. "You seem particularly intense this afternoon, my lord."

"Looking inside my mind again, Hattori?"

"Of course not." Hattori answered. "Attempting to listen to your thoughts would be insulting."

"Indeed..." Okubo nodded in agreement, not that he was worried about a mind reader stealing his secrets. He had already demonstrated on more than one occasion that attempting such a thing had terrible consequences. In fact, an attempt had been made by a Qing spy only a few days before. The man had been subtle in the ways of magic, but when Okubo had sensed the intrusion, he had surged his own Power and ruptured vessels in the spy's brain so forcefully that blood had squirted from the man's ears. "Insulting, and sometimes fatal."

"Of course. That too." Hattori chuckled. "I do not need magic to know what is on your mind when your concerns are so plain to see upon your brow."

"I will have to work on that," Okubo stated. A warrior had to control his public face at all times. To display anything other than complete control was a weakness, and weakness was the one thing that Okubo could not accept. "Yes, Hattori, only a fool would not be concerned. Soon we will find this invader, and the outcome of our struggle will determine the fate of the entire world. I do not fear death, but I will not tolerate failure."

Passing his horse's reins to his subordinate, Okubo slid from the saddle with practiced grace. He knelt next to one of the huge red stains in the sand. Having fought in countless battles, Okubo was exceedingly familiar with blood and could usually estimate how long ago it had been spilled. "We are only a few hours behind it."

"I believe you are correct." Due to his criminal background, Hattori was also no stranger to blood, most of it shed in the darkened back alleys of Edo by flashing knives. Hattori had once been an honorless collector of debts and inflictor of violence, but Okubo had still recruited the young man into the Brotherhood of the Dark Ocean. Okubo did not care what station his warriors had been born into, only that they were useful, and Hattori was extremely useful. "The gap has closed. We are gaining on it."

Okubo heard his warriors returning from the fort. They were silent as ghosts, but Okubo had no difficulty hearing ghosts either. He did not bother to look up. "So it is like the others?"

"No bodies," the lead scout, Shiroyuki, reported. "Just like every village along its trail. The entire garrison is missing, at least a hundred soldiers. The armory has been stripped of rifles and ammunition."

Hattori spoke. "Judging from the tracks leaving the other villages, the creature has recruited a force of at least a thousand men."

Okubo nodded. Hattori was forgetting the women and children. The Pathfinder did not care. It could manipulate all flesh.

"Pathetic," said the other scout, Saito. Like Okubo, he was a former member of the samurai caste. Saito had once been an officer of the shogunate. There were new fabric patches sewn onto his clothing, hiding where his clan insignia had once been worn proudly. Some of Dark Ocean's members had sacrificed much in order to follow Okubo's grand vision. "Conscripting villagers over a few days does not make an army. I'm not worried about peasants."

"They will not be peasants anymore." Okubo shook his head. No matter how brave his men were, they could not understand the horrors Okubo had witnessed the last time such a creature had walked the earth. "It will shape their flesh and control their minds. They are nothing but tools for the beast now. We may not even recognize them as men."

"Lord Okubo is correct," said Shiroyuki. "The footprints are odd. The bare feet especially, as if they are changing as they walk. The first gathered, they are more like animal tracks—"

Okubo held up one hand to silence the warrior. "Do not speak of this to the others."

"But the men of Dark Ocean fear nothing!" Saito shouted.

"Of course. I picked them because they are the strongest there is, and I made them stronger. There is no need to trouble their thoughts before this fight. Man or not, the Enemy's slaves can still die. That is all that matters." Okubo adjusted his armor and climbed back into the saddle. "If we ride hard we can intercept the creature before it reaches Yining."

Saito looked to the sky. There was not much daylight remaining. "Is it wise to fight it in the dark?"

Okubo scowled. "It is not *wise* for men to fight an alien god at any time, but that does not change our duty."

Saito, clearly realizing that he had just committed a terrible breach of etiquette by daring to question his superior's decision, bowed deeply.

Okubo could respect his subordinate's caution, but the more lives the Pathfinder consumed, the stronger it would become, especially if it found anyone else with magic it could turn against them. The only reason he'd been able to defeat the last creature was because it had arrived in such an unpopulated area. Giving it access to more time, more lives, and potentially more forms of Power, could prove disastrous. The others could not comprehend the madness that awaited them if the creature grew strong enough to send a message back to its creator.

"We must catch the Pathfinder before it reaches that city. It must be stopped at all costs. If we die in the process, then so be it, but let them speak of our deaths with reverence for generations to come."

Okubo had faced this sort of creature once before, back during the decades he had taken to calling his wandering time.

He had been the first that the Power had chosen as a vessel in this world, and his sudden, uncontrollable abilities had been a cause of political embarrassment. He had been cast out of his family, his name—Tokugawa—stripped away. Once free of his homeland, he had taken upon himself the name Okubo, in honor of a friend who had argued, despite considerable personal risk, against his banishment. As a masterless swordsman he had traveled the world, first across Asia, and then Europe and Africa, and finally even the distant Americas, selling his skills to whichever petty warlord made the most interesting offer. The wandering time had helped him explore his strange new magic and introduced him to others that shared his burdens. As the years had passed, the Power had chosen more vessels, and he had found more and more people like himself, none as strong, a few close, but all useful to learn from.

It was during one of the many minor wars he'd participated in that he'd first come across one of the creatures. It was as foreign to this world as the Power itself. His magic had given him an instinctive fear of the new arrival. The Power actually feared the creature. It was a predator, and anyone with magic was its prey.

Yet, even as impressive and dangerous as it was by itself, the creature was merely a scout for a much greater being. If not eliminated quickly, it would alert its master to the presence of magic here on this world. Okubo began to think of the creature as a pathfinder of sorts, blazing a trail for its master. If the master followed, everyone with magic would be destroyed in the ensuing feeding frenzy, and the Power would flee this world as it had fled other worlds before. The Enemy would leave the Earth as nothing more than a lifeless husk.

The presence of such a profound threat had given Okubo the Wanderer a purpose, and he had become Okubo the Hunter. He had been alone and unprepared when he'd caught the first Pathfinder in the remains of a desolate village in the heart of Africa. The encounter had nearly cost him his life, but he had come away more experienced and with the sure knowledge that more of the creatures would come in the future.

That first confrontation had proven that he was the strongest warrior in history, but there was strength in numbers. So he had set out to build himself an army. Okubo was a charismatic leader, and a warrior and wizard without peer. Some followed because they understood the importance of their duty, others for glory, or power, or money. The ultimate reasons did not matter. He now had a small army of four hundred and fifty men at his back, each one picked for their magic, skills, and courage. Recruited in his travels, most were his countrymen, but he did not turn away barbarians as well. He had Chinese followers, a handful of Westerners, and even a young Russian holy man. As long as they were useful, they could serve. All of them were fanatically devoted to his cause. Okubo had named these warriors the *Genyosha*, his Brotherhood of the Dark Ocean.

They had followed the trail of the new Pathfinder for weeks, across deep forests, treacherous mountains, and scorching sands. Since most of the men of Dark Ocean were Nipponese, the Chinese military had taken them for some mercenary invasion force and attempted to stop them. Each time the fools had paid with their lives, but every skirmish had slowed them down and given the Pathfinder that much more time to gather its strength, which meant that it, too, would be stronger than last time.

If life had taught him anything, it was that the strongest would always prevail.

❖ ❖ ❖

The army of the Enemy stretched before him like a gangrenous rot across the desert. Flesh mutilated, twisted, and regrown, the leering abominations barely retained any semblance of humanity. These creations were an insult to the senses. Their existence offended Okubo to the core of his soul. He could feel his magic within, recoiling in fear at the hungry presence of the Pathfinder.

Three words made up the totality of Okubo's battle orders to the warriors of Dark Ocean. *Kill them all.*

And then he charged.

The first wave of Enemy troops fell before him in an instant, their flesh charring, their muscles twitching with uncontrollable spasms as crackling lightning leapt through their ranks. Okubo followed, a katana in each hand, turning and slicing any creature foolish enough to get in his way. Most human beings blessed with magic had access to but one small area of the Power, but Okubo alone could instinctively choose from many, and as one type of magic was exhausted, he would pick another. The second wave of soldiers burst into flames, the third froze solid and were shattered by his blows.

The men of Dark Ocean followed, but they were mere mortals. They could not keep up, but as Okubo cut a path of blood through the army, the Dark Ocean mopped up the chaos left in his wake.

The fourth wave was channeling their stolen magic, trying to shield themselves from his fury. These poor slaves had been Actives once. So Okubo quickly picked a different point from the tangled geometric mass of the Power, bent space, and stepped through to appear behind them. Another shift, and now he had the strength of ten men, and his swords cleaved through limbs as if they were grass.

The fifth wave had firearms. Time seemed to slow as ball and shot streaked through the falling bodies around him. The Power answered his plea, hardening his flesh to the consistency of rock as the projectiles ricocheted away to tear through more of the twisted peasants. Moving faster than the gunners could aim, he attacked. Okubo broke one of his swords cleaving through a pelvis, so he picked up the dropped musket, shot another corrupted solider, then used the musket as a club to bludgeon four others to death.

Sixth wave. This Pathfinder was a manipulator of living flesh, and did not limit itself to humans alone. The mighty beasts before him may have been oxen or horses at one point in time, only now they loomed over him like the oni from stories used to frighten children, but they burned like anything else.

He stepped through the fire. Seventh wave. Okubo turned his body to mist and stepped through a shield wall. A wave of telekinetic force rolled outward, flinging the troops away. His other sword had been left lodged in the skull of an ox-man-beast, and his musket club had been reduced to splinters, so he took up a spear and returned to his work.

Move. Slash. Lunge. Stab. Block. Repeat. The Power was a living thing. It needed time to rest and regain its strength just as any living thing would during such exertion. So Okubo took a moment to simply rely upon his own natural skill. The spear moved in a blur, piercing hearts and slashing throats. He stepped between the blades, relying on years of training against the clumsy yet incredibly strong attacks of the Enemy's forces. *Move. Slash. Lunge. Stab. Block. Repeat.*

Yet no warrior, no matter how well trained, could survive for long in such a storm of steel and lead. They were closing. The enemy strokes were drawing nearer. His arms were tiring. The Power refreshed, Okubo reached deep inside and caused the very energy in the air to collect and then explode.

There were no waves now, only a red circle in the middle of the Pathfinder's army. The world was carnage. The desert was wet with slaughter. Okubo was its king.

"Face me, coward!" Okubo roared.

The Pathfinder itself appeared.

The warrior Okubo prepared for the greatest fight of his life.

Okubo knelt on the rocks, facing the rising sun, deep in thought. Over half of his Dark Ocean had died gloriously in the battle, their bodies strewn across the desert, intermingled with the corpses of the Pathfinder's army. Okubo's armor was broken and hanging loose on his body, his clothing was tattered, and all of it was coated in sticky blood, though not a single drop of it was his. His body had suffered wounds sufficient to kill a mortal man fifty times over, but the Power had saved him, hardening his tissues against blows and immediately healing any internal damage.

The Power had kept him alive for a reason... It required a champion.

He recognized Hattori by the sound of the young man's footsteps upon the rocks. "You may approach." Okubo did not open his eyes, but he could feel the new sun on his red-stained face. Okubo was already scanning the skilled mind reader's thoughts, a feat that he had not been capable of even a few hours before. "No, Hattori. I do not need food or drink, nor do I need rest." In fact, Okubo was fairly certain that he would never need any of those things again. He was the greatest protector the Power had ever had. He understood now that as a reward for this victory, the Power had rendered him functionally immortal.

"Very well, my Lord." Hattori joined him on the rock overlooking the battlefield. Okubo could sense Hattori's well-earned pride. "After all that . . . We did it. We won."

"Temporarily."

"But . . . We slaughtered their army. The Pathfinder died by your own hand!" Hattori's questioning tone could be taken as disrespectful, but Okubo understood and forgave his subordinate. No warrior wished to be stripped of their glory after such a battle.

"There will be another, and should we win, surely more after that. I think I know our Enemy better now. This creature was far stronger than the last, and as the greater Enemy's hunger grows, so will the desperation of the Pathfinders it sends forth."

"I do not understand, my Lord."

Of course he didn't. How could he? He was not in direct contact with the Power like Okubo. He knew now that it would continue to escalate, each new Pathfinder being greater than the last, as the Enemy grew hungrier, until either it found the Power, or it starved. Things had become clear. Because of this victory, the Power would grant Okubo even greater access to its magic, allowing him to become far stronger. Even this very minute he could feel new areas, new spells, new geometries opening up to his mind. The Power now knew that Okubo was its best chance for survival, and it would entrust him with all of its secrets. There would be no limits set upon him any longer. The Power would allow him to take whatever he wanted, whatever he needed, to ensure their mutual survival.

Such magical ability would be vital. Dark Ocean would need to succeed every time. A Pathfinder would only need to be successful once.

No. Okubo needed something greater than a small brotherhood of warriors for the next time. He would need a mighty army. *No.* He would need an empire . . .

Nippon was rotting from the inside, hollowed by weakness, led by the corrupt. There was no one there strong enough to oppose his will. With Dark Ocean by his side and fueled by the Power's favor, he could conquer and build the army he needed to ensure Man's survival. But why stop there? Why conquer only Nippon? *Why not the entire world?*

Nippon would be first, but only a united world would be sufficient to defeat the Enemy once and for all. "It is time to reclaim my name."

"I do not understand," Hattori said again, sounding exhausted.

"I am the only one who can truly understand." Okubo opened his eyes and looked to the east, toward his homeland. "But that is all that matters."

⚜ Chapter 1 ⚜

It was not so many years after magic first manifested in this world that the first members of the society gathered. We were to be a shield against injustice. We were motivated by righteousness. We become Grimnoir in order to become heroes, to sacrifice our lives in the pursuit of a higher cause, to defend the defenseless . . . I've found that means attending a lot of funerals.

—Toyotomi Makoto,
knight of the Grimnoir,
testimony to the elders' council, 1908

Paris, France
1933

FAYE THOUGHT that Whisper's funeral was very nice. Even though it was a rainy afternoon, there was a huge turnout, which was still to be expected since Whisper had been such a friendly girl. It made sense that she'd been popular. There had to be a hundred people down there all dressed in black. Faye hoped that when she died, she'd have a funeral this nice too, with all sorts of people coming from all over to say pleasant things about her before they stuck her in the ground. Dwelling on that thought gave Faye a touch of melancholy, since her friends probably already did think she was dead, blown to bits along with the God of Demons in Washington, D.C. Only Francis knew that Faye was still alive, and she was counting on him to keep her secret.

For all she knew, they'd already held her funeral and she'd missed it. Hopefully it had been well attended.

She couldn't make out the carving from this far away with the

11

spyglass, but the tombstone would have the name Colleen Giraudoux carved on it. Nobody Faye knew had ever called her Colleen, it had always been Whisper. It had been months since Whisper had died, but she'd died far across the Atlantic Ocean, and Washington had been in a terrible state at the time, what with a big chunk of it being ruined or set on fire. Sadly, there had also been a lot of other bodies to sort out, so Whisper's corpse had been stacked in one of the overflowing morgues along with thousands of others for weeks before Ian Wright had identified her and had her remains shipped back to her home in France for a proper burial like Whisper would've wanted.

Faye had made a solemn promise to Whisper right before she'd died. So Faye had crossed the ocean, stowed away with the coffin in order to make sure that promise was fulfilled. The long journey across the sea had given Faye time to ponder on what Whisper's sacrifice had meant. Whisper had taken her own life in order to save the city from the big demon's rampage. Whisper had given up her magic in order to make Faye's stronger.

Faye was special, even by Active standards. She had known that for quite some time now. Her connection to the Power seemed positively endless when compared to anybody else. Blessed with what she figured was the best kind of magic ever, she was maybe the strongest Active around, especially after she'd managed to kill the Chairman and he wasn't competition anymore. Everybody had said that Okubo Tokugawa had been the strongest in the world, but she'd shown him. *Greatest wizard ever, I don't think so.* Faye snorted as she thought about it. The Chairman wasn't so tough after she'd Traveled his hands off.

Faye was unique. The problem was that he had never realized just how come she was that way, and why her magical abilities had grown so quickly, but Whisper had told her the secret. A long time ago, a terrible spell had been created, one that stole people's connection to the Power as they died. The man the spell had been bound to gobbled up more and more magic until it had made him crazy. They called him the Spellbound, and he had done some horrible things to make his magic better. The Grimnoir had finally killed him, only the terrible spell hadn't died along with its creator. It had simply moved on and found a new home.

For some reason, it had picked her. She really wished that it hadn't.

Faye was the new Spellbound. There was no way she could have known it at the time, but it was the spell that had enabled her to defeat the Chairman and save the *Tempest*, just as it was the spell that had let her defeat the big super-demon Mr. Crow had turned into. It seemed like she'd inherited a gift, but Whisper had made it sound like a curse. The fella that had created the spell had started out as a good man with noble intentions, but the more he used it, the more evil he'd turned.

The Grimnoir elders were so scared of what a new Spellbound might do that they'd been ready to murder her. It probably didn't help that they already thought she was kind of crazy anyway, so she figured she was already halfway there in their eyes. They'd even secretly sent Whisper to keep an eye on her and to kill her if she turned bad. Instead, Whisper had made Faye promise to stay good, and then shot herself in the heart to save a city.

Faye had held a bunch of very complicated one-sided conversations with Whisper's coffin on the trip over. Now they were lowering that coffin into the ground, and Faye had hidden herself several stories up on the rooftop of a fancy old church between some very ugly gargoyles. She was studying the mourners through a spyglass, trying to decide which one of them was supposed to become her teacher.

Jacques Montand was the expert on the Spellbound, and Whisper had asked her to seek him out. Jacques was one of the Grimnoir elders, one of the seven leaders of their secret society. Faye was proud to be a member, a knight as they called themselves, since they did a whole lot of good heroic stuff, but she did object to the part about preemptively murdering her just in case she decided to turn evil. That made it sorely tempting to teach them all a lesson . . .

Faye refocused on watching the funeral. Those kinds of murderous thoughts were probably the evil sort that she should be trying to avoid. It was hard not to think that way, though, because she was just so very talented when it came to killing folks. She'd *borrowed* the spyglass from the ship she'd stowed away on. She moved her focus from face to face around the coffin, studying each one, trying to figure out who was the secret magical warrior who had trained Whisper to be a Grimnoir knight, and which ones where just friends from Whisper's normal, not-secret life. It was hard to tell, especially with all of those darn umbrellas. Plus, on half of the people, she could only see the backs of their heads, but Faye didn't dare go down there. She had to stay hidden. The only way this was going to work was if the elders still thought she was dead.

Which did raise another question. What if, after she talked to Jacques, he decided to rat her out to the other elders? Then she'd either have to kill him to keep him from blabbing, or let the same folks who'd sent Whisper to kill her know that they needed to try again harder. She knew which one made more sense, but that sure seemed to go against her promise to Whisper to stay good, and she really didn't want to get into the habit of murdering other good guys, even if it was in self-defense.

This sure is complicated.

Being picked to be one of Grimnoir elders didn't mean you were old, just that you were supposed to be wise; but Jacques had to be older. Old enough to have beat the last Spellbound when Faye was still a baby, but there were several grey-haired men in that crowd. Faye knew from meeting a couple of the others that the elders were crafty and tended to keep a lot of protection around, which was understandable since the Imperium, the Soviets, and who knew who else was always gunning for them. So she tried looking for people who looked like bodyguards. There were a few tough-looking fellows, but for all she knew, they were just some of Whisper's multitude of boyfriends. And besides, in Grimnoir circles, you didn't have to be a side of beef like Jake Sullivan or Lance Talon to be dangerous. Faye, being skinny and unremarkably plain, was a perfect example of that.

One nice thing about her particular Power was that she was able to see the world around her so much better than everyone else. It was basically like a big map inside her head. It wasn't like Faye could see through walls with her eyeballs, but she instinctively knew perfectly well what was on the other side of those walls. For example, this big church, or cathedral, she supposed it should be called, had fifteen people moving around inside of it, and she could even get a feel of what was in the first level of tunnels beneath it. *Rats and bones mostly.* She could sense danger or any objects large enough to hurt her if she should Travel into them.

Faye hadn't known too many other Travelers in her life, as they were the rarest of the rare. Grandpa hadn't known how to do the trick with the head map like she could, none of the Grimnoir books knew anything about it either, and the few Imperium Travelers' she'd met, well, they'd been too busy trying to kill each other to talk about how their Powers worked.

Her head map could sense life, and she could pick out magic. If she tried really hard, she could even sort of trace the individual links back to the Power. Faye concentrated, drew in the width of her head map, and focused on the people at the grave site. Sure enough, there was magic in that crowd, several different kinds in fact. And a few the Actives had connections to the Power that were quite strong.

Was this how the last Spellbound turned evil? Since he was a Traveler too, did he have a head map of his own that could show him who had Power and who didn't? And was that what tempted him to kill folks and steal it? Though Faye could sort of understand the appeal of gaining even more magic, the thought sickened her.

She had to pause to wipe the raindrops off the lens. The spyglass blew up the faces of the magical folks, and she studied each one. It was easy to pick out the Grimnoir. Sure, they were sad, just like everybody else. The difference was that they all shared this same look of resignation, like they'd been to way too many funerals already. She supposed that was to be expected, since members of the society were getting themselves killed all the time. Those had to be Whisper's fellow knights.

The spring rain shower was annoying, and you can't exactly sneak around spying on folks while carrying an umbrella. Plus the rain had softened up the years of pigeon poop on the roof so everything was slick and her traveling dress was a mess. *Come on, Jacques... Which one are you?*

Faye had focused her head map so intently on the mourners that she hadn't even sensed the danger until it was almost on top of her. *There was somebody else on the roof!*

She hadn't heard him approach, which was saying something since the top of the cathedral was slick as a milk-barn floor and anything you could stand on was at an obnoxious angle. She'd simply Traveled up this vantage point, but the newcomer was climbing up the tiles behind her and slinking along around a gargoyle. He'd scaled the side of the cathedral and wasn't even breathing hard. If it hadn't been for her head map, he would easily have been able to creep right up next to her.

Well, this mysterious fellow had picked the wrong girl to try and sneak up on. She carefully collapsed the stolen—*borrowed*—spyglass and stuck it into a pocket so as not to accidentally scratch it. Faye picked out a narrow ledge just to the side of where the stranger had crawled onto the roof. Her head map confirmed that it was safe to Travel there. Rain drops were soft and easily pushed aside by her passage, so she focused on the spot and Traveled.

Faye appeared out of thin air and landed easily on the ledge. She didn't even need to put out one hand to correct her balance. Faye was rightfully proud of her Traveling skills. The science types had taken to calling her form of magic with the much fancier name of Teleportation, but she still preferred to think of it as Traveling. That name had been good enough for her adopted grandpa, Traveling Joe, God rest his soul, so it was good enough for her.

The climber was still focused on her last position. Faye studied him for a moment. It was hard to tell since he was all crouched over behind a gargoyle, but he seemed to be a tall, thick fella, gone soft around the middle. He must have lost his hat on the climb, because all men wear hats, and he didn't have one on. It was hard to tell his age, because though he looked old, he wasn't moving like an old fella. He was magic all right, she just couldn't tell what kind yet. His hair was stark white, thin, and plastered to his head by the rain. He was wearing what appeared to be a nice, dark-colored suit, but it was now smeared grey because of the stupid pigeons. *Well, serves him right for skulking around like an Imperium ninja.*

Still unaware of Faye's new position, he collected himself, reached inside his suit coat and came out with a small black pistol. Faye had a gun too, though hers was a much bigger .45 automatic, but she figured she wouldn't even need it. She watched, bemused, as the stranger rose from behind the gargoyle and pointed his pistol at nothing.

She Traveled, appearing only a few inches behind the man and shouted, "Boo!"

Startled, the man turned toward her with lightning speed. Faye had figured he'd be some sort of physical Active in order to have made his way up here so easily, so she was ready. The gun turned in her direction, but she was already gone, appearing effortlessly now in front of him. Even if he was a mighty Brute, he was in a rather bad position, what with being so close to the side of a really tall building, and so Faye simply reached out and gave him a shove.

Arms windmilling, his dress shoes squeaked on the rain- and pigeon-shit-slick roof as he tried not to fall over the edge. He almost would have made it too, but the tiles cracked and gave under his heels, and, top-heavy, he started going over the edge. *"Merde!"*

She knew a similar word in Portuguese, since Grandpa had used it a lot on all things relating to dairy cows, and apparently the exclamation translated over in French.

Before he could fall, Faye reached out and snagged his skinny tie with her right hand and a gargoyle's wing with her left, managing just enough of a grip to stop them both from tumbling to the street below. Of course, since she could Travel, only one of them would be going splat if she let go of that gargoyle.

"Whoa there, mister." She loosened up on the tie for a split second, just to demonstrate who was in charge. She snagged it again and kept him from falling. He grabbed her arm with both hands, nearly crushing it, though she could tell he was holding back—he was probably a Brute. Only his toes were still touching the edge of the roof and even Faye was mostly hanging over open space. She hoped he spoke English. "Don't do anything stupid. Let go of my arm."

He shook his head, then spoke with a light French accent. "If I fall, we both fall."

She'd been right to begin with. He was older, probably in his fifties, maybe sixties, but age was hard to tell with some folks. Eyes wide, the man looked first at the ground, then back at Faye, and then back at the ground. He was leaning back way too far to do much of anything except fall. A sufficiently skilled Brute might survive a fall like that, but it probably wouldn't be much fun. He'd dropped his pistol in a vain attempt to grab the gargoyle. He looked forlornly at the gun sitting in the rain gutter. "I did not see you coming."

"They never do."

Faye realized that the old man was studying her face, specifically her odd grey eyes. All Travelers had grey eyes, and there weren't very many Travelers. "You must be Sally Faye Vierra."

"That's me."

He looked around. *Faye. Ground. Gun.* Then, realizing that he was in a very bad way, he settled on looking at Faye. "Please pull me up?"

"Maybe." Faye answered, noting the black-and-gold Grimnoir ring on his gun hand. "Why'd you try to sneak up on me?"

After the initial shock of almost falling, the old fellow had regained his composure. "Why were you spying on us?"

That was a fair question, though she was rather disappointed that her spying skills weren't turning out to be very good. "I'm looking for somebody in particular. He was a friend of Whisper's."

He was a distinguished-looking man, well dressed, despite the pigeon poop and new tears that he'd put into his clothing trying to sneak up on her. He probably would have been rather handsome in his youth. It was hard to tell if he had the commanding presence of a Grimnoir elder, since nobody really had much of a commanding presence when the only thing keeping them from falling off a roof was a little girl holding onto their tie. He was old enough to have fought the last Spellbound. "Are you Jacques Montand?"

"I am . . . You've come to kill me, then?"

Not really, but he didn't need to know that yet. "I'm thinking it over."

"So you know what you really are?"

"The Spellbound. Whisper told me before she died."

"I see . . ." Jacques sighed. They both knew there wasn't a whole lot he could do right then if Faye decided to just let go of the gargoyle. She could easily Travel to safety before hitting the ground and Jacques knew it. He slowly released the death grip on her arm. "I do not know everything she told you, but I would ask you to leave the other members of the Grimnoir leadership out of this. They voted to leave you alone. Our last instructions to Whisper were to observe you but to take no action. The majority of the elders thought that though you had been cursed, you yourself were innocent of any wrongdoing."

"Uh huh . . . On this vote, how close was it?"

"Five against two."

Well, she was even more popular than she expected. "How'd you vote?"

He looked her square in the eye as his shoes slipped a little further. "I understand more about the threat of the Spellbound than the others. I voted to have you eliminated immediately."

"I didn't ask for this!" Faye exclaimed. It would have been so easy to just let go of him. That big of a fall might've even killed a Brute as tough as Delilah or Toru. Then Faye could simply take Jacques' link to the Power and make it her own. But then again, that was probably just the mean side talking. Faye had made a promise, and Faye always kept her promises. "I should drop you, jerk."

"It was nothing personal. I have seen what the spell will eventually cause, and I have evidence which makes me believe this will happen again. I do not regret my decision." He closed his eyes and waited for her to let go. "Do it. I am not afraid."

Faye was impressed. The Frenchman had guts. "I didn't come all this way to kill you, Jacques." Faye pulled hard. It was enough to shift both of their centers of gravity back over the edge, and he stumbled forward onto more solid tile. It was also hard enough for the tie to choke the heck out of him, and he had to stop and adjust it before he could breathe a sigh of relief. Jacques stood there on trembling legs. He may have been a Brute, but he didn't have near as much physical Power as some of the others Faye had met. By the time he opened his eyes, Faye was ten feet away, sitting on a gargoyle's head, just in case he tried to do something stupid and heroic. "I came here so you could teach me."

Billings, Montana

ROCKVILLE WAS JUST AS UGLY and godforsaken as he remembered it.

The Special Prisoners' Wing was separate from the rest of the prison, and from the road it looked like one massive, windowless concrete cube. The ugly fortress sat in the middle of an open area that seemed unnecessarily big, but was that size to make sure that an escaping Fade would run out of Power or have to come up for air before he could reach the perimeter. Around the yard was a brick wall tall enough that even a Brute would have a hard time hopping it and thick enough that it would be tough to crash through. The wall was topped with concertina wire and had a guard tower on every corner. It had been said that the riflemen in those towers were all expert shots, and not of a hesitating nature. He'd never been in one of the towers, but he'd been told that, in addition to the thirty-caliber machine guns, they also had elephant rifles and even bazookas in case one of the tougher prisoners decided to take a stroll.

There had been two dozen escape attempts since the Special Prisoners' Wing had been built. There had been only one success that anyone knew of. The rest had ended up back in their cells or in the facility's crematorium.

Rockville was simply ugly. Rockville was a monument to ugliness. It served the ugly purpose of keeping dangerous criminal Actives away from the world. Its name served as a warning to any Active who thought about using magic to break the law. Rockville was a synonym for hard time. If any normal person ever passed by they would have to stop and gawk at the sheer *ugly* of the place. Good thing it was in the middle of nowhere.

But no matter how nasty Rockville looked on the outside, it was nothing compared to the monotonous hard-labor hell that was life on the inside.

Been a long time. He'd never thought he'd be back here, certainly not as a free man.

At least this time he wasn't here as a convict. He was here as a recruiter.

Jake Sullivan parked the car before the gatehouse and waited, feeling the eyes on him. The Special Prisoners' Wing of the Rockville State Penitentiary didn't get very many visitors. Cautious guards approached from both sides, polite enough, but carrying Thompsons and ready for anything. There was no such thing as a complacent guard at a facility where the average prisoner could have super strength or set you on fire with his mind. From what Sullivan knew, at least one of the gatehouse men would be deaf, and therefore immune to the manipulations of any Mouth trying to con his way through.

Papers presented, he waited while they triple-checked everything. It only took a few minutes. Of course they'd known to expect him. The Warden was thorough like that.

The gate was built solid enough to stop a bulldozer, and it took a good five minutes to get it open wide enough for his car to make it through. There was a second fence inside the first, this one made of wire, and he had to wait for that gate to be pulled aside as well. Originally they had kept attack dogs inside the wire, but had been forced to get rid of them after a Beastie had used them to maul some of the guards. After that they'd electrified the wire, until one day a

Crackler had sucked up the extra voltage and used it to blow a hole in the main wall during an escape attempt. So now it was just a fence.

That was the thing about containing criminal Actives. You just never knew what they were going to come up with next. Rockville collected the worst of the worst, the most violent, dangerous, magically capable hard cases that a judge couldn't come up with a good enough reason to just execute.

There was a loud clank as the main gate began to close behind him. A cold lump of dread settled in his stomach. He took a deep breath and waited for the guard to wave him through the secondary fence. He wasn't the sort to get rattled easily, but Jake Sullivan had served six long years inside that wall. Just over there was the rock quarry where he'd spent thousands of hours doing backbreaking manual labor. He'd killed a lot of men inside these walls, all in self defense, but regardless, that sort of thing lingers with a man.

The gate closed like the lid on his coffin.

The Warden's office was exactly as he remembered it, dusty and old-fashioned. Every flat surface held stacks of books and papers, most of which were about magic, all taken from the prison's extensive library. Sullivan had read them all at one point or another. Since the Special Prisoners' Wing was dedicated to holding Active felons, no expense had been spared in the collection of information about magic. The Warden was a scholarly man, not out of any sort of innate curiosity, but rather because his job required it. It took a keen mind to come up with defenses for all of the various ways his special prisoners could cause trouble, but the Warden took his job very seriously and was now something of an expert on the topic.

The last time Sullivan had been in this room was when he'd been offered J. Edgar Hoover's deal for an early release, his freedom in exchange for using his own Power to help capture wanted Active criminals. Sullivan had jumped at the chance. Some of the other cons had called it selling out, but they were just jealous. Anything beat breaking rocks.

The Warden had greeted him warmly and waved the escort guards away. After all, the Warden had known Sullivan had enough respect for law and order to not be scared of him trying anything while he'd been a prisoner. So he certainly wasn't about to worry about him doing anything now that he was a free man. Sullivan took a seat in a chair meant for a normal man, and it creaked dangerously under his extra mass.

"You've been busy since we last met," the Warden said from across his wide desk. He was a squat, thick-necked, wild-haired fellow who always seemed to have the stub of a cigar clamped in one side of his mouth. In his six years here, Sullivan had never actually seen the Warden with a *lit* cigar.

"Yes, sir." There was no need to be so deferential anymore, but old habits were hard to break. "It's been eventful."

"In addition to what I've read in the papers, I've heard a few rumors. They're saying you're responsible for exposing the OCI conspiracy and catching the bastards who tried to kill Roosevelt."

He couldn't exactly tell the Warden about how he was now part of a secret society that had saved the entire east coast from a Tesla superweapon. "I played a small part is all."

The Warden leaned way back in his chair and chewed on his cigar. "Then that would mean my arranging your release was a good idea."

It had been the Warden who had suggested to Hoover that Sullivan could be of some use in helping capture criminal Actives. He wouldn't go so far as to say that they were friends, since the Warden was the man responsible for keeping him caged like an animal in a prison full of violent madmen, but once he'd understood Sullivan's nature, there had been a certain level of respect. Plus, if the Warden had not allowed him access to the library, Sullivan would've gone crazy a long time ago. "I personally think it was a good idea. Can't speak for anyone else."

"Well, I do suppose it depends on who you ask. Some seem to think you're a national hero while the rest say you're a menace to society. I was a little worried about keeping my job when that whole Public Enemy Number One thing happened." The Warden chuckled. "Luckily, nobody in their right mind would want my job."

"Yeah, that was real amusing." Being framed for an attempted presidential assassination and becoming the most wanted man in the country hadn't exactly been a picnic.

"I imagine," the Warden agreed. "For a few days there I was under the impression I might once again be able to enjoy your sunny company here at beautiful Rockville."

There was no way the OCI could have taken him alive, but that went unsaid. Sullivan merely gave a noncommittal grunt.

"It isn't often that I get to speak to one of our rehabilitated fellows. So, what brings you back to my fine establishment, Mr. Sullivan?"

"I made a request to the Bureau of Investigation."

"Yes, I received the letter from Director Hoover. It was rather cryptic, but gave me the impression that you are working on a rather important project. He was clear that it wasn't one of his projects, but something that could prove to be vitally important nonetheless."

"It is." Sullivan didn't think that Hoover was entirely convinced as to the reality of the Enemy's existence, but after his political victory over the OCI, Hoover had felt like he'd owed Sullivan enough to at least humor his request. Not to mention that the BI director was happy to have the volatile and now infamous Heavy Jake Sullivan go off someplace where he wouldn't be able to talk to reporters anymore.

"I'll admit, I am curious. So what's the nature of this mysterious project of yours?"

Track down a horrible monster from outer space before it can send a message home to its daddy to come and destroy the whole Earth. "I can't really say."

"Hoover said you'd say that." The Warden leaned forward suspiciously. "So what do you want from me?"

"Not what. Who." Sullivan reached into his coat, pulled out the paperwork, already signed by a federal judge, and passed it over.

The Warden took it and read, disbelief growing on his face. "You can't possibly be serious? This prisoner... Released? Why—"

"There's an important job that needs doing. I'm putting together a team to do it. Real talented bunch, if you get what I mean. In fact, there ain't much we can't do. However, this particular fella's got some rare skills I need."

"He's dangerous."

"Which means he'll fit right in."

"You know about..."

"Heard about him. He got here after I left."

"Don't think you can control him, Sullivan. He'll get inside your head."

"He ain't a Reader."

"Might as well be." The Warden rolled his cigar to the other side of his mouth. "He's not like you, Sullivan. Letting you out was one thing. Anybody who has studied the law could look at your case and see you were railroaded. You were a war hero who stomped a crooked sheriff in a crooked town, and because you were a scary Active, you were made into an example. I just wish I'd read your file sooner. The vast majority of the rest of my convicts, on the other hand, are in here for damn good reasons. This man Wells, for example. He's a killer, nothing but a mad-dog killer."

"Sorry, Warden. I'm afraid where I'm going, mad-dog killers are exactly what I'm gonna need."

Solitary confinement was by the gravel pit. Sullivan had spent quite a bit of time in solitary. It was where you got put automatically after a fight. Didn't matter if you started it or not. Get in a fight, go in the hole. And Sullivan, having had the reputation of being the toughest man inside Rockville, had no shortage of upstart punks who'd wanted a shot at the title, so Sullivan had spent a lot of time in the hole. Usually, he hadn't minded. The quiet had helped him think.

The holes lived up to their name. They were just shafts that had been dug ten feet straight down into the solid rock with a four-hundred-pound iron plate stuck on top for a roof. The holes weren't even wide enough for a tall man like Sullivan to lie all the way down. Inside was just enough room for the prisoner, a bucket to shit in, and a whole bunch of rock. Once a day they'd send down a clean bucket with food and a can of water in it, and pull up the old bucket to hose out to send back with your rations in it the next day. Once they'd decided you had enough they'd roll down the rope ladder. It hadn't been too awful in the summer, but being in a hole during the Montana winter was miserable. There tended to be fewer fights during the winter months.

The Warden had telephoned ahead, so there were ten guards waiting around one hole in particular. Some were carrying nets, and the rest were armed with strange Bakelite batons with metal prongs sticking out the ends.

"What're those?" Sullivan asked, gesturing at the unfamiliar weapons.

The guard patted the big square end of his baton. "Electrified cattle prod. Gotta have something. Bullets just bounce off this guy."

"It won't be necessary. Stand back while I talk to him."

"Warden said you'd want it that way. Your funeral, pal." The lead guard shrugged. "Stand away, boys."

The guards complied, a few of them giving him dirty looks that suggested they remembered him from the old days. Even cleaned up and without the striped prisoner suit and the ball and chain clamped around his ankle, he was still an easy man to recognize. He'd never given the guards any trouble. They were just men doing a hard job, so Sullivan held no grudge, but to them, once a convict, always a convict, and only a sucker trusted a convict.

Waiting until the guards were safely away, Sullivan walked up to the hole and kicked the iron plate a couple of times to announce his presence. "Morning."

The voice was muffled through the plate. "What do you want?"

"I want to talk, Doctor."

There was a long pause. "So it's doctor now, huh?"

"You got a medical degree and you're an alienist, so that's your title, ain't it?"

"I suppose I've rather gotten used to my title being 'Convict.'"

Sullivan remembered his own stays in the hole, how only the tiniest bit of light could creep through the air slots cut in the iron plate, and the painful blindness that came with freedom. "Cover your eyes. It's bright today." Then Sullivan used a tiny bit of his Power to effortlessly lift the rusting iron slab and toss it to the side.

Sunlight filled the hole. "Aw. That really stings."

"Warned you." Sullivan kicked the waiting rope ladder down into the pit. "Come on up."

"Give me a minute to make myself presentable."

"Take your time." Sullivan waited patiently as the prisoner rubbed the feeling back into his limbs then struggled to make his way up the ladder. He didn't offer to help pull him up, since the man was filthy after several days in the hole, and Sullivan didn't particularly feel like getting his suit dirty, or worse, ending up in a wrestling match with a Massive who had a reputation for violence.

Like I got room to talk. Sullivan didn't just have a reputation for violence, he'd gained national notoriety for it. *Still ain't getting my new suit dirty though.* He folded his arms and waited for the prisoner to pull himself over the side. For being able to alter his density, and being so good at it that he could even make the Rockville guard contingent nervous, the prisoner didn't look like much. He was of average height and thin build, not particularly remarkable at all. Sullivan was half a foot taller and twice as wide in the shoulders.

Wells blinked for a moment, adjusting to the sunlight, then the two men stood there, sizing each other up. It was hard to guess the age of someone that dirty, but the OCI's file had said that Doctor Wells was thirty-five, so fairly close to the same age as Sullivan. Though right then the convict looked about ten years older. The hole had that effect on a man. The doctor had a widow's peak, and rubbed one hand through his thinning hair, seemingly bemused when he discovered how matted with dried blood it was. "Please, excuse my appearance. The facilities leave something to be desired."

For some reason Sullivan expected the convict to be a twitchy one, since his OCI file had repeatedly used the term *erratic genius*, but instead Wells seemed cool, almost *too* collected. Sullivan nodded politely. "Let me introduce my—"

"Wait." Wells held up one hand, which was still scraped and raw from the altercation that had landed him in the hole in the first place. "Don't tell me. I've had nothing new to keep my mind occupied for three days now. Allow me to deduce why you're here."

Sullivan was in no hurry. The *Traveler* was on its maiden voyage, and Captain Southunder was still shaking her down and checking systems. She wouldn't be ready to leave the Billings airfield for another hour or two. "Knock yourself out."

"I take it you don't work here?"

"Nope."

Wells glanced over to where the squad of guards were fidgeting. "You're talking to me by yourself, and the Warden is far too thorough to not have informed a visitor of my capabilities, which suggests you're not afraid of me, nor do you seem even the slightest bit nervous."

Sullivan let him have his fun. "Should I be?"

"That depends." Wells saw the discarded iron plate. Normally it would take three or four strong men to move it into place. "You're obviously a Brute . . ."

"An interesting hypothesis."

He went back to studying Sullivan. "No. Not a Brute . . . You have the morphology of a Heavy. All known Heavies are physically robust, big-framed specimens."

Sullivan nodded. "I prefer the term Gravity Spiker. It's more dignified."

"And I prefer the term *psychologist* over the term *alienist*; however, most Heavies wouldn't care. Statistically, Heavies tend to score rather low on the Stanford-Binet intelligence scales. They're *slow*. You're an oddity. More than likely a self-taught man . . . Don't look at me like that. Your pronunciation of *hypothesis* suggests that you've read the word, but not heard it spoken very often, which means you've not attended school. It isn't hypo-thesis . . . It's *hýpothésis*."

Sullivan shrugged. "I'll have to remember that." He hadn't had much schooling, and frankly, some of the dumbest sons of bitches he'd ever met had been the ones with the fanciest educations and the most degrees framed on the wall. Despite that, you'd be hard pressed to find anyone who'd read more books in their life than Sullivan had. It helped that he could put down a fat tome in the time it took most men to read a newspaper.

Wells talked fast. His brain ran faster. "Your clothing is new, expensive, but you seem unused to it. It would suggest that you make a good salary, but that isn't right. Nice suit, but you didn't care enough to shave today, nor does your hair reaching your collar suggest you care much for grooming. But I have been out of circulation for a year, so I may have fallen behind on what is fashionable. You strike me as a man too busy to care about his appearance. The clothing was purchased for you so you'd look presentable, perhaps by an employer?"

"Close, but no cigar." Francis Stuyvesant, knowing that Sullivan was going to be doing a lot of recruiting for his mission, had ordered one of his legion of functionaries to hook Sullivan up with a good suit. It was nice to have something tailored and not bought from a secondhand store.

"But I'm close. It was a gift. Your shoes were not. Your shoes are too sturdy, picked for comfort and durability rather than style."

"A man never knows when he's gonna have to chase somebody down."

"Chase, rather than run from . . . The choice of words demonstrates your mindset. Either way, they don't match your suit." Wells' eyes darted back and forth, then he took a few steps to the side. "Though you don't have it on you now, your coat has been tailored to hide a firearm on your right hip. Something rather large apparently. So you are in the habit of carrying a large handgun, not a little gentleman's pistol, but a serious working weapon. The clothing is too nice for a policeman's salary."

"Maybe I got a rich uncle?"

"You don't talk like a man with an inheritance. You have less-refined enunciation. You don't strike me as *nouveau riche*. You have the face of a boxer."

"I've stopped a few fists with my nose."

"A fighter then. Your knuckles are scarred." Sullivan unconsciously clenched his fists. "And you are a former soldier. You can always tell by how they stand when they are being made uncomfortable..."

"I'm starting to see how you end up in so many fights around here."

"Yes. It's a good thing I'm indestructible."

"*Virtually* indestructible," Sullivan responded. "Everybody dies, Doc. Some folks, you just got to try a little harder."

"Great War, judging by your age... The most likely use for the common Heavy during the Great War was as manual labor. Heavies are a dime a dozen."

"Yeah. Lots of us around. Not so many of your kind."

"Odds are you've never met another like me," Wells said with a bit of false modesty.

He resisted the urge to smile. Wells was a smart man, just not as smart as he thought he was. Sullivan was one of the only Actives alive who'd learned how to blur the lines between different types of magic. He was no stranger to manipulating his own mass. "Naw. I met a Massive once. No big deal. They squish like anybody else."

"*However*," Wells said sharply, "you were no laborer during the Great War. Your combative stance suggests the second most likely statistical probability for a Heavy, which was mobile automatic rifleman."

Wells was as astute in his deductions as the OCI file had suggested. "Machine gunner," Sullivan corrected.

"First Volunteer then," Wells said, noting Sullivan's surprise. He waved one filthy hand dismissively. "AEF used different terminology. Machine gunner there would suggest having worked on a crew-served weapon, but nobody would waste a Heavy in that role when they could be used as walking fire support on their own. General Roosevelt used Heavies as machine gunners. I'd wager you were no stranger to a suit of armor either."

"I should've said I was a blimp mechanic, just to see what you'd say then."

"Lying, and the types of lies the subject chooses, only help me understand the subject's thought processes." Wells was circling him now. "You're not a Rockville employee, but you don't have the nervousness that an outsider to Rockville would normally have. No... You're used to this place, but for reasons—*Convict!*" Wells suddenly bellowed, using a command voice like a guard would have.

Sullivan raised an eyebrow.

"Hmmm...A slight reaction. Maybe I was wrong, or maybe you are just not the sort given to dramatic reactions. But I'm never wrong...I know who you are...Mr. Heavy Jake Sullivan."

That was impressive. "Very good, Doc. You do that trick at parties?"

Wells gave a little bow. "It's nothing. You're a legend in Rockville."

"Beating a dozen men to death will do that."

"Only a dozen over six years?" Wells' smile was utterly without emotion. "Why, I'm halfway to your record in only one."

It was only an estimate. In actuality, he'd hadn't really kept track. "Congratulations?"

"So, Mr. Sullivan, would you like me to figure out what brings you all the way back here to beautiful scenic Montana to speak with me? I will admit, I was expecting to reason out the why of this visit long before I reasoned out the who. I wasn't expecting a celebrity."

"Save your parlor tricks. I've got a job to do and I think I might need somebody like you on my crew."

"A Massive? My type of Power *is* incredibly scarce."

"That could come in handy, but no. I need an alienist."

"Psychologist," Wells corrected.

"As long as you keep calling me a Heavy I'll keep calling you an alienist."

"Why pick me, Mr. Sullivan? Sure, I'm the best, but I have many capable peers who aren't incarcerated for the next twenty years. That could pose a logistical problem."

"You think you know about me? Well, I know a bit about you, too. I know you got bored, screwed over a bunch of gullible patients, and lost your medical license. Then somehow you wound up making a million bucks running cheap Mexican hooch across the border before you got caught. According to the Rockville doctors, you're what they call a sociopath. I know you don't give a shit about anyone other than yourself. I know that you'll kill somebody the minute it's convenient for you. You think life's a game and everybody else is just pieces on a board. Normally, none of those things would sound like attractive qualities to an employer.

"But the important thing is I know you're a genius at predicting folks' behavior. Word is, as long as you think it's a challenge, nobody is better at guessing an opponent's moves than you. You come highly recommended in that regard."

"By whom?" Wells asked suspiciously.

"A former colleague of yours had a file on you a quarter-inch thick." That was an exaggeration, but there had been a few pages in the armful of evidence Faye had snatched before Mason Island had been sucked into a black hole. "Dr. Bradford Carr."

For the very first time, Sullivan was pretty sure he caught a genuine display of emotion from Wells, and it wasn't a pleasant one. Wells quickly contained the hate and managed to give a pleasant smile instead. "So...how is the *good* doctor?"

"Dead...Oh, that's right. You boys don't get to read the papers in here. Me and my friends ruined him. That's how I got my hands on his files, and how I know that you're one of the only men he ever actually feared. He committed suicide. Hung himself with a shoelace in his prison cell a little while ago."

"How delightful. *Now* I'm slightly intrigued. What is it you're proposing, Mr. Sullivan?"

"I've got paperwork from a federal judge releasing you into my custody. Each week you work for me knocks six months off of your sentence."

"I see." Wells seemed to be mulling that deal over, but Sullivan knew that was just an affectation he'd adopted to make normal people feel more comfortable around someone whose mind worked too fast.

Brain like that? Wells had already run the numbers. "And despite what you read about me in Doctor Carr's files, you trust me not to betray you?"

Sullivan snorted. "Compared to some of the folks I've got on this, not particularly. Look, I'll save us both the time with the pointless threats. If you do anything to sabotage my mission, we both know I'll kill you, or one of my extremely dangerous pals will kill you. You can make the same threat to me, but then we'd just waste a bunch of time, and we're both too busy for all that posturing nonsense."

"Refreshing. And what happens if I try to escape?"

"You won't. You'll stick around till we're done, and after that I don't particularly care what you do."

"Why would you possibly expect me to do that?"

"A man who thinks life is all a big game needs a big challenge. Hell, you're probably enjoying Rockville because at least surviving here takes some cunning."

"I'll admit, it can be thrilling at times." Wells looked down at his striped clothing. "Though it does leave something to be desired in the style and hygiene departments. Despite that, your offer of freedom isn't as interesting as you'd think." Wells glanced over at the nervous guards. "I'm confident that when I tire of this place, my next challenge will be figuring out a way to escape."

"I only know of one person that's ever made it out of Rockville alive, and he was a Ringer."

Wells chuckled. "If any old schlub could do it, then it wouldn't be much of a challenge."

"If you want a challenge, I've got a challenge like nothing you've ever seen before. I've got an opponent that even somebody as smart as you will have a hard time getting ahead of." *A little flattery never hurt.*

Now Wells did appear to have to roll that one over for a moment, and since he seemed to have a brain like a Turing machine, that was saying something. "And what would this challenge be?"

"Saving the world."

Wells chuckled. "You must have mistaken me for an idealist, Mr. Sullivan. I don't give a damn about the world. The world is filled with small-minded fools. If you've brought me some war or conflict or another, whether starting it or preventing it, that's simply boring. I'd rather live out my days as a Rockville gladiator. If there's some warlord or politician that needs killing, save your breath, that's the sort of pointless manipulations Bradford Carr used that animal Crow for."

"Crow's dead too. Long story."

"A deserving death, I'm sure . . . Best of luck, Mr. Sullivan, but I am not particularly interested in subjugating myself to the whims of another again. I'm going back in my hole now. The sunshine was nice, but solitary is where I like to recite poetry."

Sullivan had used his time in the hole to ponder on gravity. Turns out it had been time well spent. "Suit yourself, Doc."

"I'm sure you'll be able to find a Reader or some other mentalist to outwit this opponent of yours."

"Hell, I've got a Reader, but I don't know if their magic will work on a thing like this. If I wait until it acts, then I'm already too late. I need someone who can figure out how it thinks so that we can get ahead of it."

Wells paused at the top of the ladder. "It?"

"Too bad even with all your fancy deductions you assumed the Enemy was *human*."

That got his attention. "I am now slightly more intrigued," Wells admitted.

"Our opponent isn't from Earth."

"Another super-demon then? Even in here, I heard about what happened to Washington."

"Hardly. This thing is why demons exist. It eats magic and leaves dead worlds behind. It's an entity that's pursued the Power across the universe, and the ghost of the Chairman told me it's on the way. If it ain't here yet, it'll be here any day now. We're gonna stop it."

The doctor gave a low whistle. "And they called me crazy . . ."

"The challenge is for you to help figure out how to track down this thing so we can kill it. The most advanced airship in the world is waiting for us in town. Once our captain's feeling confident our experimental dirigible won't just explode, we're going to invade the Imperium. Want to come?"

Wells let go of the ladder. "I'd like my own private cabin."

"Space is tight on the dirigible. You get a bunk like everybody else."

"Top bunk?"

"Deal."

Faye in
the Rain

⊰ Chapter 2 ⊱

"FDR can go to hell. I'm a man. Not a type, not a number, and sure as hell not something that can be summed up as a logo to wear on my sleeve. A man. And I ain't registering nothing."

—Jake Sullivan,
quoted in *the San Francisco Examiner*, 1933

Washington, D.C.

THE CHAIR OF THE CONGRESSIONAL Subcommittee on Active Registration was clearly furious. He was red-faced, with veins standing out on his forehead, and he kept blinking his left eye far too much. The man looked like he was about to have a stroke. Francis Cornelius Stuyvesant prided himself on being able to have that effect on statist bureaucrats, and they were only fifteen minutes into this particular hearing. If they managed to make it the full scheduled hour, he could almost guarantee that the chair would go into an apoplectic fit. "What did you say?"

Francis banged his hand on the table. "You heard me right the first time, congressman, but I really should rephrase my remarks. Calling you and your OCI lackeys whores is insulting to hard-working prostitutes everywhere."

There were gasps of outrage from the gallery, though a few people laughed, including several members of the press. Dan Garrett was sitting to his right, and he just put his face in his hands. Poor Dan, but he should have known what he was in for when they had asked Francis to attend.

"How dare you make a mockery of these proceedings, Mr. Stuyvesant!"

"Mockery? Let me define mockery. The OCI taking innocent Americans to secret jails without any due process is the real mockery. Holding them prisoner without trial is a mockery. What Bradford Carr did made a mockery of the Constitution of the United States. I was kidnapped, beaten, and set up as a patsy while one of your employees tried to blow up Washington, and then a *government* demon rampages across the city, and you accuse *me* of making a mockery of your proceedings? How dare *you*? Keep your manure, Congressman. I don't feel like shoveling."

Several people in the gallery cheered and began to clap. A smaller number booed Francis.

"I am warning you. You will be held in contempt of Congress!"

Francis turned and looked theatrically to Dan. "Is that even a real thing?" And then back to the panel. "Do I at least get a public hearing this time, or do you just throw me in a secret prison because I've got magic? How does that work?"

"Please calm down, Mr. Stuyvesant," cautioned another of the congressmen.

"You calm down!" Francis shouted. Dan reached over under the table with his foot and tried to kick Francis in the shin. It didn't do any good. "Any bum off the street can tell you what the OCI did was wrong, but then Roosevelt comes along and signs a law that says we should do it again, only bigger and more official, and we're supposed to respect that? I say hell no!"

The cheering section had gotten a little out of hand, so there was quite a bit of gavel pounding and shouts for order, until the Capitol policemen forcibly removed some of the more vocal Active supporters. Because of the nature of the crowd, and the fact that Dan Garrett, a known Mouth, was also testifying today, there was a single Dymaxion nullifier spinning on the congressmen's long table. The Capitol building was a magic-free zone today. Even though he now owned the only company capable of manufacturing them, Francis hated the anti-magic device on principle. But if he'd protested the use of one during this hearing, the press wouldn't have believed a word he or Dan—especially Dan—had to say.

Dan leaned over during the chaos and whispered to Francis, "This isn't helping our case. Seriously, leave the diplomacy to me and just state the facts."

"We've already lost with these bozos," he whispered back. "Let the press get some good quotes."

Despite being born into a political dynasty, Francis had always hated politics and despised politicians. After all, his good-for-nothing father had been a very successful politician, which told young Francis pretty much everything he had needed to know about the lot of them. However, since being dragged into the spotlight, despite an instinctive hatred of the political game, it had turned out that he was actually pretty good at it. It must be in the blood. Being one of the richest men in the world surely helped.

He'd leave the diplomacy to cooler heads like Dan, but Francis had discovered a gift for demagoguery. The OCI had screwed with the wrong man, and as a result, Francis had declared war. Not a literal war, but if Roosevelt got his wish, then they'd have that too eventually.

The audience had been quieted down, and a congressman from South Dakota went on a tirade about the destruction wrought against Washington, thereby proving that Actives were far too much of a menace to society to remain uncontrolled, and *blah blah blah*. Francis wasn't really paying attention. He'd heard it all before.

Franklin Delano Roosevelt had already given the executive order pertaining to the official monitoring of everyone with magic, not long after taking office. The climate in Washington after the great demon rampage had made it easy. The Active Registration Act was just icing on the cake. Right now they were only going to round up the Actives they considered to be the most dangerous, but anybody with half a brain knew that was the tip of the iceberg. America was going to follow in the steps of the Imperium and the Soviets, treating magical people like just another resource to be cultivated and controlled, and the Grimnoir would be damned if they'd get away with it.

The really hard part about being a secret society was who you tended to be secret, which meant that the few of them which had been exposed as members got the unenviable duty of becoming their public face. Dan was their most eloquent speaker, but he hated this sort of thing. Luckily, Francis had discovered that he sort of enjoyed it.

"Save us the platitudes," Francis cut the congressman off midsentence. "Sure, Roosevelt is just trying to protect us Magicals from ourselves like we're children, which is mighty nice of him, since the only reason he's even alive is because I used telekinesis to chop an assassin's head off with a serving tray while my friend used his Fade magic to carry the president to safety . . . By the way, do you know how the government paid my friend back for that?"

"Your peanut gallery has been removed, so you don't need to entertain the mob." The congressman leaned toward his microphone. "We have all read the court transcripts, Mr. Stuyvesant. There's no need to dwell on—"

"They paid him back by beating him mercilessly and torturing him in a cell on Mason Island." He didn't need to add that Mason Island had been sucked into a black hole. Everybody knew that. Luckily, hardly anybody knew that the giant magical vortex had been Francis' doing. He didn't particularly want that bit on the Congressional record.

"That was an anomaly. Bradford Carr broke the law—"

"Oh, so now you make that sort of thing legal and it is all supposed to be okay? You are simply validating every horrible thing Carr did. Roosevelt's new act is the first step toward putting a hundred thousand Americans into camps. That's despicable."

"No one wants to hear your tired conspiracy theories, Mr. Stuyvesant. The government would never do such a thing. Enough of your slander."

"The government already *has*—"

"Gentlemen," Dan chimed in. Even when he wasn't using his magic, he always managed to keep it smooth. "You must understand the reaction of the Active community. The destruction in Washington was caused by an out-of-control agency of the federal government, yet it would seem that we the people are being held accountable for it. The fulfillment of Roosevelt's proposals will deprive many law-abiding Americans of their rights and property. This is an extreme and unnecessary act."

There was one man on the panel who hadn't spoken yet, the new Coordinator of Information. He was a composed, middle-aged fellow with a stern look about him that suggested he was not a man to be trifled with. He didn't bother with his microphone. "If I may?"

"The Chair recognizes William Donovan, newly confirmed head of the Office of the Coordinator of Information."

Dan and Francis exchanged a quick look. This man was an unknown quantity. He had been a decorated hero in the Great War, and had been involved in New York politics for years, having even run and lost a bid at the governorship, but his opinions, if any, on Actives had never been made public. The word was that he was an old college chum of Roosevelt's, brought in to clean up the "corrupt" OCI.

"Mr. Stuyvesant, you mentioned your friend, who was unfortunately and illegally mistreated by my predecessor. I believe his name was Heinrich Koenig, a German immigrant . . . Is that correct?"

"That is correct, sir," Dan answered quickly.

"He's the one in that picture that was in all the papers. You know, the one where he's fighting your gigantic out-of-control government demon," Francis added smugly.

"Yes. The infamous photograph of the Fade with the pickax. It is a very moving image, especially since it happened right down the street from here. Yet, I have to wonder, as Mr. Garrett and Mr. Stuyvesant have protested so vehemently about Actives not being any more dangerous to the fabric of American society than any other particular group, and that there are no Actives plotting any sort of insurrection against the United States, where it is your friend Mr. Koenig has gone . . ."

"I have no idea," Francis lied under oath. He was sure the OCI man already had the answer anyway, especially since Sullivan had already tried and failed to get the government to believe him about the Pathfinder. Of course he lied. It wasn't like Francis could warn the Imperium that his friends were on the way.

"Pardon me. I was not finished. I was about to say I wonder where Mr. Koenig has gone, along with several dozen other extremely powerful Actives, including a former public enemy number one, the infamous Heavy Jake Sullivan? A number of them were last seen boarding a heavily armed experimental warship provided to them by United Blimp and Freight. A company which, I might add for the record, you are the president and CEO of."

There were even more gasps and murmurs now, and a whole bunch of reporters started scribbling in their notebooks. The new Coordinator looked rather smug.

Maybe I'm not very good at this after all, Francis thought to himself.

After maneuvering through the mob of shouting reporters and cameras, Francis and Dan made it down the Capitol steps.

"So that went better than expected," Francis said.

"You must not have been in the same meeting as I was," Dan muttered. "That Donovan fellow played you for a fool."

Francis grinned. "At this point, any time I have a meeting with the government and come out of it without having somebody like Crow working me over with brass knuckles, I consider that a home run."

"Thankfully, Donovan shut you up before you said anything really stupid. It wasn't like he didn't use something everybody already knew anyway." The Washington Mall was still under heavy construction. Many of the buildings were still being repaired, and a few had needed to be torn down, leaving gaping fenced-in holes where there had once been landmarks. "And to think, last time I was here, I was about to get stepped on," Dan said.

"How's that different than this time around?" The great claw marks were still visible on the Washington Monument, as nobody had really come up with a satisfactory method to fix that damage yet. *No wonder everyone is so scared now.*

Dan sighed. "I suppose it's a different behemoth doing the stepping, but we're still getting squished."

"That's not very optimistic." But who could blame him? Soon it was going to be the law of the land that every person in America with magic was going to have to wear an armband identifying them as an Active and what type of magic they were capable of, all in the name of public safety. "You're starting to sound like Sullivan ... Or worse, Heinrich. Come on, let's get a drink. I've had enough nonsense for one day."

There was a car waiting for them on the street, only it wasn't Francis' regular car, and it certainly wasn't his regular driver. This driver was far too pretty. The lady was tall, statuesque, and doing her best to hide her good looks behind big dark glasses and a floppy hat. "Hello, gentlemen," she said, gesturing toward the open rear door of a plain government Chevrolet. "Someone important would like to have a word with you."

"Why, Pemberly Hammer." If Dan was surprised to see her here, he played it cool enough you'd never be able to tell. "How nice to run into you."

She tipped her big hat at Dan. Between it, the silver-blonde wig, and the fake glasses, nobody from the press would recognize the now-infamous corporate-espionage expert turned BI agent. "Why, Mr. Garrett,"—She sounded sweet, with just a hint of east Texas— "Why, bless your heart, you know you can't lie to me." Hammer was, after all, a Justice, and since Justices could always recognize the truth, lying to one was simply a waste of time.

"Got me there. It's not nice to see you. It's frankly a bit suspicious... Nice car. Not as nice as that fancy Ford you used to have though." It was a dig, and not a very subtle one, since Dan had been partially to blame for her last one getting wrecked by an Iron Guard.

"Actually, before he up and disappeared off the map, Sullivan wired me some money to replace my car that he stole."

"He promised he would."

"Well, it was his fault the last one wound up on its roof." Hammer smiled. "Imagine that, a man who keeps his word."

"Jake always keeps his word. He's old fashioned like that, reliable as gravity."

"Yep. Good old Jake. Though I do wonder, where did he get off to with that fancy new warship of his?"

"You should ask your boss. I'm fairly sure Jake asked for his help and got turned down."

"He didn't ask me for my help," she sniffed.

"Okay, enough. *Agent* Hammer..." Francis didn't know her very well, other than that Sullivan had vouched for her character, and she'd helped rescue him from Mason Island, but she worked for J. Edgar Hoover now, and it would be a cold day in Hell before Francis trusted Hoover or anybody on his payroll. "Where's Sidney?"

"Your driver was sent away, Mr. Stuyvesant. He tried to argue, but I did that whole flash-the-badge thing and he moved right along. I ever tell you how much I enjoy that? Don't worry, I'll have you back to your hotel in time for your dinner reservations. In the meantime, you need to come with me. Important top secret government business, that sort of thing. You know how it is."

"Oh, I know how that is." Francis looked to the street and lifted an arm. "Taxi!"

"All right, all right," Hammer lowered her voice. "Look. I know you've had some bad blood in the past with my new boss, but this is legitimate."

"I'm not in the mood, lady. I'm way past trusting your people."

"It was the OCI that kidnapped you, not the BI."

"All a bunch of letters from the same damn alphabet."

"And to think, they sent me to pick you up because of my positive relationship with the Grimnoir." Hammer sighed. "I wish you could just read minds, Dan, so we could just get this over with, and you'd know I'm telling the truth. You Mouths can do that a little bit, can't you?"

"Sort of. I can get a sense of things, a handle on someone's emotions, how to move them better, sort of an instinct about where they're swayable, maybe little bits of images of thoughts that are right at the top, if I'm burning a lot of Power..." Dan said. "Not that I'd do that to you, of course. That wouldn't be very gentlemanly."

"Of course it helps that you know I'd plug you in the knee for poking around in my head." Hammer patted the revolver-shaped bulge beneath her floral-pattern blouse. "But we're wasting time, so go ahead. You need to know I'm being earnest here. We need to get away from those reporters before one of them decides to take my picture. I need you to come with me now. It's important."

"Very well. Just keep that Colt holstered because I like my kneecaps the way they are." Dan closed his eyes to concentrate. He was about the best Mouth in the business, and usually he could play it so cool you would never know when he was using his magic on someone, but now Dan was obviously pushing hard, not even bothering to be subtle. Dan's eyes popped open. "Seriously, Hammer?"

"Serious as can be."

"I wish you would've just come out and said so. Hell . . . Get in the car, Francis."

"She's legit?"

"She's legit." Dan seemed upset. "Get in the car now."

Their destination was only minutes away, but Hammer insisted on driving around for a little bit to make sure they weren't being followed before circling back and taking them to the White House.

"You've got to be kidding," Francis muttered.

"Nope. Afraid not," Hammer answered as they stopped at the gate. They were keeping it low-key now, but the Army had been handling security in the Capitol ever since the demon rampage. The soldiers at the perimeter looked at Hammer and checked her ID while other soldiers gave Francis and Dan the once-over, then they were waved right through. They were definitely expected.

Francis had been to the White House before for social events. His father had been an ambassador and a man of considerable authority, he had uncles who'd been senators and governors, and of course, grandfather Cornelius had bought politicians like a farmer would buy pigs at auction. That said, attending a secret meeting with the president was still a little intimidating.

"Let me do the talking," Dan warned.

"I won't screw this up," Francis answered.

"No, you won't, because I'm going to knock you over the head, tie you up, and hide you in the trunk," Dan warned. "Oh, you think I'm kidding? Wipe that smile off your face. This isn't some congressman from Podunk, North Dakota you can shout at."

Hammer chuckled. "Dan, I never get tired of seeing you sweat."

"Yuck it up, Hammer. You know damn good and well what Carr had planned for Actives in this country. You saw the evidence Faye pulled out of Mason Island. Do you think for one second Carr was *alone*? Do you think he was the *only one* in the whole government who thought the Imperium and the Soviets were off to a *good start?*"

Hammer's smile died. She knew that Dan was right. Deep inside, every Active in the country did. "I don't think it is going to come to that."

"You hope it doesn't come to that?" Francis snorted. "It sure seems to have come to that damn near everywhere else in the world."

"You're a walking lie detector," Dan said. "You tell me what you really hear when they start talking about public safety and national security, and monitoring and *controlling* Actives for our own safety. I've not got your gifts, but I'm pretty good at snowing folks with words, so I can darn sure recognize when somebody else is doing it to me."

"Well..." She sighed. "I hear a lot of folks who don't know better. They're afraid and they figure we've got to do *something*, but since they don't understand the topic, their proposed *somethings* don't make a whole lot of sense, and then I hear a lot of no-good rat liars willing to take advantage of Do Somethings... Honestly, it scares the hell out of me." Hammer pulled the car to a stop. Men were already waiting for them. "All right, this is it."

Francis' door was opened from the outside. "Welcome, Mr. Stuyvesant. Come with us, please." Dan started to get out his side, but that door was politely caught by another functionary. "I'm sorry, Mr. Garrett. The President wishes to speak with Mr. Stuyvesant in private."

That was unexpected.

"Aw, hell," Dan muttered. "Do *not* screw this up."

"Don't worry, Dan. I can handle this."

"Francis, wait." Hammer looked over the seat at them as they were getting out. "Good luck in there."

He'd heard they were building a new, nicer Oval Office, but either it wasn't done yet or Francis didn't rate it, because he was led to the same old office that he'd visited before. Besides the obviously increased security, the White House hadn't changed much since the first time he'd been here, tagging along once when Grandfather had gone to visit Wilson. He barely remembered Wilson, except that he'd seemed very tall and a little frightening, like a leathery scarecrow, but in Francis' defense, he'd only been a kid.

Another man was leaving the Oval Office as Francis approached. They made eye contact, and the fellow looked familiar for some reason. "Mr. Stuyvesant. What a pleasure to meet you." The man nodded politely and extended his hand. Francis shook it. Firm and businesslike. Tall, humorless, he had the look of a banker. Francis knew a lot of bankers, but that wasn't where he recognized this man from. It was from the front page of the papers. "I am Nathaniel Drew."

They came from the same social circles, but Francis hadn't been paying much attention to those lately. "The architect?"

"I prefer to think of myself as the designer of the planned communities of the future."

"Of course. I hear you're quite the visionary." That was the polite way of saying that all Francis knew of the man was that he was another one of those opinionated collectivists who felt the world was somehow entitled to a bigger share of Francis' money, all in the name of progress, but Drew was also a Cog of some renown, which explained why he was meeting with the President. In fact, Drew was even wearing a white armband on his suit coat bearing the meshed gear logo of the Cog. Francis frowned when he saw that. The mandatory armbands were part of the Active Registration Act, so the architect was probably sucking up to the President, and Francis automatically hated suck-ups. "Those armbands aren't law yet."

"Oh, this?" Drew glanced down at it. "I stand behind Franklin's proposals and merely wish to set an example for others of our kind."

"No, seriously..."

"Easy identification is in the best interests of public safety and builds better relations with the general public."

Cogs were beloved celebrities. Of course he didn't mind wearing it on his sleeve, but tell that to some poor Shard who didn't want to be known as a freak, or a Reader who'd spend the rest of their life a pariah. "Personally, I'll be damned if I ever wear one of those things. Like cattle with an ear tag."

"We are all entitled to our opinions." Drew gave him a forced smile.

"Yeah...It's a free country. For now...Nice to make your acquaintance, Mr. Drew. Maybe I'll give you a call the next time UBF needs another skyscraper."

"Sadly, I am afraid my time has been too consumed with other altruistic humanitarian projects to bother with any commercialism, but please, I was just leaving..." The architect stepped out of the way. "I do not wish to keep you." And then he was whisked away by the functionaries, and Francis was escorted into the inner sanctum.

Franklin Roosevelt was already seated behind his mighty desk, waiting. "Well, hello, Francis. It has been a long time." The president extended his hand to shake, but he did not bother to stand. Francis gave him a firm handshake and found himself hoping that his palms weren't too sweaty.

"Good afternoon, Mr. President."

The functionary hurried out and closed the door behind him, leaving the two of them alone. Roosevelt looked like a kindly man, with an easy smile, even a bit of a twinkle in his eye, but Francis had grown up in the brutal knife fight that passed for New York politics, where various rich families played at Machiavellian games, and he knew that this man had been ruthless enough to earn the grudging respect of Grandpa Cornelius, who had been as cutthroat a rat bastard as there had ever been. That meant Roosevelt was not to be trusted.

"Last time we spoke was at a gala event put on by your father. You were about to leave for Boston for school. How time flies."

"Yes, it does, sir." When they had last spoken, Francis' greatest questions in life had been how to bed the best-looking girls and where to get the best-quality alcohol. Since then he'd been drafted into a secret war, engaged in intrigue, espionage, and outright combat against all manner of nefarious magical forces, lost good friends, been shot, beaten, and briefly imprisoned, and unexpectedly wound up as the head of one of the most powerful corporations in the world. Francis was still a very young man by most standards, but the last few years had been very *full.* "Yes, it does."

The president gestured at one of the high-backed chairs which had been arranged before the desk. "We were supposed to have spoken in Miami before the unfortunate events there . . . Please, have a seat." Francis did. The chair was remarkably uncomfortable. He wondered if that was on purpose. Roosevelt was smoking, and he gestured at a golden box on his desk, but Francis shook his head politely. "You know, I've never been able to thank you personally for what you did in Florida. You and your German friend, Mr. Koenig, saved my life."

"That is no problem at all. We've all been very busy since then." The assassin had already struck before the two Grimnoir could react, but if Heinrich hadn't Faded the already badly wounded Roosevelt through the hotel steps, the assassin Zangara would've finished him with the next magical blast. "Are you well? There are rumors that the Healers weren't able to—"

Roosevelt waved his hand dismissively. "No, no. I assure you, I am quite all right."

"Heinrich and I were both glad to help."

"Of course. Allow me to thank you now. Miami was just another warning of things to come. This has been a time of crisis for our nation. I've got a country to get through difficult straits. Things were bad enough as it was, our people low on hope and long on debt, and that's before the added complication of assassins' plots and their schemes within plots. The greatest among those plots would not have been exposed if it had not been for your help."

Yet the Grimnoir were still being painted as the bad guy, as if only they hadn't been there to be scapegoated in the first place, then none of this would've ever happened. "It would be nice to hear you say that in public."

The president laughed, even though Francis had not been joking.

"You remind me of your father. That's exactly the sort of angle he would've taken. He was hotheaded, a bit impulsive in our youth, of course, but there was a stalwart Democrat for you." Francis only nodded along. He was a Republican, but that was only because when he had first registered, he had declared he was the opposite of whatever his father had been. "Has anyone told you how much you look like your father?"

Not lately. Thankfully. Francis was also told that he resembled Cornelius before he'd gotten fat. "I don't think you had me summoned here to trade pleasantries about family."

"Of course." Roosevelt's smile went away too quickly for it to have been real in the first place. Regardless of the fact that Francis had helped save his life, this was politics now. "I must remember that you are a titan of Wall Street, a captain of industry. Your time is *so* very valuable."

"No offense intended, Mr. President."

"You are correct though. Time is of the essence, and every day my proposals are stymied makes our situation that much worse." The pretenses were gone, and now Francis was clearly speaking to the man who thought it was a fine idea for Actives to have to wear identifying badges like they were livestock brands. "I heard about your testimony earlier."

By the time the evening papers went out, the whole world would hear his inflammatory testimony. "I stand by what I said."

"You may want to tread more carefully in the future. You are not making yourself any friends."

"If they don't like the truth, then maybe I don't really desire their friendship."

"Regardless . . . One needs friends in this town."

"That's a shame. Whoever will I play bridge with?"

Roosevelt chuckled. "I see how this will be . . . Then let me clarify a few matters for you, young man. I now know quite a bit now about your *society*. I am familiar with your code and your manifesto. You see yourselves as chivalrous defenders against tyranny, I grasp that and I appreciate the sentiment."

"Thank you, sir."

"*However*, I do not believe you grasp the magnitude of the situation before us. This nation teeters at the brink of ruin and the world stands at the edge of chaos. I inherited a mess. Our industries and businesses are failing, our people are broke and hungry, and above all, they are worried about terrible events such as Mar Pacifica, Miami, or Washington. We must take firm, decisive action to assure the people that steps have been taken to prevent future acts of this nature."

Francis gritted his teeth and cut off his angry retort. "I've seen your proposals. I don't think they'll have the outcome you're looking for."

"And on that point we are in disagreement. I believe my proposals will ensure our liberty and our safety."

Now Francis couldn't help himself. "Look, I'm not some yokel you're going to sway through a fireside radio chat. What is it that you really want?"

"The American people deserve to be kept safe from the magical menace."

"Magical menace?" Francis sputtered.

Roosevelt smiled. "I understand your antagonism toward the term, but men like you are not the problem. You're one of the good ones, Francis. You will be able to go about your life and your business with no undue extra burdens. Every other great nation in the world either has or soon will take steps toward better utilizing and protecting their Active population. We are at a crossroads of history. America must do the same."

"Like the Imperium and their torture schools?"

"Of course not. That is barbarism." Roosevelt acted offended by the suggestion. "However, you bring up an important point, which I fear you fail to understand. The world stands at the brink of war. World peace is threatened. I know you are far more aware of that than most of our countrymen. You are in the business of building the machines of war, and I know of your personal vendetta against all things Imperium. If it does not happen soon, I can promise you it will happen within the decade. The Soviets have turned their attention on a vulnerable Europe, and we both know the clock is ticking toward our collision against the Imperium in the Pacific."

"I would not disagree with you there. I'd be surprised if we make it that long." Francis leaned forward in his chair. Roosevelt knew damn good and well who was behind Mar Pacifica, not that he would ever admit it since the country wasn't ready for a war. The event was still being blamed on Active anarchists. "We're headed for a confrontation all right, and it will be a big one."

"Obviously, a student of General Pershing's would understand this. Not to mention, I have no doubt the Navy will need many new UBF airships...Yet, no matter how capable our military becomes, both of those nations have utilized their Actives and developed their magic to heights as yet undreamed of here. You're no doubt familiar with Second Somme. You know how incredibly dangerous a concentration of magicals can be during a war. We are in an arms race, and America hasn't even found the starting line yet."

"So the ARA is just an excuse to catalog us...See who's useful, who's not. Probably get rid of the dangerous oddballs while you're at it. That's what Stalin does. Stick them in camps, out of the way, where they can't hurt anybody, until you need to use them as weapons against another country."

"There is no such plan—"

"Granada, Minidoka...I'm a Mover, so I guess that's where I was supposed to go. Gila River, Topaz...Ringing any bells, Mr. President?"

"Save me your sanctimony. Those were the plans of Bradford Carr's cabal. I was as much a victim of his machinations as you were."

"But you're continuing his dream! You're putting the framework in place to accomplish all of his goals. All your talk of safety is just an excuse to take advantage of people's fears. Actives are citizens. You're taking powers never meant for your office."

Career politicians never liked to be called on their bullshit. "How dare you..."

"Oh, I dare all right." Francis was getting rather upset. "Carr had an *extermination* list, and now you want me to trust the same government? Even if I trusted your administration, which I *don't*, what about the next one, or the one after that? Hogwash."

"Do not take that tone with me." Roosevelt was certainly not used to being spoken to like this, maybe in an editorial, but never to his face.

Francis hadn't realized he'd raised his voice. "Forgive me. Extermination orders get my blood up."

"We must modernize."

"What you call modernity, I call slavery."

"A loaded but misleading term." Roosevelt sighed and shook his head sadly. "We simply have a difference of philosophy. Whether you like it or not, there will be a compromise reached. The more unreasonable your side is, the more likely you will not like that compromise."

"I had this same conversation with Bradford Carr, in his dungeons, while I was chained to a wall... He thought that the government owned people. I say the people own the government. There is no *compromise* between those two positions."

Obviously angry, the president put both of his hands down flatly on his great desk. "Oh, there will be a compromise. I will get my reforms and you will not stand in my way."

"Is that a threat?"

And now the knives came out. "I'm the President of the United States. You're the petulant spoiled brat of a blimp merchant."

"I'm a very successful blimp merchant," Francis corrected.

"Though I'm not sure how long you would be able to retain that position if the full weight and attention of the federal government was to be turned against UBF. Many have been clamoring to me about how UBF is a monopoly, and how breaking it up would do wonders for the economy. If that were to happen, you might find yourself in a new line of work rather quickly. That would be unfortunate."

Not only was that a threat, that was one hell of a threat.

"I called you here so I could appeal to your senses, Francis. I need something from you. You can either cooperate, or you can be obstinate."

"And what would that be, exactly?"

Roosevelt put away the knives and went back to being the kindly radio grandpa who just wanted everybody to be prosperous and happy. "Simple. You own Dymaxion."

So that was what this meeting was really about. Francis bit his lip. Buckminster Fuller's Dymaxion Nullifiers were the only thing in existence which could completely block an Active's access to the Power and there were only a few remaining in existence. "You want more magical nullifiers."

"I've been informed that you refuse to sell them."

"If I had a device that made people with good eyesight go blind, or made folks with excellent hearing go deaf, I don't think I'd sell those either. I'm practically one of your consumer safety activists."

"I've been told these devices are vital to national security. The OCI still has a couple, and it is only a matter of time before some Cog is able to reverse engineer them. So any bullheaded foolishness will ultimately prove pointless. In the meantime I would be greatly appreciative if you would begin selling those to the government again. I understand these are valuable, time-consuming works, each one practically a work of art, so I can see to it that you are *extremely* well compensated for your labor. Surely, if UBF is supporting the government in this endeavor, then there would be no point to my new regulators paying your company any particular mind."

Because if threats don't work, you can always try bribery. Francis smiled. "Because without Dymaxions you can't round up and enslave a bunch of ticked-off Actives?"

Roosevelt's eyes narrowed. He hadn't liked that one bit. "Out of a long-time respect for your family, I tried to be reasonable, but you are being a very unreasonable man. You will turn your remaining stock of Dymaxions over to the government, and you will show us how to make more, or there will be severe repercussions."

Francis had once boarded the Imperium flagship to slug it out with a platoon of Iron Guards and the world's greatest wizard. Franklin Roosevelt had seriously underestimated his ability to *not give a shit.* "You said I remind you of my father, but there's one big difference between him and me. He had flexible principles. *I don't.* Do you want to go to war with me, Mr. President? Because if you think you can just seize my property without due process, then that's where we're headed."

"Very well, Mr. Stuyvesant. If you want to do this the hard way, then that's how we will proceed. History does not look kindly upon those who stand in the way of progress."

Dan Garrett was *so* not going to be happy. "Well, this meeting is over." Francis stood up. "Good day, Mr. President."

Roosevelt pushed a button on his desk. The doors opened and a functionary came in to escort Francis out. The president's icy glare left no doubt that Francis had made himself a formidable new enemy. "I have one last question before you go."

He was still red-faced and angry, but he was trying to maintain some respect for the office. "I'm happy to help," Francis lied.

"Only one man has been able to successfully nullify magic, and he works for you. Where is this Buckminster Fuller?"

Oh, there was no way in hell I'm letting these vultures sink their claws into my most valuable Cog... "You know how those Cogs can be, what with their heads in the clouds. If I see him, I'll tell him you inquired about his health. Last I'd heard he was taking a vacation."

◈ Chapter 3 ◈

It is an odd affliction, this Cog magic. In most ways I am a man of average aptitude. Pertaining to most subjects I can reason as any educated man should, but when my intellect turns toward the topic of airships my mind simply ignites as if on fire. Thoughts pour in unbidden. Reason reaches new heights. The abstract becomes clear. Shortcomings are corrected. Weaknesses are exposed and turned into strengths. Years of scientific reasoning are completed in a matter of fevered days, and when the fire dies down I discover that I have once again revolutionized the whole world. I must wonder if I had not been born with this form of magic, would man be confined to forever using inferior forms of transportation such as aeroplanes?

—Ferdinand von Zeppelin,
personal correspondence, 1915

UBF *Traveler*

BUCKMINSTER FULLER was obviously not a happy Cog. "Mr. Sullivan! Mr. Sullivan! A moment of your time?"

Sadly, Sullivan had not been able to escape through the hatch in time to avoid their resident magical supergenius. It was like the Power picked the smartest human beings around to be Cogs. All Cogs were bright, even before the magic came over them, but for some folks the Cog magic arrived later in life, and they were an extra special sort of fun. "Yeah, Fuller?"

"I'll have you know these working conditions are completely unsafe. I am dealing with potentially dangerous magic combined with lethal chemical mixtures in a laboratory the size of a closet, all of fifteen feet away from a bag filled with explosive hydrogen! My quarters are totally unsuitable for regenerative occupancy! My roommate is a pirate! A *pirate!* But that is not the worst. Oh no. The worst is that this is no scientific expedition. You have turned this vessel into a veritable warship! A device designed in the pursuit of killingry!"

"Killingry?" Jake Sullivan cocked his head to the side. "Is that a real word?"

"Of course it is! Killingry. Meaning such as weapons and implements which are in opposition to livingry, or that which is in support of spaceship Earth life! And do not try to obfuscate the subject, Mr. Sullivan."

"I'd never dream of... obfuscating stuff... Ain't Francis paying you a whole lot of money to come along?"

"I need the funding to maximize my life's work, but please recall you promised me this trip would provide incredible opportunities to look into new forms of magical research."

"Yep."

"This is an engine of destruction, filled with violent, coarse, barbaric men!"

"Yep."

Fuller was fuming. "I will have no part in any endeavor which intends to deprive life from—"

Sullivan held up one big hand to stop him. "Okay. Look. I'll keep my word. You're going to see magic that no westerner has ever seen before, and if we get... *lucky,* you'll probably get to see magic that nobody has seen ever. We need you. We need your big old brain and your ability to see magic, or else maybe all the livingry or whatever the hell you call it on *Spaceship Earth* is gonna get eaten. Got it?"

The Cog nodded thoughtfully. "I can comprehend the necessity to protect a biological continuation of intelligent life, but I must demand to know where we're—"

"Nope. Secret. You'll hear it in the briefing, same as everybody else." Sullivan patted Buckminster Fuller on the shoulder. "Don't worry. All the famous scientific expeditions had lots of men with guns on board. Lewis and Clark had guns. Magellan had guns. Hell, Charles Darwin carried himself a Walker Colt on the *Beagle.*"

"He did?"

Sullivan had no idea. He'd just made that up. "Sure. You're in good company. I've got to go talk to the captain." And then Sullivan hurried down the ladder before Fuller had a chance to respond. He breathed a sigh of relief when he saw that their resident genius didn't attempt to follow.

The *Traveler* was the most advanced airship to ever come out of Detroit. Originally designed as a new technology test bed and UBF's attempt at breaking the world altitude record, its speed and maneuverability were shocking, and it was capable of ridiculously long voyages. The *Traveler* was the smoothest meshing of mechanical engineering and magical know-how in history. Their dirigible was a prototype, and according to United Blimp & Freight CEO Francis Stuyvesant, *the future of air travel.*

However, Fuller was right, the *Traveler* had not originally been intended to be a warship. John Browning and a crew of creatively malicious pirates had been given three months to turn the *Traveler* into a fighting vessel. Browning knew more about weapons than any man who had ever lived, so for its relatively small size, the *Traveler* now packed one hell of a punch. Fuller had been adamant against using his Power to create anything offensive, but he was a Cog genius when it came to designing defensive or life-saving magic systems. In theory, the Traveler could now go higher, faster, and farther in worse weather than any other airship in history.

Bob Southunder and his pirate crew had managed to harass the greatest navy in the world using nothing but a Great War-era zeppelin cobbled together out of spare parts and creativity. Given access to the actual UBF plant, Southunder had forced through a lot of changes on the *Traveler*, some of which the engineers had disagreed with. It was a case of craft theory versus real-world experience, but since Pirate Bob was the one who would be in charge should it go down in flames, Francis had backed the captain's ideas more often than not.

One of Southunder's demands had been to use hydrogen instead of helium, Imperium style. Helium was safer, but it provided less lift and it was a scarce commodity in most of the places their mission might take them. He'd argued that the crew's Cracklers could use their magic to power machinery capable of processing water into hydrogen to fill the bags and for fuel. Worst case scenario, in case of a catastrophic failure, that's what their Torches were for.

It took a while to maneuver through the narrow corridors. The *Traveler* had two separate, lightly armored, compartmentalized bags, each one nearly three hundred feet long, with a superstructure that filled the space between them and an armored command deck at the very front. To Sullivan's untrained eye the *Traveler* looked like a bigger version of the *Tempest,* which had struck him as a mighty fine dirigible for the few brief moments he had been able to ride on it before it had corkscrewed into the ground in central California. It reminded him of two footballs, side by side, only with wings, and several great big engines on the back.

And the engines... They were like something out of the science-fiction magazines; their engines were awe-inspiring and completely terrifying at the same time. Sullivan had never seen, or more importantly, *heard* anything like them before. The roar was incredible. Francis called the new designs *turbo-jets.* They were an invention of one of the Cogs, a Brit by the name of Whittle, from the R&D department at UBF. Sullivan had never known that the British called their Cogs *Boffins* before. It was a pretty innocuous name for a wizard who could come up with an engine that could suck a man in and spit out confetti, an unfortunate event which had happened to one poor UBF engineer during initial testing. Captain Southunder had called the Boffin-designed turbo-jets a tool of the devil, at least until he'd taken the *Traveler* out for its first test flight, and then he'd done nothing but sing their praises ever since. The *Traveler* was just that damn *fast.* During the test run from Michigan to California they had broken the world airship speed record by going just over a hundred miles per hour. The UBF Cogs estimated that the *Traveler* was capable of a hundred and twenty. Since Southunder's magical power was manipulating the weather, up to and including hurricane-force winds, he was already betting on a hundred and fifty with the right tail wind.

Sure, there were airplanes that could easily do three times that, but none of them had the range or could carry the amount of men and cargo Sullivan thought they might need. With the *Traveler,* Sullivan had a hybrid airship with firepower just shy of a Great War heavy cruiser, which could fly most of the way around the world without stopping, and was loaded with every nifty device UBF could stuff onboard, including a teleradar powerful enough to let them detect aircraft miles away. Cog superscience sure was something. *Popular*

Mechanics could get a year's worth of articles just out of one ride on the *Traveler*.

Francis had made him promise to bring the *Traveler* back in one piece. The young head of UBF had fought an uphill battle against his board of directors in order to fund the Pathfinder expedition. As far as the board was concerned, the name *Pathfinder* was because this was a scientific expedition to test the boundaries of what an airship was capable of. They were unaware that the Pathfinder was simply the name the Chairman had assigned to an outer-space monster. That might have caused a few problems for the shareholders. If they'd known that their multi-million dollar experiment was being crewed by a gang of pirates and a magical secret society, they'd probably have tossed Francis out on his ear.

Well, they could certainly try, but the last few years had changed Francis Stuyvesant. He was no longer just the mouthy young punk Sullivan had kneecapped with a .32 the first time they'd met. Francis was proving to be as ruthless and capable at running a business as his grandfather had been. Their recent hardships had molded Francis into an actual leader of men. Sullivan approved. So Francis had put his foot down and gotten Sullivan a fancy airship.

It sure was nice having rich friends.

Sullivan found Captain Southunder on the bridge, readying the *Traveler* to leave the airfield. Before meeting Southunder, he had sort of assumed that a pirate captain would have been loud, barking orders, wrangling a group of rowdy privateers, that sort of thing, but Pirate Bob, as he was affectionately known by his crew, was a quiet and understated man. There was no drama with Pirate Bob, he simply had no tolerance for the stupid or lazy, so every man on his crew learned his job and how to do it without him having to babysit them, or they got tossed over the side.

Southunder had been easy enough to convince about the threat of the Enemy. This was a man who had spent a big chunk of his life protecting part of the Geo-Tel from the Imperium, so the concept of a world-ending event wasn't that farfetched for the good captain. "Welcome back, Sullivan," Southunder said without turning away from the window. "We lift off in thirty minutes."

"How's it shaking out?"

"It? Ships are *she*. Not *it*. Don't hurt her feelings, Mr. Sullivan."

Sullivan chuckled. "Aye aye, Captain."

"Any problem picking up your psychopath?"

"Sociopath," he corrected.

"There's a difference?"

"Well..." Despite his addiction to reading scholarly texts, psychology wasn't one of the fields Sullivan had ever bothered to study. If it hadn't been for Bradford Carr's morbid fascination over Wells' supposed effectiveness, he wouldn't have bothered with an alienist at all. "I actually don't know."

Southunder turned from the window. "With the bunch you've put together, one more crazy shouldn't hurt."

The captain's tone suggested that there had been trouble. "Toru again?"

"Your Jap is a popular fella, but no. He's been quiet, probably trying to avoid ticking my men off enough so that they won't put a knife in his back."

"Good luck," Sullivan said. "Stabbing Toru's likely to upset him some."

"I've warned them...Still can't believe I'm on a ship with an Imperium Iron Guard." Southunder moved closer to Sullivan and pretended to check the navigation chart. Some other members of the crew were coming up the ladder, so the captain lowered his voice so only Sullivan would hear. "You'd be hard pressed to find one of my marauders that hasn't lost family to those cold-blooded bastards. If somebody doesn't try to do him in by the time we get to Canada, I'll have vastly underestimated their restraint. "

Having a former Iron Guard on the crew wasn't good for morale, but Toru Tokugawa was the expert on the Pathfinder, and for that fight at least, he was theoretically on their side. "Keep them focused, Captain. That's all I ask."

"I'll do my best, Sullivan, but I'd recommend you learn everything you can from that Imperial sooner rather than later...You know, just in case he has an *accident*. The sky is a dangerous place."

"More dangerous with us in it, I imagine," Sullivan said. "You get us there in one piece. I'll take care of the rest."

"Speaking of *there*. Most of these men don't know your plan. They know bits and pieces, so they're filling in the blanks with bad guesses and rumors, even your fellow knights. They need to know. This one ship is going to declare war on the entire Imperium soon. Once we cross that line, there's no going back."

"They'll be all in. There's too much at stake not to be."

"When are you planning on briefing the whole crew?"

"Right after dinner. It's harder to mutiny on a full stomach."

Southunder smiled. "I'll have the cook prepare something hearty."

The *Traveler's* crew was made up of one hundred men. *Correction,* men and one woman. It might be offensive to some or scandalous to others, but Sullivan was too pragmatic to dwell on it. The idea of having women in what was fundamentally a military unit was completely foreign to him. Sullivan was of the mindset that the fairer sex should be protected, kept from harm whenever possible, but the lone woman aboard the *Traveler* was here for a damn good reason. Hell, Francis had even named the ship in honor of one of the most dangerous Actives anyone had ever known, and she'd been a girl. Not to mention Sullivan's last girlfriend could pick up and toss an automobile, so he wasn't one to underestimate the fairer sex.

Nonetheless, having men and women serving on the same boat was an odd concept to somebody old-fashioned, but Pirate Bob's marauders had a woman onboard for years without any problems. Though, it probably helped that Lady Origami had been their only Torch and had kept the *Bulldog Marauder* from being engulfed in flames and crashing into the ocean on several occasions. Plus, nobody was going to get fresh with a girl who could set you on fire with her mind.

There were a few women he knew who he would've loved to have along on the expedition. Jane was about the best damn Healer there was, but was one of the backbone members of the American knights, and she and her husband Dan were now stuck serving as something akin to ambassadors for their kind, dealing with all of the liars and rats in Washington. Sullivan didn't envy them and would much rather go battle Iron Guard any day.

The other woman he'd thought about asking had been Pemberly Hammer. As a Justice, her magic was rare and powerful, but she was a BI agent now, and answered to J. Edgar Hoover. Even though Hoover was technically almost an ally, maybe on a good day, all the Grimnoir knew he'd turn on them the instant the winds blew wrong . . . Or maybe that was just what Sullivan had told himself, so as to justify not dragging Hammer along on a mission this dangerous. He knew damn good and well that if he'd asked her, she would've volunteered. Hammer was as tough as anyone, had a Power that was half polygraph and half perfect compass, yet he hadn't asked for her help. That said a lot more about what he thought their odds of surviving were than any commentary on Hammer's abilities. It was difficult for a man like him to admit that he might be soft on someone.

Sullivan leaned against the wall and took the opportunity to enjoy a cigarette while he waited for the crew to finish their chow. Because of the fire danger on board the *Traveler,* and considering that their Torches were still only human, smoking was only allowed in certain areas, the galley being one of them. Because of that, the air was thick with smoke.

One of the reasons the whole damn hydrogen-filled ship wasn't a complete death trap walked past him carrying a tray of food. He could tell that the diminutive Japanese girl had to resist the urge to bow when she saw him. Old habits die hard, but Pirate Bob's Marauders weren't big on any habits born in the Imperium. "Hello, Mr. Sullivan."

Sullivan tipped his fedora. "Lady Origami." He didn't know her real name, doubted anybody did actually. "Good to see you."

"And good to see you, Mr. Sullivan," she answered. "Captain speaks highly of you. Our journey is very important. I look forward to this journey."

Either she was lying, or she was a lot harder than she looked, which would be easy, since she looked like a porcelain doll. But rumor was she'd escaped an Imperium school, and she'd certainly spent the last few years keeping a gang of rowdy pirates alive, so looks could be deceiving. "Your English has gotten a lot better."

"Thank you. I have been practicing a lot." The marauders didn't have any sort of official uniform, though most of them wound up wearing coveralls and tough work clothes. Lady Origami was the same, grease-stained and with her hair covered in a bandana, only she'd decorated her *uniform* with bits of silk, surely looted from Imperium vessels. She reached into a sash and pulled something out. "I made this for you for our journey. It is for good fortune."

"For me?" He held out one hand and she placed the tiny object in the center of his palm. It was made out of paper, but the paper had been folded hundreds and hundreds of times, until it had been perfectly and intricately shaped into a tiny three-dimensional animal. "That sure is something."

"It is a frog."

"Yeah. I can tell. It even has toes. You're really good."

"Paper burns the fastest of all. That is why I like it most. The frog means we will return. I do not know how to say this correctly." She looked down, embarrassed by the gift. "I must go."

"It's okay. I understand. And thank you."

And then she hurried off. It was a little awkward, but that was to be expected, since the first time they'd met she'd tried to seduce him for some unfathomable reason. *Except that had been right after Delilah . . . Never mind.* He needed to focus on the present, not live in the past. Sullivan carefully placed the paper frog into his shirt pocket. Their female crew member was an odd one.

The floor rocked beneath his feet, a reminder that they were actually moving. The *Traveler* was so smooth that sometimes it was easy to forget they were in the air, and after a time you even began to tune out the unearthly howl of the engines. Heinrich Koenig walked *through* the wall and appeared next to him. Sullivan was now used to the Fade doing that, so it didn't startle him nearly as much as it used to. "Heinrich," Sullivan greeted.

"Everything is ready," Heinrich said, keeping his voice low.

"Good." The young German was one of the most paranoid of the Grimnoir, and that was saying something. Heinrich had a Fade's natural mistrust but his upbringing in the treacherous environment of Dead City had taken it to new heights. Regardless, Sullivan was glad to have Heinrich onboard. "Let me know what you find out."

"This should prove enlightening."

"Try not to kill anybody until *after* we interrogate them."

Heinrich grinned. "I cannot promise this, my friend." He clapped Sullivan on the shoulder, and then went to join the other Grimnoir.

Word had spread through the ship that Sullivan was going to brief them on their next move. Since they were still in the US, and the winds were mild, only a handful of the crew weren't in the galley. Normally they would have eaten in shifts, so the narrow room was far too crowded, almost standing room only. Captain Southunder had the bridge. Sullivan suspected it was because he wanted to see how

Sullivan would handle the marauders without Southunder's calming influence present.

It was expected, but still disappointing, to see that the crew had segregated themselves into a few distinct groups. The biggest crowd was made up of members of the Grimnoir society. Sullivan knew many of them, and had fought alongside several. Lance Talon was the senior member, Heinrich was his second in command, but since this expedition was Sullivan's idea, they were both deferring to him. The knights as a whole were oath-bound to do their duty. Every single one of them was an Active with fighting experience against the Imperium, the Soviets, or, more recently, his own government's OCI. Since many members of the Grimnoir society still thought the Enemy was a figment of Sullivan's imagination, these knights were volunteers. The society as a whole was torn about the Pathfinder mission. They were few in number as it was, and their threats were numerous. To have forty of their best leave on what could be a wild-goose chase inspired by one girl's crazed ramblings and the word of their greatest foe's ghost was seen as a fool's errand by many of the elders.

The next corner of the room was filled with the surviving crew of the *F.S. Bulldog Marauder* and the soldiers of fortune who had worked with Southunder in the Free Cities. These were more of an unknown quantity, originally united by nothing more than their hatred of the Imperium. They were made up of every race, creed, and color, but then again, the Imperium didn't discriminate when it came to invading countries and ruining lives. The marauders were dangerous and crafty, and knew how to wring the most out of an airship. Sullivan figured they were mostly in it for the money, a few for the adventure, and the rest because they'd follow Bob Southunder into hell if their captain thought it was a good idea. A handful of them were magical, and only a couple of those were strong enough to qualify as Actives, but every last one of them knew how to fight, and nobody could run an airship like the marauders.

The smallest group was the UBF employees, mostly made up of engineers and technical experts. Francis had picked out his best and brightest, given them the pitch, and then paid them large amounts of money to come along. This was the part of the crew that Sullivan was the least familiar with, but Francis swore up and down that they were all extremely good at their jobs.

The *Traveler* was outfitted with every high-technology device produced by Cog science short of a peace ray, and that was only because John Browning hadn't been able to figure out a way to attach one to a ship this size. Cog science could be tricky. Browning was too busy keeping America from falling apart to come on this journey, and for that Sullivan was thankful because he thought John was getting too dang old for this sort of business. The UBF men knew enough to keep their magical alterations working, and one of the Grimnoir was supposed to be a very talented Fixer.

The UBF would keep them in the air, the marauders would get them there in one piece, and the knights would take care of business. *Simple.*

The fourth and smallest group wasn't really a group at all, but rather the individuals who had either been forced on him or those he felt he needed who didn't fit in with anybody else. Wells was the newest addition to that list, and the alienist had picked a spot in back where he could observe unnoticed. Cleaned up and with a fresh set of clothing, Wells looked even more unremarkable. Toru was another one that fit in that category, but their former Iron Guard didn't eat in the galley with the others. It was probably safer for everyone that way. Sullivan checked his watch. Toru was supposed to attend the briefing, but he hadn't arrived yet. He probably wouldn't even show, just to prove some point.

Unofficially, Sullivan had no doubt that the newly reformed OCI had a snitch onboard. With all of the controversy about the Active Registration Act going on, this many powerful Actives doing who knew what with a private warship? Hell, the *Traveler's* armament alone was violating several of Roosevelt's new federal laws, but he'd like to see the Treasury agent dumb enough to try and enforce them. Even though OCI was under new, supposedly noncorrupt management, it would have been surprising if the secret police didn't have somebody on the inside. You couldn't put together an expedition of this magnitude without word getting out. However, Sullivan wasn't currently worried about the OCI sort of spy. Let them report back. Then maybe the fools in Washington would realize what they were really dealing with and pull their heads out of their collective behinds. Luckily the *Traveler* would be leaving the OCI's jurisdiction, and frankly, Sullivan was a lot more worried about the Enemy than he was about a bunch of bureaucrats meddling in his affairs. Not that he wouldn't deal with them when—or if—he got back. After Mason Island, Sullivan was done playing games, but first things first, he had to save magic before the petty bureaucrats could try and control it.

No, the spies he was worried about were the Imperium kind. When this many people knew about the mission, it was inevitable the Imperium would find out, and those bastards would sabotage everything, but Lance and Heinrich had come up with a plan for them.

Chowtime was over. The conversations had died down. All eyes were on him. Sullivan finished his smoke, ground it out in an ashtray, and walked to where a world map had been stuck to the wall. The Grimnoir knights who had been leaning on it quickly got out of his way. They were as curious as everyone else.

It was pointless to ask for everyone's attention. They were eager to begin the hunt. "Let's get to it." When he'd led men into battle, he'd preferred to just lead by example, from the front. The words had always come hard, but since he'd wound up in charge of this expedition, it felt like he should say something motivational. "Most of you don't know much about what we're after, or where we're going, just that it's dangerous as hell, but you were all man enough to volunteer to do what has to be done . . . So thanks."

And that was as good as the motivation was going to get. "You all had a chance to back out. You're still here, which means you're stuck. Captain Southunder runs this ship. I run this operation. You all know who you answer to and you know the chain of command. You got a problem, I'll listen, but if you don't like my decision, too bad. Questions? No? Good. So let me tell you what we're up against."

Toru had silently entered the galley while Sullivan's back had been turned. The Iron Guard was big for a Japanese, all solid muscle, and the other members of the crew automatically parted around him like fish with a shark in the water. There were a lot of uneasy or hostile glances sent Toru's way. He simply stared back, daring them to try something. Sullivan gave him a small nod in greeting. "Our expert's arrived."

The Grimnoir's normal strategy for taking on Iron Guards was to try and outnumber them five to one. That usually made for a fair fight. There were a handful of Grimnoir, like Sullivan himself, or Faye before she'd gotten killed, who could beat those odds, but they normally held true. Toru was outnumbered ninety-nine to one on this ship, and he still didn't seem to give a shit. Toru nodded his way. "Please, do not stop on my account."

All of the volunteers had been told about the true nature of magic before they'd signed up, so there was no need to waste their time. They wanted details. "You all know what we're after. It is a little chunk of the thing that is chasing the Power. The Chairman called it the Pathfinder, so that name will do as good as any. We'll have one chance to kill it before it calls home. Other Pathfinders have come here twice before. Toru here knows all about how the last ones worked."

The former Iron Guard surveyed the crew menacingly. "Each one has been different, but they are all creatures of nightmares, so deadly that Okubo Tokugawa, the greatest warrior of all time, barely achieved victory. They eat magic and then use it against you, kill everything, and then turn the corpses into weapons. The strongest amongst you may have a small chance of survival." The room was dead quiet except for the sound of the engines. "Most of you will surely perish."

Sullivan sighed. He should have known better.

Lance Talon broke the silence. The burly Grimnoir wasn't about to take attitude from an Iron Guard, former or not. "What the hell? You son of a—"

"I do not care if you take offense, Grimnoir." Toru snapped. "I have vowed to defeat this threat to honor my father's final command. Lying to you will only encourage overconfidence, which will lead to our defeat. Believe my words. The Order of Iron Guard were formed specifically to combat this Enemy."

Lance stood up from behind the dinner table, revealing that he had a big revolver hanging from a gun belt. Sullivan remembered—a little too late to do any good—that Lance's wife and children had been burned to death in an Iron Guard attack. "Easy, Lance."

Lance's hand was casually hovering over the butt of his Colt. "Except your precious Iron Guard are too busy raping and pillaging their way through a bunch of peasants to do their job, now ain't they?"

"Yes." Toru's eyes narrowed dangerously. "The Iron Guard have become distracted from their true purpose. I will convince them of the error of their ways." He slowly turned and addressed the entire room. "I will teach you everything I know before we engage the Pathfinder. It will devour your Power, rip the life from your bodies, and then twist your remains into weapons. Yet, as capable as it is, it can still be defeated. Hopefully your inevitable deaths will not bring shame upon our cause."

"That'll do, Toru."

Toru gave Sullivan a small bow. As proud and stiff-necked as Toru was, he had still sworn that he would obey Sullivan's orders. "I will be in my quarters until you need me." Toru left the galley. He seemed to take the tension with him.

"Wait... How come he gets his own room?" Doctor Wells asked.

Sullivan was just close enough to hear someone's whispered answer. "Because everyone is terrified of him."

"Hmmm... So that's all it takes?" Wells responded thoughtfully. "I see..."

Sullivan looked at Lance and shook his head. Lance returned grudgingly to his seat. "We can't count on those Imperium bastards to fix this problem for us. The US government doesn't believe us. So we're gonna have to do it ourselves. All systems are go. Captain Southunder says that the *Traveler* is in top shape." There was a chorus of cheers and hoots from the pirates and the UBF. *Good.* They had pride in their ship. "We're ready to head out."

"Head out where?" a young knight shouted.

And that was the big question everybody was so eager about. Sullivan went to the map and jabbed his finger into Montana. "We're here. We're going to cross into Canada, and once night falls, we're going to kill the lights and head west, then up the coast, along the Aleutians, into Kamchatka." Sullivan thumped the map. "Get your cold-weather clothing together, 'cause I hear it's not nice."

"That's deep Imperium territory," said one of the marauders. Sullivan knew this one, Wesley Dalton, or Barns to his friends. He was Pirate Bob's best pilot, and since he was an Active Lucky, he was the only reason any of them had survived the *Tempest* crash. "Sounds fun."

"The Japanese have locked it up tight since the Siberian resistance surrendered. We're not expecting them to have much there in the way of defenses. There's a small Imperium garrison up in the mountains by the name of Koryak. Expect high winds and nasty cold. That's where we think the Pathfinder is gonna land shortly."

"How do you know?" asked one of the UBF men.

Sullivan looked around the room. Fuller wasn't around, which made this convenient. "Have you met Buckminster Fuller?" Several of the UBF engineers had visible reactions, ranging from shaking their heads sadly to rolling their eyes. Fuller was squirrely as all get out, but the important part was, his stuff worked. Even while driving you nuts, you had to admire the brilliance of his magical creations. "Yeah, I know, but he's the most brilliant Cog ever when it comes to reading magic. He came up with a spell for us. I saw it myself, clear as day." Sullivan's reputation for quality spellbinding preceded him. "Trust me. That's the place. We're taking our time, conserving fuel, but the weather looks good, so we should be there in forty-eight hours. The knights will go down with me. We'll take the base while Captain Southunder covers us from the *Traveler*."

"What about the space monster?" asked a pirate.

"For the next two days, Toru will be conducting training in the cargo hold." He didn't know that yet, so informing the Iron Guard would be amusing. "The Jap doesn't think we can do this. Let's prove him wrong."

"The Chairman killed this thing before, and we killed the Chairman," Lance said. "I like our odds."

Traitor.

That was what they were calling him now. The word stung.

Toru was one of the thousand sons of Okubo Tokugawa. He had served with distinction in the elite Imperium Iron Guard and had once even been in contention for the vaunted position of First. He had served in several war zones, winning multiple commendations for his bravery and tactical prowess. He had then been assigned to the Imperium Diplomatic Corps and been a student of Ambassador Hattori, one of the original members of the legendary Dark Ocean. Toru's integrity should have been above reproach.

He was following the final command of his father, a command so important that even death could not keep the Chairman from issuing it. He alone was honoring the wishes of the greatest man who had ever lived. It was the Imperium which had lost its way. They were the fools who were blindly following an imposter. Ambassador Hattori had given Toru his memories at the moment of his death. Toru knew the truth. Only Toru understood that the Enemy was coming. The vulture that was profiting from the real Chairman's death was hiding that dreaded fact. Who were these dogs to question his honor? Who were they to call him traitor?

The Grimnoir had intercepted the Imperium communication in San Francisco and brought it to him for translation. It had been a test. He had no doubt that since the Grimnoir did not trust him, they would have his translation checked for accuracy. There were no Imperium secrets in the letter to protect, so he had given them the truth.

The message had been a warning to all of the cells working within the United States that Iron Guard Toru was a traitor to the Imperium, and that if that he was spotted, to alert their handlers at once. It had then gone on to list his many crimes, a few of which were even true. It had read that one of the thousand sons of Okubo Tokugawa had fallen in with the Grimnoir Society. This was an insult to the Imperium and a shame upon the Order of Iron Guard. He had murdered Ambassador Hattori and several of his own men. Since Toru had only murdered one of the men, that made him suspect that the assassins that had been sent by the false Chairman had removed the other embassy staff who had known too much.

Gold was promised to anyone who could provide information on Toru's whereabouts, and anyone who managed to erase this shame from the world would be given a wealth beyond their dreams and a position of importance within the court bureaucracy.

Toru Tokugawa was now the most wanted man in the Imperium.

The worst part was that every espionage plan he'd been involved with, and there were many that had originated at the Washington embassy, were now compromised. Cells would be rearranged. Undercover agents would be pulled. The Chairman's mission of conquest in America had been dealt a severe blow. The message implied that Toru had been a Grimnoir agent, and that he had been recruited years ago after losing face and shaming himself as a coward during the occupation of Manchuria. That was nothing but an insult. Toru truly loved the Imperium. He would never betray the Chairman's mission of purification. He believed in the doctrine of strength above all else. His integrity would never allow him to give valuable Imperium secrets to the Grimnoir. He was only here because his father's ghost had demanded it.

His attempt at meditation was a failure. Peace would not come. His mind would not clear. Toru's bed consisted of a mat and a few blankets thrown down on the cold metal floor, and now, meditating only seemed to focus his discomforts. The small portion of the cargo hold which he had claimed for himself was permanently chilled. The constant thrum of the *Traveler's* unearthly engines grated on his nerves. He had given up his position of status for *this*?

What he really wanted to do was take up his steel tetsubo and start smashing things, but a warrior did not disgrace himself with displays of emotion, especially when among his people's enemies. He would not show weakness in front of the wretched Grimnoir...Also, the interior of a fragile dirigible was a terrible place to go mad with an eighty-pound club and superhuman strength.

How *dare* they bring up Manchuria? Yes, he had questioned his leaders, but it had not been because of cowardice...It had been... *What?* He had disobeyed those orders why? *Compassion?* No...That was not what had cost him his promotion and gotten him removed from the front and sent to serve with the Diplomatic Corps in America. That was not why he'd disobeyed.

It had been guilt. It had been *conscience*.

He crushed the letter in his fist and tried to go back to his meditations. After a few minutes of futile mental exercise, he decided to concentrate on physical exercise instead. The one thing the *Traveler* had in abundance was pipes sticking through the walls, and he'd already found a few solid enough to do chin-ups from.

Careful not to tap into his own Power or any of the eight magical kanji branded onto his skin, for that would have been cheating, Toru began doing repetitions. The stronger his own body was, the harder he could push his Power without damage. Since it was discovered that he was a Brute, the Imperium schools had made sure he'd spent hours a day doing physical training, every day, for a decade. Toru was no stranger to exercise. Besides, it helped him think.

The Imperium had wanted him to read this message. Diplomatic Corps training had taught him that a message such as this would have been encrypted. This message had not been. Surely, as soon as they discovered that he had faked his own death, the code key would have been changed. He should not have been able to read a real, current message.

They were trying to shake him. They were trying to insult him, make him angry, to cause him to do something foolish. If that was the case, they had underestimated his resolve. It would not work. Okubo Tokugawa's final command had been to Jake Sullivan, ergo, Toru was honor-bound to see Sullivan's mission completed, no matter what.

If the imposter wanted a fight, so be it. He might look and sound just like the Chairman, but it was doubtful that he would be nearly as invincible.

"Toru."

Distracted and purposefully limiting his magical senses, he had not heard Sullivan approach. The Heavy was quiet for his size. Toru let go of the pipe and dropped to the floor. "How long have you been there?"

"About thirty chin-ups."

Toru had counted forty-two and hadn't yet begun to sweat, but with so many men who hated him on this vessel, allowing someone to sneak up on him was unacceptable. He would have to pay better attention in the future. "What do you want?"

Sullivan wandered into the storage room, idly inspecting the pile of weapons stacked on the floor. The broken remains of Toru's Iron Guard katana were on top of the stack. Thankfully, Sullivan did not remark on the broken sword. He'd been there when Toru had smashed it to demonstrate his resolve. "It's about the crew."

"If they cannot comprehend the enormity of the task, then they will fail."

"Fighting in the Great War taught me a few things. I've seen what happens when you kill a unit's morale. You might as well kill their bodies, 'cause next time they go into combat, they're either useless or good as dead."

"Irrelevant." Toru snorted. "It should not matter. Imperium men do not have this problem. Superior warriors embrace death in order to fulfill their missions. The greatest honor a warrior can achieve is dying in his lord's service."

"These ain't Imperium men. The Chairman's bullshit won't fly here."

Toru returned to his uncomfortable patch of floor and took a seat. "One of our nations has conquered a tenth of the planet over the last two generations while the other has grown fat, complacent, and apathetic. Please, share more of your opinion on which of our differing methods is the superior."

Sullivan frowned. Toru knew he had him there. Sullivan, despite being a product of a weak culture, was still a true warrior. Trying in vain to convince the American authorities of the danger of the Pathfinder had left Sullivan infuriated and baffled. Toru had just won the argument before it had even begun, and Sullivan didn't even know it yet. The Imperium school's education hadn't all been physical.

"Only the fools in charge are like that. Don't underestimate a regular American's backbone."

"Yet here we are. One lonely ship ... Did you really come here simply to debate philosophy?"

Sullivan pretended to take in the room. "Riding around on a blimp named after the little girl that killed your father ... That's got to stick in your craw."

It was a rather astute observation. Despite appearing to be an oaf, the Heavy could have made a passable diplomat. "Is there a point to this visit, Sullivan?"

"Yeah. Take your head out of your ass so you can see the sunshine. Whether you like them or not, these men are our only hope of beating the Pathfinder. You best start acting like it."

"That is an order?"

"It is."

The things that I do to fulfill my father's commands ... Toru nodded. "So be it."

"Good. You'll get them up to speed then. These ain't Imperium. They're free men, and they'll fight better if they know they can win. Convince them they can."

"You wish me to lie?"

"You won't have to. I intend to win."

"Optimism is such an American trait. Optimism is a lie."

"And pessimism lowers morale."

"Not pessimism. Pessimism is another weak western concept. I speak of *fatalism*. A warrior accepts his fate. He willingly does whatever must be done to complete his task and accepts whatever consequences that entails. That is the only true way to assure victory ... Yet, I will do as you order."

"You're a real piece of work." Sullivan moved to leave, and then paused in the doorway. "Listen . . . This thing with your own country out to get you . . . I heard about the letter. I know how you feel."

Indeed, Jake Sullivan had once been declared a traitor to his country, a scapegoat for a conspiracy of ambitious fools, but Sullivan had a child's understanding of honor, and though he was a powerful combatant, he had no comprehension of the true warrior's code. Sullivan's country was corrupt and weak; he should have expected to be betrayed by it.

"You know nothing."

Traveler

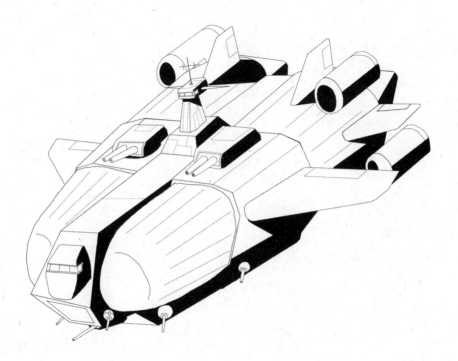

⫷Chapter 4⫸

Wyatt Earp was one of the few men I personally knew who I regarded as absolutely destitute of physical fear. I have often remarked, and I am not alone in my conclusions, that what goes for courage in a man is generally fear of what others will think of him. In other words, personal bravery is largely made up of self-respect, egotism, and apprehension of the opinions of others. Wyatt Earp's apparent recklessness in time of danger is wholly characteristic. Personal fear doesn't enter into the equation, and when everything is said and done, I believe he values his own opinion of himself more than that of others, and it is his own good report he seeks to preserve . . . He never at any time in his career resorted to shooting excepting cases where such a course was absolutely necessary, such as when combating those with wizard's magic . . . Wyatt could scrap with his fists, and had often taken all the fight out of bad men, as they were called, with no other weapons than those provided by nature . . . Yes, you've heard the stories, but you do not know the half of it. Why, this one time back in '08, we helped out Jack Pershing and his Knights of New York with a problem involving a stolen Tesla weapon and some of those branded Japanese bastards. You should have seen—Wait. Strike that. That never happened. Forgive an old man's ramblings.

—Bat Masterson,
Interview in the Baltimore Mercurium, 1921

UBF *Traveler*

A FEW HOURS LATER, Heinrich floated down through the ceiling and woke Sullivan up. "It is time." The Fade pulled the chain and the small room's single lightbulb lit up. Despite this being considered the officer's quarters, there were still five other bunks, most of which were currently occupied, and the men all began to grumble and mutter at the sudden light.

Sullivan maneuvered himself out of the tiny hole his cot sat in and managed to not hit his head. At least he'd gotten the biggest bunk aboard, which meant that it was still far too tiny for a man of his stature. The floor-level bunk beneath him was filled with equipment rather than a person, mostly because nobody was brave enough to sleep below a man whose magically augmented mass made him weigh in around four hundred pounds. Sullivan's watch was sitting next to his .45. He picked them both up. "One in the morning. That didn't take long..." He'd figured it wouldn't, so he hadn't even bothered to take his boots off before going to sleep. "Who is it?"

"One of the UBF men, Skaggs."

Sullivan had only spoken to him once. He remembered Skaggs as a round-faced, gravel-voiced fella, one of Francis' mechanics. "Where?"

"Aft rope room," Heinrich answered. The Fade was excited. He enjoyed this sort of thing far too much. "Lance has eyes on him."

"I'm glad you boys didn't just pop him."

"It was so very tempting."

Their conversation was starting to wake up the others in the officer's quarters. "Wha, huh?" asked Barns, sitting up in bed and automatically reaching for the shoulder holster hanging from a peg on the wall. "Wha's going on?"

"Go back to sleep," Sullivan ordered the pilot before he could pull his machine pistol. Pirates were a jumpy bunch. "I'll tell you in the morning."

"Kill the damned light, will ya?"

Sullivan pulled the chain, then followed Heinrich out into the hall. Unlike most UBF vessels, the *Traveler* hadn't been built for comfort, and the corridors were dimly lit, with bare metal walls. He had to duck every few feet to avoid banging his skull on a random pipe. The rope rooms were at the very bottom of the ship, so they'd have to hurry to catch him in the act.

Nabbing Skaggs alive meant that they'd be able to question him, and if you were going to question somebody, might as well do it with your human polygraph machine around. "You fetch a Reader?"

"Lance sent a mouse."

"He'll love waking up to that in his face. Best get the Mouth too, just in case our spy don't feel like talking."

"Way ahead of you, Jake. You forget how much more practiced at this treachery business I am than you." Heinrich looked back, eyes wide as he thought of something. "The spy is an engineer."

"So?"

"Skaggs knows the guts of the ship. If he gets orders back to sabotage us, who knows what he could harm?"

"I really don't feel like crashing another one of Francis' fancy blimps." He was just holding Heinrich up, what with his having to walk around solid objects instead of through them. "Go. I'll catch up."

Heinrich nodded, then his features seemed to blur and turn grey, and then he sank through the floor and disappeared. It was a good thing too, because it then saved Sullivan the indignity of trying to maneuver his bulk down the narrow stairwell in front of witnesses. His feet barely fit on the steps. "UBF designed this thing for pygmies," he muttered.

He reached the rope room a few minutes later, but judging by how Skaggs was lying in a crumpled heap with blood all over the side of his face, and Heinrich was standing over him with a pipe wrench in hand, Sullivan hadn't needed to rush.

He nudged the fallen UBF engineer with his toe to make sure he was still alive. Skaggs groaned. "He give you trouble?"

"Nothing a wrench to the face couldn't fix." Heinrich answered. "But I suppose a wrench to the face solves most personnel issues."

"Check this out." Lance's deep voice came from an empty corner of the room. "Down here." Sullivan stepped over the piled coils of rope and spotted a small brown mouse running around in circles. The floor gleamed from shards of broken glass.

Sullivan knelt and carefully picked up one of the biggest pieces of glass. It was mirrored, and someone had scratched lines into it. "Communication spell?"

"Yep," the mouse answered, impossibly loud for a critter that could fit in the palm of his hand. Since Lance Talon was a Beastie, and his Power allowed him to take control of animals, they'd made sure that the *Traveler* had a mice problem for occasions like this. Sure, they'd eventually make a mess of things, but then they'd just have to get a cat... Or he supposed Lance could just take over all the mice and have them jump overboard. Beasties probably didn't really have trouble with pests. "That spell detector Fuller put together went nuts. I found our friend here telling somebody about how we were heading for Siberia."

Heinrich had dragged the semi-conscious Skaggs upright and was patting him down, looking for weapons. A quick search wouldn't matter if their spy had some form of offensive magic. "He an Active?"

"Not that I am aware of." Heinrich paused long enough to slap Skaggs hard on the cheek. It caused a cascading ripple through the fat of his face all the way to his extra chins. "Hey! Hey, wake up, *scheisskopf.* You try anything, I even feel a bit of magic, I feed you into a turbo-jet." Heinrich hit him even harder to make the point. "Do you understand?"

From the all the flinching as Heinrich slapped him around, it was obvious that Skaggs wasn't used to that sort of rough treatment. "Okay, okay! Stop, please." Skaggs was blinking his way back to coherence. Finally realization dawned as to just how much trouble he was in and the begging started. "Oh no. Oh no. I didn't do anything! Please don't hurt me. Please, I'm begging you."

Either he was legitimately terrified, or he was a damn fine actor. Sullivan wasn't in the mood for either. "You're getting off this blimp. Only question is if you're taking the fast way or the slow way."

"This is all a mistake!"

Sullivan held up the piece of glass. "The mistake was you thinking you could rat us out and not get caught." Skaggs' eyes flew back and forth from the piece in Sullivan's hand to the remaining bits littering the floor. He was done and he knew it. "Who're you working for?"

Skaggs might have been tougher than he first let on, or he might have just been that desperate. "Go to hell."

"Want to play it hard, huh?" Sullivan tossed the piece of glass back on the floor. "Your call." There was movement in the hall, and Sullivan looked back to see a few Grimnoir waiting at the hatch, the Reader and the Mouth he'd asked for. They were men Heinrich recruited, so Sullivan didn't really know them well yet.

"What's going on?" the tall, thin young knight asked.

"Which one are you?" Sullivan asked.

"Mike Willis. I'm a Reader."

"We got a spy," Sullivan said simply. "Let me know when he's lying." He turned back to Skaggs. "This fella is a Reader. So I'm gonna have the truth from you even if they have to suck it right outta your brain."

"Go to hell," Skaggs repeated himself through gritted teeth.

Heinrich had picked up a rather stout length of rope. They were in the rope room, after all. He looked over at Sullivan and raised an eyebrow. Sullivan shrugged, so Heinrich began to beat Skaggs with it about the head and neck. The UBF engineer rolled into a fetal position and tried to protect his face.

"I'm a Mouth," said the other knight. He was a short, downright skinny, almost frail-looking dark-haired man. "I can talk it out of him if you want, so that's not really necessary."

"You offended?"

"That depends entirely on who he's working for." The Mouth scowled. "If it's Imperium I'll want a turn beating him too."

"What's your name?"

"Genesse."

"I like that attitude, Genesse." Sullivan gave Heinrich a minute before holding up one hand. Heinrich stopped the beating. "My Teutonic friend here has very little patience for folks wasting his time. The only difference your attitude makes is determining how bad this hurts. So who were you talking to?"

Skaggs picked himself up off the floor, and tried to show a little dignity. He gave a bitter laugh. "I told them you were coming. You better let me go. The Japs will tear you apart."

Sullivan looked to the Reader, who nodded. Skaggs was working for the Imperium. It never ceased to amaze him how many fools the Imperium managed to recruit in America. He could ask why, but that was pointless. The reasons varied, but they always came back to power, greed, or worst of all, the true believers who'd caught the Chairman's twisted fevered vision of the future. The why didn't even matter.

"You on your own?"

He spit a mouthful of blood on the metal floor. "As far as I know."

Sullivan looked. Willis nodded.

"What was your mission?"

"Keep an eye on the traitor Toru. See what you were up to. Call it in."

"That's it?"

"That's it. They don't tell me much, okay?"

The Reader seemed to agree. "I'm getting a lot of thoughts about how this seemed like a good idea at the time."

It was as Sullivan had expected.

"It wasn't anything personal. I'm no Imperium nut. I've got debts. I've got problems. One of their boys, one of the scary ones with all the magic scars, he made me an offer. What was I supposed to do? They paid me a lot of money."

"You think that makes it *better*?" Heinrich snapped.

"I get any last words?"

"Only if you manage to say them real quick," Lance said through the mouse. "Heinrich, would you do the honors?"

"The fast way down?"

"Works for me."

"Wait!" Skaggs screamed, but Heinrich had already put one hand on him. The two of them turned grey, drifted through the floor, and disappeared. There was nothing but a few thousand feet of open air beneath them and the mountaintops.

"Good Lord," Willis whispered.

"That's what he gets for falling in with the Imperium," Genesse said without emotion. Now there was a man who was used to dealing with the Imperium.

Willis was horrified. "Just like that?"

"Just like that. When you're at war, and you catch a spy, you don't hold a trial. You execute them and move on." Sullivan just shook his head. "If he'd got his way, we'd all be dead. Him too . . . The idiot."

"It's not like the Japs would have stopped shooting long enough to let him off. They have no loyalty to their snitches," Lance said. Being a very long-time Grimnoir, he didn't seem quite so moved over the death of an Imperium stooge.

Genesse was looking at the broken glass. "There'll be an armada waiting in Siberia for us now."

"Good thing we weren't going there to begin with," Sullivan said. There was a brass phone mounted on the far wall of the rope room. Sullivan went over, cranked the handle a few times to charge it, then picked up the mouthpiece to raise the bridge. "Captain? This is Sullivan. It's done. You know what to do."

"I was wondering why you were lying during your briefing," Willis said. "Hey, can't blame a guy for using his Power a little. I didn't delve in or anything, but the idea that the whole thing was a setup was right at the surface during your talk."

"Not bad." Sullivan hadn't felt any intrusion. The kid was good. He'd have to watch himself better in the future.

"Fuller never built a device that could spot the Pathfinder. Fuller's brilliant. He can see magic and tweak most any design to get results, but he didn't know near enough about how that sort of spell worked to even try," Lance's mouse said. "Once Fuller sees how their magic looks, maybe, but until then, he's stuck."

"But according to Toru, the Chairman's Cogs have already built some sort of Enemy detector," Sullivan finished. "That's where we're heading."

Heinrich swam back up through the floor, alone. He solidified, then knocked his hands together, as if dusting them off. "I for one am curious to see how many more Imperium swine we have aboard."

Lance's mouse chuckled. "However many are left, you can bet your ass the next one will be a whole lot more careful."

The *Traveler* creaked and swayed as they changed course.

The Reader was still confused, but was probably too scared of the other knights' dangerous reputations to try and read their minds now. Curiosity was great and all, until you were palling around with the knights who'd fought the Chairman and lived to talk about it. "So where are we going?"

"Santa's workshop," Lance supplied, which just seemed to confuse the poor Reader even more.

Sullivan just shook his head. He was never much for secrets anyway. "The North Pole."

Paris, France

INSIDE A LITTLE CAFÉ IN PARIS, Faye sat impatiently across from the Grimnoir elder who'd voted to have her murdered, while he took his sweet time sipping a fancy little coffee and watching people walk by in the rain.

"Are you about done yet?" Faye asked him.

"You have asked me that five times already," Jacques answered pleasantly.

"Six. Because we've been here *forever*." A few of the other patrons seemed to have overheard her, but nobody seemed particularly curious about someone speaking English. Jacques had said that this part of town had lots of American tourists and *ex patriots*—whatever that meant. The staff all seemed to know Jacques, like he was a regular here. "All you do is sit around and watch stuff and drink coffee."

"Watching *stuff* and drinking coffee is how I choose to spend my time, my dear. I am retired."

Faye snorted. Retirement was a crazy European idea where you just stopped working when you got old. Who'd ever heard of such a thing? Grandpa had been older than Jacques and he'd still milked cows until the day he'd died. And if he hadn't been murdered by Madi, she knew Grandpa would still be milking cows today. "Retirement... You guys are funny. You're still Grimnoir." She pointed at the black and gold ring on his finger. It matched hers. "Grimnoir don't *retire*."

"That is not my job. That is my life. It is different."

"Come on. You promised to teach me to be the Spellbound."

Jacques took another sip. "Now you are putting words in my mouth. I promised you no such thing. You nearly flung me to my death, and I was nice enough to say I would try to help you in your quest for knowledge. I gave you my word that I would keep your presence secret from the society, and that I would help you as best I could. That is what I am attempting to do. I am a kindly old man and you are a bossy girl."

"Bossy?" By Faye's standards she hadn't even been particularly threatening. Jacques still had all his limbs. "You're supposed to be the big expert on this thing."

"Indeed. I am..." He let that hang, but after she stared at him expectantly for an eternity, he finally sighed and gave in. "I will tell you everything I know about the Spellbound. Since the elders have decided not to interfere unless you begin to make bad decisions, the very least I can do is help you comprehend what you are dealing with. However, I believe the spell's results are a direct reflection of the character of the user. Thus, in order for you to understand the Spellbound, I must first understand you."

Faye waited. Jacques took another sip, then watched a young

couple with colorful umbrellas walk by outside. The pretty young waitress came back by and Jacques smiled at her. He was a flirty old man. Then he went back to drinking and watching.

"Well?"

"My, you really are an impatient little girl, aren't you?"

Faye groaned. "That's because y'all are so *slow.*"

He nodded. "Interesting . . ."

"What?"

"You say that often. You find everyone slow. Don't you find that at all peculiar?"

"Don't blame me if all your brains don't go fast like mine." Even the smartest people she knew, like Mr. Browning or Mr. Sullivan, made decisions like their heads were filled with molasses. "Nothing personal."

"I find that fascinating. It isn't like you have been consorting with anyone slow-witted. I am at least passingly familiar with Pershing's American knights. They are an intelligent, driven, some would say *too*-decisive group. Yet everything I've learned about you suggests that they seem sluggish to you. Every report I've read about you has mentioned it. The astute have commented upon the speed of your intellect, while most have merely dismissed you as being *odd.*"

"Reports? What reports?"

"After you came to our attention, we learned as much as we could about you. Travelers who live to adulthood are rare enough as it is, but anyone who could survive the *Tokugawa* and the firing of a Peace Ray becomes a person of interest. I have been speculating about the return of the Spellbound for a very long time. Of course I asked for reports about you. Did you think that I would vote on someone's fate without knowing everything I could about them first? I am no barbarian." Jacques paused to eat a cookie, and then washed it down with more coffee.

"I swear Jacques that if you don't speed this up I'm gonna Travel out of here and take your head with me."

He raised a single eyebrow. "Like you did with the Chairman's hands? Now that was quite the impressive feat."

Faye blushed. It was nice to get some credit once in a while. "Yeah. That was pretty neat."

"Did you know that trick would work?"

She shrugged. "It seemed reasonable. I guessed it would work. It wasn't like anyone else was having any luck."

"Yet, you had never teleported and only taken part of an object before. So how did you know you could do this, especially against one such as the Chairman?"

Faye scowled. "It's hard to explain. I just looked at everything that was going on, and everything that I'd heard, and I sorta just put it all together real quick."

"Define *quick*."

"Maybe a second, I guess." That sounded reasonable. Time just sort of seemed to slow down when she got to thinking real hard about stuff. "I don't know."

"That is the sort of report that crossed my desk that made me originally suspect you were the Spellbound. It sounded so far-fetched that many of my peers dismissed the idea that you had done it at all."

"But I did do it! I beat the Chairman!" The last time she'd met with Grimnoir elders their disbelief had annoyed her to no end.

"Indeed. But you must understand their doubts. You were nearly untrained, you had never done anything like that before, yet you found a way to defeat the greatest wizard of all time. A man who had proven impervious to every assault, a man who had survived dozens of assassination attempts by extremely skilled Actives, yet you extemporaneously outwitted him. And then when you teleported the *Tempest* across the entirety of the Pacific, how long did it take you to decide you could do that?"

"You gotta think fast when you're about to get burned." Faye realized Jacques was staring at her intently and she was struck by how much smarter he was than he acted. It made her a little uncomfortable. "Okay...Well, I saw the *Tokugawa* getting blown up by the Tesla thingy, so I had to see how much the *Traveler* weighed, how much the folks on it weighed, you know, so I didn't get them stuck together, where we were, how fast we were going, I even had to look at the wind and how everything was turning, then how fast the pillar of light was coming, and then I figured that I needed to take us further than I could see with my head map, so I just hurried and sorted it out and did it before the Tesla beam got us. But since I only had a second, I kind of messed up and pushed a little too hard. I'm lucky I didn't just kill us all."

Jacques was still looking at her, but now his mouth was open just a little bit, like he was kind of surprised. He quickly closed it.

"You doing okay, Jacques?"

"All of that . . . Before the pillar of light reached you?"

"Yeah."

He drained his coffee in one quick gulp, pulled some money out of his pocket and left it on the table. "That concludes our lesson for the day."

"Lesson? That was supposed to be a lesson?"

He picked up his hat and set it on his white hair. "Yes. It was your first lesson in mastering the most dangerous spell the world has ever known."

"Well, I'm no expert on schoolin' and such, but you're not a very good teacher."

"I never claimed to be. Meet me here tomorrow at ten." And then Jacques quickly walked out of the café and into the rain without looking back. He didn't even bother with an umbrella.

Faye sighed and polished off the cookies.

Chapter 5

Facing the heroes' band
Devil in the Oklahoma sand
Let it rain, let it rain
In that place so dry
He made the angels cry
Let it rain, let it rain
Lighting strikes, feel the pain
Hey Grimnoir, let it rain

—Author Unknown,
Lyrics from the Ballad of the Hero George Bolander, 1933

UBF *Traveler*

THE VIEW OUT THE FRONT of the ship was green forests and blue rivers as far as the eye could see. Sullivan was leaning on the rail and making up for interrupted sleep with strong black coffee. The night watch was wrapping up and being replaced by their luckier day shift brethren. Barns Dalton entered the *Traveler's* bridge, took one look around, scratched his head, and asked, "Are we heading north?"

"Yep," Sullivan answered.

"Isn't Siberia that-a-way?" Barns gestured out another window.

"Yep." He took a drink of the nefarious liquid and let it burn its way down. Captain Southunder's idea of coffee could degrease an engine. "Change of plans."

"I'm only just the main guy that drives this thing," Barns muttered. The marauder from the night shift gave up the helm, and Barns slid into the chair. "It isn't like anybody needs to tell me anything."

Sullivan had no idea how any of the complicated new navigational equipment on the *Traveler* worked, but Barns hadn't seemed to have any trouble learning it. He'd been a biplane stunt pilot before falling in with the marauders, and according to Southunder there wasn't anything Barns couldn't fly, and with his Power being related to the manipulation of probability, nobody that he couldn't *outfly*. The young man tapped the glass to make sure the gauges weren't stuck. "Good to see my sense of direction's not broken. Where the hell are we going?"

Captain Southunder returned to the bridge, sliding down a ladder like a man half his age. Put him on a moving airship and he was as surefooted as an Imperium ninja. "Eighty-two degrees north, eighty-two degrees west, Barns. Near the northern shore of Axel Heiberg."

"Hmmm..." Barns had to think about that for a moment. "Sounds cold."

"It's a secret base on top of a glacier. Conditions shouldn't be much worse than what everyone was already expecting in Siberia. Freezing cold, horrible winds, man-eating polar bears, and murderous Imperium bastards, all in one convenient location."

"I should've stayed in the south Pacific," Barns grumbled. "But hey, at least we've got a fancier blimp."

"Indeed we do. The *Traveler* may be a technological marvel, but a man will always remember his first love with fondness," Southunder said. "The *Bulldog Marauder* was a real beauty."

"She was held together with baling wire and pitch tar."

"She had *soul*." Pirate Bob turned to Sullivan. "Winds are good. If you want me to manipulate them, I could have us there quicker, otherwise we'll be there near midnight."

Landing and making their way across a glacier in the dark would be dangerous as hell, but it beat being spotted and taking antiaircraft fire. They needed to capture this place, not level it from the sky. "Save your Power, Captain. We'll do this at night."

Southunder laughed at him. "You've never been this far north before, have you, Sullivan? Night is a relative term this time of year. There won't be a lot of cover to work with."

"No cover, eh?" He'd forgotten about that. That was the problem with book learning compared to practical experience. Facts were recalled a lot faster when it was something that made life harder. They still had a few weeks before the solstice, but even now, being a few hundred miles from the pole, there would only be a few hours of night, and none of them particularly dark enough to conceal an incoming dirigible. "Can you provide us some?"

"Of course." The captain had to think about that for a moment. "But up here, that'll test the limits of my magic. Thing is, I manipulate the weather enough to give us sufficient storm cover, there's repercussions. Further out you get from where I twisted the system, the less control I've got."

"What're you getting at?"

"When I cause enough disturbance to hide this ship, there's no telling how nasty the weather may get down on that glacier."

Sullivan simply nodded and went back to his coffee. "I'll tell the boys to wear their mittens."

Barns shuddered. "I really should've stayed in the South Pacific..."

"We are ramp down in five minutes!" the marauder shouted from the catwalk. "Five minutes!"

The *Traveler* shook hard as a strong gust of wind hit. Ian Wright had to hold onto one of the cargo nets to stay upright as the dirigible careened to the side. They said that landing was the most dangerous part of any dirigible flight, so doing it in a storm, especially one that you'd inflicted on yourself, was completely reckless. Another gust struck and took them in the opposite direction.

Twenty-five Grimnoir were going on the raid. Most of them were clustered in the cargo bay, dressing in incredibly bulky winter clothing and doing last minute checks of their equipment. The wind changed again, spinning the *Traveler* sideways. An open ammo can toppled, spilling rifle cartridges everywhere. One of the knights stumbled to the side and vomited on the floor.

A red bulb began to flash off and on. The marauder on the catwalk shouted orders to some of the other crew, but he was cut off by a terrible grinding noise.

"What's going on?" Ian asked the knight next to him nervously. After all, Chris Schirmer was a Fixer and a protégée of the great Cog John Moses Browning, so he had more experience with mechanical goings on.

"How would I know?" he answered, busy stuffing loaded

magazines into pouches on his belt. "I was a gunsmith, not a blimp builder." But then he watched the running crewmen, analyzed where they were going and what tools they were scrambling for. "I think one of the landing skids is stuck."

"Isn't that bad?"

"It's not good. I better go see if I can help." Schirmer got up and made his way across the wildly tilting deck.

Ian closed his eyes and concentrated on everything but his growing nausea. "I volunteered for this? Why the hell did I volunteer for this?"

"To fight an outer-space monster," answered someone. Ian opened his eyes to see that it was Steve Diamond, one of the knights he had fought alongside against the OCI at Mason Island. The Mover was cheating and using his Power to gather up all of the spilled cartridges. The .30-06 rounds rolled across the floor like they were being swept, and then the pile floated up and neatly into the ammo can. Diamond used his real hand to close the lid. "That's something special."

"Assuming that this Pathfinder thing is even real in the first place."

"Come on, Ian. Not this again." Diamond sighed. "This is an adventure."

Another knight looked up from his cleaning his rifle. They'd been told to rub down their bolts with powdered graphite, since the temperature outside would freeze grease or oil and cause their weapons to malfunction. "Hey, are you the Summoner who was trying to talk the elders into stopping this mission?"

"Yeah. I'm the Summoner."

"Genesse," the knight introduced himself. "Mouth. Easy..." He must have caught Ian's flinch. "I'm not trying to sway you." He was a short, thin man with an olive complexion. Ian thought he might be Italian, but he sounded like an American. Then again, Ian was a Scot who talked like an American, since he'd spent so much time there. Grimnoir tended to be well travelled. "If you don't think it's real, why volunteer?"

"I changed my mind." Ian didn't elaborate. He'd had this out with the others before. There was no need to rehash old arguments five minutes before an attack on the Imperium.

Jake Sullivan was persuasive for a Heavy, or maybe it was because he was a Heavy. The man just would not move on an argument. It was like arguing with a boulder. He was so adamant about what he perceived to be the truth that he'd convinced many of the Grimnoir of the existence of the Pathfinder. To Ian, that information had come from the Chairman, and was thus tainted. Only a fool would believe anything that came from a madman, and it was even worse when it came from a madman's ghost.

To Ian, they didn't need to look out into space for an enemy. There were plenty of real enemies right here at home. While a big chunk of the society's best wasted their time on a wild-goose chase, the OCI was registering Actives in America, and registration was sure to lead to camps or pogroms. While they were attacking a useless Imperium installation on an iceberg in the middle of nowhere, real Imperium schools were torturing and killing innocents all over Asia.

Like Beatrice.

He wouldn't argue with the knights that Sullivan had already convinced. That was pointless. Ian had volunteered for this mission for other reasons entirely. "Regardless what happens, at least we'll give the Imperium a black eye."

"That's the spirit," Diamond said.

Diamond had a sort of constant understated enthusiasm that Ian found annoying. The elders called it a can-do attitude. It was probably also why Diamond had always found himself in positions of leadership while Ian had been bounced around from one petty assignment to another, even though they'd joined the society about the same time and were about the same age.

Of course, it was easy for Diamond and the others like him to have a can-do attitude. It hadn't been his wife who had been tortured in an Imperium school until she'd gone insane. None of them had been forced to Summon a demon to sneak in and put her out of her misery.

Ian looked around the room at the knights surrounding him. He knew many of them. They were all volunteers, and each of them was here for his own reasons. The Reader, Mike Willis, was the noble heroic type, and an old friend of George Bolander's. Willis was here because that's what his mentor would have wanted. Mottl was an Icebox and Simmons was a Torch; they were Diamond's men, and that whole bunch was always looking for a scrape. Their lone Healer, Dianatkhah, had the reputation of a lady's man with a thirst for danger. He only knew the others in passing, but the lot of them were capable, dangerous Actives. Regardless of what had gotten them on this ship, heaven help anyone who got in their way.

While the knights had been talking, Schirmer had used his Power to quickly understand the complex mechanism of the landing gear and exactly how it had broken. The Fixer temporarily corrected the problem with some bubble gum and a length of wire. He gave an *okay* sign to the crewmen on the catwalk.

"Ramp down in two minutes!" the lead marauder shouted.

Jake Sullivan appeared in the cargo bay, holding a bullpup Browning Automatic Rifle, surely enchanted by the master himself. The Heavy seemed even larger and more intimidating than normal all wrapped in fur. Give him a helmet with cow horns and he'd look like a Viking. "All right, boys. It's time to go."

The assembled knights cheered. Ian played along even though it made him sick. The society had truly been blinded by Sullivan's story. They were wasting their time on a fairytale while Actives suffered. Ian's father-in-law, Isaiah Rawls, had understood who the real enemies were, and he'd sacrificed his honor, but in doing so had won the greatest victory against tyranny the Society had ever seen.

Genesse had asked why he'd volunteered. The Mouth would never understand. Ian's real mission was to make this fool's errand of an expedition count for something. For too long the society had been holding back, being cautious. This mission was the most overt action the Grimnoir had taken in years.

Ian didn't believe in Sullivan's Pathfinder, but he did believe in killing Imperium.

Axel Heiberg Island

THE PATROL never knew what hit them.

Sullivan had been a soldier. He understood what cold and monotony could do to a man, and winter in a trench in France was a tropical paradise compared to this blasted place. It didn't matter how tough or how well trained a soldier was. There were only so many hours someone could stare off into a field of nothing and stay alert. There were only so many days you could guard something that no one knew, nor cared about, before it began to seem pointless. Even for

Imperium soldiers, men so fanatical that they'd follow any order without hesitation, the freezing monotony would erode that sense of duty. It would dull you down until you were only pulling your patrols because your superiors demanded it, but even then, you'd just be punching a clock, freezing your ass off, staring at ice, until it was your turn to go back inside.

Until one night you got eaten by a polar bear.

Sullivan tensed as the gigantic white beast came lumbering through the snow. Even with the magically summoned snow storm, it was still far too bright to be the middle of the night, but it was surprising how close the animal got before he saw it, and Lance wasn't even trying hard now. The polar bear's face was dripping red, and much of its dirty white fur was stained pink.

"Got 'em. You should've seen their faces," Lance said through the animal. The bear seemed unnaturally happy, not that Sullivan had ever had a conversation with a bear before. Did the animals Lance controlled still experience things like joy? He'd have to ask Lance later, assuming he didn't freeze to death first. "Four men, and she put them down before anyone could even fire a shot. Polar bears are great like that. Her nose says that's it for the perimeter. You're clear rest of the way in."

"Good work," Sullivan said through chattering teeth.

"Work? Hell. My body's back on the *Traveler* warm and toasty, sitting by a heater vent. Follow her tracks and I'll take you to the door. Stick to the tracks. There are crevices all over the place." The polar showed all its teeth in a terrifying smile, then staggered to the side and ran away. It was invisible within two seconds.

He was wearing a mask, but the cold had already leached through and his face was numb beneath it. It was so cold that his eyeballs were freezing in their sockets beneath his goggles. Sullivan's nose had filled with snot and frozen so bad that it wasn't until after the bear was gone that its foul, musky odor finally registered. Turning back, he could just make out the next few men, crouched, weapons ready. He signaled for them to follow. The first man who reached him was wearing so much clothing that he was simply unrecognizable. Sullivan repeated what Lance had said about sticking to the tracks, had the knight repeat the words, and then had him pass it back down their single-file line. The last thing he wanted was to lose a man by something stupid like falling in a hole. They should've tied ropes to each other like Heinrich had suggested.

The snowfall was so thick he could barely see the bear's fresh tracks. Each step was treacherous and slick. They'd brought snowshoes, which had been a good bit of planning, but he'd underestimated how damned hard it was to walk in the things without practice. The muscles in his legs burned, which made him sweat, which then simply froze on his skin, making for a truly miserable situation. Luckily for Sullivan, he could cheat and alter his own gravity a bit, so he quit sinking so deep with every step. He could have made himself light as a feather, but didn't want to burn through too much Power. There was no telling what exactly they would face inside the Imperium base.

He should have taken out the Spiker armor. It had spells engraved on it to regulate the wearer's temperature. But it was big and weighed a ton, and the last thing he wanted to do was clumsily fall off a cliff. Sure, he would probably live, but then everybody else would've had to get him unstuck, and that would've just been embarrassing.

Always being the experimental type, Sullivan decided to try using his magic to increase the density of just his skin. It seemed to work at holding his body heat in, but it took quite a bit of Power, so he let it drop. He'd have to play with that more later. It could come in handy if he fought another Icebox. And while he was thinking about not having enough Power, it made him think of the spell he'd copied from Bradford Carr's spellbook, which was hidden beneath his bunk. With that thing on his body, he'd probably have Power to spare, but that spell had such a dangerous track record, he'd only try it if he had no other choice.

Cold made the thoughts wander, so Sullivan got his head back in the game.

Toru hadn't known much about the polar stations other than the fact that they existed, and that all Imperium soldiers dreaded being assigned to such a godforsaken hellhole. Twenty years ago, the Chairman had built them, one in the Arctic and a second in the Antarctic, as an early warning system for a Pathfinder's arrival. For whatever reason, his Cogs had declared that they needed to be built as close to the poles as possible. This was one of the last bits of solid ground in the region, so one of the many companies secretly owned by the Imperium had bought the land from the Canadians. It wasn't like they were using it for anything.

The station's magic was untested. It had been nearly fifty years since the last Pathfinder had come, so it was unknown if it would even detect the creature. The Iron Guard hadn't been counting on them working well, if at all. This type of magic was odd and untestable. However, when it came to understanding spellbound items, the Grimnoir had a secret weapon...

Sullivan's goggles were fogging up, which was making it even harder to follow the tracks. He was thankful for Lance's Beastie magic, because running into a patrol of soldiers conditioned to this would have been a nightmare. He never wanted to get into a gunfight when he was wearing gloves too thick to work a trigger, assuming his BAR's action wasn't frozen solid anyway.

There was a lump ahead of him, and the tracks led right over the top of it. He was already at the top before he realized that it had actually been a wall at one point in time before the wind and ice had simply devoured it. On the other side was a big lump of snow... *No. That's a building.* There were other lumps nearby, probably smaller buildings.

Someone joined him on top of the wall. "We're here." And he could only tell it was Heinrich because of his voice. He was indistinguishable from the others in his masked mound of furs. Heinrich's goggled head scanned across the smaller buildings. "I bet those are their antiaircraft batteries."

"It would've taken them half an hour to chip one loose. I'm thinking we could've just parked right on top of this place and been fine."

"Yet we would have missed that wonderful nature walk." Heinrich looked back the way they'd come. "Magnificent, isn't it?"

Sullivan looked back. With Southunder's magical obscuring snowfall, there really wasn't much to see. Dead City must really have set the bar low. "You say so."

"I am glad we were able to come during the spring."

Another shape joined them. This one was easily identifiable even before he said anything. Only Toru was strong enough to make the trek carrying that many weapons. Sullivan figured that he was only hauling the big metal war club and the sword to prove some point to the Grimnoir. "I am cold."

"No kidding . . . What do you think?"

Toru studied the compound. "Their cannons are obviously inoperable. If I had inspected this station, I would have ordered the commander executed for dereliction of duty. This is unbecoming of Imperium military."

"You sound disappointed," Heinrich said.

Toru might have grunted, but it was hard to tell in the wind.

Sullivan counted the figures as they appeared through the snow. They were clumping up, huddling together for warmth. A dumb tactic in case the Imperium had eyes on them, but he was so cold he couldn't rightly blame them. It looked like they'd all made it. *Good.*

"I see an entrance," Heinrich said. The polar bear had walked right up and over the mound of the building. There appeared to be a depression where the last patrol had dug their way out with snow shovels.

It was time. "Heinrich, ready the men." The Fade nodded once and slid back down the wall. Readying the men would consist of taking off their snowshoes and making sure the actions of their weapons would actually cycle. He waited until Heinrich was out of earshot. "Toru, you can stay out here if you want."

"Do you question my resolve?" he snapped.

"It's not that." Sullivan remembered his own hesitation before they had fought the OCI. "Those are your countrymen in there."

"Yet they stand in the way of fulfilling my father's final command. It is unfortunate, but their deaths will serve a higher purpose."

"If they surrender, they don't have to die." That was foolishness, and he knew it as soon as the words left his mouth.

"They are Imperium. They do not understand *surrender*. Even if we were to take this facility without bloodshed, they would commit suicide for the shame of allowing it. Dying in battle is always preferable . . . Come. It will be warmer inside."

They'd brought dynamite in case the door was hardened, but who needs dynamite when you have a Fade?

Heinrich Koenig dropped through the ceiling and landed gently on the floor. There was a single soldier leaning against the wall, struggling to stay awake. Heinrich caught the young man mid-yawn. A candle burned on the table next to him. The base was wired for electricity, but Heinrich reasoned that since fuel for their generator had to be flown in, they probably used it sparingly.

The soldier blinked stupidly, not understanding how a man in unfamiliar winter clothing had suddenly appeared right before him, but before he could do anything Heinrich had gotten one hand over his mouth and driven a punch dagger under his ear.

They stared at each other for the briefest eternity. The violence was so sudden that the Imperium man had not yet realized that he was dead. Heinrich looked into his eyes, seeing the same look that he'd seen dozens of times before, but a survivor of Dead City never hesitated.

Twist. Even if the soldier was wearing one of the magical kanji that granted increased vitality, it would not survive the severing of the spinal column.

Wait a moment. Then Heinrich slowly lowered the body to the floor without a sound.

The exterior hatch had been locked from the inside. There was probably some sort of signal the returning patrols would use to have it opened. There was a rather sturdy padlock on the inside. Heinrich bit one glove to drag it off, then simply took hold of the padlock and imagined it as an extension of his hand. He willed himself to go grey, and the lock went with him. It was just like Fading with the clothes on his back, and he'd done it so much that it was second nature. The lock pulled through the metal and popped out the other side.

It was very difficult to keep out a determined Fade. He rapped his knuckles on the hatch to tell the others to come in. Sure, he could have waited for them, but where was the fun in that? Besides, Fades worked best on their own. Heinrich took up the fallen soldier's submachine gun, an Arisaka model that he had some passing familiarity with, so he checked to make sure it had a loaded magazine and retracted the bolt. He'd brought his own firearm, but it never hurt to use up the enemy's ammunition first.

The first room was closed off from the rest of the building with a heavy door, surely to mitigate the heat loss. Heinrich crept through the wall to find a shadowy hallway. It had to be fifty degrees inside, a temperature which now seemed achingly hot, and his skin began to prickle.

Something knee-high and white scurried past. He recognized the now-familiar shape of Ian Wright's favorite demon. The Summoned hurried down the hallway, surely off to cause some mayhem. Hallways were fatal funnels. Only a fool would walk down a hallway when it was much faster to simply go through the walls, so he did, through supply rooms and empty offices, until he found himself in the barracks.

There were six soldiers in the room, either getting dressed for work or getting undressed to go to sleep, he was not sure. There were no beds, merely woven mats on the floor, and a very meager amount of furniture, which also meant there was no cover. All of them looked up in surprise at his sudden appearance.

Heinrich opened fire.

The room was narrow, so he just held the trigger down and jerked the muzzle side to side. It was a wasteful use of ammunition, but he emptied the Arisaka's entire magazine. Only one of them reacted in time to try anything useful, but Heinrich put half a dozen bullets into the man before he could get his pistol free of the holster.

Surveying the scene, they appeared to be done for. Heinrich took up the dropped pistol, one of the nicer Nambu models, checked to make sure it was ready, and then stood in the corner where he would be concealed by the opening door. Heinrich had been in Imperium buildings before, and knew they preferred to use sliding doors. Those must not be as efficient at regulating the heat, since this facility used normal doors. He mulled this thought over idly as the Imperium soldiers bled to death at his feet.

There was shouting on the other side of the wall, so he forgot about architecture and concentrated on business. They would want to rush in to see what had happened, but that had been far too much gunfire for it to have been an accident. They would hesitate until there were a few of them, and then they would rush inside. Their attention would be focused. They would have tunnel vision in the direction they assumed danger would come from.

Heinrich smiled. Fades liked to come at you sideways.

Shouting in Japanese. The door flew open. Heinrich stepped through the wall and came out behind them. There were three responders, and sure enough, they were all focused on the room he'd just left. Heinrich had an easy shot and got one of them in the side of the head. The second lurched away while Heinrich fired at him. The

Nambu fired an anemic 8mm round, so Heinrich had to hit him several times before he was happy that the soldier was done for. Heinrich was turning to shoot the last when he realized that the Nambu had malfunctioned. A brass case was sticking out the side of the ejection port like a stovepipe, taunting him. The last soldier was spinning around, slipping in a puddle of blood. There was no time.

Heinrich could control the degree to which his body became insubstantial. It did not take much effort to push his way through solid objects, and bullets were no different. He went grey as the first rounds penetrated his clothing. The bullets left a track of warmth through his torso before they exited out his back. The soldier quit firing, mouth agape, and Heinrich reformed, solid, and flung the jammed Nambu toward his face. The soldier flinched away, but that was all Heinrich had needed. Drawing the push dagger from inside his coat, he knocked the soldier's muzzle aside and then struck him in the chest. Once, twice, the third slipped through the ribs, and the Imperium man fell gasping to the floor.

There was more shooting from the hall. The other knights were inside. The Imperium man was still struggling to fight, even with a perforated heart, so Heinrich kicked him brutally hard in the side of the head so he could bleed to death peacefully and not cause any more trouble. Heinrich took up another subgun and went toward the sound of gunfire.

The knights were making fast work of the base's defenses. Normally the Imperium would have put up a better fight, but they had not expected this, and if Heinrich could pick only one advantage to have in a fight it would be surprise.

Jake Sullivan, on the other hand, if he could only pick one advantage, would surely choose overwhelming force. And he was demonstrating that philosophy rather well when Heinrich found the Heavy one floor down, twisting gravity in order to fling a group of Imperium soldiers around like leaves in the wind. Heinrich came through the ceiling in time to catch the last bit of the gravity spike, and even that was enough to almost put him through the next floor.

"How goes it?" Heinrich asked.

Sullivan paused to shoot one of the rising Imperium with his BAR. The .30-06 was incredibly loud in the enclosed space. He jerked his head down the next hall. "Got a bottleneck."

Heinrich gave a quick look. It was a metal pathway. No cover, at least nothing that would stop a bullet. At the far end was a muzzle flash, and Heinrich instinctively went grey as the bullets zipped by. "Want a grenade?" he asked as he reformed again behind cover.

Sullivan shook his head. "I think that's where the device is. I don't want to put any holes in it. We need to grab it before one of those assholes does something crazy."

That was always a danger with the Imperium. When they thought all was lost, they would not hesitate to take their own lives in a spectacular manner if there was a chance they could take some of their foes with them. Heinrich thought about the distance he needed to cover and the relative density of the materials. It would be tight, perhaps at the ragged edge of what he could accomplish with the amount of Power he had left, and if he ran out while still inside a solid object, he would be fused within it. A fate which he'd witnessed and knew to be an excruciatingly painful way to die. "Give me a moment, Jake."

Heinrich dove into the floor.

The harder he burned his Power, the faster he could move through solid objects; however, he needed to maintain enough solidity to gain traction in order to move forward. The nearest analogy he could come up with was that of swimming, though that wasn't right either, but it was the quickest way to explain his abilities to a non-Fade.

This was the bottom floor and it extended out into the solid bedrock, so Heinrich couldn't just fade up one floor and drop in behind them. He had no choice but to pass through solid rock.

So Heinrich found himself in the pitch-black darkness of the foundation. The endless cold of the frozen earth was beneath him. He drove himself through the dark, pushing as hard as he could. The Power was dwindling, like a bucket with a hole punched in it, and when the bucket was empty, he would die. The extra eight pounds of steel and wood were slowing him down, so he let go of the stolen Arisaka. Its molecules instantly fused into the matter around it, a fate he would share if he did not hurry.

Many Fades died the first time they'd attempted something like this. Of course, he could not ask them why, because when you were fused entirely into solid rock there wasn't even enough of you left for a Lazarus to question, but he thought it was because they'd panicked.

Heinrich had grown to manhood in a city filled with the hungry dead. Panic was a foreign concept to him.

There was open air above, beckoning, but if he came up too early the Imperium would simply shoot him to death. No. It was better to brave the dark. It was always better to brave the dark.

Power dwindled to nothing, Heinrich made one last desperate push. He clawed his way through the floor, body solidifying from the top down, until he came out on his hands and knees in a wide-open room. At first he thought the thing above him was a chandelier of some sort, and he blinked at the searing light. As his eyes cleared he realized it was a massive, luminescent globe. Surely, this was the device which had brought them here.

But there was no time to admire the scenery. There were two Imperium firing wildly down the hall. A third, wearing the red sash of an officer, was ordering a fourth and a fifth to stuff wires into a big metal barrel. The officer was screaming orders in Japanese. Heinrich did not need to speak the language to know they were going to blow the place up.

Good. I would hate to die trapped in a glacier for nothing.

They had not seen him yet. He reached into his coat and drew his Luger P.08 from its shoulder holster. Even though he counted John Browning as a personal friend, sometimes carrying a weapon manufactured in one's homeland became a matter of national pride.

The ones with the explosives were the most dangerous, so they had to be stopped first. He walked toward them, gun extended in one hand. The closer the better, as he really did not wish to accidentally shoot the contents of that barrel. He was within ten feet before they spotted him, and he paid that alert Imperium soldier back with a single round through the face. The next absorbed two rounds before he was convinced to let go of the explosives. The officer turned and snarled something, and Heinrich gunned him down mercilessly.

The two soldiers turned toward him as he aimed at them. There was no way he could Fade through any more bullets, and there was no way any of them could miss at this range. He fired as they did, pulling the trigger wildly until the toggle locked open on the empty Luger.

The room was quiet. The air was choked with carbon. *I am not hit?* Heinrich blinked, but refrained for checking himself for holes. He'd struck one in the cheek and took the base of his head off. The brains sliding down the wall confirmed that. Then he realized that he was still alive only because a doughy three foot tall albino demon had launched itself onto the other soldier and was beating him mercilessly. Heinrich looked up to see where a heating duct was hanging broken from where Ian's Summoned had crawled through, probably devoted to the same task that Heinrich had just risked his life to accomplish.

Heinrich walked over to the little demon. It looked up at him with four blazing red eyes. "Ian, if you can hear me through this beast, the drinks are on me."

The demon nodded in a very human like manner, and then went back to pulverizing the soldier's skull with its two doughy fists.

Sullivan at Role

◄ Chapter 6 ►

Dear Doctor Kelser, if you are really a doctor at all. Forgive my impertinence, but it must be said. You are a fool and a fraud. It was with great amusement that I read your recent paper detailing your new theory on the origins of magic amongst the population beginning the mid portion of the last century. Atlantis? Really? You cannot scientifically explain the origin of magic so your first assumption is that the lost continent of Atlantis must somehow be involved? Did your medical degree come from a box of Cracker Jack? Every reasonable man of science understands that magic comes from crystals.

—Orson Flick,
Letter to the editor, Scientific American, 1921

Axel Heiberg Island

TORU KNEW right where to go.

He had lied to the Grimnoir about having never visited this base before. Toru had passed through once, accompanying a supply drop, mostly as an excuse to get away from the embassy for a time.

Only a washed-up Imperium officer would end up in charge of such a horrible duty station, but at least the last one had some vestige of professionalism, or had at least managed to act convincing in time for Toru's inspection. This current commander was pathetic in comparison. From the speed of the assault, it appeared the Grimnoir might not even take any casualties. It was shameful that Imperium men would be steamrolled so easily. Regardless of how inept this officer may have been, there was still something that Toru needed from him before the Grimnoir killed everyone.

While the main body of Grimnoir were distracted, Toru took a side passage and made his way down a ladder. Utilizing his Power, moving with lightning quickness, Toru crossed the basement level of the facility in seconds. A powerful enough Brute could run down a gazelle, and Toru was the best of the best. He intercepted an Imperial soldier on the way. It did not please him to do so, but Toru snapped the man's neck with a single quick strike before the warrior could even begin to react. *It is for the best, my brother.*

The officer's quarters were next, and Toru intercepted the young men as they woke up and went toward the sound of the guns. No Actives would be wasted on a post such as this, but all Imperial officers were branded with at least one kanji, so they could prove dangerous enough to thwart his mission. Toru fired his Power and lifted the steel tetsubo.

Toru killed them all.

Blood dripped from the spikes on his club. Toru turned in a slow circle. The walls were painted red. Broken bodies lay in piles.

It is for the best.

The commander's chambers were locked, so Toru kicked the heavy door from its hinges. An unshaven, bleary-eyed Imperial captain was still trying to get his shirt on. Toru looked in disgust at the garbage strewn about the room and the empty sake jugs, and then broke every bone in the captain's hand when he reached for his pistol. Toru grabbed him by the neck, lifted him off the ground, and slammed him hard into the wall.

The captain was red-faced and struggling to breathe. He blinked rapidly and begged for mercy like a peasant. "Please don't kill me! I surrender," the captain squealed in a manner that offended Toru's philosophy about what it meant to be a warrior. It was easy to see what caliber of officer would be sent to a dead-end post such as this.

"I am Toru Tokugawa," he stated. The captain's tear-filled eyes widened. "My name is known. Good. You will activate your emergency communication spell to the Edo court *now.*" Toru squeezed just a bit harder, letting the captain know the price for noncompliance, then he dropped the man to the floor. "I need to have a word with them."

Every Imperium base in the world was equipped with prepared kanji so that a quick message could be sent back to the high command.

They bypassed all levels of the military bureaucracy and went straight to the top, to the Chairman's inner circle. They were to be used only in the gravest emergency, and using one for anything short of an apocalyptic crisis unnecessarily would mean a death sentence for the officer activating it.

Trained as an Iron Guard, Toru knew how to prepare such a spell himself, but when he'd tried it months ago, it had simply not worked. He had hoped to send a message home, warning them about the false Chairman, but his particular spell had been purposefully blocked somehow. The imposter was obviously trying to limit the contagion of the rogue Iron Guard.

Toru understood now that even if he could get a message to high command, it would be pointless. No one would believe him. Who among them would doubt the word of the Chairman? It was for an entirely different reason that Toru had decided to send this message.

The captain hesitated, so Toru used the blankets from the man's bed to wipe the blood from the tetsubo. That was all it took for the captain to wet himself in fear. The worm crawled away, wincing as his broken hand touched the floor. A screen was moved from the far wall, revealing a large mirror, and the captain went to work activating it. His spellbinding was sloppy, as would be expected just from looking at him, but these mirrors were created by Unit 731 Cogs, masters of the individual kanji. Even an imbecile could make one of their spells work.

Toru waited, watching himself in the mirror. His reflection stared back, splattered with the blood of good Imperium men who should not have had to die. It was a waste of precious resources. That was on the imposter's head, not Toru's. The captain was jabbering on the whole time, begging, pleading, groveling... If Toru had been in a merciful mood before, the pathetic display of cowardice would have removed any lingering doubts. The mirror flashed and a new, familiar scene appeared on the other side. He had seen this view of the Imperial Court many times before.

A functionary appeared in the mirror, obviously confused as to why the most isolated base in the world would be calling for the high command, but then he saw Toru standing there with the captain cowering at his feet, and his mouth fell open in surprise. Sick of the captain's piteous mewling, Toru raised one boot and stomped on his neck, silencing him forever.

"I demand to see Okubo Tokugawa. Bring me the Chairman."

The shocked functionary stared on in silence. His mouth moved, but no words came out.

"Tell him that Toru Tokugawa wishes to speak with him."

The metal globe was six feet across and floating six feet off the ground. Sullivan couldn't tell what it was made of, but he had to admire the remarkable craftsmanship as it slowly rotated under its own power. The continents didn't look quite right; they were sort of stylized. He didn't know if that had been necessary for the kanji spells carved all over it, or if it had been because the Chairman had liked for his gizmos to have a certain artistic flair, but either way, Sullivan had to admit it was kind of pretty.

"This floor is locked up tight. Only a few of us wounded," Diamond reported. At some point in the fight he'd gotten blood on his glasses, so the Mover took them off and cleaned them on his coat sleeve. "We've got a few pockets of resistance left, but they're pinned down."

"Keep 'em that way. Don't waste any of our boys trying to dig them out. We got what we came for. How about our path out?"

"We control it. Some of the guys got hit, nothing too severe. I sent them all back to the main floor to that funny air lock room. Dianatkhah is seeing to them."

Sullivan nodded. Healers were so rare that they only had a single, precious one on this expedition. That was probably the safest place in the whole place to put their wounded. At least they had an exit if something went wrong. "Good. Spread the word to watch out for one of them suicide charges." The Grimnoir knights had done well. For not having worked together much beforehand, they'd performed better than he'd expected. "I hope this won't take long..."

"It'll be done five seconds after you quit asking me how long it will be," Schirmer said. Their Fixer was their most talented spellbinder, and he'd been preparing the communication spell. Since they'd been unsure how much glass would be available at the site—and unbroken after they took the place over—they had hauled a bag of salt along on the hike. Schirmer had poured the salt out on the floor and was drawing designs in it. Sullivan had turned out to be pretty darn good at that sort of thing, but he had to admit that the Fixer from Texas was better.

Sullivan checked his watch. Ten minutes from entry to taking over the place. Not a single fatality, just a couple of minor wounds... *Not too shabby.* He turned to Heinrich, who was supervising the looting of the Imperium command center. The knights were grabbing every scrap of paper there, just in case there was some piece of valuable intelligence. That was a lot of paper, and they only had a couple of folks who could actually read Japanese, but it was worth a shot. "Alert the *Traveler*. Southunder can kill his storm. Have Barns pick us up right outside."

"You do not wish to walk back?"

"I'd prefer to keep all my toes... Schirmer?"

The Fixer cracked his knuckles. "Done."

This next part, which Sullivan was the best at, involved connecting someone's personal Power to the designs in the salt. And Sullivan had the most Power of any of them. *Just lucky that way I guess.* The symbols represented the various geometric designs that made up the living thing they called the Power. Sullivan knew more about it than most people, but even he couldn't wrap his brain around all the abstract concepts of a critter that weird.

However, there was one person they knew who seemed to have no problem understanding all of it.

"Hurry and drag these corpses out of here," Heinrich ordered some of the knights as he pointed at the dead Imperium. "Our genius does not handle violence well."

"He gets spun up real easy," Sullivan explained as the magic connected. There was a flash of light as the pile of salt was fused into a solid mass. It floated off of the ground as a disk and rotated until the flat surface came to face him. No matter how many times he did that, the trick never got old. It was like looking through a window, and on the other side was Fuller's laboratory on the *Traveler*.

"Mr. Sullivan! Right on time." Buckminster Fuller pointed at the four wristwatches he was wearing on one arm. "I was assured you would be prompt in the execution of your duties!"

Cogs... Sullivan sighed. "We found it."

"I am eager to see what you have for me!"

The view was remarkably clear. The strain on his Power wasn't too bad. Schirmer did damn fine work. "Here you go, Fuller." Sullivan allowed the communication spell to turn until Fuller had a view of the Chairman's globe.

There was a moment of silence as the Cog took in the sight. Fuller's Power was an odd one, even by the standards of the Grimnoir. He was the only man they knew of who could actually see the geometries of the Power, and even see how it connected to individual Actives. Others of their kind could only feel their own, and then they sort of messed around until they maybe figured out how to draw little bits of magic to bind onto things. For most of them, spellbinding was like blundering your way through a room full of sharp edges and pointy bits in the dark. Fuller was in the same room, but he had the lights on.

"Remarkable. Astounding. Phenomenal! *Brilliant!* It is spherical. You know how I feel about spheres!"

Fuller did have a thing for domes. "I guess that means you like it?"

All of the knights in the room had stopped their looting to come and see Fuller do his thing. It took a lot to get jaded Grimnoir riled up, but hell, Fuller could actually *see* magic. Who could blame them? Since Francis Stuyvesant had found the man last year, the Society had made huge strides in improving their spells. Fuller's weird, super-magical brain had become a bit of a legend in Grimnoir circles.

"Like it? I love it. They may be ruthless in the extreme, but the Chairman's Cogs create items of such mastery, such flawless elegance. One must wonder how individuals capable of such savage mutilations can, on the other hand, create such a work of art. It would seem that such diametrically opposed features would be mutually exclusive. I can see why they needed to place this near the poles. The omnimultiple directionality of the Power manipulations alone are— "

Sullivan had already learned to stop Fuller before he could get on a roll with the big made-up words. Long rambling dissertations on magic could wait for a time when they weren't holed up in an Imperium base with a bunch of fanatics who were sure to try and banzai charge their way out any minute. "Sorta on a deadline, Fuller."

"My apologies, Mr. Sullivan, but I do occasionally succumb to my enthusiasm. The map is obviously a measurement device displaying the natural life-cycle processes of the symbiotic parasite, in other words, the relationship between the Power and the host, i.e., mankind."

Most of the knights seemed bewildered by this, but Sullivan understood what Fuller was saying. The globe was producing its own light, which was far brighter in the areas of the world that had the most population. That made sense, because that was where the most

Actives would be dying. He wondered idly just how bright France had burned on this thing during Second Somme.

"When an Active passes away, their now grown and developed magic returns to the Power. That is how it feeds and expands. This device is simply displaying a macroview of that process. It is rather brilliant in its simplicity. It would detect and then provide the location of any subversion...I will call it a detectlocator."

Sullivan rubbed his face in his hands. At least it was only two words this time. Captain Southunder had vetoed Fuller installing anything with more than ten syllables in its name onto the *Traveler.*

"The detectlocator is monitoring this flow of energy, watching for anomalies. Gaps. Blank spots, a place where the natural order appears to have been suborned. Places where magic is no longer flowing as it should. It would be like watching a water system and discovering that a river was suddenly flowing uphill." Fuller scowled. "However, this particular design is flawed. It is broken."

Sullivan looked over the complex kanji. It was truly the most advanced magical device he had ever seen. It was far over his head, and he'd even managed to engrave spells onto his own body successfully. How would it be to be able to see the world like Fuller? "Can you make it work?"

"I believe so. You will need to follow my instructions exactly, but we should be able to manipulate it to perform as designed." Fuller's brow furrowed as he looked over the kanji. "I can tell what they were attempting to do...This symbolical representation is a real-time display of the flow of magic from its hosts back to the Power and vice versa. It lacks refinement. It lacks true accuracy, but would at least point you to the correct region, which is enough for your intent. It should work, but this is flawed. This makes no sense. I do not understand what has been done here. The initial design would have worked, but there are more recent modifications that have subverted the parameters."

Sullivan scowled. "Recent?"

"These clever kanji were changed within the last year. I believe that this detectlocator of the Chairman's has been sabotaged."

Toru did not have to wait long. He'd held no doubt that such a brazen move would attract the ire of the imposter. The man that next appeared in the mirror looked like the Chairman, moved like the Chairman, even sounded like the real Chairman, but he was certainly not the Chairman. "Traitor! What is the meaning of this?"

"Who are you?" Toru demanded.

"You dare to question me?"

"I do. The real Chairman is dead."

"Silence, treasonous dog! I am Baron Okubo Tokugawa, Chairman of the Imperial Council and chief advisor to the Emperor. I am—"

"Spare me your lies. You are not my father, Okubo Tokugawa. You are an imposter." Toru pointed two fingers at his temple. "The memories of Ambassador Hattori belong to me now. He realized the truth before he died, and now that truth is mine."

"Hattori was a fool," the imposter spat. "You are the even bigger fool to have believed him. You were always naïve, Toru. Your cowardice was an embarrassment to my name in Manchuria and your continued existence is an insult to the Iron Guard."

It took all of Toru's restraint to not smash the mirror. "I did not summon you to trade barbs, imposter. It does not matter who you really are, for the Enemy has returned," he said through gritted teeth. "A Pathfinder is coming. The ghost of the real Okubo Tokugawa has confirmed this. The dishonor you bring upon my family pales in comparison to this danger. Continue your charade and I will not expose your lies, but you must alert the Iron Guard to its presence."

The imposter glanced about the court. "Leave me," he ordered some unseen functionary.

"You may rule the Imperium. Only I know the truth, but my father's final command was not to see to the Imperium's fate or to overthrow you. It was to stop the Pathfinder." Toru struggled to keep the emotion from his words as he continued his plea. "Anything else is irrelevant. Keep your stolen throne, but for the love of the Imperium and all it stands for, you must warn the Iron Guard. Let them fulfill their destiny. Send them to hunt the beast. I implore you. Do not destroy the dream of Dark Ocean."

The imposter's handsome face was an unreadable mask. "You are in the northern monitoring station."

"I am beyond your reach for now. If it makes any difference to your decision, on my honor as an Iron Guard—"

"You are no Iron Guard."

"I am Iron Guard!" Toru bellowed, finally losing control of his temper and unconsciously reclaiming something which he had forsaken. "I am the only one fulfilling our real mission! I only care about the destruction of the Pathfinder. Once that is done, you need not worry about me being a threat to you. Awake the Imperium. Tell them the Pathfinder is coming. Once that is done, I will take my own life and trouble you no more."

The false Chairman chuckled, and then it turned into full-blown laughter. "The memories of Hattori have changed you, Toru. You are no longer the selfish boy that I knew. Such a futile yet noble gesture. Killing yourself to protect the Imperium... I was not aware you had it in you." The imposter's voice had not changed, but his manner of speaking had. "Certainly, I could see you killing yourself out of pride, or in some misguided protest, but on behalf of others? Impressive. However, it is far too late for that now. The Imperium's course is set. The end is inevitable."

He sounded familiar... Toru had listened for hours in the academy as the proud history of the Iron Guard had been drilled into their impressionable young minds by one of its original members. "Master Saito? It is you?"

The imposter gave him a malicious leer. The expression seemed completely alien on the Chairman's normally composed face. "You were always a quick study, Toru. One of my better students. You could have been promoted to First, but you lacked resolve. I can see that has changed."

Dosan Saito had been one of the senior members of their order, one of the Chairman's trusted inner circle of advisors, and a master sensei of the Iron Guard Academy. Toru knew this from his own memories and Hattori's before that. "But you were Dark Ocean!" Toru was stunned. "How could you betray him?"

"You know so little..." the imposter shook his head with exaggerated sadness. "I have been preparing for this for a very long time. When Okubo died, events were set in motion."

Saito had seen the last Pathfinder with his own eyes. He had been there during the final battle in China. The memories of Hattori confirmed that. "Then you know I tell the truth. You know how serious this is. You must unleash the Iron Guard!"

"There is much you will never understand. There was much that

Okubo failed to understand as well. You have a few things in common with your father after all."

"It is coming!" Toru shouted.

Saito chuckled as he made a subtle motion with his fingertips. "Foolish Toru . . . It is already here."

There was a flash of red. The mirror exploded.

The Grimnoir knights were clustered around the floating sphere. None of them could believe their eyes. They'd done as Buckminster Fuller had instructed, carving corrections onto the magical sphere until Fuller was satisfied that every mistake had been corrected. At first Sullivan thought they'd accidentally broken the gizmo worse, but Fuller assured them that this was the right setting. They were seeing the truth.

There were tiny red dots spread across much of Asia.

Ian Wright reached out one hand toward the sphere, but then snatched it back, almost as if the stains burned. "I know some of these places. I know this one for sure."

"Imperium schools," Heinrich muttered. "These are all the places where Unit 731 conducts its experiments on Actives."

There were dozens of them, spreading like the lung cancers that Jane kept warning him about because of his smoking. The Healer would surely call this *advanced*. "The Pathfinder's already inside the Imperium . . ."

"Sullivan!" The shout tore his attention away from the floating globe. Toru was limping down the hall, his heavy coat shredded, leaving a trail of blood behind him. "There is danger."

"What happened to you?"

Toru stopped, surveying the globe. He took in the red splotches without comment. "There is something here with us. Gather your men." There were shiny bits embedded in his face. *Glass.* It took a moment for Sullivan to realize that the hand pressed to Toru's side was actually holding his guts in. The former Iron Guard grimaced. "There is little time."

Anything that could tear up a Brute like Toru was not to be trifled with. "You heard the man," he snapped. "Prepare to move out." The knights were efficient and smart enough not to argue. The Grimnoir were a loose organization, yet they had the functional equivalent to

NCOs. These men, like Diamond and Heinrich, began shouting orders. The gathered Imperium papers were hastily shoved into backpacks, and weapons were readied. Schirmer moved to the ring of salt. Sullivan took one last look through it. "We've got to go, Fuller. Tell the Captain about what we just saw and have him contact Browning."

"I shall. Good luck, Mr. Sull—" but then Schirmer smashed the salt with a rifle butt and it crumbled into glowing bits. Sullivan felt the Power shift inside his chest as he regained that small bit back.

Toru coughed blood, but when somebody had as many Healing spells on them as Sullivan or Toru did, you either killed them outright or not at all. "I do not know what it is. It came through a mirror."

"You gonna make it?" Sullivan asked. Toru removed his hand and displayed his wounded side. The claw marks made it look like he'd been mangled by a piece of farm equipment. Any other man there would've been dead on the spot, but his Healing kanji were burning so hard that standing next to Toru felt like standing next to a radiator. "Damn..."

"I will live."

The Mouth, Genesse, came running up. "The *Traveler* is on the way. Southunder's ended the storm. It looks clear."

Sullivan looked at Toru. Anything that could overwhelm a Brute like that wasn't to be underestimated. "We better off fighting this thing in here, or out there?"

"It was faster than me."

Sullivan gave the order to move out.

The knights were quick on their feet. It only took a minute to get everyone off the lower floor. As they passed the men holding the choke points against the remaining Imperium, they'd gather those silently and move away, leaving the soldiers holed up against nothing. If they played this right, they'd be long gone by the time the Japanese mounted a counterattack.

Sullivan led the way up the stairs, Browning's bullpup automatic rifle in his big hands. He already knew that he'd get them to the entrance, and then hold it until everyone else had made it out and been accounted for. Once a leader of men, always a leader of men, and the habits he'd formed during the Great War had come back fast. Or maybe they'd never really left at all.

Whatever had attacked Toru hadn't made a move against the rest of them yet. Sullivan's eyes darted back and forth, checking every corner for threats. It kept his mind occupied enough to not dwell on the thought that not only was the Pathfinder already here, but also it was somehow already spread throughout the entire Imperium with nobody knowing. *Survive first, deal with that later.*

He froze when he saw the footprint made of blood. "What the hell?" It might not have gotten his attention if it had been shaped like a human's, but this one was all twisted up and wrong. Sullivan held up one hand to stop the line of knights. He glanced back and spotted Ian Wright, and signaled for the Summoner to come forward. Pointing at the blood, Sullivan asked, "One of yours?"

The Summoner shook his head. "I don't know what that is."

Sullivan lifted his rife. That meant the thing had gotten ahead of them. "It's here—"

There was a long scream, which echoed down the halls. It came from the direction of the entrance and it certainly didn't sound like it had come from a human being. Then there was another scream, this one entirely too human and filled with unmistakable pain. There was a gunshot, and another, and then a rattling barrage of automatic weapons fire.

He set off at a run. Sullivan was fast for a Heavy, especially when driven by the thought that his men were counting on him. Several knights were right behind him.

But they were too late.

Diamond had called the entrance an airlock. Whatever it was, the room had been built tight, with solid doors to keep the cold out and the feeble warmth in. Now, that heavy door had been ripped from its hinges and was lying on the floor in pieces. The room had been painted red, floor to dripping ceiling. The crumpled lumps of winter clothing were all that were left of their wounded knights and their Healer. A haze made of particulate blood and bits of shredded goose down hung in the air. And in the center of the room, a thing made out of nightmares turned and hissed at them.

In the dim light, it could be mistaken for a person. *Briefly.* As it turned, wet muscles rolled beneath a thin, translucent covering. There were bullet holes puckered across its torso, weeping black, but it didn't seem to notice. It dropped the severed leg it had been gnawing on when it heard Sullivan's heavy footfalls, and when it turned and opened its jagged face to scream at them again with that horrific banshee wail, Sullivan let the thing have it.

Gravity shifted, magnified a dozen times, hurling the creature back and crushing it into the wall. It screeched and tried to push away, struggling to reach for him with long, pointed fingers. Sullivan aimed the BAR at its heart and squeezed the trigger.

Chapter 7

Healing the sick, walking through walls? Sure, that's neat an' all, but I met this one brother who could play bagpipes you could swing to. Now that's real magic.

—Duke Ellington,
Interview, 1927

Paris, France

FAYE WAS WAITING for Jacques Montand to arrive at the little café, rather patiently, she might add, when she realized that she was being watched. She had spotted the man on the sidewalk that morning. Then when she'd caught a glimpse of his reflection in a window a few blocks later, she'd gotten suspicious. Taking a seat in the front of the same café ten minutes after Faye had arrived had been the final straw.

He was a fairly average-looking fellow, tall, lean, older than her, but not by more than ten years at the most. His overcoat and fedora were dark, nothing that would stand out on the street, and he was pretty good at looking like he wasn't watching her from behind the newspaper he was pretending to read.

A quick, focused check of her head map confirmed that the man had magic. He was an Active. She tried not to feel smug as she congratulated herself on picking out the tail. Lance had called that sort of thing *field craft*, which made sense, since, like hunting, it was all about paying attention. Faye's initial reaction to suspicious men following her around was to greet them, preferably with sudden, overwhelming violence, but today she refrained. If he was Imperium, he'd show it soon enough.

But what if the stranger was using her to find Jacques? There were all sorts of nefarious groups that wanted to murder the leaders of the Grimnoir. Mr. Browning had tried to warn her about that many times. But everybody thought she was dead, so using her to find them didn't make much sense either.

Well, if he was an Imperium spy sent to find the Grimnoir elders, it would serve Jacques right for not helping her find a place to stay where she wouldn't have to worry about being spotted and followed. She'd been forced to get a hotel room. Which was annoying, both because she didn't know her way around Paris at all and didn't understand a word of the language, except that a lot of the words sounded like mumbly versions of Portuguese words, and also because hotel rooms in this part of town were expensive, and she had only *borrowed* one stack of money from Francis' walk-in safe before she'd left America. To be fair, all of Francis' money stacks tended to be really thick and made entirely out of large denominations, so she was in no danger of running out anytime soon, but it was more the principle of the matter.

Jacques arrived fifteen minutes late with a briefcase in hand. He smiled at the pretty young waitress, asked for something in French, and then took his time strolling across the room. She discreetly kept an eye on the stranger while Jacques took a seat across from her. The stranger's eyes flicked over toward them briefly, and then back to the newspaper.

You're pretty good, buddy, but I'm better. If he so much as twitched wrong, Faye would Travel him up to the top of that big funny-looking metal tower with the funny name and drop him off it.

"Good morning, my dear. You appear rather enthusiastic."

She was always enthusiastic when she was thinking about how to take care of bad guys. Faye kept her voice a whisper. "The man by the window, he's been watching me."

Jacques didn't even bother to look. "Well, you are a rather pretty young lady, Faye."

Faye didn't think of herself as pretty, but the compliment made her blush. "That's not what I meant. He tailed me here."

The senior Grimnoir nodded. "I see." The waitress brought Jacques one of the fancy coffees and a plate of intricate little pastries. *"Merci."*

"You ain't worried?"

"Do you believe I should be?"

"What with all of the assassinating and whatnot, yeah, probably."

Jacques' eyes twinkled when he smiled. He cleared his throat loudly. The stranger looked up, Jacques looked over and nodded at him once. The stranger folded his newspaper, got up, tipped his hat at Faye, and walked out.

"He's one of yours?"

"Of course," Jacques said as he popped a pastry in his mouth.

"You were having me tailed?"

He finished chewing first. It would have been impolite to talk with his mouth full. "Only for your own safety. There are many international elements within this city that would be very interested in someone with your reputation."

Faye snorted. "I don't need protecting. I spotted him no problem."

"Yes. You did. Did you spot the other three I sent, though?"

Faye looked around the room. None of these people seemed familiar in the slightest. "No . . ." He might have just been making it up to mess with her, but now she would be on the lookout just in case. "Way to go, Jacques. You know I was pretending to be dead."

"No need to fear. These knights are as loyal to me as your friends are to John Browning or General Pershing before him. They will not say a word to anyone, especially the other elders, because I have asked them not to. I merely wanted to keep an eye on you. I'm curious to see if you will be able to spot the others now. They are compatriots of Whisper's, and if I may be so bold as to say so, extremely talented individuals. That should prove to be an amusing challenge for you, no? So, are you ready to continue your lessons?" He did not wait for his response, but rather opened his briefcase and began shuffling through papers. "We will start with a small test."

"What? Why?"

"Something you said before intrigued me." Jacques placed a piece of paper and a pencil before her. A complicated maze filled the page. "Solve this."

"What?"

"You have never solved a maze before? It is a children's game."

The whole thing seemed stupid to Faye. "No. Why would I have?"

"I forget myself, your upbringing was rather harsh on the frontier. I would imagine that any papers you had were saved for the outhouse."

Faye's eyes narrowed dangerously as she picked up the pencil. She contemplated stabbing Jacques with it.

"I joke. Please forgive my impertinence . . . It is simple. There is an entrance and there is an exit. Draw a line from one to the other. I wish to see how long it takes you."

"This is dumb." Faye folded the paper in half so that the two ends were touching, and then jabbed the pencil through. Problem solved. "There."

"Heh . . . Just like a Traveler." Jacques shook his head. "No. Not like that. *Through* the maze. Those are walls. You must not cross any of the existing lines."

"Why?"

He thought about it for a moment, and then laughed. "The rest of us have to put up with walls. Please, just humor an old man and do it again."

Faye studied the map. It was too easy. She put the lead down. "Why are you wasting my time on this stuff?" Back and forth, up and down, twenty-seven separate turns, and done. She passed it back. Jacques' mouth was agape. "You've got that surprised look again, Jacques."

"Fascinating . . . Here, do another."

This one had twice as many lines inked on it. Faye sighed as she took it in. It took longer to actually draw her way through it than it did to analyze it. Sixty-eight changes of direction, and she was done.

"You did not backtrack once, not a single mistake."

"Why would I? Jeez, is this what normal folks do for fun?"

Jacques' eyes were opened a bit too wide. He was flabbergasted but trying not to show it. He skipped several other papers and went to the bottom part of his stack. "Try this one."

This page was absolutely full of twists and turns, not just square edges. Faye simply put the pencil down and drew the path through it, seventy-four turns and eighteen points where she had to choose from divergent paths, but she could instantly see which ones were dead ends, so she just skipped those. Dead ends were for suckers. "Really, Jacques. When do we get to the part where I master magic?" And by the time she said that, she was done.

He took it from her and traced his finger over the pencil line. "Unbelievable."

"You French folks must be entertained super easy. In America we've got this thing called radio . . ."

"One more." Jacques handed her the very bottom sheet from his stack. She'd thought the last one had been as full as possible, but this one was absolutely filled with tiny corridors. It must have taken hours to draw. The paper was actually heavy with ink.

Her eyes flicked over it once. "I can't. Not your boring, normal walk-around-stuff way, at least. It's all blocked."

Jacques took the paper back slowly and sat it on the table in front of him. He stared at it for a long time.

"You trying to figure it out, because trust me, I already—"

"No. I know it is, but you figured that out in a second . . . There are hundreds of possible paths there."

"Yeah, but when you know what you are looking for, some stuff fits, and some stuff don't. It's not hard to figure out."

He was still looking at the maze with a funny look on his face. "How does the world appear through your strange grey eyes?"

Faye didn't know how to answer that, other than seeing a little bit better in the dark than most folks she knew, Faye didn't think her eyes were any big deal. They made it so she had to wear dark-lensed sunglasses out in public to keep people from recognizing her as a Traveler, but other than that, no big deal. "I just see stuff normal, same as anybody. I just think about how it all goes together better, I guess. I've got this map in my head—"

"Yes. You've mentioned that, but in other Travelers, it is more of an instinct. For you, it is something more." Jacques seemed distant, distracted. "Very few Travelers live long enough to get very good at their peculiar form of magic. This thing in your mind, it is really like a map?"

She couldn't imagine what it would be like to live without a head map, or even worse, how terribly limiting it would be, not having the freedom to Travel. "Well, that's the best way to explain it I guess."

Jacques was quiet for a really long time. She thought about asking him another question, but he seemed to be thinking really hard about something. Whatever it was, something must have clicked, because he started talking, all while still staring at that maze.

"Whisper confirmed for me that you were not born with grey eyes. All Travelers are born with grey eyes, but you were born with blue eyes. Your eyes turned grey on September 18th, 1918, the day we killed the last Spellbound."

"I don't remember..." As far as Faye knew, she'd always been a Traveler.

"Yes, you were far too little. He was named Anand Sivaram. What do you know of him, Faye?"

"Just what Whisper told me. He was a real bad man. He was a Traveler, but real smart."

"Smart is an understatement. He was an astonishingly brilliant man, perhaps one of the greatest minds of our time."

"It sounds like you respected him."

Jacques chuckled. "How could you not? One must give respect to those who deserve it because of what they are capable of, even as you despise them for how they use their capabilities. Sivaram was born in one of the poorest slums in a very poor nation, with a rare form of magic that everyone around him saw as a malicious curse."

"I know the feeling."

"The parallel had not escaped me. Sivaram mastered teleportation, Traveling, as you are fond of calling it. As you are well aware, most Travelers do not live to adulthood. It is a form of Power most unforgiving of mistakes. Perhaps it was the complicated and dangerous nature of his Power that honed his curiosity so, but Sivaram embarked on a lifelong quest to understand magic. He was one of the first to discover that you could fashion spells and bind bits of the Power to them in order to create various effects. He went on to invent many of the spells we take for granted today, such as using the Power as a method of long-distance communication. He fashioned many others, great and marvelous spells that have since been lost to us. It was his greatest spell that pushed him over the edge into madness and murder. His notes have since been scattered around the world, but I sought out every last piece I could in order to better understand him."

"So you could kill him better?"

"Of course. I may not look it now, Faye, but I was once quite the dashing leader of Grimnoir. The task of stopping his reign of terror fell to me. As you know, a Traveler can be a wily foe. Now imagine, if you will, a Traveler who came to hunger for death, and did everything within his considerable ability to cause death on a massive scale."

The thought made Faye uncomfortable, mostly because she knew she'd be super good at it. She tried to hide her discomfort by nonchalantly eating one of the pastries. It was delicious.

"Sivaram's earlier works were rational, coherent. He was a compulsive letter writer, and there was so much correspondence to choose from. I read so many of his words that I began to feel like we were old companions. I truly believe he started out as a kind, generous, gentle man, but the more he delved into the mysteries of the Power's true nature, the more it changed him. By the time he'd fashioned the spell that you would come to inherit, his character had fundamentally changed. He believed the Power was talking to him, actually communicating its will and wishes. He became delusional, erratic, and eventually driven mad with homicidal urges."

"That ain't a real long drive for some folks." Faye could immediately tell that her attempt at humor had failed.

"This spell's burden was more than any one man could bear."

"I intend to prove you wrong."

Jacques paused. "My apologies. I did not mean it that way."

"It's okay. He went crazy and started killing good folks. I wouldn't be here talking to you now if I was planning on doing the same thing, now would I? I've got to know, though, what did he think the Power was asking him to do?"

"By that point, Sivaram's writings had become far too difficult to understand. They were simply the babblings of a madman."

"But…"

"If I were to guess, he thought that the Power had chosen him to be its protector."

Considering what Faye now knew to be out there, that was a sobering thought. The Chairman had thought the same thing about himself, and look how that had turned out.

Jacques took one last look at the complicated, unsolvable maze. "We must go on a journey, Faye. There is someone I would like for you to meet."

UBF *Traveler*

"WHAT THE HELL is this thing?" Lance asked as he stared at the body. "Some type of demon?"

"It isn't a Summoned..." Ian Wright was standing a few feet away, keeping one hand over his mouth. "Summoned have a feeling of... How can I explain this? *Connection.* This thing isn't linked to any Summoner. Plus it would've dissipated back into smoke and ink when it was killed. The insides of a Summoned are basically smoke and goo, all kept in a shell based on the imagination of somebody like me. This thing has guts."

"I realize that. I know demons pretty well." Lance absently tapped his permanently damaged leg. He had been mauled by a Summoned when he was younger. "But you got another explanation for this critter?"

There were half a dozen of men assembled in the sick bay. The corpse had been dragged in and dropped on a tarp. Sullivan hadn't said a single word while they'd examined the thing that had attacked them at the Imperium monitoring station. He'd only leaned in a corner, smoking and thinking over the implications of their discovery, angry at knowing that he'd been used.

It was hard to look at. Sullivan had skinned plenty of game in his youth, so he was no stranger to the sight of bare red muscle, but you shouldn't be missing your skin and still be running around. And this thing had been fast, fast enough to take apart three wounded Grimnoir and their only Healer. It looked like a man, but its limbs were too long, its chest too big and its spine was all curved and bowed. The toes looked more like fingers, and its teeth... The bodies of his dead men showed what those teeth could do.

Dr. Wells knelt next to the corpse, poking at it maliciously with a length of pipe. None of them actually wanted to touch it with their bare hands. "It isn't like anything I've ever seen in my travels. However..." He squished the pipe into the hole in the ribs and rolled the purple and red bits around. "I'm fairly certain this was once a human being."

Lance snorted. "You've got to be kidding me."

"I can assure you. I've seen many, many human organs in my day, and these, no matter how deformed some of them have become, are clearly human organs."

Lance wasn't convinced. "I know you've probably read a lot of anatomy textbooks, Doc—"

Wells pried some of the ribs a bit further apart. "Textbooks?

Hmm . . . *Yes,*" he replied absently. "Yes, of course that is what I meant . . . In textbooks."

"But that ain't no man. Look at those teeth! Damn thing's got jaws like a hyena. And those claws . . . I've hunted damn near every corner of the world, and the closest thing I've seen to those were on an anteater."

Heinrich had been nearly as quiet as Sullivan for most of their rushed autopsy. "We know the Imperium has performed terrible experiments. We've seen with our own eyes how badly Unit 731's failures can be. Perhaps this is the next step in their eugenic madness?"

"It's not one of theirs," Ian stated with grim finality. "I've seen their work. They twist people, but not anything like this. I've been to one of the schools. My . . . Somebody I knew was lost in one of them. This isn't how 731 works. There's no brands on this body, no spells at all. Those Jap Cog bastards can't twist flesh without magic."

"Wright and Wells are both right," Sullivan finally spoke. Toru had warned them about what had happened the last time around. He just hadn't expected to see it again this soon. "This was a man, and it wasn't Imperium magic that did this to him. This was something worse. You agree, Fuller?"

The Cog had been completely silent so far, standing in the corner, as far from the skinless man as possible. At first he'd seemed disgusted by the broken carcass, but then he had focused in on trying to understand the creature's magical nature, and had been off in his own world ever since. He had a small notebook in one hand and a pencil in the other, and he was either writing quickly or sketching, or maybe a little of both. "Fuller!" Sullivan snapped his fingers.

Fuller's head popped up, for a split second seemingly bewildered by the distraction. He looked back down at his notes, and then back up at Sullivan. It seemed to take a moment for his brain to shift back to reality and away from esoteric formula and odd geometries enough for him to form actual human language. "You promised that this expedition would witness magic like mankind has never before seen. You were true to your word. This . . ." and for once the man who had extra words for everything seemed stymied. "This *thing* is bonded to magical elements the likes of which I have never even dreamed of."

Dr. Wells had given up on his autopsy and let the bloody pipe fall on the floor with a clatter. "What does that mean?"

"It has magic, but the power geometries are multistacked across planar elements!"

The rest of them exchanged confused glances. Wells ran one hand through his thinning hair. "You say so."

"No, no. What you think of as magic is cords of omnidirectional energy capable of distorting physical law and probability. These cords have been tied into a knot. My Power can see the connection, but my mind is unable to untangle the knots. How? Why? I do not know." Fuller looked back at his notes. "I need time to think."

"Think quick." Sullivan said. "I got a feeling we'll be running into more."

"You think this is the Pathfinder's doing?" Lance asked.

"I know it." Sullivan ground his cigarette out in a nearby ashtray, turned, and strode out of the room.

Sullivan's words were left hanging in the air like the cloud of tobacco smoke.

"Hey!" Wells shouted after him. "What do you want us to do with this thing when we're done?"

"Burn it."

It was hard to keep his cool when he was that furious, but luckily nobody spoke to him as Sullivan made his way to the cargo hold. He found Toru in his *quarters*, standing in front of a mirror he'd hung from a wall pipe, pulling shards of broken glass out of his face with a pair of pliers.

The Iron Guard healing kanji had done its work, and Toru's jagged lacerations were mostly closed, though Toru still seemed shaky from blood loss. "Sullivan." He gave a curt nod into the mirror. "What do you—"

Sullivan grabbed Toru by the shoulders, spun him around, and slammed him back into the wall. The mirror shattered. Surprised, Toru didn't even have time to use his magic before Sullivan's elbow landed on his throat. "Talk, you bastard!"

Toru's face turned red. "Unhand me."

"What do you know?"

"I said unhand me," Toru answered, his calm visibly slipping.

"That thing came for you. The Pathfinder's already inside the Imperium. What do you know?"

Toru flared his Power. The impact of the hand against Sullivan's chest hit like a sledgehammer in a Rockville quarry. Sullivan called on his own magic in time and absorbed the hit. Gravity twisted and Toru hit the wall hard enough to bend the metal.

"I lost four men back there!"

"Do you think that makes you special?" Toru shoved him again, driving his magic harder. The grating under Sullivan's boots screeched in protest against the extra gravity. "You will lose more before this is over!"

"You Jap bastard—"

"Gentlemen." Neither of them had seen Captain Southunder walk in. The old man seemed relatively calm, but his words were hard. "If you two are going to fight, you will take it off my airship. I will not tolerate a Heavy and a Brute carrying on and wrecking my fine new vessel. The rest of us do not particularly relish the thought of being stranded at the North Pole, nor do I wish to walk home. Either one of you two wants to start violating the laws of physics and common sense, you will take it outside, or my marauders will escort you outside. Is that understood, Mr. Sullivan?"

Sullivan stepped away from Toru. "All right."

"I expect a more level head from you, Mr. Sullivan..."

Normally, that would be true. It took a lot to rile somebody who was as constant as gravity. "I can't abide losing men."

"A noble sentiment, but breaking my ship will not bring them back...Mr. Toru?"

Toru looked like he was ready to fight, but he paused, realizing that using his Power had caused the wound in his side to partially split open again. Blood was seeping out. "Look at what you have done."

"Walk it off."

"Mr. Toru?" Southunder asked again.

"Very well." Toru glared at the old pirate. *"Captain."*

"Splendid." Southunder folded his arms and leaned against the wall. "That nonsense out of the way, I'd also like to hear an answer to Mr. Sullivan's questions. It seems there have been some *complications.* So Fuller fixed the Chairman's toy and it showed the Pathfinder is already inside the Imperium, I take it."

"Something is eating magic all over the Imperium." Sullivan gave Toru a suspicious look. "Camping on top of every single place that's got itself an Imperium school. Then some sort of hyena-ape-man came through a mirror and attacked Toru here before it slaughtered a few of my men."

Toru gave a small nod. "A passable summary."

"You want to tell me how that is possible, Mr. Toru?"

"A sufficiently skilled spellbinder is capable of sending small amounts of physical matter through a communication spell. My mastery of the kanji is insufficient to perform such a feat. I was unaware of anyone who could send living matter through a mirror, thus I was caught by surprise. It will not happen again."

In better circumstances, Sullivan would have been excited to learn about this new magic trick of the Imperium's, but these were not better circumstances. "I know Faye did something like that once, Traveled right through a communication spell." In fact, she'd even done it to try to kill Toru. "But why were you using one? Who were you talking to?"

"The imposter."

Toru was lucky Sullivan needed his help, or he would have just eaten a .45 slug right there. "You better have a damn good reason."

"As a result of leaving my order, I have been cut off, unable to send word to my former brothers. This base had a mirror prepared to directly reach the high command. The Iron Guard are far more suited to deal with this threat than this puny expedition. Of course I used it. I challenged him to do his duty to the Imperium to stop the Pathfinder, and I offered my suicide in exchange. Apparently the imposter disagreed."

"What the hell were you thinking?"

Toru frowned. "Would you not have done the same thing?"

Probably. But he wouldn't give the smug Jap bastard the satisfaction. "You shouldn't have been alone."

"Yes... Because the Grimnoir are so trusting of me that they would have no problem with me manipulating powerful Imperium kanji under their noses inside a secret base."

The anger, though still there, had lost some of its direction, and now Sullivan just felt tired and frustrated. He took a seat on a nearby crate. "So what's going on at the schools?"

"School, my eye," Southunder said. "Torture chambers is more like it."

Toru looked like he wanted to argue, but was wise enough to let it pass. "I do not know. Whatever is happening, it began after my father's death. The imposter revealed himself to me. He is a senior Iron Guard named Dosan Saito, one of my *sensei*."

"*Sensei?*"

"Teacher. Saito was one of Okubo Tokugawa's closest advisors and a highly respected member of the cabinet. The betrayal of a man so honored is unexpected."

"You assholes and your *honor*. He's got your whole empire snowed, and good." Sullivan took out his pack of cigarettes and lit up. They were in one of the areas of the dirigible where smoking was frowned on, but Southunder let it go. Which was good. Sullivan was willing not to fight Toru for the safety of the ship, but the smoking was nonnegotiable. "So is this Saito a Ringer or something?"

"No. Like me, he is a Brute, a relatively common type of magic. I do not know how he is capable of such a compelling disguise. He has deceived men who have known Okubo Tokugawa for decades."

"Well, I hope he enjoys himself," Southunder said. "I frankly do not give a damn which tyrant is in charge of your gang of tyrants, as long as he does his part to destroy this space monster before it is too late."

Toru took a deep breath, as if composing himself before saying something difficult.

Sullivan's cigarette dangled from his lip. "Oh, what now?"

"I believe Saito is in league with the Pathfinder."

The three men were quiet for a very long time. Things had just gotten a whole lot worse, and sometimes that took a moment to really sink in. That explained the sabotage of the detector, and also their surprise guest. Sullivan closed his eyes and listened to the hum of the engines. They were lifting off, leaving Axel Heiberg. In a few minutes Barns would be calling, asking for their new heading, and frankly, Sullivan didn't have a clue what to tell him.

Toru broke the silence. "Each Pathfinder has been different than the one before. The last creature worked quickly, gathering an army as it went, consuming Power as rapidly as it could until it was strong enough to send its message. It was direct, simple. This one is different. It seems to be working through subterfuge, building its forces gradually in the dark."

"Your point, Mr. Toru?"

"All is not lost until it is strong enough to send for its master. The last creature was based upon strength and was defeated through strength. This one works through cunning, and therefore must be defeated with cunning. There seem to be plans afoot that we are only now discerning. The key to our victory is through disrupting those plans."

Captain Southunder shook his head. "And how do you intend to accomplish that?"

The threat was inside the Imperium, but the Imperium was also the one force best prepared to stop the threat. "We give them a wake-up call. We expose the Chairman as a fake," Sullivan answered.

"It is the only way. The Pathfinder's forces are spread across the Imperium schools. Alone we could never cleanse them all. When the Iron Guard understand that they have been deceived and that the Pathfinder is among them, they will strike back, and they will win. We have a hundred men. They have a hundred thousand."

"Like the Iron Guard will believe the likes of us." Southunder was incredulous. "The Grimnoir are a thorn in their side, I've been raiding their shipping for decades, and Toru's a turncoat. You couldn't even convince your own government, Sullivan. How are we supposed to convince them?"

"They think the Chairman's immortal." Sullivan looked to Toru. The Brute nodded. They were on the same page. "So we kill him again."

Toru had the smile of a shark. "In public."

Skinless Man

⚞ Chapter 8 ⚟

Hunger—real hunger—not your going-without-afternoon-tea, nor no-eggs-at-breakfast sort of affair—can, when a man is utterly without occupation, make life one continual aching weary desire. If the desire is not satisfied, or does not abate of its own accord (as it very often does), it can have disastrous effects on a man's mind. It has been known to make men think very seriously about the rights of property, and a few have become so unbalanced as to become socialists.

—Geoffrey Pyke,
Memoirs of a Boffin in a German Prison Camp, 1918

New York City, New York

"RAT BASTARDS!" Francis hurled the whiskey bottle into the fireplace. It failed to shatter, so he concentrated his Power and reached out with his mind, and the bottle exploded in a properly dramatic manner. "Filthy, no-good thieves! I can't believe this!"

"What part of this came as a shock to you? The part where you told the President of the United States you wanted to have a fight with him and that he was happy to oblige, or the part where you thought you could tell a bunch of crusading busybodies to shove off and you didn't expect any consequences?" Ray Chandler, CFO of United Blimp & Freight and Francis' confidante, covered his glass of whiskey protectively while Francis looked for something else to throw across the office. "Come on, Francis. You should have seen this coming a mile away."

His office on top of the Chrysler Building was a temporary safe haven from the army of auditors, investigators, bought-off reporters, union activists, and other various teat-sucking pawns of Roosevelt's who had been making his life a living hell, but they'd be back again tomorrow. Francis had no doubt about that. It was seventy degrees outside, so it wasn't like he'd needed to light a fire, but throwing things at the chimney always made him feel better, especially when it was lit. As a side effect, however, he'd had to order the air conditioning turned up to compensate, but what was the point of being rich if you weren't allowed a few idiosyncrasies?

"They're accusing me of selling warship designs to the Imperium? *Me?*"

"Well, your grandfather did violate the embargos. It doesn't take a Cog to point out that their *Kaga* class look suspiciously like the Super Tri-hull we've been trying to sell to our Navy."

"And I put a stop to that nonsense as soon as I got back from *killing* a bunch of Imperium navy." Francis picked up the evening paper. "Look at this! It's even the same reporters who wrote all the anti-Grimnoir propaganda after the assassination attempt. Why do people still believe proven liars?"

"Are you kidding? You've been wearing a big target on your back all year. They probably already had these articles about what a crook you are prepped from the last time you were getting the frame job from the OCI. They just had to haul them out and dust them off when Roosevelt asked." Chandler chuckled. "Hell, they'll probably win the Pulitzer for their hard hitting investigative journalism."

Francis angrily wadded the evening paper into a gigantic, ball and threw it at the fireplace too. However it hit the logs, caught fire, and then rolled out onto the floor. "Shit!" He ran over and desperately stomped out the fire before it ruined the Persian rug.

Chandler just shook his head, finished his drink, and then poured himself a refill. "I'm sorry to say, Francis, that it looks like you are the subject of a very savage public-relations campaign."

The scorch mark wasn't *too* bad. Francis used his magic and rolled the newspaper remains back into the fire. "Well, buy some newspapers, then. I'll beat him at his own game."

Chandler laughed hard. He'd had a bit too much to drink, but in his defense, he'd been fighting National Recovery Act auditors all day and their allegations of UBF price fixing. "Beat him? The man's a master manipulator. That's like Donald Duck saying he's going to outmaneuver Black Jack Pershing on the battlefield."

The mention of Pershing made Francis sigh. His old mentor would have known what to do. Francis was up to his eyeballs in trouble, getting attacked from every angle short of gunfire, and it was frankly overwhelming. "We're in bad straits, Ray, but I'm not giving up those Dymaxions. I'll burn this company down before I let those conniving bullies take them away."

"The board may disagree about the whole burning-everything-down strategy. You've done well, made them buckets of money, way better than they ever expected, and they sure love making money, but they like heat even less, and they're getting a lot of heat right now. I give it two weeks, tops, before they're calling for your resignation."

"It doesn't matter," Francis muttered. Ray was a financial wizard, and even if Francis got run out of the family business, Dymaxion was still his, and that's what Roosevelt really wanted. Federal agents had already seized all of that little company's assets under various legal excuses, mostly related to lies about his taxes, but they hadn't found a single Nullifier, Nullifier part, diagram, or note on their creation. Francis had told one of the Treasury agents that, sadly, all of those items had been lost in a tragic canoe accident. "The only thing that's really of value is what's stored in Fuller's brain."

"And when Fuller gets back from *holiday*, do you plan to hold him hostage somewhere so the government can't take him too?"

"If I have to. You don't get it, Ray. The world's changing. We're one of the last places where Actives aren't property. I'm not going to let my people become property."

"Canada and England's magical types are fairly well off...Okay, okay, I get you. So what do you aim to do, then?"

Francis leaned against the fireplace and studied the pattern of broken glass and curling newspaper. "I should run for president."

"You have to be thirty-five, so twelve or so years from now, I'm sure that'll be a fine idea."

"What? Seriously? When did they make that a law?"

"Wow." Chandler took a long drink. "Now there's a testimony about the quality of our finest prep schools."

"That's what I get for spending most of school chasing skirts." Francis walked back to his desk. "Look, I may not know the finer points of constitutional law, but I damn sure know right and wrong."

There were only a few framed photos on his desk, mostly of close friends since none of his family members rated the space. Francis picked up the one portrait of Faye and sighed. He'd loved a lot of women, but he only cared about one of them. That was because Faye was special. Faye owned *special*. He was the only one who knew she was still alive, and he had no idea where she was, but he found himself wishing hard that she was here now. Even without any of his resources or connections, but with her drastically uncomplicated view of the world, she would probably be doing a lot better than he was . . . Of course, the White House would probably be in flames and half of Congress would be dead, but Faye certainly knew how to get results.

The intercom on his desk buzzed. "Mr. Stuyvesant, Mr. and Mrs. Garrett are here to see you."

"Send them up."

"Grimnoir business, I presume?" Chandler asked.

"No earthly idea."

"Then I'd better be going," Chandler polished off his drink and got off the couch. "Dan doesn't like when I ogle his rather lovely wife, which is remarkably difficult not to do even when sober. Tonight? He'd probably *suggest* I take a stroll off your balcony and I'd probably find that a brilliant idea. I think I've had a touch much."

That was a lie. Chandler could outdrink a sponge, though he had been dealing with auditors all day, and if anything was an excuse to drink to excess, it was auditors. "You don't have to leave. It isn't like that whole secret society thing is particularly secret anymore."

"Ha! You think I *want* to know? Please. Once Roosevelt has his way with you all, I've got to try to figure out how to include this job on my resume without mentioning our association, Mr. Blacklist . . . Either that or I'll just embezzle a bunch of your money before Roosevelt steals it all and then retire to a beach in Cuba."

"Night, Ray."

"Night, Francis."

Francis passed the time waiting for his associates to arrive by coming up with inventive new curse words. They entered a few minutes after Chandler had left. Jane immediately came over and gave him a hug, because that's just how Jane was, and she could probably tell he was having a bad day. Chandler was right: Jane was a beauty. Francis had always thought she looked and even sounded a little bit like Marlene Dietrich. Also, Jane really was a sweet heart, just an all-around nice person to the core of her being. "I saw the papers."

"Hard to miss that big cartoon of me on the front page, holding up the sacks labeled *blood money* while standing on a pile of corpses titled *equality* and *prosperity*."

"They were never one for nuance," Dan agreed.

"I thought the cartoon made you look cute," Jane said. "I've never been famous enough to warrant a caricature. You and Dan are in the comics all the time now."

"They don't use you because they don't want to put a pretty face on the *Active menace*. They always make me look like a troll," Dan complained. "And fat, too."

"I prefer to think of you as attractively plump," Jane said as she patted her much shorter husband on the stomach. Dan did look a bit troll-like to her in Jane's company, but in comparison, so would most men. Not that it mattered to Jane, since, as a Healer, everybody looked like see-through meat bags filled with pumping organs and blood. But she always said that one simply got used to it. "Now hurry, Francis, fetch your hat. We must be going."

"Why? You guys taking me out for a night on the town?"

"Sadly, no." Dan spread his hands apologetically. "I just received word from Browning. His contact inside the government gave him a heads-up. There's been a new development on the registration front."

"Oh, what now?" Francis grabbed his shoulder holster, threw it on, and then tossed his coat over it. The .45 sitting on top of his desk went into the holster. There had been talk about a new executive order, but he'd been too busy trying to keep his business holdings in one piece to pay much attention to the rumors. "They rounding people up already?"

"It is a special holding area for Actives, all right," Jane answered, "but it isn't a roundup, Actives are supposedly *volunteering* for this."

"*What?* That's got to be a lie. The propaganda machine isn't even trying hard."

"We need to head over to New Jersey to check it out."

"New Jersey?" Francis thought about it for a second. He went back to his desk, grabbed another .45 auto and several extra loaded magazines. Jane raised an eyebrow. "Hey, don't give me that look. It's Jersey."

Drew Town, New Jersey

IT WASN'T AT ALL what he'd expected. It wasn't a prison camp. It was a town, and a rather cozy one at that, nestled in the forest, next to a serene lake, all within commuting distance from the city. The signs even said that they'd be putting in a bus line, the lake was stocked with fish, and the forest even had hiking trails. There were signs everywhere, all talking about how wonderful Drew Town was and would be, and every sign had happy families on it doing happy family things. Some of the art had been stolen from the *Saturday Evening Post*.

The houses were nice. Most of them were still under construction, but the first two hundred were already finished in their neat orderly rows, on perfectly level streets laid out in a grid. Numbers north and south, letters east and west. Lawns were still going in, but every finished house already had a white picket fence around it.

There was no barbed-wire fence around the perimeter. No spotlights or guard towers. Sure, there was a gatehouse on the road with a couple of bored security men inside, but that was it. They'd simply gone around the gatehouse and followed a dump truck up a dirt side road. Even in the middle of the night the construction crews were working at a feverish pace, with hundreds of workers toiling away beneath the spotlights. More signs proclaimed that these men were employed because of Roosevelt's Works Project Administration.

"WPA?" Dan asked as they drove past dozens of homes under construction.

"It stands for We Poke Along," Francis answered. "It's a new billion-dollar agency that pays the unemployed tax money to dig holes and then fill them back in."

"Why, Francis, I'd never known you to be so political," Jane said.

"I've got a right to complain. When I get mugged, I'm not expected to thank the mugger." There were electric lights on every corner. They'd already broken ground for several large buildings. The signs around those sites said that those would be schools, hospitals, churches, and even factories. It was like a massive, planned-out company town, only far nicer. "What the hell are they up to?"

"I've not heard a word from the news about this place," Jane said.

"According to Browning's government informant, this place is supposed to hold Actives."

"They're expecting thousands of people to live here, that's for certain." Dan pulled the Packard to a stop in front of one of the finished houses. The lights were on inside. "Hang on. I'll get us some answers." Dan got out, and Francis and Jane followed him.

Their Mouth went up the steps and rang the doorbell. Insects were buzzing around the porch lights. Jane paused to admire the flower beds. Francis noted that there was a bronze plaque on the door. It was a floating anvil. "You see that?"

Dan scowled at the plaque. "That's the sign they want Heavies to wear on their armbands." He rang the bell again.

There was noise from the other side, and then the door opened to reveal a tall, extremely broad-shouldered, thick-necked man. The fellow towered over them and had callused worker's hands that looked like they could entirely engulf Dan's head. He certainly looked like a Heavy. "It's late. What do you want?"

"Are you the resident?" Dan asked.

The Heavy's beady eyes narrowed. "Huh?"

They needed to remember that most Heavies weren't known for their smarts. Jake Sullivan was an anomaly in that respect. "Do you live here? Is this your house?"

"That's a dumb question. Of course I live here ... Who are you guys?"

Dan turned up his Power. "We're friends from out of town, come by to visit."

"Oh hey!" the Heavy grinned. "Good to see you guys. Come in! Come in! Hey, Alice, we got company!" Totally defenseless against the Mouth, his demeanor changed. "You guys want some cookies?"

"Naw, we're good." Dan smiled. *Pushover.* "We've only got a minute so we can't stay."

"Aww, but I haven't seen you guys in forever."

"We just wanted to know, friend, how did you end up living in this nice house in this lovely little town?"

"It is real nice, ain't it? Lord knows I couldn't afford this on a steelworker's wage. The government folks sent me a letter. Alice helped read it. Said since I had magic, we could come and live here for free. Even said that if you didn't have work, you could live here for free until they found work for you. Everybody in Drew Town's got magic of some kind. Mr. Drew says only magical folks get invited to live here."

"The architect," Francis muttered as he remembered bumping into the man in the White House. "Son of a bitch."

"Aw, he's perfectly nice," the Heavy said. "He just wants to keep Actives safe from the folks who don't like us. You know how those League types can get."

Francis knew that he was talking about the League for a Magic Free America. Like most groups of bigoted fools, they loved lynching and firebombs. It still chapped his hide that he'd gotten shot saving a bunch of those ungrateful bastards from a truck bomb. "Those hoods are nothing a tough guy like you couldn't handle, I bet."

The Heavy shrugged. "Yeah. I'm tough, so what? But I got a wife and little kids. Here, we don't have to worry about nothing. My kids don't even have to worry about getting treated different for being weird, and they can go to school like I never got to. I ain't alone. Bunch of folks already signed up. Mr. Drew says pretty soon this town will be all filled up with magical folks and they'll make more towns like this across the whole USA."

"Thanks, friend," Dan said. "Have a nice night, and forget we were ever here."

"Okay. Buh-bye." The Heavy closed the door.

They walked back to the Packard. Francis turned, went across the lawn, hopped the fence, and ran up the next porch. There was a Crackler plaque on that door. He crossed the street to find the crossed bones of a Shard. He pulled a flier off of one of the light poles. Beneath the Norman Rockwell painting was a reminder that Actives could get monetary bonuses for suggesting their Active friends and family for membership in Drew Town to the town administrators. Francis ran back to the car and got in. "All the houses are tagged."

Dan was drumming his fingers on the steering wheel. They were all thinking the same thing, but it was Jane that spoke first. "It appears that President Roosevelt understands that you can catch more flies with honey than vinegar."

"You can also catch flies with bullshit." Francis held up the flier. "This is Bradford Carr's master plan all over again, only with a happy face, a two-car garage, and a fish pond."

"They won't need to round up Actives if most of us volunteer," Dan stated. "We know the OCI was making lists, and now they'll just send invitations. I bet once this place is all beautified and full up, it'll be all over every newspaper, magazine, billboard, and radio program. That's how I'd do it. They'll have every fed-up, tired of being picked on, or out-of-work Active in the country beating down their doors."

Francis looked out the car window at the white picket fences and imagined them replaced with razor wire. Once again, the men in charge were trying to herd magicals into easily controlled groups . . .

But why?

Somewhere in France

JACQUES HAD SHOWN UP the next morning with two train tickets and asked Faye to gather her things. She didn't have much in the way of *things* so it hadn't taken very long. The Grimnoir elder had been as enigmatic as ever when quizzed about their destination. Faye couldn't read French, but it helped that there was a very rough map printed on the back of the ticket. It looked like they'd end up in Germany eventually. She didn't know much about Germany, other than that the Kaiser had been on the other side during the Great War, and men like Mr. Sullivan had fought there until its capital had gotten blown up by a Peace Ray. Heinrich, the only German she knew well, had made his homeland sound pretty nice, actually, except for the parts about the starvation, poverty, anarchy, and, of course, all those zombies.

"Come now, Faye. Why so sullen? You have done nothing but stare out the window all this time. You should be happy. We are traveling!"

Faye snorted. "You call this traveling?" Regular folks would never be able to understand the glorious freedom of her magic. Traveling was like pure bottled *happiness.*

"Admit it, my dear. You are only content when you are in motion."

"This ain't traveling, Jacques. This here is some rich folks took a room out of a mansion and stuck it on rails." Faye pointed at the table between them. "Heck, we even get served cookies. What is it with you and big sugary things?"

"I am a big sugary person." Jacques patted his belly. "Come now, perhaps this method of transportation is not as fast as you are used to, but this way we get to enjoy the scenery."

She had to admit Jacques had a point. Europe was rather lovely. Everything she'd seen so far in France was neat and green. *Very pretty.* Sure, Faye was a fancy world traveler now, but that was all a recent development for her. Most of her life had been spent in two places. First was Ada, Oklahoma—and most of what she could remember about that was it being a barren, dry, horrible, mean, ugly wasteland. Then she'd gone to El Nido, California, which had been a paradise of alfalfa fields and happily chewing cows in comparison. France reminded her a lot more of California than it did Oklahoma. She'd never seen a fat person until she'd gotten to California. The sun and the wind burned the fat right off you in Oklahoma, left you hard and mean. Mr. Bolander had changed that, since his death had unlocked the rain and saved Oklahoma. Faye had heard on the radio that grass was starting to grow there again, but that wasn't the Oklahoma she remembered. She'd been glad to get out. Didn't miss it one bit.

"It's nice I guess."

"Besides, we have this all to ourselves." Jacques picked up a cookie and used it to gesture around the luxury car. "Being a retired man of wealth has its benefits."

"My boyfriend owns UBF."

"Indeed. How could I forget? I am but a penniless hobo in comparison to young Francis Stuyvesant, but I reserved this car because it was the only one which gave us privacy. It will give us time to talk."

"So I can continue my lessons?"

"I do not know if there is actually a lesson to continue. That was Whisper's notion. I will tell you what I know of the Spellbound. Hopefully you will manage to not turn into a rampaging murder machine in the process."

It was a little too late for that, but Faye figured she could keep her murdering and rampaging confined to just the bad folks at least. "That's mighty hopeful of you, Jacques."

The old man grinned. "I am by nature an optimist, my dear."

"So where are we going?"

"Do not trouble yourself. I will tell you when we get there. Just know that we go to speak with an old friend of mine. He helped me to understand what the Spellbound was truly capable of. I hope that he will be able to do the same for you." Jacques reached into one of his bags. "We will not be there for many hours."

Hours? And to think that normal folks considered this *Traveling*... "I'd like to know—"

The thump of a thick stack of papers onto the table interrupted her and threatened to knock the giant plate of cookies onto the rug. The papers were bound together with string, and Jacques quickly untied it and let them spill outward in a mass of chaotic correspondence.

Faye picked up one of the old letters. This envelope was discolored with age and had been damaged by water at some point. The handwriting was very swoopy and hard to read. "What is this?"

"I told you Anand Sivaram was a prolific writer. Perhaps if you can get a glimpse into the one who first bore the mantle of the Spellbound, you will understand more about your own Power. You had best get started."

Hours and miles flew by as Faye read about Anand Sivaram.

It was in my twenty-fifth year, while still mastering my own connection to the Power, that I received my first glimmer of understanding. I have read the words of the learned and respected, scientists and philosophers, zealots and eugenicists, and yet it was in a pathetic excuse for a hospice where I came to understand that all of them were wrong. They did not understand magic because they could not experience magic. Magic must be lived. It must be breathed. It must be part of your soul. Only through immersion into this river of magic do we truly commune with the Power.

It was during an extended convalescence, healing from an accidental misuse of my own magic, that I spent the time necessary to let my mind roam to truly formulate my understanding of magic. I had injured my back after foolishly placing myself in a precarious situation. Barely able to walk, I had been forced to lie still, with nothing else to do for days but turn my thoughts inward.

All Travelers, as they have taken to calling my kind, develop some instinctive form of sensory ability relating to the area in which we are set to appear, or we die in short order. It is that simple. Despite being faithful to the methods I had developed in order to protect myself from injury while using my magic, I still found myself injured. On the day of my accident, I had done as I had taught myself, and opened my mind for any sense of foreign bodies which could potentially impact or embed themselves in me—the single greatest cause of death among young Travelers is flying insects—before Traveling. Yet in a moment of distraction I had foolishly landed and placed my feet upon slick stones, slipped, and wrenched the vertebra of my lower back.

Thus confined to bed for weeks on end, I had set myself to the mental task of improving my methodology. I meditated upon this at great length. In time, my mind seemed to expand beyond my physical presence, and for the first time in my life, I saw the Power as it really was.

My eyes were opened. My journey had begun.

Jacques chuckled, and it broke her concentration. Faye looked up from the note. "What's so funny?"

"You move your lips when you read. I just noticed that. You really shouldn't do that. Terrible habit to have in the field, secret messages to you won't be very secret if there is an Imperium spy around who can read lips."

"I'm not afraid of Imperium spies."

"You should be. The really clever ones will seduce you and then leave you to pay the bill. Ah, never mind. That is a story best shared with more mature company. Speaking of spies reminds me, though, you have yet to spot all of my men."

Faye scowled at him. She had never been particularly good at reading, and if it hadn't been for Grandpa, she wouldn't have known how to at all, so going through the letters of Anand Sivaram was a difficult, frustrating, time-consuming process.

But she simply couldn't stop.

"Shut up and eat your cookies." Faye picked up another paper. This one was an amazingly complex drawing of a spell. She recognized it instinctively. Faye didn't need Buckminster Fuller's Power to tell that all of those complicated shapes stuck together represented the part of the Power that controlled Traveling. Sivaram had been bored in a hospital and his mind had wandered until he'd first seen the Power. Faye had once followed Mr. Sullivan's dying spirit to the place where the dead people dream in order to see the Power itself. She liked

Sivaram's way better, but it did make her wonder, did it take somebody who could Travel to actually see the Power? Without dying first and getting dragged back first like Mr. Sullivan had, at least? The Chairman had been visiting there for years, which explained how come Imperium magic sometimes seemed so much more advanced than theirs, but then again, it seemed like the Chairman had been able to do whatever he felt like.

Many of Sivaram's letters had been dated, so she'd put them into order as best as she could. Then there were loose pages, random scribbles, doodles, old photographs, and even napkins with hasty notes scrawled on them. There were huge gaps in time, obvious spots Jacques hadn't been able to fill in, references to things Sivaram had written that there was no record of, but despite those handicaps, she could follow his path, clear as day. Sivaram had been consumed with a desire to understand the way things worked, and it had dragged him across the whole world.

The majority of the letters were to his wife. The love there was obvious, especially in the early letters, but that began to fade as he became more and more distracted, and his devotion changed from people to magic.

Dearest Devika. I will not be returning home this month as planned. I can only hope that you can endure my continued absence. I cannot give up when I am this close. The journey must continue. This week we went even further in the jungle. When I first heard the British ambassador speaking of this man known as the wizard, I knew I had to seek him out. What manner of man could manipulate magic into all new forms? It has taken years for me to even begin to understand my own Power, yet I cannot conceive of such a skill. As a Traveler, I can catch but the tiniest glimpse at times of what magic really is. I have learned so much, but the things they attribute to this wizard, if even only true in the smallest measure, could drastically increase our understanding of magic. They say that he has learned to draw magic. Draw it? As if it is so easily manipulated! They say that he has engraved magic upon his own body, giving himself whole new types of Power. Surely this is impossible, but I simply must know for myself.

There was a quickly drawn map of a place she didn't know, and the margins were filled with geometric doodles that were obviously Sivaram's guesses at what the Power really looked like. It seemed that even before he went and broke his brain and went full-on murder crazy, he was already wound a little tight.

Dearest Devika. I know this letter must come as a surprise, as so much time has passed that surely you must have thought me lost and dead in the jungles, but I have prevailed. My journey to the colonies has been a success. I found the man I have been looking for. The stories about the wizard are true. All of the stories are true. It is magnificent. It is not the creation of new magic, for the magic is already there, we are simply reaching out and taking more of it for ourselves. The Power is an incredible entity, made up of thousands and thousands of intersecting nodes, each one of those capable of some small shifting of the supposedly immutable laws of the universe. I have taken new forms of magic to myself, as many as my frail mortal body can bear. With each one, the mysteries have become clearer. Reality is far more beautiful and far more terrifying than we have ever imagined.

There were dozens of letters to his wife, yet not a single one written to Sivaram in response. She wondered if Jacques had simply never found those, or if she had never bothered to respond at all. The thought made her sad, but then she delved back into the world of the Mad Traveler.

The magic is wasted. It grows so strong while we live, but then it is all lost when we perish. If only there was a way to save this, to keep it, to nurture it and mold it across the generations. All that I have learned, all that I have gained, it cannot be learned through a book or through lecture or pathetic human language, it can only be mastered through immersion in the river of magic. But why must this precious river flow? It must be dammed. It must be stopped. I will not die like this. Pointless.

Faye's journey continued. Notes and alchemical solutions, chemistry diagrams and mathematical notations that were far over her head, yet each one became increasingly erratic. Now the geometric representations of the Power had become darker, uglier, harsher. Where they'd been elegant before, these lines seemed twisted, the paper had often torn beneath the fury of Sivaram's quill. There were long dried droplets of blood on the pages, as if he'd gotten a nosebleed and not noticed because of the intensity of the concentration needed for his calculations.

Jacques came back from lunch. She had not realized that he had left, nor had she heard him ask if she wanted anything. He placed some meat, cheese, and bread next to her, and she ate it without tasting it.

The next letter was addressed to no one. His handwriting had been shakier, harder to read.

I am close to a breakthrough. The wall between our world and the Power is thin here. My mind is unable to comprehend that which must be done. I am weak. No one else understands. Their Power is wasted. Fools. They stumble blindly, not understanding what must be done. I will take their Power, take it and use it as it should be used.

I do not believe in gods. Gods have never helped me. Everything I have done, I have done through my own intellect. Yet now as my mind fails me, I have prayed for help.

I think something has answered.

Faye did not understand the next drawing at all. It was half math, half shapes, and it made her head hurt just looking at it. She had to force her eyes away and let loose an audible groan.

Jacques was sitting across from her, watching, sipping from a glass of wine "Yes. I see you found the rough draft of the spell which would become your curse."

"Is that what it is?"

He took a sip. "I believe so. Do not feel bad. It has that effect on everyone." There was a sharp knock on the door. Jacques spoke loudly in French. A coachman stuck his head in and asked Jacques a question she couldn't understand. She did understand that Jacques' answer of *oui* meant *yes*, and then the man left.

"What was that about?" Faye asked.

"He merely wanted to make sure we had all of our windows closed for our safety. Do not worry." Jacques took the bottle out of the bucket of ice and poured himself some more wine. "Please, continue."

Dearest Devika. I have succeeded where all others have failed. They called me mad, but I have confirmed the truth. The Power is alive. What we call magic is the means by which it feeds. It grants a piece of itself to some few of us, and as we exercise that connection through every manipulation of the physical world, the magic grows. Upon our death, that increase returns to the Power. It is a symbiotic parasite. Grown fat upon us, the process repeats, more Actives are created, the cycle continues. The Power itself has a certain measure of awareness. Aware? Yes. I do not know yet if it knows that I have stolen from it, and if so, how it will react to my petty thievery. As the Power is using us, I intend to use it. I beg your forgiveness for what I must now become.

There was an old, badly damaged photograph of a very young woman. Nobody could smile in photographs back then because your face muscles would get worn out before the picture took, but she was still rather pretty.

"That was when I became involved," Jacques said softly. "She was one of us. A knight and a . . . friend . . . Sivaram was a vulture at first. When people died around him, he would snatch up their magic. Even those who are considered normal are not without some small touch of magic, for the Power would often touch them, find them wanting, and then move on. The Spellbound would steal even that, but it was not nearly enough. He needed more, and the stronger the Active, the better."

As the stack of papers dwindled, there were fewer notes and letters, but it was made up for with newspaper clippings, and Faye read every single one. Murder. Murder. Murder. Accidental Death. Mass Murder. Drowning. Plane Crash. Theater Fire. Ship Lost at Sea. It went on and on and on . . .

"There were more. Many, many more. Travel in, cause something awful, Travel back out. I suspect that many of the assassinations that helped speed along the Great War were his doing, his insatiable hunger for chaos, and the hope that a great modern war would bring tremendous death with it. That's finally how we caught him. I set a trap. I simply went to the greatest slaughter the world had ever seen and waited for him to show up. Normally I would ask if you had any idea how deadly an assassin a motivated and highly skilled Traveler could be . . . but you know, Faye. You know very well."

Faye could only nod. She tried to only used her Power to do good things, but for her, killing folks was a snap. But this . . . she flipped through the newspaper clippings. This was unimaginable.

"Yet even then we underestimated him. Sivaram was no longer a mere mortal Traveler. The spell he'd carved into himself saw to that. He was hard to catch, even harder to kill. He massacred my men and anyone around him. I believe the Spellbound became our greatest threat."

"More than the Chairman?"

"It was arguable, but I was in the minority. There was at least a cold logic to everything Okubo Tokugawa did, and yes, I know he killed far, far more people that Sivaram ever dreamed of, by an order of magnitude. The Chairman's Imperium has made butchery and slavery into a bloody, emotionless trade, mechanized, unfeeling, something only an all-powerful government can do. Sivaram was alone, most of the elders saw him only as a mad dog that needed to be put down. However, after studying the man and following him for years, I came to understand the true threat. Read his last letter. It had never been posted. Read, Faye."

Dearest Devika. Much time has passed since I have written. I have been consumed by my work. I write this letter in a brief moment of lucidity. I do not know how many more I will have, as they are becoming fewer by the day. Do not let my sons listen to the rumors of what I have become. The rumors are true but they must never know of the evil created by my hand. I was blinded by pride. One does not steal from the Power without paying a price. It is more intelligent than I suspected and it is learning. Though I thought I was using it, I was truly the one being used. Human emotions are not sufficient to describe the Power, but it was not upset when it discovered my theft. My resourcefulness gave it hope. The Power tried to prepare me for a task, but I was unworthy of its gifts. I have failed the test. Now all that remains is the hunger.

The failure of understanding the Power's true nature is upon my head. Though incomprehensible to our pathetic minds, it has its own mysterious desires and purposes. It is using mankind for something, developing and steering us in the hopes of accomplishing its goals.

When I was young and naïve, I thought to master the Power by toying with geometries beyond human understanding. I was nothing, but I stepped before the Power and presented myself as a sacrifice, as a science experiment. The Power utilized me, and though I have failed, it will try again, for I surprised it. I showed it what mankind is capable of. This spell burned into my flesh is too strong to die now. The Power will find a new subject to toy with.

What an interesting phenomenon. Look at the laboratory rat. What a clever thing. This rat's pathetic mind discerned new avenues that the observer, even with its far superior intellect, could never see. Of course not, it is hard to see when you are on such a lofty perch. Behold the rat's tricks. The rat dies, but the experiment is incomplete. We will train more. The experiment will begin again. There will be more rats. The rats must be fed.

The madness I have wrought is nothing compared to what will come. Please forgive me for what I have done.

The ink had run in spots, as if his tears had watered the paper as he'd been writing. Faye slowly returned the letter to the stack. "I don't get it," she lied. Not understanding everything was not the same as not understanding anything at all.

"Very few members of the Society ever saw that, and among those who did, most dismissed it as the ravings of a madman. I disagreed." Jacques put his glass on the table between them. The usual affable, pleasant demeanor he tended to wear was gone, having been replaced with the face of a very cold, very discerning investigator. "Mad? Perhaps, but driven mad because he understood just what he had unleashed upon mankind. I see in that letter the same thing I saw in the letters of criminals giving their deathbed confessions, a stark realization that actions have consequences."

"You ain't really worried about what the Spellbound *does*..." Faye muttered. "You're worried about what the Power is up to."

"Sivaram thought his actions, killing in order to steal magic, *pleased* the intelligence behind the Power. We are talking about a being which feeds off of us, uses us, changes us, gives blessings and takes them away without a shred of anything we recognize as logic or decency. It would appear that Power is an advocate of evolution, let the strongest survive, and let the weakest perish. Magicals were a new step in evolution, one brought about by the Power. The Spellbound was one of those magicals taking evolution into his own hands, and it seems that the Power approved. Sivaram said he did not believe in gods." Jacques snorted. "Heh. It seems to me he found one that believed in him. And it is neither a merciful nor wrathful god, but rather an ambivalent intelligence that cares only about itself."

Faye had never thought of the Power that way, and it made her a little uncomfortable. "I'm gonna stick with Jesus, thanks."

"I ask you, Faye, what happens to us if the Power decides to take this experiment to the next stage? What happens if you, the second generation of this spell, continue to further its goals?"

"I don't—"

"It will create more like you, probably many more. And they will steal magic from anyone who is weaker than they are. At least the Chairman is an orderly form of destruction. This other path is one of utter chaos. We can contend against the enemy with understandable goals, but it is nearly impossible to fight one that exists only to cause chaos. Now do you understand why I voted the way that I did?"

Maybe. Yes, but Faye still didn't like that one bit. Anybody else who voted to kill her would have to deal with her veto power, which would probably consist of a round of 12-gauge buckshot to their face. "And what if you're wrong, and the Power is right? I told y'all what the Chairman said about the Enemy coming to eat the Power. I can feel it myself once in a while, like a big weight hanging over us all. Maybe the Power was trying to save both us and it."

"So we should tolerate a known risk in order to protect against a risk that may not even exist? The Chairman was the king of lies. Why should I expect him to be any more truthful in death than when he was in life? You wish to risk this because it is your life which is at stake. You are biased. Perhaps you can control the Spellbound curse, perhaps not. That still remains to be seen. You have been in this world for such a short time. Those letters you read from Sivaram span over thirty years. It took decades to wear him down and turn him into the monster that he became."

"But I won't do that."

"And why would you not? Strength of character? Love for your fellow man?" Jacques gave a bitter laugh. "Sivaram loved his family and his people with all of his heart, but the curse wore him down eventually. It cut him to the soul, stole his humanity, and soon everyone around him, especially those with magic, were in danger. They were mere vessels holding the Power he sought . . . And he took that Power, oh, did he take *so very many* lives."

"I'd never do anything to hurt my friends!" but even as the words left her mouth, she felt the sting of doubt.

"The Spellbound does not get to have *friends*, or family, or comrades, or lovers. The Spellbound is alone. The Spellbound is a *force*. Sivaram started out as a pacifist and a scholar and look where he wound up. You have been known to us for only a short time, but already look how many other Actives you have killed."

"And every one of them deserved, it too." Faye snapped. "You can think I'm dangerous all you want, but I'm also the best we've got. If it hadn't been for me, the Chairman would still be around. If it hadn't been for me, Washington D.C. would've gotten squished by a demon. You think I'm dangerous, Jacques? Well, so is a gun." She gestured rudely at his coat. Of course, she hadn't bothered to check, but she assumed he had one on, as any properly attired gentlemen should. "Being dangerous is their job. Ain't much call for one that's not dangerous, now is there?"

Jacques looked her square in the eye. "Look out the window."

Faye did, and it nearly took her breath away. The beautiful farmland they had been passing through was gone, and now as far as her eye could see was nothing but a swath of sick, grey dirt. An odd, uncomfortable feeling settled into the pit of her stomach. "What is this?"

"This was part of the battlefield left over from the battle which you have heard referred to as Second Somme. A geographic misnomer, to be sure, but that is the name which has stuck."

Of course Faye had heard of Second Somme. She'd even seen a glimpse of it, since that was the personal hell which Mr. Sullivan had consigned himself to after she'd shot him in the heart. "It's lifeless."

"Worse than Oklahoma was?"

"Yeah. That was a drought. Sure it was a drought caused by magic, but this is different." Faye shivered. There wasn't even a breeze that could blow a tumbleweed across that grey bit of hell. Not that a tumbleweed could've grown there, either.

"It has been a generation, but look at it still. This land was defiled by magic, utterly ruined. The eastern half of my country was a muddy wasteland of trenches and barbed wire as far as the eye could see, but all of that, other than the occasional unexploded artillery shell that some poor farmer still occasionally turns over with a plow, has gone back to normal. This place, it never has, and never will. Too much magical energy was used here. Too much Active blood was spilled. The land was *changed*."

She could feel the cold in her bones. There weren't even buzzards, and the only thing close to plant life were broken, petrified tree stumps that had been that way since she'd been a baby. "It's just dead, ain't it?"

"Not quite. There are horrors which roam the wastes. A few living things were changed, warped. That much magic usage always has consequences. It twists the very fabric of our bodies. Even breathing this dust will make you sick. It is best to pass through here quickly."

Faye had thought she'd seen ugly before. The blackened circle that had been Mar Pacifica had been ugly, but it had been a fresh wound. This was an old scar; a scrar that had never fully healed.

"You have not seen real war, Faye. You have seen skirmishes. This is what happens when magic truly goes to war against magic. You have not seen the utter savagery that comes from something of this magnitude. Second Somme was one of the largest battles in history, and it was the greatest loss of Active lives ever. Day after day they killed each other, magic being flung back and forth like nothing you could possibly imagine. The laws of physics were broken. Men became something more, and sometimes something less, and afterwards the land was so blighted that we could not even stay long enough to bury the dead without growing ill. We gathered what we could, and most of the rest were left to sink into the mud."

"I've heard it was real bad."

"If it had not been for General Roosevelt sacrificing his American Volunteers, then my country would have been conquered by the Kaiser's undead hordes. It was only through a combination of luck, courage, and tenacity that this line held. Oh, how the Power must have grown fat on us." Jacques sounded tired. Bitter and tired. "It must have been a feast."

In the distance, Faye could see hills with living plants on them, so thankfully the battleground didn't go on forever. All scars had to end somewhere. "You were here?"

Jacques was staring out the window. "For part of it, but I was drawn away when I received word of the Spellbound's whereabouts. I missed the final offensive because I was a few miles away hunting Sivaram. He had been difficult to track during the war. With all of that death to choose from, there had been little need for him to strike out on his own, so this opportunity could not be missed. I was not alone. Knights from both sides deserted in order to assist me. All of us put aside our war in order to stop the greater danger. I was the only survivor, so perhaps in some sad way, Sivaram saved my life."

"Because you missed this?"

"Yes. We caught him minutes after he had murdered Whisper's entire family. She had no one else, so I took her in and raised her as my own." Jacques wiped his eyes. "I loved her very much."

"I didn't know all that," Faye said.

"All you need to know is that it is only because of Whisper you are still alive. You see that, Faye? If you are wrong, if the Power decides that the Spellbound is the next step in its relationship with mankind, then it will be Active against Active, killing and taking, no better than animals. It will reduce us to predator and prey." Jacques glared out the window at the tainted wasteland. "If you are wrong, then *that* is our future."

✦ Chapter 9 ✦

No one who, like me, conjures up the most evil of those half-tamed demons that inhabit the human breast and seeks to wrestle with them can expect to come through the struggle unscathed.

—Sigmund Freud,
From *Interview with a Reader:
An Analysis of a Case of Hysteria*, 1905.

Wannsee, Germany

THE BERLIN WALL was much taller than she'd expected. She had heard of the great wall which had been erected around Dead City to keep the zombies inside; everyone with access to a radio had heard stories about it at some point, but maybe it was because she'd spent those years on the Vierras' dairy farm that she'd always figured it would have been more like the sort of fences they used to keep cows in than an actual giant wall made out of stone. If she'd thought that through, she would've realized how naïve she'd been. After all, cows and zombies were very different in temperament.

"So the man you want me to talk to is inside *there?*"

"That is correct, Faye," Jacques said.

Was he trying to get her killed on purpose? Faye had dealt with the undead before, so she knew how dangerous they could be. Was Jacques trying to get rid of the Spellbound again? Skip another elder's vote, send her on a wild-goose chase into one of the most dangerous places in the world, and just let the ravenous zombies get her instead? It made a sick sort of sense. "Are you crazy?"

Jacques chuckled. "Can anyone who has lived for this long in this field truly be sane? I think not."

The train station was on the outskirts of the city which had once been known as Berlin. It, like most of the wall's surroundings, seemed grey and worn. Faye had always assumed that Heinrich always wore grey simply because he was a Fade and it helped him blend in everywhere. Now she wondered if he always wore grey because that was the only color he had seen growing up. Maybe grey was just his favorite color?

She hadn't spoken out loud, but Jacques knew what she was thinking. "The people on the outskirts of Dead City do not use bright colors. Should any of the undead make it over the walls, those who still have eyes are attracted to bright colors, just as those who can still hear are attracted to noise."

Now that he mentioned it, Faye realized it was abnormally quiet here. Obviously there had been the noise of the train engine, but after it had rolled out, the city was oddly silent. The porter who had carried their bags had spoken in muted tones. There were no loud announcements, no music playing anywhere, no loud conversations from the locals. It was like being in the shadow of the dead sucked all the life right out of a place. The grey stone walls loomed over the town, so she supposed it would be hard for anyone to forget. "That's too bad."

"Most of the undead have gone so mad that they are not capable of rational thought. Should some get out, which I have been told is not too uncommon an occurrence, it is better to let them wander aimlessly for a time rather than to have them hone in immediately on the living. It gives the tower guards more time to spot them."

"What about the ones that are still smart?"

"Thankfully for us and them, there are not so many of those left anymore. If an undead who has retained his reasoning truly feels the need to escape into the world of the living, heaven help us all. Hunting down the occasional wrathful undead who escapes these walls is a specialty of our German Grimnoir brethren."

The feeling in the air was not that different from the fields of Second Somme. This was a place where magical energy had torn a hole in the world and left a gaping wound. She had been in Mar Pacifica, and had survived the Peace Ray impact there—a hit which had been a tiny fraction of the size of this one—but when she'd come out of the ground, Mar Pacifica had felt different. Everything had still been smoking and burning. It hadn't had time to turn grey and dead yet.

She hadn't been back to Mar Pacifica to find out what it looked like now, but in her gut she knew it would be another dead, blighted place forever... And it had been so pretty once.

"I can't believe we're going in there."

"We? I plan on renting rooms for the night and enjoying a warm meal. In the morning, *you* are going in there and I will stay in my room and enjoy a good book. If you are not back in twenty-four hours, then I will simply assume you are gone, board another train, and head back to Paris."

"That's awfully yellow of you."

"Says the girl who can teleport to the portly old man with bad knees who could not outrun the slowest of shamblers. I was only a Brute of medium talent in my prime. Now, I would be consumed in minutes."

She knew he was exaggerating. He'd still managed to climb a cathedral just fine. "Oh, come on, Jacques. Even zombies don't eat that fast, and there's plenty of extra helpings on you."

He looked offended and tried to suck in his gut.

If he was going to send her into Dead City to get murdered, she didn't feel any particular reason to be polite about it. "I'm sick and tired of you not telling me anything and keeping secrets. You need to spit it out right now. Who is it I'm supposed to talk to here and why? It better be a good answer or I'm leaving."

"Feel free; you came to me, remember?" She could have simply Traveled away and never looked back, but she didn't, and they both knew why. Faye did not want to end up a homicidal madman like the last Spellbound. Faye put her hands on her hips and waited.

"Very well then. The man you are looking for inside those walls was once a knight of the Grimnoir. His name is Zachary. He assisted me in my original investigation of the Spellbound. If anyone can answer the questions regarding your curse and if you are doomed to follow in the footsteps of Sivaram, it is he."

She looked in disbelief at the walls, and then back at Jacques. No living person would be caught dead in there. "He's a zombie..."

Jacques nodded. "Sadly, yes. Several years ago we were battling some Soviet agents in Hungary. Zachary was killed while under the effects of a Lazarus' curse, so he came back from the dead."

Faye winced as she remembered poor Delilah. "I'm familiar."

"When the pain became too much to bear, and he felt he was becoming a danger to those around him, he banished himself here. Zachary possesses an extremely rare type of magic, one which the forces of evil would go to great lengths to secure for themselves if they realized it truly existed. His Power was one of our best kept secrets, and very few knights knew of him. Zachary came here to live in solitude and secrecy. Since then, he has still offered his knowledge willingly to the society when asked, but no one has spoken to him in quite some time."

"How do you know he's still..."—she almost said alive, but that wouldn't do at all—"*around*?"

"I do not know for sure. It has been years since his last contact with the outside world. The last time I tried to speak with him was when the question of your identity was raised. Alas, he did not answer the summons on his ring. I do not know if that was because he was unable, or if he no longer cares enough to bother."

Faye sighed. So not only was she going into Dead City, she was going to do it for somebody who might not even be sane enough to answer her questions. It wasn't like the undead were known for their *calm*. "So this fella knows more about Sivaram than you do?"

Jacques shook his head. "I am afraid not. I am the expert on that sad individual."

"Then why—"

"Zachary can see the future."

Jacques Montand was true to his word. He would wait the twenty-four hours before leaving Germany, never to look back. It was deeply troubling that he was so willing to abandon the poor girl to such a dark fate, but that was only if he was thinking of her as Faye, the helpful, earnest, courageous young woman, rather than as the Spellbound, a lethal vampiric curse bound in flesh, destined to turn into an engine of homicidal madness, and a prototype of things to come. Then the idea was not so difficult to bear.

She had gone alone into the city. It would be exceedingly dangerous, but he suspected Faye would come back. She was one of the only Actives in the world capable of traversing Dead City alone and making it back alive. It would surely be lethal for almost anyone else, as had been demonstrated by a more than a few foolish treasure-hunting expeditions into the interior. Faye was different, though. Her combination of natural craftiness, quick thinking, and seemingly limitless Power made her an unstoppable force. She was quite the weapon for good. It was so tempting to believe that she could stay on a righteous path, but Jacques had seen far too much in his long life to hold to such naïve idealism.

The hotel room was too quiet, but such was the nature of the suburbs of Dead City, a place of perpetual nerves and whispers. The quiet made it too easy to think, and he was not a man at ease, for those who had difficult decisions to make seldom where. He had kept his word and Faye's continued existence was still a secret to the other elders. His knights had been sworn to secrecy, which had been easy to do since none of them realized just what was at stake. The idea that he was somehow assisting the greatest danger to mankind gnawed at his conscience.

It would have been so much simpler if she had been a snarling killer instead of a charming young girl.

Assuming Zachary was still available, he would be able to help give her direction. His Power was unreliable at best, but perhaps their fortunes had shifted, and his visions would show some good possible outcomes for Faye to work toward. *Doubtful.* Jacques took another shot of bourbon. It was more likely that Zachary's visions were still the same as they were before. Then, Faye would come to understand just how dangerous she really was. It would either serve to temper her recklessness and prolong the inevitable, or sadly, but perhaps for the best, Faye would simply kill herself and spare them the trouble of having to deal with the Power's dangerous manipulations for another generation.

Before he had been lost, when their Soothsayer had foretold the coming of a new Spellbound, all of the potential outcomes had ended in rivers of blood and skies of fire. He had never foretold any otherworldly Enemy or hypothetical Pathfinder, but then again, none of them had known to ask.

Letting Faye live was an incredible risk. Jacques took the vial from his shirt pocket and studied the unassuming liquid through the clear glass. The girl was trusting. It would be so simple to place a few drops of this into her food or drink. Her death would be swift and nearly painless.

Why did you have to put me in this predicament, Whisper?

There was a sudden warmth in his body, and it wasn't from the alcohol spreading through his bloodstream. His Grimnoir ring was burning with sudden magical energy. Someone was attempting to contact him, and by the amount of Power being channeled, it was someone rather capable, more than likely another of the seven elders. *Had they found out?* Did they know he was sheltering the Spellbound?

Placing the lethal toxin back in his pocket, Jacques went to his luggage and removed a small pocket mirror, which he had already engraved and bound with spells for just such an occasion. He set it on the bed and willed his own magic to connect. It only took a second for the Power to activate and for the communication spell to take hold. The mirror began to glow as it lifted from the covers to hover at eye height. It seemed to spin about as others joined the conversation. He recognized many of his longtime compatriots from around the world and various other prominent knights, some of whom appeared to have just been woken from sleep. A few of the faces seemed to be blurred and dark, much as his would appear to the others, a magical protection to conceal the identity of the elders. So this was not an interrogation, but rather an emergency conference. He breathed a sigh of relief.

And then the spell settled on the man who had called so many from across the entirety of the Earth. It was not one of the seven elders looking back at him, but rather it was the hard, square-jawed face of Heavy Jake Sullivan, who, despite his relative inexperience, displayed a subtle mastery of magic which already rivaled or surpassed many of the elders. Sullivan was a dangerous, dedicated, and passionate individual, and his adamant insistence on the existence of the Chairman's mythological Enemy had caused many of their best young knights to join his futile quest.

"Evening," Sullivan said. There was a chorus of responses, some more positive than others. Regardless of Sullivan's effectiveness against Imperium forces, he was a controversial figure at best.

"Hello, Mr. Sullivan. Have you found your white whale yet?" Jacques asked.

"Read that book. Don't want to ruin it for you, but the whale turned out to be real. I'll keep this brief as possible. We raided the Imperium monitoring station at the North Pole."

"You did *what*?" someone blurted. They'd known Sullivan was chasing his unicorns, but apparently not everyone had realized just how far he was willing to go in order to catch them. Of course, Jacques had already thought this through, so he wasn't surprised in the least. Sullivan's decisions were proving no more shocking than those of the man who had recruited him. Black Jack Pershing would have approved of such decisive actions. "The Imperium will retaliate against us all!"

"I'm talking to dozens of people all around the world, so I don't have the Power or the inclination to debate this again. We took a few casualties, but we learned that the Enemy is already here. It's all over the Imperium, hiding at every one of their schools. The invasion has started."

There were some angry cries from the disbelievers, but Jacques cut them off. "The schools are beyond our reach. What do you intend to do now, then?"

"We think the imposter Chairman is somehow in on this. Toru figured out who he is. I'll have your knights send you the details. In the meantime, I plan on taking out the Chairman, in public, so that the Iron Guard will know they've been compromised. Once they realize that, they'll have no choice but to clean out the infestation for us."

"Another attempt on the Chairman? Every such action has always caused a terrible response," one of the elders shouted. "Permission denied!"

"Good thing I wasn't asking for any." The Heavy was not so easily riled. "We're already on our way. The Pathfinder's got a head start, so we need to act fast. Exposing the fake Chairman is our only fast option."

Jacques nodded. It wasn't like they had not already tried to assassinate the Chairman many times before. The most recent attempt had been a disastrous plot, which had rocked the elders' council, murdered Pershing, cost Harkeness his life, and sent Rawls into banishment. "It will be a shame to throw away the lives of forty knights."

"And a far bigger shame to have the Power flee and all of us be eaten by this Enemy," said another elder.

"Assuming it is even real!" declared the American elder. He was the newest member of their leadership, and it had been a difficult decision for the others to choose between this man or John Moses Browning. Both had been capable candidates, but it had been felt that Browning had been getting up in years, which seemed an ironic reasoning for a position called *elder*. "You want to risk the lives of our men, *my* men, all on the word of an Iron Guard? Absurd."

"Button it," Sullivan ordered, which was a rather surprising breach of etiquette, but Sullivan was, after all, an American too, and they tended toward direct speech. "We're making the attempt whether you like it or not. Anybody on this airship who doesn't want a piece, I'll let them off before we hit Japan. But one way or the other, we're going in. So the society can either help, or it can get out of my way."

There was a long silence as the most powerful and influential Actives in the world weighed the consequences. Their stated purpose was to protect Actives from the world, and to protect the world from Actives, and it had been clear for generations that the Imperium was the greatest threat to human liberty in history. Attempting to assassinate the Chairman was practically a tradition at this point. "It isn't like the Nipponese can possibly come to dislike us *more*," said a British elder with a laugh. "I say good hunting, Mr. Sullivan."

One of the more cautious elders interjected, "Are we willing to lose so many valuable knights over this?"

Fool. They are going regardless of our opinions. They were young, idealistic knights, eager to strike a blow against tyranny. The elders were old, looking at the big picture yet unable to grasp the passion which inflamed their soldiers. Whether Sullivan realized it or not, he had inspired many. They would follow him, and this task would be seen through to completion, regardless of the outcome. Personally, Jacques thought the entire concept of the Enemy sounded implausible, and, in fact, he had doubts that Okubo Tokugawa had ever been killed to begin with. The Chairman had easily destroyed all of the knights who had come against him before, so why would this time be any different?

Yet, he could still feel the weight of the poison in his breast pocket, and the thought occurred to him that this suicide mission offered other opportunities. If it could not be stopped, then it should at least be utilized in the most effective manner.

Jacques cleared his throat. "I agree. It is a risk, but the Society is already at war with the Imperium. Regardless of the actual existence of this Enemy, if the Chairman is truly dead, then Sullivan's expedition may well succeed and throw the Imperium into complete disarray. If the Chairman is, in fact, still alive, then perhaps this time we will get lucky and kill him once and for all. The knights on this mission are all volunteers. Since they go willingly toward this end, who are we, so far from the actual danger, to deny them their courageous attempt... You have my full support, Mr. Sullivan."

With Jacques' statement, the balance had shifted. There were a few murmurs of assent, and the dissenters were quiet. It was close enough.

"Thank you," Sullivan said. The Heavy may have been uncouth and unflinchingly violent, but he was also struck Jacques as an honest man. "I need up-to-date intelligence and I could use any local support you've got to help us get close. I've heard we've got a few knights hidden in Japan."

"That may not be necessary, Mr. Sullivan," said the British elder, his face shrouded in magical shadows, but still obviously gnawing on a cigar. "Setting foot on the home islands is a death sentence. Japan is locked up tight as a vault. However, there may be another opportunity in the near future, which will offer you better odds. It is also deep within enemy territory, but it is not quite the belly of the beast."

"I'm listening."

"My sources have told me that Okubo Tokugawa is planning an inspection tour to China within the month, mostly military bases along the front, but his itinerary includes a lavish award ceremony for his officers in Shanghai. Perhaps he will be presenting trophies for *most butchery* or *best torturer*. The knights in that city have faced terrible setbacks over the last few years, so there are not very many of them left to help, but it is still a far more approachable, and more importantly, *escapable* place."

"I'm not exactly set on this being a one-way trip myself, sir."

"Indeed, Mr. Sullivan. Some of my men volunteered and are with you on your fool's errand. I am rather fond of them and would prefer for them to return home in one piece."

"Shanghai's one of the Free Cities. That's got possibilities." Sullivan mulled it over. "It could work. I'll talk to the captain and see what we can do. I'll be in touch." Abruptly, the communication spell was broken. The mirror instantly lost all of its unnatural color, fell, and landed safely on the bed.

Jacques watched the silent mirror for a time, thinking about what he'd just done through a few simple words. He'd never been much for politicking, but he had just thrown his considerable support behind an assassination attempt that would almost certainly fail. Jacques returned to his chair, picked up the glass, and poured himself another finger of bourbon. He pounded it down in one gulp. His words had just authorized many good knights to end their lives in a futile attempt against an immortal.

And Faye, poor cursed, Faye... Once she knew her friends were going into harm's way, even if it meant certain death, she would join them.

Such was Faye's character.

When she found out—when he told her—she would go, and when Sullivan's hunt inevitably ended in blood, Faye would be destroyed by the combined might of the Iron Guard, then the danger of the Spellbound curse would be postponed for another generation. At least Faye's magnificent Power would be able to strike a great blow against the tyranny of the Imperium in the process. Let the candle burn the brightest right before it is snuffed out. Maybe he was just trying to justify his decisions, but he suspected that Faye would prefer it that way.

Jacques poured another. *I am so sorry, Whisper. I do not know what you expected me to teach her. I have failed you.*

UBF *Traveler*

IT WAS ONE of Hattori's fondest memories of his treasured master and teacher.

Lord Okubo sat upon the sand at the edge of a cliff and watched the sunrise. His loyal commanders knelt before him in the semblance of a makeshift court. Only a few days had passed since their battle against the Enemy in the deserts of Xinjiang, and Okubo was spending much of his precious time passing his accumulated wisdom on to his closest followers. It was as if during their struggle Okubo had achieved a new measure of enlightenment and now he wished to share it with his Dark Ocean.

"I was mistaken to think of it as a scout. That implies that the

Pathfinder is a separate being from the greater Enemy. Do not think of it as a scout. Think of it as a tendril, a feeler. It is detached, but still part of the whole. Do you understand the vastness of space, Hattori?"

Being singled out from the group made him uncomfortable. "I... I have not dwelled on such things. I can look at the sky and see the stars..." *An understanding fitting for a mortal man, but Okubo was no longer a mere mortal man. The Power had seen to that. Hattori was certain his answer would be insufficient.*

"The heavens are larger than you can imagine. There are a multitude of worlds like unto our own, and then copies of those worlds existing in parallel, and realms between them beyond counting. We are only one of a multitude. Actions of significant enough consequence can be felt in these other worlds, like ripples across a pond."

This would have been a blasphemous view of the universe coming from anyone else, but Okubo's vision was not to be questioned, and none of the warriors voiced a disagreement. Their Russian monk seemed intrigued by these ideas, but he was a very philosophical individual, when he wasn't molesting the peasant women, at least.

"The Power was born from one of these realms between. It was chased from its home, and has been chased from many others since. Like all prey, the Power avoids its predator. Like all predators, the Enemy must feed, or it will starve and perish. They are part of an eternal cycle, and because the Power came here, we are part of that cycle now as well. Tell me, Saito, how do we end this cycle once and for all, preferably in a manner which does not end all life in this world?"

"We kill the Enemy in battle!" Saito answered immediately. That was the proper answer for a member of the warrior caste to give.

"Incorrect. That is currently beyond our capability. How do we end this cycle?"

"I... I am unsure," Saito said. Hattori was glad to see that the haughty former samurai was obviously ashamed by his ignorance. He had been badly injured during the battle and it had given him some measure of humility. "I do not know the answer, my Lord."

Okubo gave Saito a patient smile, like a father would to an exuberant but inexperienced son. "Then it will be our sacred duty to find the answer."

"I will." Saito touched his forehead to the sand.

The master of Dark Ocean continued his lesson to his disciples. "The

Enemy pursues the Power because it must. It spreads bits of itself across the vastness of space, searching on all worlds, hoping, waiting for one of them to discover magic, so that the rest of it may come and eat. As time passes, it starves and becomes more desperate. It will send ever greater portions of itself out, searching with increasing desperation, because it must find the Power, or it will die."

He could not help but ask. "Can the Enemy truly die?"

"Anything can die, Hattori."

"Even you?" Hattori was doubtful about that.

"Of course I can die. It is inevitable that something stronger will eventually take my place. That is the way of things. But back to the Enemy; it may seem incredibly strong. So strong, in fact that an incomprehensible being such as the Power quails in fear of it. Yet what happens when a predator starves?"

The Russian spoke for the first time. "It becomes more ferocious. It holds nothing back. It does nothing but seek food."

"Exactly."

"So there will be more, and stronger than this one?" Hattori asked in shocked disbelief, as if trying to comprehend how such a being could possibly be worse.

"Yes. It is easy to think of the Pathfinder as needing to absorb magic in order to send a message home. That is not the case. Rather, it is gathering the strength needed to put down roots. The Pathfinder is a seed. It is an anchor. If it becomes set, it will inevitably draw the rest of itself across the realms, until the greater whole of the Enemy is here, and when it does, we will all die."

"So defeat is assured?"

"I do not think so. A starving predator is a ferocious predator, but it can also be a stupid predator. Desperation causes mistakes. Perhaps in time, if we can continue to defeat these Pathfinders, these desperate tendrils, we can starve the Enemy to the point that we can destroy it once and for all."

And that concluded the lesson.

Such greatness. Such selflessness. Such honor. Toru was humbled to have descended from and been tutored by the warriors of Dark Ocean. To think that Saito was insulting their sacred cause filled him with righteous anger. *He had been there!* Yet it also caused Toru to ponder upon his own failings. He knew abandoning his order had been the correct course of action, but if he was honest with himself, his dedication to the ideals of the Iron Guard had already slipped before that. He had been found wanting, and that weakness had taken him from the front lines to the Diplomatic Corps in Washington. It had been a fortunate circumstance, because otherwise he would never have been able to serve under Ambassador Hattori, but it had still been as a result of his weakness.

And now they were flying directly to the site of his past failings.

Toru's meditation period was over. Someone had entered his section of the hold. He kept his eyes closed, listening to the creaks and the pops of metal shifting and the constant noise of the engines, but beneath all of that had been a footstep. His hands were resting on his knees, but near at hand was the hilt of the sword which had once belong to Sasaki Kojiro. As a Brute, he would be able to unsheathe the mighty blade and cover the length of the cargo hold before most men could react and pull a trigger.

Many of the crew had personal issue with Toru's presence, and he knew it was only a matter of time until one of them broke their oath to keep the peace. Being forced to kill someone in self-defense could hardly be held against him. Another nearly imperceptible footstep vibrated through the floor grates. Toru had to resist the urge to smile. Let them come. He would slice them in half. Would it be a Grimnoir, angry at some loved one dying at an Iron Guard's hand? Would it be the female Torch, who tried to hide the brands which marked her as an escapee from the schools? Or would it be a foolish pirate, bitter at having lived in fear of the Imperium? Did it matter? A third footstep. Toru relaxed his mind and prepared his magic.

"Mr. Tokugawa? May I have a moment of your time?"

Damn it. He probably wouldn't get to kill anyone today after all. "Come in."

The blanket which served as a privacy curtain was moved aside, revealing the former prisoner, Wells. He did not look like much of a threat, but Toru had been led to believe that he was a capable Massive, which was a rare and truly dangerous form of magic.

The Diplomatic Corps had taught him how to read the subtle nuances of a man's expression, his stance, his manner and attitude, these things were all clues to his true nature. Americans were especially easy, considering their complete lack of propriety and inability to control their faces, which was perhaps why Toru found that this Wells made him uneasy. Wells could control his face as well as any longtime member of the Imperial court, and often wore upon it a mask showing only that which Wells wanted to display.

What is under that mask, strange American? Toru gestured for Wells to come closer. "What do you want?"

The thin man was holding a notepad. "I wished to ask you a few questions."

"Why?"

"Let's just say I'm looking for a challenge. It'll only be a few questions."

Toru remained seated. "Of what nature?"

"I wish to know about the man you believe is impersonating the Chairman." Wells made a show of looking at his notepad. It was an unnecessary gesture, but one designed to give an aura of human fallibility. "Saito?"

"Dosan Saito was a young samurai warrior who abandoned his family to become one of the first members of Dark Ocean and disciples of my father. He was a founding member of my prior order, and served as First Iron Guard for over a decade. He led with great distinction during the invasion of China and Russia. He went on to be the master sensei of the Iron Guard Academy and valued advisor to the Imperial Council. Now he is a traitorous dog in league with our greatest enemy, and I will end his life with my bare hands."

Wells stood there awkwardly. There was no place to sit. Toru did not care to make the American comfortable. Perhaps the more uncomfortable he was, the sooner he would leave.

"Is that all?"

"How old would you say he is now?"

Toru scowled. Hattori's memories suggested that Saito had been quite a bit older than he had been. "He would be in his eighties."

"Remarkable. Yet he's still a threat?"

"Yes."

"That hardly seems likely."

"Do you question my honesty?" Toru asked with a bit of menace.

"Of course not. I meant no offense." Wells was very convincing at acting afraid, but Toru could tell Wells had no real comprehension of fear. This was not a normal human being. This was an abnormality skilled at feigning humanity. Toru had known Shadow Guard and Unit 731 Cogs like this Wells, brilliant men with far too much sophistry to serve as honorable Iron Guard. "But his age..." Wells just kept standing there, ready to take notes.

Toru sighed. "The methods are secret, but many of the Chairman's most valuable subjects have lived capably far beyond their natural lifespans. It has something to do with the kanji they have been branded with. Okubo Tokugawa did not age at all. Many of his closest advisors aged at a slower rate. Saito especially, since Brutes tend to be extremely fit. Should I not be killed in battle, I would more than likely live to an extremely advanced age."

"That's not likely." Wells chuckled. Toru's expression remained frozen. "Never mind. Please continue."

"Iron Guard do not retire. They either die in service or they are assigned somewhere where they can still be of value to the Imperium. Saito was an advisor to the council. I have not been home for many years, but when last I was there, Saito would often still join martial exercises at the academy. He is aged, not nearly the man he once was, but not yet feeble."

"Can he still fight?"

"Whatever his current level of skill, it will not be enough to stop me."

"So he's a Brute, not a Ringer." Wells scribbled some words. "How do you think he managed to change shape and appear like your father?"

"I do not know. Some manner of foul sorcery. It will not matter when I remove his head from his body."

"Hmm... I'm sensing that you have a bit of pent up aggression relating to this man. Saito also seems capable of fooling nearly everyone with his impression, suggesting some form of mental control..." Wells began chewing on his pen, a disgusting habit of absent-minded Americans, but merely another act in this case. Toru was impressed. This Wells would have made a fine Shadow Guard. "He even fooled you into thinking he was your father. That has to be the ultimate betrayal, the sacred trust between a boy and a father. How did that make you feel?"

Toru's eyes narrowed dangerously. "What kind of doctor are you, again?"

"A psychologist. I specialize in understanding—"

"I am familiar with the term. I believe it to be a form of chicanery best suited for manipulating self-indulgent Europeans into not being disgusted by their obvious flaws. I am a warrior, born and bred to fight and die on behalf of the mightiest order of warriors of the mightiest nation in history. If you ask me about my *feelings* concerning my father again, I will kill you. Is that clear?"

"If it makes you more comfortable, then we can leave that topic off the table." The person mask slipped. Rather than being cowed, Wells gave Toru an odd, absent little smile. *Yes.* Wells was eager for a confrontation. "As for killing me, you could try, but that would prove rather interesting since I'm indestructible."

"I am not some Rockville miscreant wielding a sharpened spoon, Dr. Wells. You may be slightly more difficult to harm, but we are over the middle of the Pacific Ocean. How long can you tread water?"

The mask returned, and Wells appeared to think it over like a reasonable man should. "Valid point...Let's put that aside for a moment, though, and concentrate on helping me better understand our mutual adversary."

"Why?"

"Wasn't it said by Okubo Tokugawa in his own book, and forgive me if I do not get this absolutely correct, because I had to read the English translation; In order to assure victory, a warrior must understand his enemy better than the enemy understands himself. Anticipate their move before they make it and the tip of your sword will be there waiting to meet them. Is that about right?"

Toru nodded, suspicious. "That is approximately correct. In my experience. Westerners who memorize my father's words have either come to truly believe in his vision or they are academic contemplators trying to understand greatness that they can never hope to achieve."

"Perhaps I am a bit guilty of omphaloskepsis at times..."

"I do not know that word."

"Navel gazing...Never mind. I will not be pigeonholed in either of your narrow categories, my good man. I memorized that quote because your Chairman was describing my career. You see, I seek to understand motivation and substance—"

Toru held up one hand to stop him. "Much like a theater actor must study their character, you began studying the way normal people think in order to better appear as one of them."

Now that had gotten Wells' attention. He nodded slowly. "You are a more perceptive man than I was led to believe, Mr. Tokugawa..."

"It is because I have known men like you. Your minds are twisted from birth. You are an outsider."

"Something like that," Wells answered slowly.

"There is no need for shame. In the Imperium, men such as yourself would be highly valued for your unique intellect. I have been led to understand that many members of Unit 731 share your specific mental affliction. It enables them to conduct their experiments on human subjects without hesitation or remorse. You do not feel what others feel, but your analysis of how they think has made you a very capable mimic."

"Then you know why I'm good at my job." Wells gave him that odd little smirk again. "Regardless of my original personal goals when I embarked on my particular path of study, today my understanding Saito better enables you to kill him better. Tell me everything about this bastard and I promise I will help deliver him into your hands."

"That is intriguing..." Toru stroked his chin. It could help, and he had nothing better to do on this accursed tub. "Very well. If it helps me end Saito's life, then I will put up with all manner of nonsense. Continue your questions."

Wells looked around again for a spot to sit, but then finally gave up and sat on the hard metal floor. The pen went back to the notepad. "I think I'm going to enjoy our sessions together, Toru. May I call you Toru? Now where were we?"

Chapter 10

Germany has the strongest army in the world, and the Germans don't like being laughed at and are looking for somebody on whom to vent their temper and use their strength. It is 38 years since Germany had her last war, and she is very strong and very restless, like a person whose boots are too small for him. With the formation of this great legion, a momentous hour has struck. The Ninth Army is an indestructible blend of technology and magic. Every last soldier is a mighty wizard. Nothing can match us. Nothing. Our rivals are envious of our magic, and they force us to legitimate defense. Germany will triumph. Bear yourselves as Huns of Attila. For a thousand years let the French tremble at the approach of a German!

—Kaiser Wilhelm II,
Speech at the Magical Services Branch Headquarters,1914

Dead City, Germany

DEAD CITY was a horrible place.

Faye didn't like zombies one bit. To be honest, they scared the heck out of her, and she was a very difficult to girl to scare. She hadn't allowed herself to be scared very much since the day Madi had murdered her Grandpa, and the times she had been afraid since had been more about being scared for her friends and very rarely for her own safety. There simply wasn't much out there that she couldn't handle if she just kept calm and took care of business, and being scared never helped that. Zombies were different though. They were unnatural. They were just nasty, gross, make-your-skin-crawl, make-your-stomach-hurt, make-your-hair-stand on end, scary, and in this awful city, they were *everywhere*.

She tried to move fast, never staying in one place for too long. Luckily, Dead City was a mess of broken edges and fallen walls. Very few of the buildings were in one piece. The only ones which had been repaired was from back when the people were still trying to make it decent and livable, by the living people like Heinrich, back before the Kaiser's million undead soldiers had gotten too crazy and too hungry.

Faye appeared on the fifth-floor window ledge of what had probably once been a bank. At least she thought it looked banklike, since there had been big stone columns out in front. Only one of them was still standing and the others had fallen to lie broken in the road. The columns were whiter than the grey ground, so they looked a little like bleached bones. Not that there weren't plenty of real bones lying around.

Scanning for threats, Faye leaned out around the corner. The gritty dust under the soles of her shoes crunched. At least this ledge didn't break like the last one she'd landed on. The place was positively falling apart. The coast was clear. The poor hungry zombies who'd been chasing her around the first floor were still down there screaming and throwing a fit. She figured they'd forget soon enough and go back to their shuffling and muttering.

Jacques had given her a map. On it he'd marked the spots where he thought Zachary might be staying. It was a big, clumsy, hard-to-fold mass of paper, so she'd simply memorized the whole thing in a few seconds and was trusting in her far superior head map. It didn't help, however, that Jacques' map had been made from back when this place had still been Berlin, and things had made sense. Some of the roads on the maps were flooded canals now. Others were filled with buildings that had fallen. But even then, there were a lot of places to check, and so far she hadn't had any luck.

Her search would be totally pointless if it turned out that the zombie she was looking for had gone crazy and wandering aimlessly like most of the undead around here. She didn't mind the wanderers so much; they showed up on her head map just fine so she could stay one step ahead of them. The talkers and jabberers were nice too, because she could hear them coming. It was the ones who were holding still that worried her. Already she'd nearly Traveled right into two of them. Living things positively glowed on her head map, moving things too. Dead and still? That was a problem.

The windows on this floor had no glass in them. Come to think of it, she didn't think a pane of glass had survived anywhere in the city. Hadn't seen a single one yet, matter of fact. Had the Peace Ray shattered them all? Or had the undead smashed everything they might see their ugly reflections in? Either way, she could see inside the dusty room. There was nothing that she could spot with her grey eyes or that she could sense on her head map that suggested there was any danger.

Jacques had said that Zachary would gravitate toward "living" in the tallest places. Back when he'd been alive he had been some sort of artist, and he'd even drawn illustrations in the pulps, of cowboys and Indians and spacemen and pirates and gangsters. Surely it was in an artist's nature to like rooms with a view. Jacques had also given her a package to deliver, should she find him. She didn't know what it was, but the satchel was really heavy and felt like it was filled with books. Either it was a gift, or maybe Jacques thought that the more weight she Traveled with, the faster it would use up her Power, and he was simply trying to get her caught and eaten. Well, fat chance of that, because Faye was still the best Traveler *ever*. So she'd show him.

"Zachary? You in there?" Faye stuck her head through the window hole. "Hello? Anybody?"

She hadn't seen the dead woman. She'd been still for so long that it was almost like she'd been stuck to the floor. The zombie sat up with a screech, spilling a choking cloud of grey dust. It startled her, but more than anything Faye really felt sorry for these poor dead folks. She would've loved to do them all a favor and kill every last single one of them, but zombies didn't die easy. You could even cut them into pieces and the pieces just kept on twitching and screaming. She'd heard that they kept on feeling hungrier and hungrier, but nothing could ever feed them. They moved only because magic had stuck their souls to their bodies like some horrible glue. What would it be like to get hurt, but to never get better, and to always feel whatever it was that killed you? Delilah had been the toughest person Faye had ever known, so she'd handled it for a bit, but in the end getting turned into ash by the Peace Ray had been for the best.

The zombie lurched for Faye, but her legs really had been fused to the floor from sitting for so long, so it took her a second to tear free. Like most of the undead Faye had seen so far, this one was weathered, all dry and shrunken, and naked, clothing long since rotted off, and too crazy or in too much pain to care about dressing proper. There was a great ripping noise, a bunch of leathery leg and butt jerky was left on the floor, and then the zombie was coming right at Faye.

She had already picked her next stop. "Sorry to wake you, ma'am," and then Faye stepped off the ledge and Traveled safely away.

Faye was really thankful for her particular abilities right about then. She'd been blessed to be a Traveler, as it really was the best kind of magic ever. When she'd first started meeting other types of Actives as she'd sought out the Grimnoir, she'd been a little jealous of the other's seemingly more useful abilities, like super strength or healing or controlling animals. But now Faye knew that she was the lucky one. Nobody else would be able to get around Dead City in one piece... Not that she could imagine anybody ever wanting to.

So many walls had fallen over that it had created a maze where the streets had been, and in some spots it was hard to tell where the streets ended and the sewers which had been beneath began. It wasn't like the roads were level anymore, with big piles of spilled brick like the buildings had puked their guts up before they'd died.

There was lots of graffiti at ground level. It looked angry, but it was all in German, so she couldn't read it. None of the graffiti was new, though. So the dead had probably done that sort of thing at first to pass the time before they'd either given up or run out of paint.

It was in one of those tunnels created by fallen walls that somebody answered her calls. The response had gotten her hopes up, only it turned out to only be another undead having a brief moment of coherence, and though she didn't speak the language, she'd thought the dead man was asking if she were his daughter, but then he'd lost his mind again and tried to eat her.

The sun was getting high. Hours had passed, and she was getting tired, hungry, and thirsty. Dead City was *huge*. All of these years that she'd heard about the destruction of Berlin, she'd never realized just how dang big it was. She had Traveled two hundred and eighty-seven times since she'd started her search, and she hadn't even scratched the surface. Her Power was still burning bright, but her body was getting worn out.

She stopped in what had probably been a park to eat her lunch. The bench was lopsided, the trees were barren sticks coming out of the ground, the stream was dry, and the bridge that had crossed it was now just a big pile of rocks, but at least it was in the open so she could see in every direction long enough to eat the chicken sandwich she'd packed.

She supposed there had been a lot of lakes around Berlin, because when it had all gotten broken, the lakes had come spilling back in. There was water everywhere, but most of it was cloudly with muck, and she'd seen a few zombies floating all bloated and soft like, or bits of people sticking out of the muck, so she'd be darned if she was gonna drink any Dead City water. It made her glad she'd brought a canteen.

It was nice to take a minute to relax, and then she realized that there was a severed head stuck in the branches of a nearby tree. Like every other plant she's seen in the city, this tree was all blasted, black, ashy, and dead, and for once the random body part seemed equally still. "How'd you get up there?" she asked the head, but when she did, the eyes opened and it started hissing at her. The noise must have drawn attention, because within thirty seconds there were answering moans and shrieks from all around the park. Company was coming. "Thanks a lot, jerk." Faye stuffed the rest of her sandwich in her mouth and took a swig of water so it wasn't so dry that she'd choke—now that would be an ironic way to die while in Dead City—and she Traveled to her next selected destination.

How had Heinrich survived here for so long? She gained new respect for her friend as she walked the broken rooftops. Occasionally she found evidence of other mortals who had tried to enter Dead City, but usually only bits and pieces of them. Jacques had told her about foolish treasure hunters, so she figured the half-eaten man she found with a shovel, burlap sack full of jewelry, antiques and a Mauser pistol had been one of those. The C96 was all dried out and could use a good cleaning, but she kept the pistol anyway. She had her Browning .45 hidden beneath her shirt, but a spare gun never hurt.

One hour of time and forty Travels later, Faye had her first stroke of luck. Not only was this dead man mostly sane, he was rather polite, helpful, and even well dressed.

"Hello?" Faye crept across the broken floor tile, darting between the beams of sunlight sneaking through the boarded-up window slats. She'd learned the hard way in the last apartment building that sometimes the zombies could be wedged into the ceilings too. That one had nearly pulled her hair. "Anybody home?"

"*Hallo. Wer ist da?*"

"Sorry to bug you." Faye peeked around the crumbling brick corner. There was a tall, thin shape standing in the back of the next room. His stance was wary, not all hunched over and dragging like most dead folks she'd met. "My name is Faye. Do you speak English?"

There was a long pause. "Yes . . . Forgive me. I do not often receive visitors. Come in."

What luck! He didn't immediately try to eat her face and he spoke English!

It was dark inside, but her grey eyes could see just fine. He was dead all right, bug-eyed, skin all dried out and cracked-open scabby, but despite that he was dressed in a very snazzy army uniform, and his chest was covered in ribbons and medals and gold braids leading up to big golden things on his shoulders which looked like they should be used for cleaning boots, and speaking of boots, his went up to his knees and were so polished and shiny that if there was sunshine they would probably be blinding. He was even wearing a sword, and it was one of the only metal things she'd seen in town that wasn't rusty. On the table next to him was a bottle, which had been empty since Faye had been a little girl, and a weird German helmet with a spike on top of it. The helmet was darn near as sparkly as the boots. "I was getting ready for the parade."

Apparently there were different kinds of zombie crazy.

"I'm Faye. What's your name?"

"Field Marshal . . ." His voice was a hissing wheeze. The zombie tilted his head to the side. "I do not remember . . . What are you doing in my study? American, no? Have you brought the new draft of the armistice treaty? Are you with Pershing's expeditionary unit?"

In a sense, yes, her and Mr. black Jack went way back, but she didn't want to complicate matters. "I'm not in the army or nothing. I'm here looking for somebody. Maybe you can give me directions?"

The zombie general, or whatever he was, gave her a bow with a flourish. His bones creaked ominously. "Of course, young lady. How may I be of assistance?"

"I'm looking for a man who lives around here somewhere. His name is Zachary."

"Zachary, you say? I do not know this man, I think... Did you see my medals? How they gleam?"

"They're very nice. The man I'm looking for can tell the future."

"Ah, the Fortune Teller. Yes. I know of him. He moved to the top floor of the Fenstermacher building down the street."

"Really? Which one is that?"

"It is not far from here. It is the one the Kaiser had a radio tower built on top of... I went there once. All of the notable members of high society in Berlin did. An actual Fortune Teller. How marvelous, I thought. I wished to know if there was any chance the Kaiser's forces could turn this run of bad luck... Alas, there was not."

"Thank you, Field Marshal. You've been a big help."

The zombie sounded very sad. "Not so many of us visit the Fortune Teller anymore."

"Why's that?"

"I think he is a charlatan. Our fortunes were all the same. I do not remember mine exactly." His dried features seemed to scrunch up in confusion. "It was very... depressing." He shuffled around to his table and picked up his empty bottle. "Please, please don't go. Stay and have a drink." He poured an imaginary drink into the dry glass. "I could use some company for a bit."

She was rather impatient to go, but she felt bad for the old dead soldier. She took the proffered empty glass. "Okay, but just one."

One imaginary drink had turned into five, and then ten, and the field marshal had told her stories about where every one of his medals had come from, and then he'd talked about his lovely wife, and their twin babies, who were probably her age by now, but the undead didn't seem to have a real good grasp on time. It was funny how that worked out, but it wasn't like imaginary booze was going to befuddle her or the empty bottle was going to run out of anything except for dust, so Faye had sat their pretending to sip air while an old zombie held a conversation.

It was the least she could do for the good advice, and she figured an hour spent like that had probably saved her ten times that long searching the city, assuming the field marshal had given her the right address, of course. She'd made her apologies, said she had other commitments, and Traveled through the ceiling.

Faye had to dodge between two groups of particularly aggressive undead who seemed to be having a turf war over the main boulevard, and then she nearly got her head blown off when it turned out one of them still had a working rifle and was a fairly good shot with it. That neighborhood turned out to be a real pain since there were other snipers up on the roofs, so it forced her back through the building interiors and torn-up streets. A sleeper had scratched her boot with his bony fingers and a few minutes later a different one had ripped a chunk of fabric from her blouse. That one had made her angry enough that she'd shot it a few times with the old Mauser pistol, just to make a point, but the gunfire had merely drawn more attention, so she'd had to Travel fast.

She reached the Fenstermacher building. It had probably been a big factory of some kind before it had started falling apart. The radio tower the field marshal had told her about had rusted badly and was leaning over. The next time there was a strong wind, it would probably end up in the street, and she supposed any zombies that got squished underneath it would just be stuck and angry forever.

Faye picked a spot in what appeared to be a large, empty room. So far, avoiding corners seemed to be the safest method. She popped into existence, dropped softly to the floor, and looked around for any dusty lumps that could be angry dead folks. *Clear.* At least there was quite a bit of sunshine for once. Then she realized that her gentle landing hadn't disturbed any dust, because the floor had been swept.

"Hello? Zachary?" But she knew right away she'd found the right place, because pinned to the nearest wall was a sheet of paper with a picture drawn on it, a quick and simple ink drawing like you'd see in the pulp magazines.

The word *Spellbound* had been scrawled across the top.

The picture was of her.

It was a good likeness, not like looking in a mirror or anything, but she could easily tell it was supposed to be her. That was nice. Nobody had ever drawn her portrait before.

There were more pictures pinned up, lots and lots of them. The drawings were of people mostly, but also places, and things, and machines, and events, and demons, and even stuff she didn't recognize. There were hundreds of them, and when she took a few steps, she realized that all of the other walls in the room, from floor to ceiling, had paper stuck on them too.

Faye whistled. "That sure is something."

She showed up as the subject often, probably more than anybody else, but she recognized many of her friends; Francis, Mr. Sullivan, Mr. Garrett, Lance, Delilah, Jane, Black Jack Pershing; there was Heinrich hitting a demon with a pickax, and even Mr. Browning showing off some new gun. Then there were her enemies, the Chairman screaming at her to give back his hands, and Isaiah Rawls and Mr. Harkeness plotting away, and Mr. Crow both as a man and as a demon, and Mr. Madi fighting on the *Tokugawa*. Then there were people who were sometimes both, like the one of Toru beating somebody's head in with his spiky club, and J. Edgar Hoover bossing folks around.

It went on and on, so *many* faces. So many scenes from her life. Some of the papers were yellowed and crispy with age, like they'd been drawn years ago, but they showed recent events, like Mr. Bolander calling down the Oklahoma lightning, or Faye's fight with Toshiko the ninja girl, or Whisper right before she ended her life in Washington D.C.

She froze at one that showed Madi standing over the fallen form of her grandpa, massive revolver pointing down to finish him off, and then at another of haystacks burning while a poor, scared, injured girl hid under a cow trough to carve a beetle out of her foot.

Then there was page after page after page of folks she just plain didn't know and places she'd never seen. Thousands of them, and it wasn't like they were sorted into groups. One person she recognized would be squished onto a wall among dozens she didn't. The only reason she could take it all in so quick was because it only took her a fraction of a second to scan over each one, record them with her grey eyes, and sort them out with her head map. There was a stranger who could create sucking black wounds in the world like the thing that had eaten Mason Island, and a mechanical man that looked just like a real man, and an old samurai with a big shadow living inside his head.

Were these all things that had actually happened? *No . . .* There was one of her and Francis, holding hands up on a tall bridge, but she didn't recognize the moment. There was a fancy UBF dirigible going up in flames over some foreign city with Captain Southunder still bravely manning the controls. A Peace Ray firing and a skyline she recognized as New York crumbling into ashes. Mr. Sullivan and Toru about to duel to the death on a rocky beach. A little boy crying as he was carried away by a monster without skin, while behind them a whole city was getting cleaned out of people, skinless monsters picking them like fruit.

The details weren't always right. Like the artist had only seen part of the picture and then guessed the rest, or maybe he only caught a quick glimpse and then had to recreate them from memory, but they were close enough to know that Zachary's magic was real.

"Hello, Faye."

It was rare somebody could sneak up on her, but she was awfully preoccupied. "Zachary?"

"What's left of me." He came around the corner. Dead, but in much better shape than anyone else she'd seen in the city. It made sense, she supposed, since he hadn't been dead near as long. If it had been darker, she might've even mistook him for an alive person. He'd probably stayed out of the weather. "I've been expecting you."

Faye nodded. "I guess you can't really surprise somebody who can see the future."

"Sure you can. I don't see every little thing." The skin of his face was drooping and grey. There were holes in his cheeks where you could see white teeth. If he'd had hair when he was alive, you couldn't tell because all the skin on the top of his head was gone and it was just a white skull dome. His clothing was frayed and torn, but far cleaner than anyone else's around here except for the field marshal's. His eyes, still clear and intelligent, swept across the room. "Saw you coming though. Saw that for a long time. What do you think of the gallery?"

"It's nice, I suppose."

Zachary shuffled in with a bad limp. "It wasn't always like this." His voice was raspy and dry, but he still sounded like an American. "Back before I got killed, my Power was weak. Just sporadic looks into what might happen. I could only see little bits and pieces once in a while. It wasn't like I could actually tell the future... You heard of déjà vu?"

Faye nodded. It was the sort of thing that Francis had read about in a magazine and thought was amusing enough to share with her. "Like you feel like you'd seen some things before?"

"My magic was sort of like that, but a little better. Happened often enough when I was a kid that I started drawing the pictures that would come into my head. That way I could prove later I wasn't making things up. Took years to sort of get it straight, but even at my best I'd get some things right, lots of things wrong, wasn't much better than guessing. No wonder the Society never paid much heed to what I had to say. I was about as useful as flipping a coin. See, back then I didn't realize that the Power sees things different than we do, and sometimes it was showing me things that could be."

"I've talked to the Power. It's sorta weird like that."

"Wasn't until after I croaked that it really started clicking. Believe it or not, death is handy for some things. When your choices are focus on the pain or focus on your Power, you get pretty good at focusing on your Power." He made a sad noise, but then Faye realized he was laughing, so she laughed with him. "Now I can't shut it off. It's all there, all of it, all the time, from all over the world, and maybe even some other worlds that don't exist quite yet. Things that are, will be, might be, doesn't matter, the Power just keeps on shoving it into my head and I keep putting it down on paper."

"You're a good drawer."

"Thanks." He gestured absently at the walls and she realized he was wearing gloves. He must have caught her staring. "The gloves? Yeah, I don't like to leave bits of me on the paper. All that effort, my hands are getting worn out. I can barely hold a pen anymore. It really hurts."

"But you have to keep drawing?"

"Same way you have to keep Traveling. You can't even imagine what life would be like without being able to Travel, can you?"

"No." That would be horrific. Horrific and *slow*. "It's sorta who I am."

"This is different, but kind of the same. You ever have a toothache, Faye?"

"Sure."

Zachary nodded. "Being dead's like a toothache. Only for your whole body. Forever. You ever been real hungry, so starving that you'd eat anything?" She'd already seen that he'd drawn the shack in Oklahoma, so he already had the answer. "Being dead's worse, only you can't ever stop that hunger. And that gnaws at you. It gnaws at your soul." He touched his head absently with his glove, and some more skin fell away from the top of his skull. "I gotta keep drawing. Keep listening. Otherwise, that toothache will gnaw right through the rest of me and I wouldn't be me anymore. I'd just be the hunger, like the rest of this town."

That reminded her. "Jacques sent a package for you." She pulled the satchel around and opened it up. It was filled with packages of typing paper and ink bottles and pens, and then she understood why it had been so heavy.

"Thoughtful of him, but never mind that. Don't need them no more . . . My work is done. See, I only needed to stick around long enough to talk to you. This was all for you, Faye."

"For me?"

"The Power wanted you to have it. I know why Jacques sent you. Last time we'd spoke was before the Power really started talking to me. See, I think I had too much humanity in the way before to really listen good, to really see the possibilities. Jacques figured I'd show you destroying the world, because that was what I'd shown him before."

"Do I? Do I really destroy the world?"

"More often than not. There are lots of worlds and lots of Fayes, so that was just the most likely outcome. Not the only one."

Now she was really confused.

His foot made a horrible sound as it dragged along the floor, and then Faye noticed that there were crumpled up balls of paper scattered about underfoot. She hadn't paid them any mind before. She picked one up and uncrinkled it. This picture showed her, only older, and much scarier, her features all twisted up, and she was killing lots of people with all manner of magic, fire, and ice, and lightning, and from the looks on their faces, they weren't bad people at all, just innocent folks, women and kids even . . .

"See what I mean? And that one isn't the worst. Not even *close.*"

She crumpled it back up and tossed it down. "You hide the bad ones."

"Sometimes. Sometimes they scared me so bad that I tossed them right out the window, watched them float down. I saw too many good ones, so I know your heart, Faye. I prefer to think of what can be, not the worst-case scenario. Now Jacques, he has to think about the worst. Poor Jacques. I never saw your face back when I was alive. Maybe I wasn't supposed to, you know? Power didn't want me to see. You got no idea how many pictures I've got here of him, agonizing over some hard decision, staring off into space, trying to decide what to do."

"Fourteen," Faye answered without hesitation.

"He's doing it right now, I bet." Zachary chuckled, but it was a horrible sound, what with the air blowing out the holes in his cheeks.

Faye went to the nearest one of her *teacher*. Jacques looked incredibly weary in that one. "What's he doing with that vial?"

"Deciding on whether to poison you or not, I think..."

Faye was offended, but it made her more sad than angry.

"Don't hold it against him. That much responsibility on one man is a hell of a thing. It's probably my fault, you know, I warned the others about you. I showed them...I told them there'd be another Spellbound coming. He'd devoted years of his life hunting the last one, lost his girlfriend to Sivaram, even. What'd you expect him to do?"

"If I die, will there be another one after me?"

"I don't think you realize it yet, sister. Now that we've been found, if you die, there's *nothing* after you. The Power is a funny thing. It's smarter than they think. It's picked you, Faye. It picked you for a reason. With Sivaram it saw a way out, a way to break a cycle. It's been to a lot of worlds and bonded with a lot of intelligences, but humans are the first one that ever surprised it. We've got something the ones before us didn't have: *Creativity.* It didn't realize humans were that capable, and for the first time in a million years it got its hopes up. It tried, only Sivaram wasn't good enough, so it picked you next. It's directed you this whole time, guided you, put you in the path of the others it's picked. I draw them too." He gestured at the walls. "All of us have a job to do, but you're the only one that can put it all together. You are the only way the Power sees to beat the Enemy once and for all."

"The Enemy is real. I knew it." She glanced around. "How come there ain't no pictures of it? You've got its little helpers and the people it's twisted up and skinned, but no pictures of the big Enemy."

"That's the bad part about my Power being stronger now. I never saw it before. I couldn't see things without bodies back then. Now? I've tried to draw it. Take your pen, jab it through the paper, into the table even, hard as you can, and then start making a circle. You've got to cut it deep. You shred the paper. And all you get is ink bleeding out into a bigger and bigger circle. When I try to see it, I have to push so hard that blood starts seeping through my gloves. If I keep going, I start to bleed inside my head and then it comes out my eyes. The blood and the ink, that's the only way to draw the thing that's coming."

Blood and ink . . . She looked at one of the pictures of Mr. Sullivan, his shirt ripped open and the self-inflicted scars on his chest burning as he ripped an Iron Guard in half. "So the Power's picked me to fight the Enemy? I know what happens if we lose, Power runs off, and we end up like the Summoned, but what happens if we win?"

Zachary tilted his scabrous head to the side. "That's entirely up to you. It all depends on how far you're willing to go and what you're willing to sacrifice."

Faye knelt down and reached for another crumpled sheet of paper. "Don't," the zombie warned. "Not that one."

Faye opened it up anyway. She stated at the picture for a long time. It was the worst thing *ever*. "I'd never do that. I'd never become that."

"Then don't. I know you think you wouldn't now, but you could. I can see the possibilities, and you can feel the truth. You've tasted what it's like. You've taken someone else's magic from them before and made it your own. You get strong as you'll need to be, and it'll change you." Zachary turned and began walking away. "These are all for you, Faye. It wanted you to have them, to know who can help you, and who wants to hurt you. Learn them. Learn where you came from, and what might have been, and what might still be. I know it won't take you long. Nothing takes you long."

"Where are you going?"

"This was what the Power asked from me. I'm done. Now it's time to make the gnawing stop. There's a furnace downstairs. I've already stocked it full of coal. I plan to light it, then climb inside and burn until there's nothing left of this damned body for my soul to cling to. See you."

Faye looked down at the horrific picture in her hands. *I will not become the devil.* "Thank you, Zachary."

"Good luck, Faye."

Faye with Zombies

~ Chapter 11 ~

*They say I'm the best swindler there's ever been, huh? Then what am I
in here for? Most say the best cons are Yaps, Traps, Mouths, whatever
you want to call 'em, 'cause they can change how the mark thinks. Then
the Readers, Head Cases, they're next, 'cause they can tell you what the
mark really thinks. Honest truth? They ain't all that. Magic makes it
too easy, makes a con soft. They got no imagination . . . Fine. You got
me. I am the best . . . But you know what? Don't take a wizard to clean
a mark. You know the real secret to running a confidence scam? Tell
them what they want to hear. There's a sucker born every minute.*

—Joseph "Hungry Joe" Lewis,
Interview at Sing Sing State Prison, 1888

UBF *Traveler*

THE JAPANESE AIRSHIPS were right above them. Harsh rain
pounded against the hull with a rhythmic drumming noise. Lightning
flashed, seemingly just beyond the glass of the cockpit. It was blinding,
yet the afterimage made it so that Sullivan could see the black shapes
of the Imperium warships searching for them even with his eyes
closed.

They were running completely dark, but that wouldn't help if the
lightning reflected off of the *Traveler's* hull. "Think they spotted us?"
Sullivan asked.

"If they did, we'll know when the first shells hit," Captain
Southunder replied, perfectly calm. This wasn't the first time the old
pirate had run a blockade. "We're practically swimming in Impy
bastards." He looked out over his bridge crew, obviously thinking hard

about what to do next, stuck between several choices, all with bad possible outcomes, but sometimes a pirate just had to run on instinct and make a call. "Barns, take us down a thousand feet, nice and slow."

"Aye aye, Captain." Barns gently pulled a brass lever on his console.

The *Traveler* shifted violently to the right. Most of the crew had to grab onto something to keep from losing their footing. Sullivan just planted his feet and imagined that he was anchored to the deck until the tremors slowed. After several seconds of ominous creaking, the *Traveler* seemed to steady a bit, and the crew of the crowded bridge all got back to work, fiddling with gizmos that Sullivan frankly did not understand in the least. "That was nice and slow?"

Barns grinned. "We're getting sideswiped with sixty-mile-an-hour gusts. Anything that doesn't corkscrew us into the ocean is nice."

"You asked for rough air, Mr. Sullivan. I'm happy to provide," Captain Southunder said.

"All I asked was for you to get us to Shanghai unseen."

"Same thing. As sleek as this girl is, anything that's beating us this badly has got to be hell on those Imperial slabs. Shanghai's position on the coast means that this area is crawling with ships. Of all the Free Cities, it's the one I dread visiting the most. I drained my Power to unleash this unseasonable beast in the hope that the Imperium would have the sense to dock their fleet. However, it appears they don't have the sense God gave a duck. I really didn't expect to see any patrols this far out."

"Bad timing, or do they suspect what we're up to?"

"If they do, then we'll know when the entire Jap navy is waiting in Shanghai to greet us." Southunder turned to the teleradar operator. "Mr. Black?"

The pirate's eyes were glued to a picture tube. "They haven't changed course." It all just looked like green haze and glowing dots to Sullivan, but the UBF invention seemed to be working, and whatever it was showing, it was making the operator happy. "Good thing too. From the return I'm getting, one of those airships is a huge multihull. From the size, maybe a *Kaga* class."

"Bearing?"

"Seven miles ahead, two thousand feet above us. Bearing north-north-east."

Southunder rubbed his chin thoughtfully. "How we managed to get along without that marvelous device all these years, I'll never know. Bless those UBF Cogs and their pointy heads. Bouncing radio waves off of solid objects to see how far away they are . . . It's like magic."

"Says the man who makes hurricanes with his mind," Barns said as he fought the controls. "That UBF doohickey is just fancy science."

"Science which I, for one, am happy the Imperium hasn't invented yet, or our jobs would be far more difficult."

"The day the Imperium gets one of these radar thingys is the day I give up privateering to do something safer," Barns muttered, glancing at Sullivan. "Like sword swallowing or lion taming."

"Lucky guy like you?" Lance Talon chuckled. The knight had come up to the bridge to watch, fascinated by the show. "That wouldn't even be a challenge. I've done lion taming. It's overrated."

Barns' oddball Power was somehow related to altering probability and coming out with favorable results. "You're using your magic right now, I hope?"

"Don't fret, Sullivan. This part is always a little tense, but then afterwards, we have a drink and a laugh at the Imperium's expense." The look of intense concentration on the young man's face suggested he was, in fact, using his Power. "Good times."

"Shit. I'm getting a better side view," the teleradar operator said. "That's definitely a *Kaga*."

Everybody on the bridge died a little inside. That was the most advanced airship in the Imperium's arsenal. It had more conventional firepower than a Great War battleship, several hundred extra pairs of eyes on the lookout, armor that the *Traveler* wouldn't even be able to dent, and worst of all, a Peace Ray, which could vaporize anything in its line of sight. "If that thing sees us, there ain't no running." Sullivan said.

Barns grinned. "Like I said, good times."

Southunder was chewing on one knuckle. "Any signs of surface ships, Mr. Black?"

"None yet, Captain. Hard to tell. Surface is choppy as hell."

"Stay on this heading and descend to five hundred feet, Barns."

"Gonna be rough winds that close to the deck," Barns said, but it was more of a warning than an argument. The pilot had already started to comply

"Not as choppy as being obliterated by a Peace Ray. We're burning a lot of magic right now. I'd hate to pass too close if they've got a tuned-up Finder aboar—"

CRACK! BOOM!

That time Sullivan did flinch, but it was more from the flash and electrical snap than any movement of their vessel. The actual airship had barely moved, but all of the tubes and lights on the bridge had either gone black or were flickering unsteadily.

"Peace Ray!" someone shouted.

Idiot. If it had been a Peace Ray, they'd already be ashes.

"Lightning strike," Southunder stated. He turned around in his captain's chair and looked to his Torch. "Ori! Status?"

Lady Origami was so quiet and tended to always position herself so far out of sight that it was easy to forget she was even around. The Torch placed one diminutive hand on a bulkhead and closed her eyes. Torches had to have some sort of mental view of their surroundings relating to fire, much as a well-practiced Heavy did with gravity, or like Faye had with that weird *head map* she'd gone on about. Always curious when it came to magic, Sullivan decided that he'd have to interview Lady Origami for his notes, assuming they didn't blow up in the next few seconds at least. "I stopped some sparks. Bags clear and happy."

The bridge crew all quit holding their breath. Sullivan realized that all of the hair on his body was standing on end.

"So we're not going to explode. Yet." Southunder turned to the teleradar operator. "Did that strike illuminate us? Are any of the Imperium altering course?"

"Teleradar is out," Black answered. "I'm blind." He slid out of his chair and opened a panel on the side of the machine. Smoke came wafting out. The smell of burnt wiring hit everyone's nostrils. "Shit."

Without that UBF toy, they could blunder right into an Imperium ship. "One of my knights, Schirmer, is a Fixer," Sullivan said.

"Fetch him," Southunder ordered. "And the UBF engineer too."

One of the crew picked up a mouthpiece and began turning the charge handle. "Damn it. Horn's fried."

"I'll get them." Sullivan turned to leave. He was just a useless spectator up here anyway.

"Good." Southunder's attention was on keeping them in one piece. "There's a Crackler among your knights. Make sure he's awake and have him point the lightning elsewhere."

Wish I would have thought of that before, Sullivan thought as he left the bridge.

"And you've got a Torch. Have him be ready to help Ori in case things get out of hand." Southunder called after him.

"Captain!" Lady Origami sounded very indignant at the idea of her actually needing help.

The *Traveler* was being hammered by the wind. Walking down the corridors was difficult, even for somebody who was close personal friends with the laws of gravity. Barns sure hadn't been lying about it being rough closer to the ocean, and the whole ship was getting a kick in the pants.

"Just the man I've been looking for."

Sullivan turned to see Dr. Wells. The alienist had walked right up behind him without even making a sound. The fellow had to be near as quiet as Heinrich to pull that off, either that or Sullivan's ears were still ringing from the lightning strike. He had already sent Schirmer and the UBF Fixer up top, and alerted Cracklers to keep them from getting blasted again, so he figured he had a minute before he went back to being anxious and useless on the bridge. "What is it, Doc?"

"Could you spare a minute?"

"That depends. You gonna complain some more about your living conditions?"

"It's not the Ritz, but it is a bit better than the hole at Rockville. Not by much. But no, I've got something for you." Wells always talked too loud. Like he thought he was on stage or something. He held up a stack of papers. "This is a profile of our target. I've taken everything your Grimnoir spies had about him, plus I interviewed Toru rather extensively about this Master Saito. It is not ideal using secondhand and biased observations, but I believe this will help deal with our imposter Chairman."

Sullivan took the neatly typed stack of papers. "We have a typewriter on board?"

"Yes. The UBF men came rather prepared. I don't know what they expected to do with all of those office supplies in a war zone, but be thankful because you probably wouldn't be able to read my handwriting. Legible penmanship is a sign of a boring mind."

Sullivan scanned the first page, then the second, then the third. It helped that he could read faster than anyone he knew. Wells had put together a very detailed list of every action the Grimnoir knew the new Chairman had taken since the real Okubo Tokugawa's death, complete with a hypothesis about what each act meant.

The alienist seemed really proud of his work. "Toru was rather impatient with my questioning. I really don't know how anyone manages to put up with that pushy Iron Guard, but we are lucky to have someone who was once a student of Saito's."

"Bit more than that, ain't it?"

"Indeed. Our obstinate friend tried to make his observations all sound as if they were personal, but I could tell many of his opinions had been formulated by old Master Hattori. It is almost as if Toru has a whole extra person in his head with the memories that were forced upon him by the dear deceased ambassador. That is a fascinating situation, which if I had more time, and a more agreeable and less impatiently violent subject, I would love to study further . . . Oh, if only I could absorb one other person's life experiences like that, I do believe it would have to be John Keats . . . Or perhaps Jack the Ripper."

"Gibberish."

"No, really. It would be fascinating to know what made such a mind tick."

"I mean your papers. This is junk."

"Please, Sullivan. We both know the dumb lug routine you utilize is a defense mechanism of yours. Don't pretend you haven't picked up enough Latin to reason your way through the correct terminology."

"I brought you into this because Bradford Carr thought you were some sort of man-hunter. He said your results rival a Justice." Sullivan leafed through the sheets. "This is nothing but guesswork."

Wells was holding onto the walls to keep from being knocked down as the *Traveler* swayed. "Then I'm afraid you misunderstand the fundamental science behind predicting behavior. All of us are merely a sum of our experiences. Psychology isn't algebra, where you give me a few variables and I will solve for X. Psychology is an art, but I understand people as well as you know gravity. The information I have is spotty, but sufficient. It is really rather simple."

"Simple? This Saito asshole is working with an outer-space monster in order to get everybody on earth killed. How—" A powerful gust of wind struck the ship. The *Traveler* lurched so suddenly that Wells lost his balance and fell. Sullivan had to shift his weight a bit but was unmoved. Impatient, Sullivan reached down and pulled Wells to his feet. Of course the Massive was unharmed. "How can you make sense of that?"

Wells dusted off his shirt. "Just because someone's reasoning is flawed does not mean that there was no reasoning at all. Everyone wants something, and it usually isn't what they tell you it is. Once you figure out what it is that they are looking for, that gives you power over them. That's why even Readers are so often wrong. They can read the thoughts that float to the surface, but they often miss the ocean of subconscious which lies beneath. Find out what lurks in those depths, Sullivan, and you know them better than they know themselves. Once you achieve that, you can manipulate them into doing whatever you want."

"No wonder your patients loved you so much."

"I am very good at what I do. It is even easier when someone is hiding their true motives behind a false narrative, because then all you need to do is think ahead a bit to anticipate what actions they will take in order to best reinforce their narrative. Stimulus. Response. We provide the stimulus, and since we anticipate the likely response, we set a trap. Thank your lucky stars that Dr. Carr hadn't offended me so, because if I'd still been working for him, he would've easily beaten the Grimnoir."

"Trying to trap us didn't work out so well for Dr. Carr . . . And what if Saito's brain is being controlled by the Pathfinder?"

Wells smiled. "He's not."

"I don't get how—"

"I'd bet my life on it. This fake Chairman's actions are rather clearly and unambiguously human. There is nothing alien about his actions. I see a man trying to prove himself. I see a man who believes he could have been great, but was stifled in the shadow of a greater man for so very long. Everything he has done or said since he has been in control of the Imperium is a clue to his ultimate goal. It is all there, plain as that gigantic, many-times-broken nose on your face . . . And to think I was told that you were some sort of detective. What kind of detective ignores expert testimony?"

"Fine." Sullivan sighed. "Assuming we don't get blown out of the sky, we should be in Shanghai in a few days. I'll go over this and make a call before we land." Sullivan leafed through the pages. "I just need to know how to kill this son of a bitch."

"There's not sufficient information to tell you what his physical or magical capabilities are, but I can tell you how to reach him. My recommendation is in the summary. Last page."

Sullivan skimmed it, and as he did so, he came to fundamentally understand how somebody like Wells had been able to carve himself a position of authority amongst the hardened killers of Rockville so quickly. Most of the cons would've been open books to somebody like him. Sullivan gave a low whistle. "Remind me to never play cards with you. So you want us to be bunco steerers and hustle the most dangerous man in the world?"

It was nice having a Ph.D. who was also a con. "More like he's the confidence man and the Imperium is his mark. He's laid the groundwork for us. We use his own scam against him."

"You're one malicious, manipulative son of a bitch, you know that, Doc?"

"It is nice to be appreciated."

Wells' study was much deeper than Sullivan had originally given him credit for. Though the alienist was careful to put in plenty of disclaimers about how he had a limited sample to extrapolate from, consisting entirely of Grimnoir spies' intelligence reports, and one crazy former Iron Guard whom Wells was counting as two separate subjects stuck into one homicidal body, everything he'd written seemed to make an intuitive sort of sense.

The *Traveler* was still busy trying to run a blockade and survive a magical storm. Sullivan was pretty much useless in this situation, and he couldn't abide being useless, so he'd gone to his bunk, managed to maneuver himself into place, and started reading. The lights were out, something to do with Pirate Bob conserving electricity and burning less hydrogen, so Sullivan had done most of his reading by flashlight and lightning strike.

He'd pretty much memorized the whole thing in short order, but he kept pondering on it and reading each bit over and over again. Normally he preferred to do his deep thinking while doing some sort of manual labor, a trick learned while breaking rocks in prison, but there just wasn't much for someone like him to do on a dirigible.

Sullivan had been a private detective. He'd never been financially successful, barely making enough to pay the rent most of the time, but that hadn't meant he wasn't good at it. He enjoyed puzzles, and he'd often found that once you figured out the important pieces and how they fit together, the rest sort of fell into place. People were the biggest puzzles of all, but that didn't mean they were any different. As he read and reread the profile of Dosan Saito, Sullivan began to get that old puzzle solving feeling again. This *fit*.

The Pathfinder must have landed sometime after the Chairman had died . . . Unlucky for them, it had wound up in Asia again, and somehow it had hooked up with Saito. *Why China again? Bad luck, or something else?* All of those details were a complete mystery, but Saito himself wasn't. He was a man who wanted to be in control and thought he really was in control.

If Wells was right, even if Saito was being influenced by something alien, he was still a man, and he would make decisions like a man. He was the product of a foreign culture, which most of them could never understand, but he was just a man, which meant he could be reached. Now the question became what to do once they got him.

That turned his thoughts to a sheet of paper hidden under his bunk with a terrible spell copied onto it . . . It had drastically magnified Zangara and Crow, but at what cost? *Maybe that.* But only if he didn't see any other choice . . .

"Mr. Sullivan?"

He pointed the flashlight at the hatch. Buckminster Fuller had to cover his eyes. He'd been so distracted he hadn't heard the Cog come in. In fact, he'd been so engrossed in pondering on the fake Chairman that he hadn't even realized the storm had tapered off. *How long had he been thinking?* The *Traveler* was running as quiet as something with jet engines could run. The emergency lights were on in the corridor, so he killed his flashlight. It would've been too much work to try to get his big body out of the tiny bunk, so he just set the report on his chest. "Hey, Fuller."

"The knots!" The Cog seemed agitated, but then again, Cogs usually seemed agitated. Browning was the only one Sullivan had met so far who seemed collected. "I've untied the knots!"

"Knots?" It took him a second to remember. "You mean the skinless man's magic?"

"It isn't magic! It was! Not anymore. It is something else, a perversion of magic, an evolutionary monstrosity. The deceased biological specimen used to be a Brute. And it wasn't a knot at all. It was a loop! A lasso! It isn't omnidirectional, it is *multi-omnidirectional*! It's, it's, it's—"

"Okay, easy there." Sullivan decided this was probably worth getting up for. It took a few seconds, but he managed it without bashing his head onto anything metal. He pulled the chain and turned the light on. "Break it down for me, and use words an idiot can understand."

"Domes are my area of expertise, but strings are a fascinating side note." Fuller looked around in consternation, spotted a work boot under Barns' bunk, hurried over, and pulled it out. He roughly jerked the laces out of the boot and tossed it back on the floor. He held up the shoelace. "What is this?"

"A shoelace?"

"It is the omnidirectional flow of magical energy between the host, in this case, Active magicals, and the parasitic symbiote, as in the multidimensional Power being."

"Us on one end. Power on the other."

"Yes." He took an end in each hand and stretched it out. "It is still a mystery as for how it determines suitable selection criteria."

"It picks some of us and not others. What part of it we connect to determines what magic we can do. Got it." Sullivan had figured that out on his own, and he wasn't a fancy Cog, either.

"Upon connection to the human host, what we think of as magic flows down this connection to the host, where it collects, and through an unknown process of exercise through the host's life cycle, is grown, and upon cessation of biological function—"

"Death."

"Yes, when we die . . ." Fuller let go of one end of the shoelace to let it dangle. "The being then collects the now-increased magical energy back to itself in order to continue its life cycle." Fuller took all of the shoelace into one hand in a big clump.

If Sullivan had been a more mirthful man, he might have made a sound like a spaghetti noodle getting sucked up.

"Hold this." Fuller held out the shoelace. Sullivan took it and stretched it out, curious as to what Fuller was so spun up about. "Now you are representing the connection between Actives and the symbiote. When I used my magic earlier to ascertain the nature of the magical connection of the specimen you collected from Axel Heiberg, I spoke of knots, as if the connection itself had been manipulated in some heretofore unknown manner. The normal magical geometries seemed chaotic, tied into knots, if you will, but they were not knots at all!" Fuller then went to Barns' other boot and yanked the lace out of it too.

"Barns is going to be ticked when he sees somebody's been messing with his stuff."

The Cog didn't even seem to hear him. "This second string represents a new entity. Which for the intents of this discussion I shall label the Enemy. Normally I prefer not to use language which predisposes an adversarial nature, but I've come to see the point of your usage of the term." Fuller took the second lace, looped it around the cord stretched between Sullivan's hands. He tied a basic knot on his side. Fuller's loop slipped back and forth on the original shoelace. "The multiomnidirectional layering was not some new evolution in the connection between the host and the symbiot at all. There was no *knot* in our connection, only extra materials."

"It was a hijacking."

"A fine word in this case. The Enemy, to use your rough term, has entered the equation. The connection now extends into another dimension." Fuller pulled harder on the lace and Sullivan could feel the tension, so he held on tighter to keep from losing it. "It is *hijacking* the flow of magic. Now what happens when biological functions cease?"

Sullivan let go of one end. Fuller pulled it toward himself and snagged the first shoelace before it pulled through his loop. Now it was pulled tight between them.

"Your hand representing the Power being is still making an effort to hold the string. The symbiote must decide. It is tethered to the Enemy now. It will be dragged toward the Enemy. Notice, I do not drop the other end which I have hijacked from you. Why? This host's lifecycle has ended."

Sullivan figured this must be like what college was like. "They ain't really dead. Like the skinless man."

"Correct. They are now biological tools, implements of this Enemy. They are anchors." Fuller tugged hard on the shoelace, so Sullivan had to pull back harder. "And worse, especially because I lack a sufficient number of hands and extra shoes with which to demonstrate this principle, these hijacked anchors will now go on to loop around and entrap other host-bond connections! The process will increase at an exponential rate. When enough of these hosts become anchors, what will the symbiote do?"

Sullivan let the shoelace fall.

"Exactly. Deprived of enough vital energy, and being pulled inexorably toward its predator, it will cut the connections and flee."

Now Fuller had all of the shoelaces, but Sullivan still had no ideas. "Thanks for the lesson, but I'd already sort of figured that. How's that help us all not get hijacked like you hijacked Barns' boots?"

Fuller sorted out the shoelaces until he held up the loop he'd tied. "This."

Sullivan sighed. "You got me there, doc."

"This is what the Chairman's magnificent globe was designed to track. I was so distracted by the arrival of a biological specimen which still retained some measure of magical connection that I neglected to compare my notes to the design of the detector. Over the last few days, I have finally been able to layer the two together. This looping, this hijacking, that is what is displayed on that magnificent spherical device, an interruption in the normal cycle of magic. Now that I have seen the actual target, and not a mere representation of the target I can replicate—"

"You can build your own Enemy detector..."

"In a manner of speaking, yes, but *better*. The Imperium Cog's spellbinding was brilliant, but it lacked creativity. It lacked true artistry."

Sullivan had thought the big globe thing had been rather pretty, but he didn't want to derail Fuller's chain of thought. It wasn't like the Cog was seeing things the same way as a regular man did, anyway. "That's good news."

"Far better than you realize, Mr. Sullivan. With your permission, I will require the skills of all the UBF employees, Southunder's more mechanically capable crew members, and especially the Fixer Mr. Schirmer. I will need supplies procured once we land; I will provide a full list, and I will need a sufficient portion of the cargo hold for workspace. "

"You get this thing built fast, and I'll have dancing girls bring you breakfast in bed."

Fuller smiled. "As you are well aware, the idea of harming any life here on spaceship Earth fills me with a most profound dread. There are rumors aboard this ship of what you intend to do, and I am fully aware of the dire consequences these actions will have against the people of Shanghai. It does not take a fool to know that my entreaties to search for a peaceful resolution will fall on deaf ears, nor am I deluded enough after seeing the Axel Heiberg specimen to think that such a resolution would be achievable in a time frame sufficient to not prevent the extinction of all life on spaceship Earth . . . Still, every act of violence diminishes us."

"I figured we'd keep you hidden on the *Traveler*."

"Obviously! That is not my point. I am aware that you wish to expose the Chairman as a charlatan, and by doing such a thing in an expedient manner, prevent as much killingry as possible."

I don't know about that. Sullivan figured there'd be plenty of killingry to go around. "I'll try."

"My point is that I will not simply spellbind you a device which will serve as an Enemy detectlocator. I intend to build you an Enemy detectlocate*exposer*. The loops will become visible to the naked eye. The truth will be laid bare for all to see!"

"An Enemy-exposer? You're a genius."

Fuller blushed. "I'm not a genius. I'm just a tremendous bundle of experience."

That made Sullivan think of Wells' alienist profile of Dosan Saito . . . And one more piece of the puzzle clicked into place.

Chapter 12

See beautiful Shanghai, Pearl of the Orient. Experience the mysteries of exotic Asia. Enjoy the amenities of the Paramount Ballroom, catch a show featuring big stars at the legendary Grand Theater, shop at Sincere to find the rarest of gifts, or experience the luxury of Sir Victor Sassoon's Cathay Hotel. Gamble in the French Concession or tour the ultramodern architecture of the Imperium Section, whatever you choose, Shanghai is the intersection of the cutting edge and the traditional. Any unpleasantness you may have heard about is in the past, and was exaggerated to boot, but your friends don't know that and the ladies will look at you as an international man of adventure upon your safe return! A new era of peace and prosperity has been achieved in beautiful Shanghai. The Free City of Shanghai has never been safer or more affordable to visit. Book your trip with Pinnacle Tours today!

—Magazine Advertisement, 1931

Free City of Shanghai

"GOOD EVENING, Mr. Smith," the Chinese policeman said. His English was decent, and his accent suggested he'd learned it from an actual Englishman. That wasn't a surprise, considering just how many tens of thousands of Westerners ripe for a shakedown were already in the city. There were multiple coppers at each checkpoint, and odds were one of them probably spoke French, and another, German. Shanghai was supposed to be *cosmopolitan* like that. The English speaker looked over the traveling papers. "Is this your first time in Shanghai?"

"It is," Sullivan answered. According to the Free City government documents, he was a successful tool and die maker from Detroit named Fred Smith, looking for an adventurous vacation in exotic Shanghai. Well, the forgeries probably said something to that effect, but he couldn't read Chinese either. "Been here a couple of days is all."

"Yes. This says you arrived on the *Laughing Carp* out of San Francisco." The policeman was taking his time with those papers, trying to do a thorough job, but they looked nice and official, probably as good a forgery as anything he'd ever seen in Detroit or Chicago, but then again, he couldn't read all the weird squares and lines that passed for writing around here, so he was just taking Captain Southunder's word for it. Sullivan glanced up and down the quiet marketplace. If it turned out the papers didn't look official enough, there was always violence, but he didn't relish the idea of smacking around some cops and then trying to run and hide when he was a foot taller than anybody else on the street. "I hope it was a pleasant journey."

"Sure was. Always wanted to take a nice cruise."

"Of course," the policeman said absently as he held the papers up toward the Sun to check for the proper watermarks. The other three men looked bored, smoking cigarettes and leaning on their rifles. "What do you think of our city so far?"

I think that if God don't burn Shanghai down, then he owes Sodom and Gomorrah an apology. But Sullivan didn't dare share his real feelings, so instead he played like most of the Westerners that wound up here. "It seems like a real nice place. Always heard stories about the Pearl of the Orient, and it's nice as they say." The policeman nodded as Sullivan spoke. "Pearl of the Orient" was the polite title. It was usually just "Whore of the Orient."

"The casinos are the best I've ever seen."

"Have you won much yet?" the policeman asked with a sly look.

Why? You gonna shake me down for a bribe? But Sullivan just smiled and shook his head. "Nope. Not with my luck. Maybe that'll change tonight, though." He needed to get through here and fast. It was obvious why he'd been pulled out of line for a random check. The main street through this district was the place with all of the pleasures and temptations for westerners with too much cash, but Westerners stuck out on this side road. He was an anomaly, and anomalies got pulled out of line. Didn't matter if you were in a foreign land, policemen were the same everywhere.

"Why are you in this district?"

Sullivan knew if somebody caught you looking guilty, the fastest way to get rid of them was to let them think they were right. "I'm a little embarrassed, but I've got to ask for some directions. See, I heard about this place called the Golden Flower House, I think it is, but I got turned around..."

"Ah, of course. It is for clientele with special tastes." The policeman smirked, thinking to himself that he'd called it as to why the big, white round-eye was wandering around the wrong part of town. Sullivan didn't even know what kind of weird business went on at the Golden Flower House, but the Marauders who had briefed him on the city had said that it catered to things that wouldn't fly with the madams of the more respectable pleasure houses on the main thoroughfares. The policeman was giving him a look that said *pervert*.

"I'm on vacation."

The policeman handed the forged documents back over. "Turn left at the end of this street and walk one more block. It is the one with the golden tiles on the roof."

"Thanks, buddy. Seems a little weird asking for directions to a whorehouse from a lawman, but I got to remember that sort of thing is okay here."

"In this district allowances are made." Which was code for it was illegal as hell in the rest of the city, but it was okay in this part because the mobsters made big buckets of money off of it. It was said you could buy anything in Shanghai. "Enjoy your visit, Mr. Smith."

Sullivan pocketed the papers and strolled through the checkpoint. He tried to remember what it had been like the first time he'd ever visited a big city, and tried to ape that. So he took his time, making sure to gape stupidly at anything that looked odd or foreign, which was damn near everything. The district he'd entered through had worn the mask of a Western city, and if it hadn't been for all the Chinamen, could've passed for San Francisco, all neat and modern, with tall, clean buildings. Even the signs there had been in English or French. This district was a whole different world.

It was busy, busier than any place he'd ever been, positively packed with human bodies, and they were all moving fast. There weren't as many cars in this district, but the ones there were kept on honking and revving their engines to warn the pedestrians out of their way. The buildings weren't as tall, but every floor of them bustled with activity and noise, except, of course, for the blackened, empty hulls that had been shelled by the Japanese not too long ago. Every inch of sidewalk had been taken up with street vendors, which meant the people walked in the streets around them, which meant the cars honked more. The market stalls were a buzz of activity, and merchants shouted at him continuously in Chinese, showing him everything from odd jewelry to children's toys to weird Oriental items which were probably crap to them, but might make a pretty souvenir for a tourist. From all of the yelling, folks really seemed to like to haggle in these parts.

Once he was far out of sight of the police checkpoint, Heinrich appeared at Sullivan's side. It was hard to tell it was him, since he was dressed like a local, walked like a local, and was wearing a big straw hat that kept his blond hair and most of his face hidden from observers. "Very good, my friend. Just keep walking."

Sullivan checked his watch and spoke to the air like he was talking to himself. "Must be handy to just walk through the fence and avoid all those checkpoints."

"Yes. It is. It also helps to not be a giant. I am a tall man in this country. You are a sideshow exhibit. It should come as no surprise you are being followed by some Japanese secret police."

"Great." Sullivan didn't turn to look. Odds were he wouldn't be able to pick them out anyway. He could usually make a tail, but that was when he was operating in familiar territory, and there was nothing familiar about Shanghai. "Right on time."

"Turn right at the noodle stand."

It wasn't like he could read the advertising. "Narrow it down for me."

A sigh emanated from beneath the great straw hat. "The green and yellow stand just ahead with the *noodles*." And then Heinrich kept on walking, disappearing into the crowd within seconds.

Sullivan had to admit he was a little jealous. Sticking out like a sore thumb got a little old, but he'd gotten used to it over the years and had learned to work around it. In Asia, he was an extra-sore thumb. In America he was several inches taller than average. In China he was a giant.

However, sticking out wasn't necessarily a bad thing when you were trying to send a message. He turned left at the noodle stand where hungry customers were slurping from bowls. It smelled remarkably good. Southunder had warned him that it wasn't considered odd to eat cats and dogs here, but he'd grown up poor and had eaten worse. It was all meat. Cat couldn't be any worse than opossum or squirrel, and it sure as hell had to be better than Rockville's mess.

Shanghai was supposed to be one of the most populated cities in the world, and after seeing it firsthand, he didn't doubt that one bit. It wasn't as tall as New York or Detroit, but there were a lot of high rises, and many more under construction. He'd already passed through the ultra-modern, spotlessly clean new district. It was the place for the Imperium to keep up the masquerade that Shanghai was a free city and not just a conquered place that was handy for conducting business and laundering money. This side road was even older, rougher, and seedier, built for working folks and not for show, so despite not speaking the lingo, he already felt more at home. The locals were giving him suspicious looks, but it wasn't too odd to have a Westerner in the market.

He passed a meat shop. A butcher was hacking up a quarter of a pig on a big wooden chopping block with a meat cleaver. Behind him were cages filled live chickens. One of the chickens spoke to Sullivan with Lance's voice. "There's a tailor at the end of this row. Go in there. Hurry."

The butcher turned and looked at his chickens suspiciously. The birds just sat there, stupidly clucking away, but certainly not speaking English. Perplexed, he scratched his head with one bloody hand, and then went back to cutting up his pig, mumbling something that Sullivan couldn't understand, but that he was fairly sure would translate into something about how he was working too damn hard and could really use a drink.

Crowds parted around him. He didn't need to manipulate gravity to push his way through people half his size. There was a sudden commotion back in the market. He didn't know what it was, but had no doubt the knights had just caused some sort of ruckus to distract the Imperium goons for a second. Most of the people stopped to look, but Sullivan just put his head down and pushed on. There were suits hanging in the window of the shop to the side, so that had to be the place. A bell rang as he opened the door. A Chinese shopkeeper was waiting inside. He didn't say a thing, but walked right to the door, locked it, and then turned the sign in the window. He took Sullivan by the sleeve and pulled him around a corner and out of sight of the window.

The little old man looked up, way up. Sullivan tipped his hat in greeting. "Got anything my size?" The shopkeeper reached under his long silk shirt and removed a revolver. For a second Sullivan wasn't sure if he was going to point it at him or hand it over, but luckily it was a present. The piece was a bulldog version of a British Webley with a snub barrel and a cut-down grip. Sullivan took the gun. "Better than harsh language." He broke it open, confirmed the cylinder was loaded, and then placed it inside his coat. The shopkeeper gave him a handful of loose .455 rounds and Sullivan stowed those in other pockets. Magic was nice in a fight, especially his, but it never hurt to back it up with bullets. He missed his enchanted Browning automatic and its fat magazines packed with lots of extra firepower, but he couldn't risk getting patted down at one of the checkpoints on the way in. "Thanks."

The old man gestured toward the back, waving him on. There was a wooden door partially hidden behind a bunch of hanging shirts. Sullivan opened it a crack and saw that it led to an alley. The old man took off his tailor's coat, tossed it on the counter, and walked out a different side door without so much as waving goodbye. Odds were it wasn't even his shop, and whoever owned the place would never even know it had been temporarily borrowed.

With no other directions, Sullivan set out down the dark alley. "Alley" was a bit of an overstatement, since it was really more of a garbage-strewn rut between two rotting, slightly leaning tenement buildings. He looked up, almost expecting to catch a loose brick in the face. He couldn't even see the Sun through all of the many clotheslines and dangling laundry. It never ceased to amaze him just how oddly quiet a place like this could be only a tiny distance from so much noise. Half a block later he found Heinrich, Lance, and a third man waiting for him next to some stinking trash cans.

Unlike Heinrich, Lance wasn't even trying to be in disguise. Though shorter, their Beastie was so thick through the chest and arms that it would've been impossible to try to hide among the local populace, and that was before taking the lumberjack beard, which he refused to shave off, into consideration. Lance was dressed normally and had probably been smuggled in like Sullivan had. Pirate Bob had so many connections that getting forty Grimnoir into the city was a piece of cake. Lance was looking distracted, surely watching their tail through the eyes of some convenient animal. "They've lost Jake and they look mad." His eyes seemed to refocus as he came back one hundred percent. "They're searching and I think one went for help."

"Killing them now would simplify matters," Heinrich suggested.

"Only briefly," said the stranger. He was a young Chinese man, dressed in one of those big silk shirts with the extra buttons that reminded Sullivan of pajamas. "If they sound the general alarm, the secret police will turn over this entire district looking for the perpetrators."

"Of course. Save the alarms for later. We will need to snatch a few of them for questioning eventually." Heinrich's smile was the only thing visible beneath the shadows of the hat. "Forgive me . . . Sullivan, this is Zhao, one of the few Grimnoir still in Shanghai."

The young man had a warm, friendly smile, but he possessed the hard eyes of someone who'd seen a lot. "I will serve as your guide while you are in Shanghai. It is a very dangerous place."

"That's Joe?"

"Zhao," he corrected. The top of his head was barely even with Sullivan's chest. He was either still a teenager or one of those baby-faced fellows who would look like a kid forever. "My name is Zhao."

"Sorry. Good pronunciation ain't exactly my strong suit."

"My apologies, Mr. Sullivan. I struggle with it as well."

"You seem to do okay."

"In a city such as Shanghai, it is vital for the knights to be able to understand many languages. No one expects an errand boy to be able to listen in to their private conversations. I also speak Japanese, French, and a bit of Russian and German."

Heinrich's enormous hat tilted to the side and, always suspicious, he asked something complicated in German. To his credit, the kid only had to think about it for a second before rattling something off back to him. Heinrich responded, sounding pleased.

"English is my best though. An American knight lived with our family for a time while he was spying on the Imperium. I first learned

English from him. Later, I relearned to speak it when I got work in the British section."

"Relearn?"

"The American knight who taught me was from your state of South Louisiana."

"There are forty-eight states, and I'm pretty sure South Louisiana isn't one of them," Lance said.

"I lived in New Orleans for a bit. South Louisiana's a state of mind." Sullivan chuckled. "How old are you?"

"I am nearly sixteen." Zhao said, but he didn't seem offended. He was probably used to that reaction from folks. "Do not be concerned. I know Shanghai better than anyone. I have lived here my entire life. I was a courier for the English bank, so there is no section of the city I cannot get you into. I set up this meeting as you requested, and I will provide whatever assistance you need while you are in the city."

Sullivan had only been a few years older than that when he'd slogged through the blood and hell of Second Somme. When times were tough, you didn't get to be a child for long. Hell, look at what Faye had accomplished before she'd gotten killed... "I'm sure you'll do."

"I do not know what has brought you to Shanghai, but I have heard rumors about Pershing's knights and the things you have done, such as killing Iron Guard Madi and fighting the Chairman on his own ship. Madi murdered many of my friends. It is an honor to meet you." Sullivan thought it looked like Zhao wanted to bow, but he resisted the urge and instead held out his hand to shake. Apparently the kid hadn't quite grasped the idea behind an American-style handshake, because it felt like a wet fish, but the kid seemed enthusiastic. "We must hurry."

"Lead the way," Heinrich suggested. It was a perfectly reasonable idea, since none of the rest of them knew where the hell they were going, but more than likely it was because Heinrich was so paranoid that he didn't want someone he'd just met walking behind him.

"We must cross through some of the buildings which were abandoned during the Japanese invasion. The only reason they have not been torn down is because it benefits the gangs to have places to hide things. Do not speak for a time. Voices echo for long distances in the empty places." Zhao took them a bit further down the alley, through a broken doorway, and down a long flight of stairs. They hurried along a tunnel that had to go under the street, and then up a ladder and through the basement of what felt like an abandoned apartment building. There were rats scurrying along the corners, but right on the other side of the boarded-up windows could be heard the bustle and clamor of the market.

There were bullet holes in the walls. Bits and pieces of building materials were strewn about, which Sullivan recognized as the telltale leftovers of fragmentation from shelling. It had been a few years since the *free* city had last gotten uppity against their Japanese *guests*. The Imperium had bombed the hell out of the troublemakers. The parts of the city that had been badly damaged had been abandoned and left to decay. He spotted the occasional signs of human habitation, but whoever the squatters were, they avoided contact. It didn't matter how close these buildings were to falling down, if you were poor enough, at least it was still a roof overhead. It was fascinating how the neighborhoods that were for show were as modern and beautiful as any city in the world, but right next door was a wreck like this.

Fifteen more minutes of crossing back alleys and run-down buildings took them into another basement. "We should be able to speak freely now." Zhao moved aside a rotting bookshelf to reveal what looked to be a mining tunnel. "The meeting place is not much farther."

Sullivan poked his head inside. The air was hot and damp in his lungs. It hadn't been carved for someone his size. This wasn't going to be fun.

"You got a city, you've got smugglers," Lance said as he admired the tunnel's workmanship.

"And the Whangpoo River is right on the other side of the wall. Du keeps pumps running constantly. Should these tunnels be discovered, then the gangs can simply flood them for a time. Shanghai makes crime into an art form." There was an electric hand torch just inside the entrance. Zhao had to thump the battery a few times before it engaged. "If we're lucky, the *Tokubetsu Koto Keisatsu* will merely think they lost their suspicious American to one of the brothels."

"A brothel? Now that would've been a much better place for a conspiracy to meet!"

"I'm sorry, Mr. Talon. Every brothel in Shanghai that allows westerners is watched by the Imperium. They take many useful blackmail photographs that way."

"I was only kidding, Zhao. Not that I'd mind having my picture taken with the lovely ladies, as long as I got one of them to frame for myself. Hang it right on the trophy wall. On that happy thought..." Lance clapped Sullivan on the back. "How was your trip in?"

"Long." After the *Traveler* had been hidden a few hours to the south in a small village friendly to Pirate Bob's marauders, they had started secretly ferrying knights and equipment into the city. Sullivan, because he tended to stick out in a crowd, had been towards the end of the list, and his particular trip had included a midnight rowboat ride and climbing up a rope onto a freighter. "So, Zhao, what's this toku koko thing?"

"They are the Imperium-controlled special police force. They are a plague. Shanghai is a free city in name only. Nearly all of China has been conquered by the Japanese, but supposedly we remain neutral here with an independent government and many international observers. It is all a lie so that the Imperium has a place to conduct business with the west. To most, Shanghai is a city of pleasure and leisure, but the *Tokubetsu Koto Keisatsu* are always watching, murdering those of us they call insurgents, and gathering information to blackmail visiting businessmen and fools." Zhao sounded resigned. "There are pretenses made about Shanghai being free, but we all know the instant we go against the wishes of the real masters, we are crushed."

"Sounds like the Imperium way." It wasn't too different from the Chicago way, when you thought about it.

"They are merciless. They allow the city's gangs to operate, but only as long as they continue to provide useful intelligence, and sometimes, when necessary, enforcers. The men you will be speaking with are sympathetic to our cause, but are not to be trusted. The gangster known as Big Eared Du is the most powerful crime boss in Shanghai. He is my cousin, and he hates the Japanese, but he will only help us if it benefits him."

"Cousin? Really?" Lance answered.

"Yes, but I barely know him," Zhao insisted. Sullivan didn't have room to judge, since his brother had been an Iron Guard. "Du only cares about what benefits him most. Nothing ever changes here. I really do not know what you expect to accomplish with this meeting, my brothers."

Sullivan was forced to crouch. The walls were slick. Humidity collected on the ceiling to speckle them with a constant drizzle. "Okubo Tokugawa is coming to Shanghai for a visit, and when he gets here, we aim to kill him."

"That is a good one." Zhao's laughed. The others didn't. "Wait..." The hand torch turned back to face them. "You are *serious?*"

"Of course," Heinrich said, "and we will require the assistance of every knight in Shanghai to do it."

The young knight was looking rather glum. "There are not very many of us left. The *Tokubetsu Koto Keisatsu* has been very effective against the Society. We were infiltrated by a spy and our identities exposed. Most of us were taken from our homes during a single night, never to be seen again. The rest have been living under false names and moving constantly. We know of Tokugawa's upcoming visit, but any attempt against his life in the past has been a complete failure, even with overwhelming force. There is nothing we can accomplish now."

"We brought three dozen Grimnoir with us," Lance said.

"That should occupy the first few Iron Guards' time. What do you intend to do with the other hundred?"

"That's part of the plan. We want Iron Guard there." Sullivan said. "The more the better."

"We will be slaughtered!" Zhao snapped. "I do not think you Americans realize how—"

"Listen, Zhao. You're not talking to tourists." Lance's voice was level and calm. "I know your people have gotten bled, and believe me, I feel for you. We've all dealt with them before, and we've got a plan. I'll fill you in on the whole thing once it's safe. We pull it off, and we will rock the Imperium to its foundations."

"You know perfectly well how fearsome a single Iron Guard can be in battle, but you have never seen the depravities which occur when they engage in total war. I have. You are in their home territory now. They will not be discreet here. In America, they sneak in the dark and put a knife in your back. In Shanghai, they drag us from our homes during the day and execute us in the streets for all to see!" Zhao was getting worked up. "They will crush their attackers and glory in every moment as an example to the populace that they should cower. Our bodies are drug through the streets and hung from the bridges, and then every man, woman, and child they suspect of having conspired with us is purged. The fortunate, beheaded on the spot, and the rest sent to the schools to be experimented on!"

"Then you must understand how dire our mission is when I say that an end such as that sounds like an acceptable risk," Heinrich said. "And all of it is preferable to our fate should we fail. I'm afraid we bring very bad news."

"That is the only sort of news I know..." Zhao just shook his head and started walking down the tunnel. "We must continue on or we will be late. We do not wish to keep the criminals waiting. Another attempt on Lord Tokugawa, the few Grimnoir that remain here will have no choice but to flee. We will not survive another crackdown."

"Then it is time to move elsewhere, for we must do this."

"Move? This is my home. I have fought for it my entire life. I will continue to do so, but I wish to understand what you are hoping to accomplish by committing suicide."

Sullivan thought Zhao seemed like an earnest young soldier, but the Grimnoir in Asia were practically cut off from the rest of the world. They'd suffered so much already at the hands of the Imperium, it would be almost impossible to convince them that the Enemy was actually the greater threat. "Get me to this meeting, let me speak with your leader, and I'll make him understand."

Zhao's shoulders sagged. "I do not think you realize how dire our situation is here in Shanghai, Mr. Sullivan...I am the leader."

It didn't matter that Sullivan couldn't speak a lick of Chinese. Gangsters were the same everywhere, and Big Eared Du had a better stranglehold on Shanghai than Al Capone had on Chicago. His manner, the look on his face, the way he sat there, looking smug because he had something that somebody else needed and that gave him leverage, it was always the same with men like this. Du was a king, and the dark side of Shanghai was his kingdom. He ran the Yuesheng Greens, a criminal army nearly twenty thousand strong, and nothing big went down in this city without him having a piece of it.

The king's table was the only thing illuminated in the vast space of the warehouse. There was a single powerful work lamp dangling over them. The smoke from Du's cigar floated in the yellow light. He was skinny and oily, living up to his nickname with some stupidly big ears. And when he smiled, Sullivan counted three gold teeth.

The Grimnoir knights sat at one end of the table. The mobster and his lieutenants sat at the other. The rest of the warehouse was supposedly empty, but Sullivan didn't even need to use his Power to know that there were men watching from the shadowed catwalks above and that there were probably rifles trained on their hearts the whole time. Somebody like Du didn't take any chances. Sullivan wasn't big on chances himself, so he used his Power just a bit in order to inspect the world around him, breaking everything down into its components, bits of mass, density, and forces . . .

Twenty men, all bearing long bars of steel and wood. No less than six of those were pointed at the Grimnoir, braced against the railing of the catwalk above. One of them was particularly heavy, suggesting a machine gun. Even the two pretty ladies who kept on pouring them liquor and bringing odd oriental snacks had small guns hidden inside their skimpy dresses. Sullivan didn't drink the booze or taste the little cakes. Gravity couldn't sense poison. The small army of bodyguards was far enough away that they wouldn't be able to overhear the conversation. Which was wise, considering that the subject of their meeting would be considered treasonous, even by crime-lord standards.

Poor Zhao was translating. The burdens of responsibility were heavy. He may have been young, but it was doubtful if he'd ever actually been a kid. Sullivan could see that now. He'd listened to the American's plan, gotten the pertinent details, and hadn't hesitated to make a call. He'd picked a direction and run. Keep him alive long enough to gain some experience, and he'd probably go on to accomplish great things. Problem was, with what they were up to, the odds of staying alive that long ranged from slim to none.

The leader of the Shanghai Grimnoir had, as far as Sullivan could tell, told Big Eared Du exactly what they needed him to. They didn't need the big picture. They just needed to do their part. "I am afraid what you are asking is very dangerous." Zhao scowled, listening as Du's right hand man spat out a bunch of complaints. "Dangerous and very expensive."

Lance looked over at Heinrich and nodded. Their Fade reached into one sleeve, untied a knot, and pulled out a long cloth bundle, which had been wrapped around his forearm. He tossed it onto the table. The left-hand man snatched it up, dragged it over, and unwrapped it. There were a whole lot of Grover Clevelands in there. Left-Hand Man started counting. He said something to his boss, which Zhao quickly translated. "The new American gold certificates. These are all a thousand dollars each."

"Yeah, President Roosevelt is confiscating all our gold and giving us paper instead," Lance explained. "But those are legit." Zhao went ahead and translated that.

Du laughed and muttered something to Left-Hand Man. Zhao seemed puzzled. "He says that taking real money and giving you their paper money, which is only as good as they say it is, maybe your government and ours aren't so different after all."

"They're all about the same thing," Lance muttered. "Bossing folks around."

Left-Hand Man finished his count and seemed pleased. Paper money still spent, and it was easier to move through Du's gambling parlors, whorehouses, opium dens, and racetracks than sacks of gold. Left-Hand Man held up the money, and one of the serving girls snatched it up and disappeared back into the dark. Francis would never miss that much money, but on general principles, if Du sold them out, Heinrich could always walk through the walls of his safe house and get it all back.

This whole time, Sullivan could feel a gentle prickling in the side of his head. Sure enough, a man with Du's kind of pull was bound to have a Reader on staff. They were subtle, but not good enough. They'd discussed this before, so Sullivan had made sure to concentrate on the big, obvious stuff. It would simply corroborate everything they said. Sure, if Du's Reader wanted to push hard, he could come up with the rest, but that would tip their hand, and gangsters never liked to tip their hand when this kind of money was on the table.

Right-Hand Man had something to say. "Lots of pointless, polite thank-you about the money," Zhao, knowing how relatively impatient Americans could be, skipped to the good stuff. "*But*... here it comes, the sort of distraction being asked for will cause a significant disruption in the city. Disruptions are bad for business and very costly to Mr. Du's organization."

"That's half up front. The other half on the seventeenth, delivered once your diversion starts." Sullivan waited for Zhao to catch up. "The diversion doesn't start, we walk away and you don't get paid."

Right-Hand Man must have been the nuts-and-bolts guy of the operation. "And if this disruption spreads, there will be chaos. What happens if the rebels see it as an opportunity to strike against the occupiers? Shanghai could be in pandemonium for many days. Many days when nobody bets on the horses! If it is as bad as what happened in thirty-one, then the Japanese Navy could even shell the city again. If it is bad enough to get in the western newspapers, then the tourists will not come for the whores and opium anymore."

Mobsters were all the same. Du wouldn't have agreed to the meeting if he already didn't have an angle on how their request benefited him. "And if it does get that bad, then I'm sure somebody as smart as Mr. Du will be able to come up with a list of things he'd love to accomplish while the police and army were too busy to watch him." Lance said. "In fact, I'm sure many of his rivals might even have unfortunate accidents during a time of turmoil like that. And, of course, anything bad that happens was all the fault of some magical extremists."

Du spoke for a time, forcefully and earnestly. Zhao snapped back a response without bothering to translate. Lance looked to Zhao, questioningly. Zhao sighed. "He said that his mother insists he get me a real job now that I am an orphan. I politely refused."

It hadn't sounded particularly polite. "Tell Du that family is very important to us as well, and once things are in motion, I'll see to it that you, and anyone else he gives a damn about, has a ticket out of town and a good job in America waiting for them," Lance said. "Tell Mr. Du that the Chairman killed my entire family, so I understand how Imperium retribution works. I'll get your people out. It's the least I can do."

Zhao didn't like it, but Sullivan's gut instinct told him the kid translated it truthfully.

Du grinned, and it was an evil grin, not helped by the fact that his ears really were far too big for his narrow face, so he reminded Sullivan of a bat. "He says he has no love for the Chairman, may his unspeakable foulness rot in hell, and wishes you great success in your endeavors. The Chairman is bad for business and he is tired of the

Japanese bossing everyone around and kidnapping his best-looking girls to be their pleasure women. Of course, he's saying this with an inflection that suggests he expects we will fail miserably and die. He says that he has helped the Grimnoir before, and it is always a fair relationship. Of everyone he has worked with, at least we know how to keep a secret."

Chapter 13

Toughest picture? I love making pictures but I don't like talking about them. The toughest picture I ever filmed had to be Ice Patrol. Everyone knew the Captain Johnny Freeze radio program and it was John Wayne's first big budget project. Two million bucks on the line, but everybody knows Iceboxes are big, strapping tough guys. Lots of frostbite on that set. Actives are controversial right now. The League picketed the studio, but the public sure loved John Wayne freezing Apaches. Got me more awards, not that those matter. Important thing is it paid the bills.

—John Ford, Radio Interview, 1933

Free City of Shanghai

YAO XIANG was sitting at his regular table at his favorite outdoor restaurant, enjoying his tea, passing the lovely afternoon watching the people of Shanghai go about their business, when a terrifying specter from his distant past and his current nightmares walked up and ruined his life all over again.

"Good afternoon," the Iron Guard said in a completely nonchalant manner. "Do you mind if I join you?" It was not a request. Xiang's throat was suddenly too dry to respond. The Iron Guard sat down across from him anyway.

The two men looked at each other for a time. Xiang tried not to let his terror show. The Iron Guard showed no emotion whatsoever. Xiang set his cup down. His hands were trembling so badly that the porcelain made quite a bit of rattling noise against the table before he was able to unclench his fingers to let it go. The Iron Guard was young, probably around the age Xiang's sons would have been if any of them had survived the invasion. However, that relative youth was meaningless. The Iron Guard existed only as tools of war and conquest, and Xiang had personally witnessed the unspeakable violence this particular one was capable of.

"It has been a long time, Xiang."

"You remember my name, much as I remember yours." He let out a long sigh. "Have you come to finish me off, Iron Guard Toru?"

"I am no longer an Iron Guard."

Toru was not wearing a uniform, but that did not mean anything. The Iron Guard often would dress in normal clothing in order to better blend in amongst their victims and targets. Today, Toru was dressed in a western suit coat, as was the current fashion among many of the younger Nipponese working in Shanghai. If one did not know better, they would never guess that beneath such ordinary garb was a series of magical brands that turned the bearer into a living weapon. "Please have mercy, Iron Guard."

"My Mandarin must be out of practice. Do not call me Iron Guard. I have given up that title."

The fear made it difficult to speak. "Yes. Of course."

The proprietor was an old woman. She came over to see if Toru needed anything. Xiang knew that she, too, had been a refugee from the war in Manchuko, yet she was completely unaware that she was politely taking the order of one of the monsters who had ruthlessly slaughtered her relatives. Toru asked for tea.

When she was gone, Toru went back to looking at the street. Several minutes passed in silence, but Xiang did not dare to speak. Toru seemed lost in thought, watching the people come and go for a time. It gave Xiang plenty of time to contemplate all of the terrible ways that the Iron Guard would probably murder him.

"Tell me, Xiang. Are you still employed as a journalist?"

Xiang nodded. "I am the editor of the district newspaper . . . Is that what this is about? I print nothing that would offend the Imperium! I do not know what you have been told, but the censors have approved everything—"

Toru lifted one hand to silence him. The proprietor brought Toru's drink. "Thank you." She bowed and shuffled off. "I did not seek you out, Xiang. This was merely a fortunate coincidence."

"I do not understand, Iron—" Xiang quickly lowered his head. "Forgive me. I do not understand what you mean."

Toru nodded across the busy street. "I have been informed that unassuming building right over there is an office of the *Tokubetsu Koto Keisatsu*. I have come here to deliver a message to them." Xiang looked at the indicated building, which was a rather bland office. He had no idea, but it would not surprise him. The secret police were everywhere. "I did not expect to see an old acquaintance. However, I should not say this was a fortunate coincidence..."

Xiang nodded. He would never dream of using the word *fortunate*.

Toru sipped the tea. "That is *excellent*."

"Indeed. Yes it is," Xiang agreed. Hopefully, if Toru was in a good mood, he would kill him quickly and not have him tortured or humiliated first.

"Yes. This is a sign." The Iron Guard, for Xiang could never believe in such a thing as a *former* Iron Guard, stroked his chin thoughtfully. "Nothing happens by accident. It would appear that the ghost of my father has once again guided my path. As I said, I am here to deliver a message. You are a reporter."

"I am an editor."

"I do not care. Just as it has moved me, fate has placed you here for a reason. You will report what you see so that my message may be made clear. This is another sign from my father. I will tell you a story, and you will see that it is published." Toru looked at him expectantly.

"*What?*"

"You should take notes. You will need to get this right."

Zhao had only led them part of the way back down the smuggler's tunnel when Lance spoke up. "Oh damn. Damn it all to hell." He sounded distracted, which told Sullivan that part of his mind was occupied inside some other living thing.

The group froze. "What've you got?"

"You want the good news or the bad news first?"

"Good news, I suppose."

"Our big-eared gangster friend didn't sell us out."

Zhao seemed upbeat for once. "I hoped my cousin would keep his word."

Heinrich laughed. "And now, of course, the bad."

"One of his underlings sold us out. Du and his boys left in a convoy of trucks. They're still counting money and having a good time, but one of those serving girls of his walked down the street from the warehouse and started talking to a policeman. I don't speak the lingo. Way she's standing there listening, she's not a snitch or getting a bribe, she's one of them, undercover. Now the policeman's talking into a radio. Wish I spoke Chinese..."

"Don't need to." Even though the floor was damp and slick, Sullivan took a knee. It was easier on his back than standing all hunched over. He looked over to Zhao, who was thoughtful enough to keep the hand torch pointed down the other way so as to not blind everybody. "They'll be waiting for us." Sullivan pulled the Webley from inside his coat. They had passed several forks in the smuggler's tunnels. "You got another way out?"

"Yes. There are many places to exit in the ruined quarter."

"Got a rat following the girl. She's gone back into the warehouse with a bunch of those secret police. There's a diesel engine..."

"What does it do?" Heinrich prompted.

"Hard to get an angle from the floor... Wait, it's a water pump. She's killed it. Now she's trying to turn a big valve on the floor."

"She's flooding the tunnels," Heinrich snapped.

"They're not rolling us up." Sullivan put the Webley back. "They're flooding us out."

"The whole system fills very quickly," Zhao said. "We will be taking the closest exit. Hurry."

The knights set out. Lance was all distracted trying to steer more than one body with only one brain, so Heinrich grabbed him by the sleeve and pulled him along. Sullivan brought up the rear, mostly because he was too damned big to go fast all hunched over, but it beat crawling. He'd done enough of that in France.

"That valve's heavy. She's having to fight it. I'll distract her... Okay, lady. Say hello to my little friend." Lance began to laugh maniacally.

"What'd you do?" Heinrich asked.

"Had a rat crawl up her dress to bite her on the ass. Ha!" Then Lance grimaced, stumbled, and crashed into the wall. He fell on his face, moaning.

Heinrich dragged him up. Their Beastie had been floored, sure as a punch to the head. "You okay?"

"Getting stepped on always hurts." Lance was rubbing his temples. "Yeah... But we've got problems. She had more secret police with her. The valve was rusted stuck, but they're working on it."

"How much further, Zhao?" Sullivan asked.

"A few minutes."

"Keep them busy, Lance. I don't feel like drowning."

"Looking... I've got to collect my Power... Here we go, there's like two hundred rats in this warehouse... Can't control that many individuals... Hell. They've unstuck the valve. I can only provoke a couple of strong emotions in that many minds." He closed his eyes and concentrated hard. "I'm going with rage and uncontrollable hunger."

Sullivan didn't know if Lance was really going to sic a swarm of giant, vicious wharf rats on the secret police, but he was fresh out of pity. "Do it."

"Already on the way." Lance struggled to his feet. "Too late. The floodgate's open."

There was an odd sound in the distance, not quite like anything Sullivan had heard before. It sounded more like thunder than anything. The atmosphere in the tunnel changed as air was forced past them.

"We're not going to make it in time!" Zhao shouted.

They only had a few seconds. "How close are we to the river?" Heinrich asked.

The flashlight beam bounced toward the right. "I don't know. Maybe twenty feet."

"Oh... That's nasty..." Lance said through clenched teeth, his mind divided between here and the warehouse. "*So* much blood."

Serves them right, Sullivan thought to himself, but that was just out of spite because they were about to drown. Drowning was preferable to being devoured by rats.

Heinrich still had Lance by the arm. He looked to Sullivan. "Hold your breath and hang on. I'll come back for you." Then Heinrich turned grey and hazy. A split second later Lance did as well, and then the two of them disappeared through the rock.

Sullivan looked around. There was nothing to hold on to. The rumble had grown into a much bigger noise, like they were about to be hit by a train. Sullivan flexed his Power, using it to see the world as it really was, interconnected bits of matter under constant forces, and he could feel the incredible spike of energy heading their way. He instinctively did the math. His Power would be sufficient to anchor himself in place, and then all he'd have to do is hold his breath until Heinrich got back.

Then he looked to Zhao, who was staring at him in wide-eyed terror. *Aw hell.* Every time Sullivan had ever forced a significant increase of gravitational power onto somebody else, it had either severely injured or outright killed them. His body was trained to deal with it. Sullivan was a Gravity Spiker. Everybody else was fragile in comparison. Zhao would either be swept away to be battered to death or drowned, or Sullivan could anchor him in place, but if he screwed up even the slightest bit, half of the kid's internal organs would rupture under the pressure. If the water was solid, he might be able to slow it, but fluids worked differently under gravity. They'd still rush past him and get the kid anyway. Fluids were *complicated.*

"Get behind me," Zhao shouted.

It was usually Sullivan that said that to others in crisis situations. He was not used to hearing it from somebody else. Zhao roughly pushed past Sullivan, *toward* the onrushing wall of water. The kid dropped the flashlight on the floor, extended his hands, palms open, and squinted into the darkness. He began muttering in Chinese in what Sullivan could only guess was either a desperate prayer or angry profanity. It really could have gone either way.

The surge of magical energy could be felt even before the sudden drop in temperature. Sullivan had one hand against the slick, wet wall, but he snatched it away, as the stone froze so quickly that it burned his flesh. He even left some skin behind. Ice crystals formed and spread, and within seconds, the tunnel was covered in gleaming white. The dirty ice reflected and bounced the flashlight beam. The cold hit Sullivan like a hammer and his breath shot out in a burst of steam.

Zhao shouted something, but Sullivan's ears were too cold to hear it. Either that or the blast of air pushing ahead of the water took all the sounds with it. Then somehow it got even colder. The storm at the North Pole was a summertime walk in the park in comparison. Sullivan's exposed skin felt like it was on fire. His eyes didn't want to move in their sockets. His teeth felt like they were about to shatter, and the worst part of all was that Sullivan was on the warm side of the tunnel. He was only catching the aftereffects radiating off of Zhao's body. The real force of his magic was being directed the opposite way. The kid was using so much Power, so fast, that it was liable to kill him. The cold ate the batteries in their flashlight, plunging the tunnel into darkness.

When using their magic, Spikers could *see* gravity, because everything was just matter and force after all. The whole universe was simply little bits, seen and unseen, constantly moving against each other and creating energy. In all of the many years since Sullivan had begun to truly understand the nature of his Power, he had never seen the world deprived of that energy, until that one brief moment in time, when he got to see Zhao suck every last bit of heat from that tunnel. Sullivan had never seen matter be so perfectly *still* before.

And then the water was on them.

It roared down the tunnel, ready to smash them flat, but then the angry water molecules hit the impenetrable cold, and then it was energy bleeding into the complete absence of it. The top layer turned to ice and the layer behind it turned to slush, but still behind that was a million gallons of pushing death, and Zhao pushed back even harder. Thicker and thicker, the wall turned into a plug of ice with the density of a prehistoric glacier, but it still kept on coming. Releasing that much magic at once threatened to tear the kid apart, but he kept it up. The ice thickened, hardened, cracked, exploded, and reformed, slowing, but still driving onward.

So now they were about to get steam rolled by a giant ice cube.

All of his Power exhausted, Zhao collapsed. The temperature immediately began to rise as molecules began moving again. Sullivan tried to lift a foot and realized that his boots had been stuck to the floor, so he pulled harder until his soles cracked free. He was so cold he could barely think, but ice was solid. Sullivan understood *solid*.

Lumbering down the tunnel, he stepped over the fallen kid, gathered up all of his considerable Power, magnified his density, lowered one shoulder, and absolutely chained himself to the center of the Earth. The ice flow was moving about as fast as a truck on the highway, and it hit him equally hard.

Sullivan flinched, partly from the impact, and partly from the sheer, unbelievable cold. It shattered around him, and despite his magically amplified mass, it shoved him, his feet turning the stone of the tunnel floor into gravel. The cold was killing his flesh. The moisture in his skin was freezing and rupturing his cells. The Healing spells he'd carved into his chest were burning like suns, trying to repair the damage. Sullivan drew as hard on his Power as he ever had in his life, increasing his density even more, and now the cold could not penetrate as fast, though it just kept on pushing.

There was motion in the shadows behind him. Heinrich had returned. *Take the kid!* Sullivan wanted to shout, but he was so locked under the pressure of a multitude of gravities that his vocal cords couldn't vibrate. Heinrich grabbed Zhao and they were gone.

The ice cracked. It was like the plug on a pressure vessel. The edges let go. The friction lessened. Water began to spray past. The ice split again, harder this time. Water was spraying him in the face. The tunnel was filling. The iceberg was breaking apart. The unstoppable force had met the immovable object. The ice cracked, spreading out around him, and then it exploded.

Water was blasting past him, surrounding him. The current would have torn any normal man away, but Sullivan planted himself there and waited. At least the river water was warm in comparison to the Zhao's ice, but compared to that hellish freezer, everything was warmer. The pressure lessened, so Sullivan was able to ease up on how fast he was burning through his Power. He could feel the reservoir of magical energy stored up in his chest. The air in his lungs would run out long before his magic would.

Today would be nice, Heinrich.

The pain was in his lungs. How much time had passed? He really needed to breathe. No matter how dense he could make himself, there was still the delicate balance of allowing the blood and the air in it to flow to his brain. Cut that off and he was out, just like anybody else.

Come on, Fade.

A hand landed on his shoulder. Sullivan let go of his magic, and suddenly they were both being swept away.

The world was already pitch black, so he couldn't see when it turned grey, but he felt it as Heinrich pulled him through the tunnel wall. Despite the pain and the danger, his analytical mind couldn't help but marvel at the feeling of Fading. Sullivan had expanded his original magical connection with gravity into the adjoining areas of force and density, but so far the flip side of the coin, making himself insubstantial enough for his own molecules pass through solid objects, had absolutely eluded him. Maybe Fade magic just didn't work with his mentality. Nobody would ever accuse Jake Sullivan of being flighty.

They passed through the solid earth. It was an uncanny feeling, but Sullivan trusted that Heinrich knew what he was doing, though for such a supposedly short distance, this did seem to take forever... Luckily, they hit the river and he felt himself become substantial again. Immediately his body began to be affected by the currents, and not being buoyant, he began to sink like a stone.

Desperate for air, Sullivan kicked toward the sunlight.

Yao Xiang had been scribbling furious notes for an hour. It had been a long time since he had personally conducted an interview, and he found that all of the writing was making his hand cramp badly. He had suffered from arthritis ever since the Imperium torturers had broken all of his fingers during questioning, but despite that, he could not stop, because what Toru was telling him was either the most important story in the world or utter lunacy.

"That is all, Xiang. Print that in its entirety." Toru placed his teacup gently on the table. "The Imperium needs to know the truth."

"But the censors—"

"They will deny you. That is to be expected. However, the important thing is that my words have been recorded, and will fall into the hands of Imperium intelligence to be analyzed. In a short time the truth of my story will be demonstrated, and they will have the testimony necessary to sort out the reality from the lies. If not, by next week the Imperium censors will have more important things to do than to monitor your little paper, and you can print it for the masses then."

"I would never violate the censor's orders."

"Do not bother trying to lie to me. We all know that there is plenty of underground propaganda printed in this city. I used to believe it was a problem when Imperial citizens would read such subversive things, but now I see the value."

Xiang was frankly shocked by this development. *Was this all some sort of elaborate trick to test my loyalty to the conquerors?* Yet it seemed too bizarre for the normally extremely direct Iron Guard to do something of that nature. Unless this whole thing was some elaborate form of entertainment for them, which would inevitably end with Xiang getting his head chopped off and hung on a fence for decorative purposes. "You would revolt against the Imperium?"

Toru was still staring at the street, as if carefully recording every pedestrian and vehicle. "When a ship loses its way, the course must be corrected, or it will crash on the rocks."

"Your story could cause an uprising against the Imperium."

"So be it."

He simply couldn't believe it, and maybe that was why he spoke out of turn. "Such hard hearts, capable of such cruelty, I never thought an Iron Guard would betray his—"

Toru slammed his open palm down on the table. The wood cracked and cups spilled. "I am no traitor!"

Xiang cringed back. Everyone in the café looked their way, curious. The proprietor shuffled out and immediately began cleaning up the spills and apologizing for things that weren't her fault, but nobody in Shanghai wanted to risk a Nipponese customer's displeasure, even if they had no idea who he really was. It simply wasn't worth the risk.

Toru lowered his voice. "Know this. I still believe in the mission of the Imperium. I believe in the teachings of my father. Manchuria. Nanking. Manchuko. Thailand. Indonesia. I would do it *all* again. Every battle. All of it. I would follow my orders because I am a warrior. My honor requires it."

His sons had all died at the hands of someone like this. He had been tortured for speaking out against their occupiers. Xiang had been beaten down and cowed for so long that he was surprised to hear his own words tumbling out in a rush of sudden, hot anger. "It isn't the battle. It is the depravity that comes after it. Imperium troops are cruel. They do not limit their killing to soldiers. They burn and rape. They starve villages while extra food rots, simply out of spite. They murder innocents for sport. I saw it with my own eyes. They would practice using their bayonets on defenseless prisoners! They murder children. Children!" Now he knew he'd gone too far. Everyone in the café was staring at them, surprised at Xiang's outburst. He hadn't said anything that any of them wouldn't have said in private, but you didn't dare say it to someone from the faction that could rain fiery death down upon your city on a whim. He waited for Toru to strike him dead, but he would be damned if he looked away. "Do not try to justify that to me as honor. There is no honor in evil."

Toru's public face had slipped. There was anger, and perhaps something else... *Shame?* Surprisingly, it was the Iron Guard who broke eye contact first. "Sit down, Xiang."

He hadn't realized he was standing. Xiang slowly returned to his seat. Toru was quietly contemplating the street again. Gradually, the other patrons went back to their tea.

I may die today, but I die an honest man. Regardless of what happened next, Xiang was resigned to his fate. "You were there. You know I speak the truth. You approved of such—"

"I did at first, because I did not understand. I participated in the sport, the same as the rest of the soldiers. I am not proud of my actions, but I will not deny they occurred." Toru looked at his hands. "It is easy, when you are so powerful, to think of your opponents as less than men... animals perhaps. If they are animals, do what you will with them. Use them for your pleasure, throw them away when they are broken and you are done."

"Disgusting."

"Perhaps. Some among us took it for granted. It was simply what victors do. Yet... it *haunts* me." Toru's voice was a whisper, barely audible over the buzz of traffic and the constant hum of thousands of city dwellers. "I came to understand such cruelty was not what the Chairman taught. He was a warrior, ruthless against his enemies, yet he bore no animosity toward former foes. His goal was to improve us all so that we could stand as a better world against our true enemy. Only many of his disciples failed to grasp that part of his vision. When your entire philosophy is based upon the strong taking what they want from the weak, soon the weak mean nothing."

Xiang could not believe his ears. He did not know an Iron Guard was capable of regret. "You speak of him as if he was merciful, but the Chairman let those things happen."

For the first time, Toru did not look like a terrifying Iron Guard. He looked like a tired young man. "To entertain such an idea would mean that the Chairman was somehow flawed. This, I cannot accept. He was perfect. We are flawed. I was a warrior who did what he was told. Because of my strength and speed, I was a favorite in the games, and my superiors would often choose me to represent my order in competitions against other units."

"Games? You mean massacres."

"To us they were simple contests, feats of strength for the officers to display our prowess with the sword or club..." Toru was staring into the distance. "I *never* lost. It was easy when they were not real people. I imagine it is more like chopping firewood, simple manual labor. Then one day, I refused to follow such orders. I forbid this behavior among my troops. This became...controversial."

"Why did you stop?" Xiang was genuinely curious. Terrified, but curious.

"They became *real*."

Toru paused for a long time. He seemed to be staring at his hands. He curled them into fists, and then hid them under the table.

"I do not wish to speak of it further. After this incident I was disgraced and sent to America, as far from the front as possible. I had been trained since birth to serve and to fight. To be sent away from the war was an incredible dishonor, but I understand now that it was meant to be...I do not know why I tell you these things, old man."

"You are a murderer, trying to scrub his conscience clean. If these things you told me are true, then you know you will more than likely be dead soon. You cannot expect to challenge the Imperium so directly and survive. I have interviewed murderers before, hours before their executions, and you sound like one of the condemned. I am speaking to a man who knows he is going to the gallows. You seek something that can never be given, Iron Guard Toru. I will never forgive you. *We* will never forgive you."

Toru rubbed his face with both hands, and when he lowered them, his public mask was firmly back in place. Toru stood and adjusted his coat. "I do not expect your forgiveness. I merely expect you to tell the truth." He began walking away.

"My telling the truth is why you people had my sons killed."

There was a small stutter in Toru's step. He turned back. "If I could change the Imperium's past, I would."

"Liar."

Toru gave him a small, sad smile. "Witness my conviction." And then the Iron Guard walked quickly through the dining area and disappeared into the crowded street.

Xiang stayed there, trembling, the fear and anger slowly bleeding from him. Now that the murderous Toru was gone, the painful knots in his bowels began untwisting. He glanced at his notepad, filled with tales of devouring creatures from beyond the stars, ghosts, and impossible conspiracies. The Iron Guard had simply gone mad. The horrors of war had broken his mind. *Witness my conviction.* What had Toru meant by that? And then Xiang realized that in all of their discussion he'd forgotten the reason Toru had said had brought him here to begin with.

The unassuming building that supposedly housed *Tokubetsu Koto Keisatsu* agents was busy now, men hurrying in and out because it was lunch time. He caught a brief glimpse of Toru crossing the busy street, dodging between the cars, which were going far too fast. One of them honked, but Toru did not heed it. He walked quickly up behind a group of three men who had just come down the steps. Toru's manner was unassuming, his hat down to keep from being recognized as he shouldered his way through the bystanders. *What is he doing?* Though he'd said he'd come to deliver a message, he did not hail the men, and they did not see him coming.

Toru grabbed the first by the back of his coat, lifted him effortlessly, and hurled him into the street, directly into the path of a speeding truck. He hit the grill so hard that pieces went spinning off. The truck driver slammed on the brakes. Tires locked up and screeched, but the forward momentum was too much, and Xiang lost track of Toru for a second behind the truck. Then the truck was past, leaving a smear of blood behind, and Toru was twisting the last man's head *off.* The other was already lying in a broken heap. The Iron Guard dropped the head, took one big step, leapt up all of the stairs, crashed through the heavy wooden doors of the building, and disappeared inside.

There was much commotion on the street. People were shouting and pointing, but since it had happened so very fast, Xiang doubted any of them really knew what had just transpired. Two seconds later there was a gunshot. Five seconds after that, a window on the second floor of the purported secret-police building exploded outward in a gout of fire and broken glass. Now the crowd knew something was wrong. The Shanghaiese were no strangers to sudden street violence, so they began taking cover or moving away in a fashion which would seem rather casual to most visitors.

There were more muffled gunshots, and though Xiang knew it was surely impossible from here with all of the city noise, he could have sworn that he heard screaming. Then on the fifth and final floor, another window broke open and a man came flying out. He flailed and kicked until he hit the sidewalk and burst open like a melon. Papers and documents came floating down after him like lazy doves.

Xiang had no doubt that Toru had systematically slaughtered every single person inside that building, and done so in less than a minute. The fire which had somehow begun on the second floor was spreading across the entire upper face of the building by the time Toru nonchalantly came out the broken front door and walked down the steps. He was wiping his bloody knuckles on someone's shirt like it was a rag before tossing it into the bushes. The deadly Iron Guard looked across the street, right at Xiang, and the two briefly made eye contact before Toru simply strolled away to disappear back into the city.

Witness my conviction.

Chapter 14

"You have enemies? Good. That means you've stood up for something in your life."

—Winston Churchill, 1933

Free City of Shanghai

"GOOD MORNING, Mr. Sullivan." For being so little, her voice was incredibly loud when you had a splitting headache. "I brought you breakfast."

Sullivan cracked open his eyes and groaned. The light sneaking through the boarded-up window told him it was just after dawn. "You are way too happy in the morning." But then he smelled that she'd brought him coffee, and all was forgiven. "Morning to you too, Lady Origami."

He didn't like waking up in the partially bombed remains of an old tenement, but it beat not waking up at all. His skin hurt from his brush with absolute zero in the tunnels, but the healing spells he'd managed to carve into his body had been able to repair the frostbite. The ones on his chest were still gathering Power and burned with a feverish heat, which made him realize he was naked, so he quickly pulled the thin blanket up. Not that there was a whole lot in the way of privacy in the dump the Shanghai Grimnoir were using as a safe house, but Lady Origami was still a lady. "Where are my clothes?"

"You swam in the river. I hung them up to dry, Mr. Sullivan."

He could barely remember much after he, Heinrich, Lance, and Zhao had stumbled their way here in a half-drowned fog. It was like Zhao's magic had been so cold it had messed with his head. "Thank you for doing that."

"It is fine. You are covered. I work with pirates many years. Pirate ship is very small place. A difficult place to have privacy. But none of the pirates are such a big man as you."

"Excuse me?"

She looked away sheepishly. "I mean muscles. Very big muscles. Like picture in magazines. I . . ." Now she was blushing. "I mean the last page picture, where first is a skinny boy, who gets sand kicked in face by bully, and then sends away for book about how to lift heavy things. You look like last picture, with the muscles." Now she was just getting exasperated trying to explain. "Sorry, Mr. Sullivan. I should not have spoken."

"Comes with being a Gravity Spiker."

"Yes. *Omosa.* Heavies. I am familiar. They are all so very big."

"Thanks, I guess. And please just call me Jake." Lady Origami smiled, as if to say *that's not likely.* "What're you doing here anyway? Doesn't the *Traveler* need its Torch?"

"Not so much to do there now while she is parked. Whole ship is taken over by Fuller building his machine in the hold. She cannot fly until this machine is done. So until then, I come here to maybe help burn Iron Guards." She knelt by his sleeping mat and set the tray next to his elbow. Breakfast appeared to be balls of sticky rice.

He had to remember that this lady also enjoyed participating in the brutal close-quarters fighting of a pirate boarding party. "That's mighty brave of you."

She shook her head. "Not so much. I like to help. And I do not like Imperium soldiers. Not at all. And this city swims in them. You are lucky to be alive, Mr. Sullivan. The Icebox child nearly killed you."

Sullivan shrugged as he took the coffee, hot and black, perfect to warm his bones. "The kid did what he had to do."

"I do not trust Iceboxes. Their magic is . . . hmmm . . . Forgive me. I am still practicing my English. Their magic is *incorrect.*"

Of course, to a Torch, whose magic was based in manipulating the consuming rampage of fire, the absence of heat energy would seem blasphemous. If he wasn't such an analytical man, he might even feel the same way about Heinrich's Fade magic. But he wasn't feeling particularly analytical right then though, since huge Power use always left him starved. Going all *wispy* like that, just wasn't right.

Lady Origami didn't seem inclined to go anywhere, so he just started shoving rice balls into his face. They were either better than expected, or he was just so hungry that it didn't matter. She knelt there, watching him, and he had to marvel how she was able to sit like that without hurting her knees.

"How is everybody else?" he asked between mouthfuls.

"They are fine. That very loud noise is Mr. Talon snoring."

"Huh. I thought somebody had parked a truck next door and left it running."

"Mr. Koenig was already awake. I think he does not sleep."

Sullivan was normally a light sleeper, as were most who survived the Great War trenches. Heinrich's paranoia made Sullivan look like an ostrich with its head planted in the sand. "Or when he does sleep, he leaves one eye open . . . Heinrich grew up in Dead City."

"Ah . . . Then he slept in trees to not be eaten by zombies. I see. You would need to sleep lightly to not roll over, fall, and die."

Sullivan had marched to Berlin at the close of the war. He didn't think they had been many trees left there after the Peace Ray blast, but he didn't share that, because it was a sad thought, and it didn't seem fair to share that with the usually perky Lady Origami. "How is Zhao?"

"The Icebox is still sleeping. He used much Power. Too much exercise." She gestured at the now hidden scars on Sullivan's chest. "And he does not have those."

Their presence was for the most part kept a secret, but not anymore. "Lucky me."

"I thought only Iron Guard wore the magical kanji which made them stronger. At the Imperium schools, they brand the prisoners, testing such things. It usually does not work, so those prisoners are . . . thrown away."

"I've heard that. Terrible business."

"They use prisoners to get the designs correct. They twist metal brands until they are perfect. It takes many, many tries, and most prisoners die after a few tries." She rolled up one of her sleeves and showed him a terrible burn scar on her arm. Sullivan could just tell that no magic had taken to that mark. He had made a few of those failures on himself. "Once correct, they can use them on their own people."

"I'm sorry," Sullivan said, meaning the whole damn thing.

Lady Origami put her sleeve back down. "It is fine. It does not hurt so much. They give the prisoners ether, keeps them from squirming. Besides, I escape. I am still alive." She gave him that innocuous little smile again. "My captors are not so alive."

It was grisly, but he was a curious man. "I didn't think the Imperium experimented on their own people." She scowled hard. She did not consider them *her* people, but he quickly corrected himself. "I mean Japanese people. I thought all their Actives got used by the Chairman's government and they saved the dangerous experiments for the folks they conquered."

"Not everyone in the Imperium agrees with the way of things. Some are even brave enough to open their mouths..." She looked away and her cheeks burned hot. "Those who speak too much, their whole families are shamed. They are outcasts. They become not-people." It felt like there was a lot buried behind those words. She hurried and changed the subject. "So how did you learn this Imperium trick, putting spells on skin?"

"I'm self-taught..." He saw that answer wasn't going to satisfy her. "I figured out how to do a basic healing spell one time after I got shot." He didn't add that he'd learned to do it on the fly because he'd just got shot in the heart, because that made for a long story. "I got lucky. The rest were trial and error. I put on more of the healing ones, but each one adds a little less than before, so I started messing around with other Powers. I recognize gravity the best, so that's the only other area I've had any luck with."

In actuality, he was probably as talented with spellbinding as anyone outside of the mad Cogs of Unit 731 or Buckminster Fuller, and if it wasn't for this quest and all the trouble that had come before it, he would've loved to devote his life to magical study and experimentation. *If only...* Problem was, he was just too damn good in a fight, and too stupid not to volunteer for one.

"You have so *many* scars. You did this all to yourself?"

Obviously, she meant the new spells, and not the leftovers from the various bullets, knives, or shrapnel he'd picked up over the years. "I was sick of giving up the high ground to a bunch of fanatics."

"Iron Guards die too, but because of these, it takes much more work to burn them." Lady Origami seemed intrigued. "Does it hurt?"

Cutting your own flesh with a knife, searing it all with otherworldly demon ink, concentrating through the sizzle, and then channeling so much Power into it to try and get it to stick that you had to go right up to death's door ... "A little."

She did not have to ponder on it for long, which told him she'd probably been thinking about it since she'd first seen them last night. "I would like you to put these spells on me too."

"I lied. They hurt a lot." He was having a hard time imagining her surviving the process. One healing spell had damn near killed that tough bastard Lance, who had been a very pushy volunteer. Though these physical spells were useful, Sullivan wasn't exactly thrilled with spreading them around. The Imperium troops had them, but only after their Cogs had experimented, working the kinks out, and murdering untold numbers of prisoners in the process. The last thing he wanted to do was accidentally kill one of his associates. However, danger wasn't the main reason he was hesitant to share them. Rather it was because it seemed, with each spell he'd carved onto his body, he *felt* a little less. Not just pain, but everything, and he wasn't sure he wanted to do that to anyone else. "You need to be conscious the whole time or you'll die, and then you might die anyway when the new magic connects to your body."

"I am not scared of pain. Having a baby is pain, but worth it. This is same."

"I didn't know you had kids."

"I ... do not ... now."

There was a long, awkward pause. Sullivan didn't know what to say to that. He had never been good with words, or women, or people in general for that matter. So he just nodded, and then ate another rice ball.

"Besides, I knew you lied, Mr. Sullivan. When you lie it shows up on your face. Americans are not so good at lying, but you especially are bad. You are like ... like an *ox*. The ox doesn't lie. It simply is an ox. It works so hard, it does not need to deceive. You are an ox, Mr. Sullivan."

In most circumstances he would think being called an ox was an insult, but in this case he figured it was meant as a compliment. "I guess sometimes we lie to try to protect folks."

"Yes. Nipponese, we learn to not lie with our faces, only with our eyes. My polite face is the same as my lie face. Make your face polite, and lie to them in your eyes only."

"I'll keep that in mind." In his admittedly biased dealing with the Imperium, that actually made a lot of sense.

"For the spells on your body, I am not scared to die. I do it anyway. If it helps beat the Imperium, then I do *anything.*" That polite face she had mentioned had slipped a bit. Now he could see the sadness kept buried deep beneath, but deeper than that was a core of fire, just waiting to get out. "They take what they want and ruin any who speak against. I would burn them all."

"You despise the Imperium," he stated the obvious.

"Every last one," she whispered the Marauder's slogan. "The Imperium was my home. I hate it more than you can ever understand." Apparently the conversation had moved into another area she wasn't comfortable speaking about, so Lady Origami popped up from her knees. She was exceedingly graceful. "Eat. I will fetch your clothes. Tokugawa Toru is downstairs. Yesterday, he killed many secret police."

"How are you handling having him around?"

"I do not like him. Captain Southunder said he is necessary so I should not burn him . . . *yet.* Do not trust Toru, Mr. Sullivan. His face does not ever lie. He means exactly what he says. That makes him more frightening."

"You are a remarkably perceptive woman, Lady Origami."

"Thank you, Mr. Sullivan."

"Jake."

"Mr. Sullivan."

Considering the rather direct circumstances of how they'd first met, this was one odd lady. Direct when she wanted to be, demure the rest of the time, she was probably one of the most important members of the Marauder crew when they got down to business, yet the rest of the time she acted like a servant around them, all deferential and polite. Yet beneath all that, he had a gut feeling that she was wound tight as a spring. "Whatever makes you happy."

"Thank you." She folded her arms and gave him a little bow, then turned to leave.

"One thing, that little paper frog you made me, I doubt it made it through punching an iceberg and taking a swim. Sorry about that. It was nice."

Pausing in the doorway, she gave him a genuinely pleased smile.

"It was to bring good fortune. You must have used it up. I will make you another," she said as she left the room.

"I'd like that," Sullivan said to himself.

The Grimnoir knights and Marauder volunteers who had snuck into Shanghai over the last few days were staying in several different safe houses across the city. It wasn't smart to have all of their eggs in one basket, and should any one group of them get rolled up by the secret police, the rest still needed to be able to complete the mission. Only Pirate Bob knew most of the locations, and he was back at the *Traveler*.

In fact, since they were nominally in charge of this little shindig, Heinrich, Lance, and Sullivan were supposed to be staying in different places, but because of their detour through the river, this hideout had been the closest. It had once been an apartment building for dockworkers, but one of the Japanese artillery shells from a few years before had hit a nearby sea wall, and the building's foundation and first floor had been flooded ever since. It was now rotten to the core, and would probably fall over soon on its own. Heinrich and a small group of knights had already been here for a few days.

"It ain't much." Sullivan leaned on the balcony railing, but when it groaned and rust began to fall into the water below, he thought better of it and stepped away. His clothes weren't quite dry from the last swim yet.

"Compared to where I grew up, this is a rather nice neighborhood," Heinrich answered. "At least it is defensible."

"True." The only approaches were bridges fashioned from discarded lumber and old sheet metal, so it would be difficult for anyone short of a Traveler to sneak up on them unseen. There were enough of the makeshift bridges attached to other nearby buildings that it would be very difficult to surround and cut off all their escape routes. Plus, he'd been told there were a couple other escape routes available, provided you didn't mind holding your breath. "Zhao picked it?"

"Yes. He knows this city like the back of his hand. The young man shows some tactical aptitude."

"Strongest Icebox I've ever heard of, too. I once took on an Icebox, one of the most wanted fugitives in the country, and he didn't hold a candle to Zhao. Provided we survive this, the kid's got a future."

"I would say send him away, but I sincerely doubt he would go." Heinrich shook his head. "In fact, I know he would not. He reminds me of myself at that age, and no matter how lost a cause it may be, your home is still your home."

"Even you left Dead City eventually."

Heinrich shrugged. "And a lost cause is lost. Sometimes it simply takes longer for some of us to realize it. I come from a very obstinate people."

"I know." Sullivan chuckled. He had gained a lot of respect for Heinrich since he had met the Grimnoir. The German simply did not know how to quit. "I fought in a war against your bunch. Working with you has reminded me of why it was so damn hard to win, you stubborn Kraut."

"Why thank you, Jake." Heinrich took out a pack of smokes and a book of matches and offered them to Sullivan. His had been soaked in the river, so he was glad to see that someone had thought ahead to stash vital supplies. "Speaking of lost causes, Shanghai has suffered greatly under the Imperium's boot. I have tried to prepare these knights for the presence of our Iron Guard." There was a sudden crash from inside the bowels of the rotting building, followed immediately by some agitated shouting in Chinese. "And there he is now."

"So Toru's met the Shanghai Grimnoir." Sullivan sighed as he struck a match and lit up. The hot smoke felt good in the lungs, and as a bonus, Jane the Healer was back in America, so she couldn't yell at him about emphysema or cancers. "Let's go keep them from murdering each other."

The central area had once been several individual rooms, but someone had torn out many of the interior walls to burn the wood to stay warm. The walls were covered in trophies taken from the Imperium military, broken weapons, uniforms, torn flags, all the sorts of things that a resistance found motivating. In one corner was some of the equipment smuggled there from the *Traveler*. In the other corner was what passed as their kitchen area, and in it was Toru, standing there all surly, with his arms folded, while some of the local Grimnoir yelled at him. One of them was really agitated, and had picked up a meat cleaver and was pointing it at Toru's face.

"Easy there," Sullivan warned, because Toru would more than

likely just take that cleaver away and bury it in the man's skull. "What's his name?"

"I don't know. It was confusing. Zhao introduced everyone, but everyone in Shanghai seems to have three names each, and I can't tell which is first, last, or a nickname."

"Hey, Meat Cleaver!" Sullivan raised his voice, and since he still had his "sergeant's voice" when he spoke from the chest, it made the entire building vibrate. "Knock it off." Either he spoke enough English, or that got through in any language, but it worked, and he lowered the weapon. "What's the problem in here?"

"This peasant fool does not realize what he has." Toru gestured roughly toward one of the captured trophies. "That helmet is incredibly valuable."

Helmet? It looked like some weird, stylized, oriental art piece, until Sullivan realized it was upside down. It had big horns, either for decoration or a real nasty head-butt, only the horns had been pounded into the floor, and the interior of the helmet had been used as an ashtray. "Damn it, Toru, I can't take you anywhere. Let the man have his ashtray."

"You do not understand. This is part of an extremely valuable weapon system." Toru reached for the ashtray, but Meat Cleaver, who was a chunky, red-faced, angry sort, started jabbering again. Toru paused. "Out of respect for our mission, do not make me gut this imbecile."

There were a bunch of people staying at the safe house, and every one of them who wasn't on guard duty had come in to see what the commotion was about. Luckily, Zhao was one of them. The kid looked haggard, with dark circles under his eyes, which was to be expected, because expending that much Power at one time was physically exhausting. Zhao barked an order, and Meat Cleaver, though he was probably twice Zhao's age, immediately complied, dropped his weapon on the floor and took two steps back. He did not, however, stop arguing.

"What's he saying?"

Zhao looked at Toru with barely concealed hostility. "I would prefer not to translate. It may upset our *guest.*"

"He's my responsibility," Sullivan said.

"I am taking this helmet. I do not care what this wretched pig-dog has to say—"

"Shut it, Toru."

The Iron Guard clamped his mouth so tight that if he hadn't had Brute-hard teeth they probably would've shattered. It was either that or let out a response that would've surely started a gun fight. After a few seconds his jaw muscles unclenched enough for him to mutter, "Fine."

"Pang says he killed an Iron Guard in a fierce battle, and he was wearing this armor."

Toru snorted. "It is more likely they murdered him in his sleep and stole his helmet. This tub of fat could not best an Iron Guard in *fierce* battle, especially one wearing Nishimura Combat Armor. The only thing he might be able to defeat an Iron Guard in would be a dumpling-eating contest."

"Pang is a powerful Brute," Zhao warned.

Pang puffed up his chest and flexed his muscles. It didn't help his case any.

"I killed fifteen *Tokubetsu Koto Keisatsu* yesterday," Toru stated flatly. "Can he even count that high?"

Sullivan took quick stock of the observers. There were a few of the Shanghai Grimnoir present, and most had quietly placed their hands inside their clothing, surely to rest on firearms. There was another young Chinaman standing off to the side, and unlike the blustering Pang, this one was quietly confident, watching Toru, surely with some Power ready to go. That one had the stance of a fighter. There were a few Americans and one marauder, and none of them would lift a hand to help Toru out either, so he really didn't know how stupid their Iron Guard was about to get. Lady Origami had arrived, and she was surely just looking for an excuse to set him on fire.

"Now, now, my friends. Let us not be hasty. I personally find murdering people in their sleep to be an excellent method, because since they are asleep it is rather difficult for them to retaliate." Heinrich walked into the center of the room, trying to defuse the situation. "So regardless of how our friend Pang actually killed this Iron Guard, what is this combat armor you speak of?"

"It is from one of our most brilliant Cogs, the same man who invented the *Gakutensuko*. It is a suit of battle armor, perhaps the most capable design ever, each one heavily connected to the magic of the user and driven by the Power itself. Very few were ever made. They were far too labor intensive, and each one required so many kanji that they were never mass produced. Just this one piece could add incredible capabilities in battle."

"How capable are we talking about here?" Sullivan asked. "Because, no offense, Zhao. If that ashtray can help fight the Pathfinder, I'll buy Pang a new ashtray."

"Let me phrase this diplomatically," Toru said, which meant he was about to do nothing of the sort. "I have seen that glorified heavy suit which John Browning and Buckminster Fuller built for you in preparation for our mission. Compared to Nishimura Combat Armor, it is archaic junk, as if fashioned by monkeys using bones and rocks as tools. So you can see why I must claim this helmet—"

Pang shouted something.

"Ashtray," Zhao corrected.

"Helmet," Toru growled. "I will claim this and hope that it salvageable. If these barbarians did not do too much damage to it, perhaps I can still put it to some use."

Zhao translated all of that, and from the reactions of the Shanghai Grimnoir, Zhao had done so in a much nicer way than Toru had. They still seemed either angry or ready to fight, but whatever he said did take it down a notch. Zhao and Pang began debating back and forth, but at least it wasn't so heated anymore that somebody was likely to get hacked to bits.

Something brushed his sleeve. He hadn't even heard Lady Origami approach. Everybody else was still paying attention to the loud, dangerous ones. She stood on her tippy-toes, and he still had to bend a bit so she could whisper in his ear. "I understand some. I know some Mandarin."

"Really?"

"Yes. Many Marauders from China. These men are trying to save face. Pang did not battle Iron Guards. These men are brave, but not stupid. He stole a crate from an Imperium train. The armor was inside. They did not know what it was."

"There's more of it?"

"The Icebox child is saying they could not make the magic work, and it was too heavy to wear. Only Pang was strong enough to carry it all, but he was too fat to fit, so it was left in the crate and hidden."

Zhao made eye contact with Sullivan. He didn't need to be a

Reader to know they were on the same wavelength. "I would suggest that our guest apologizes to Mr. Pang, and perhaps an arrangement can be worked out."

"Hey, Toru. You heard the man. Apologize."

Toru's eyes narrowed dangerously. "Are you deliberately trying to provoke me, Sullivan?"

"Well, I ought to let you suffer for insulting John Browning's craftsmanship, but if you want the rest of this armor, then you'll apologize to Pang."

"What?"

"The *whole* suit."

That obviously got him. Sullivan had no idea if this Nishimura stuff was as great as Toru made it out to be, or if it was more of his usual smug superiority about all things Japanese, but either way, it was enough to make him swallow his pride. He turned to face the fat Brute and gave a small bow. "I apologize for insulting you." Toru had to pause to lick his teeth, like the words left a nasty taste. "I acted impulsively."

Zhao translated. While he thought it over Pang stroked his pointy little beard, which was the only thing on his entire body which could be described as thin. Pang answered. Zhao turned back to Toru. "And?"

Surely the Iron Guard had to call upon his Diplomatic Corps training to utter the next bit without laughing in Pang's face. "I am certain now that you defeated an Iron Guard in battle. You are obviously a great warrior."

"That must be some damn impressive armor," Heinrich whispered.

Zhao translated. Pang responded in the affirmative and then it was smiles all around, except for Toru, who immediately ripped the helmet out of the floor and dumped the cigarette butts everywhere. He ran a hand down one horn, almost reverentially. "Take me to the remainder immediately."

Pang just stared at him for a second, and then said something to Zhao, who didn't even need to translate.

Toru sighed. *"Please."*

Zhao was grinning. It wasn't every day you got to humiliate an Imperium killing machine. "It is stored downstairs. There are dry pockets on the first floor where no one would ever think to look. Come. We will show you." Several of the Shanghai Grimnoir filed out for the stairs, Toru right behind them, cradling his precious helmet. He would probably hold a grudge and plot their deaths, but as long as they held it together until the Pathfinder was dead, Sullivan could deal with it.

Lady Origami waited for the others to leave before addressing Sullivan. "Earlier, I made a mistake."

"What about?"

"Toru's apology. I was wrong. He can lie."

Wannsee, Germany

"I THOUGHT YOU SAID you were leaving after one day?"

Jacques jumped. He had not heard Faye enter the hotel room. But then again, Faye didn't *enter* anything in the normal sense. She simply willed herself into existence wherever she felt like and scared the hell out of whoever was there.

The elder made a big show of putting one hand over his heart. "I'm an old man. Don't do that to me."

Faye was bone-tired weary, and coated in the grey dust of Dead City. She wasn't in the mood for Jacques' banter, so she merely walked past him and flopped into the nearest chair. It knocked a choking cloud of dirt off of her clothing, but she was too tired to care. She'd spent days studying and thinking about the drawings, and then another day collecting them after she gave up on the studying. The satchel which had been filled with art supplies was now filled with Zachary's drawings, and it made a loud thump as it hit the hotel room's floor.

"I . . . I was going to take the train, but I decided to give you more time. I am glad I did. Are you alright, dear? Can I get you anything?"

Like she'd ever drink or eat anything from him again, what with all those pictures of him thinking about poisoning her. "I found Zachary."

"You did?" Jacques pulled out the other chair, sat down on it, and leaned way forward, curious and eager. "Is he all right?"

She shook her head. "He's dead. Not alive dead, but dead dead. Zombies are so complicated. Real forever dead, I mean."

"Did you . . ."

"Oh, Jacques," Faye gave a tired smile. "I'm still not the monster you think I am."

"I did not mean to imply—"

"Naw. He stuck himself in a furnace when we were done talking. He was just plain worn out and didn't want to hurt no more. Can't rightly blame him."

His expression was unreadable. "Zachary was a good man."

"I could tell."

Jacques leaned forward in his chair until his elbows rested on his knees. "What did he show you?"

"All sorts of stuff. Things that have happened, will happen, might could, maybe, heck, I don't know. I'm still sorting it out. I gathered them all up." She touched the satchel with one foot. "But I do know one thing for sure."

"That is?"

"Me and you? We're done." Faye kept her voice even, and though it was hard, she was exhausted, starving, and trying not to be emotional. She didn't deal well with betrayal. "You were aiming to kill me."

"No." Jacques looked her in the eye. "I have kept my word. You are aware of how I voted. I explained to you my reasons. That was never a secret, but I have stayed my hand since we first met."

"I know it's been hard for you. You can't shake your doubts. You've seen too much of what it means to be the Spellbound. I know about the poison in your pocket," Faye stated. "Surprised you didn't poison all those cookies, but then you'd likely have gotten yourself by accident too. I bet you never met a cookie you didn't eat eventually."

To his credit, Jacques didn't flinch or try to lie his way out it. The elder played the vapid man of leisure really well, but Faye knew he was just as hard as any Grimnoir. He reached for his shirt pocket and removed a small vial. "It is a lethal neurotoxin. The effects are immediate and painless. Of course, I thought about using it many times since we met, believe me. Yet, I have refrained. I would ask you to show me the same courtesy now. Since you did not immediately take my head upon your return, then I can only assume Zachary showed you the future, and perhaps now you understand my dilemma. Was it the same one I saw?"

"You saw *a* future, but it ain't the only one."

"So there are more possible outcomes now? That is certainly better than before." There was a glimmer of hope in Jacques' voice.

And then Faye took that hope and squashed it. "More, sure, but most are still evil. So darn many evil ones that I couldn't even guess which one it was you saw that got you spun up enough to have Whisper murder me in the first place. You're still more than likely right, and I'm more than likely going to meet a bad end. So today's your lucky day, Jacques. I get it. I know why you're willing to do what you're willing to do."

"I am so very sorry." And she knew he was totally sincere.

"So yeah, you're right. One day the society will probably have to turn on me, and the only real question is, do you do it now while you can maybe still handle me, or do you wait to see, hope against hope, that maybe I get lucky and master this thing, but if you have mercy, and wait, and get it wrong, then you know I'll beat you all. You didn't say that before, but you know I'm already stronger than Sivaram ever was. Hard as he was, you *know* I'm better. If the Power is experimenting on Actives, you know I'll show it better than Sivaram ever could manage. I scare you now. You give me time and you know you'll never be able to take me."

Jacques nodded slowly. "You are correct, Faye. We have taken an oath to protect man from magic. You understand now what your magic is truly capable of. That is the quandary I find myself in. You are not yet, but may well be, the greatest threat to innocent life we have ever seen."

"Only I've got a bigger problem for you." Faye reached down and opened the satchel. The pictures she wanted had been left right on top of the stack. They were easy to find, all crumpled up by Zachary's frustrated hands. "There's something bigger coming. Something Zachary couldn't even draw, and as scary as the Spellbound curse is, the Enemy is *worse.*"

Jacques took the picture and looked at the ragged, blood-smeared hole torn in the page. "What manner of madness is this?" But much as when Faye had studied it before, the longer you started at the chaotic patterns, the more the Enemy took shape. Jacques gasped and dropped it almost as if it burned.

"You can feel it looking back, can't you?"

"It is real, then." Jacques unconsciously rubbed his hands on his pants, as if he'd touched something icky and wanted it off his skin. "Sweet, merciful God, it is real."

"Told you so. I was right. Mr. Sullivan was right. Even the Chairman was right. Most of all, the Power was right. And all the bad endings you can imagine from the Spellbound curse won't make a lick of difference, because if we don't stop that first, then there won't be any future at all. So evil as you think I may become, that thing is evil *now*. I ain't got nothing on it."

The picture of the Enemy had fallen on the rug. Jacques was still staring at it, like it wanted to crawl out of the ink and eat their souls. "What do you intend to do?"

"I don't know yet. Win...Somehow."

He was shaken, but he found his spine. "What do you want from me? What can I do to help?"

"Tell the elders I'm still alive, and then tell them to stay out of my way. Convince them that we're about to get attacked, everywhere, and that we'll need to be ready. Convince *everybody*. The pictures show men that ain't really men, and they're hiding, waiting, all over the whole wide world, ready to start collecting Actives. I need to find my friends before it's too late. They don't know what they're getting into against this old samurai with the shadow living inside his head. They're in the pictures, in a city with funny buildings and oriental writing on the signs."

Jacques was still distracted by the idea that he'd been wrong, that magic was about to be chased from the world, and all life on Earth was about to be extinguished. "Shanghai. Jake Sullivan's expedition is in Shanghai," he mumbled.

Faye got up and gathered her meager belongings. "Power made me the Spellbound for a reason. Some of the other folks it picked before weren't good enough, so I need to set things straight, take back things that have been done wrong. I've got some things I need to do first, then I'm going to Shanghai to beat this thing once and for all," she stated with grim determination before she Traveled away.

Then she nearly scared Jacques to death for a second time when she reappeared a moment later. "Wait...Where is Shanghai, anyway?"

Evil Fay

Chapter 15

If there is one lesson which I could pass down it is this: It does not matter what situation the adventurer finds himself in, from stalking lions in the tall grass, to living among cannibal tribes in New Guinea, or riding a raft over a giant waterfall. If you expect to survive, you must keep your wits about you. You must keep your firearms clean, your knives sharp, and—if you are lucky enough to have it—your magic ready, but no amount of Power or equipment or fancy kit will make up for a lack of brains and guts. When danger looms, don't hesitate, commit.

That reminds me of a story about this one time I was mountaineering in Tibet . . .

—Lance S. Talon,
Journey Into Danger, 1923

Free City of Shanghai

IT WOULD BE THE LAST TIME the commanders would meet before the attack. The main floor of the rotting safe house was absolutely packed. It was dangerous to put them all here, as a single Japanese artillery shell could cut the head right off their conspiracy and end their hastily laid plans in one ugly strike, but it was necessary. Sullivan would trust any of these men with his life, but he hadn't been able to brief them on all the details before leaving the *Traveler,* partly because they'd been worried about somebody getting rolled up by the secret police, but mostly because at that point he hadn't really worked out all the details.

The seventeenth was the date of the riot they'd paid for, and it was coming up fast.

Luckily, a coded message had arrived from Buckminster Fuller, and it had contained the last thing he'd been hoping for. The note had read: *It works. Mostly.* And then there had been a handful of doodles and numbers which would have seemed like gibberish to anybody else, but Sullivan had gotten the idea. It wasn't perfect. Not even close, but it might give them a shot.

Sullivan had sent for the others. It had taken another two days to move everyone out of sight of the stepped up patrols and army of snitches, but he'd gotten them all here. It was good to see them. Luckily they hadn't lost a knight to the city yet. Shanghai was such a large, busy, crime-ridden city that even though the Imperium had the local government under their thumb, they couldn't possibly watch everything.

The senior members of the expedition were still committed as ever. A week hiding in Shanghai's slums hadn't dulled the knights' enthusiasm. Barns had come representing the *Traveler*. Sullivan had hoped to leave the ship out of the assassination attempt, but that wasn't looking likely, considering how Fuller's gizmo worked. Fuller's plan sounded nuts, but Barns swore up and down the Marauders could pull it off.

So far they'd covered the basics, assigned duties and decided who would best serve in which element of the assault, determined their areas of responsibilities, and planned their potential escape routes. If the Grimnoir were going to succeed in exposing the false Chairman, then they would need to execute the plan flawlessly, and that meant that they needed to go over every last detail with painstaking care.

Lance whistled at a particularly bad detail. "The hell you say. *How* many Iron Guards?"

"I did not misspeak. For a ceremony such as this, there will be at least forty, perhaps as many as one hundred," Zhao answered. "Our spy at the last event counted sixty Iron Guards that he could see. Plus he suspected there were more hidden in the crowd, dressed as regular soldiers or administrators."

"Those were not Iron Guard," Toru interjected. "Any of my former order would be proudly wearing his best uniform at such an event. It would be shameful and dishonorable to do otherwise... But the Shadow Guard, on the other hand... I would expect at least a squad of Fades and Travelers to be present and most likely in disguise."

There were five thousand Imperium soldiers garrisoned around the "Free City" of Shanghai, but the only ones he was really worried about were the ones who would be at the ceremony. If Big Eared Du's Yuesheng Greens did their job, the majority of the Imperium military and police would be too busy to interfere. Twenty thousand criminals throwing a riot was pretty hard to ignore, even in Shanghai. "And how many regular Imperium troops will there be at the estate?" Sullivan asked. "Just because somebody isn't a magical heavy hitter don't mean they can't still put a bullet into one of us. What're we talking about?"

"There are five platoons of Imperium scum..." Zhao caught himself and looked over at Toru. Luckily, Toru didn't seem to be paying attention, or he was working on his diplomacy and had simply let it pass. "Five platoons of Imperium soldiers have been taken from the front, and are now traveling with the Chairman. Normally there are two such groups stationed at the Imperium Section in New City."

Sullivan walked slowly around the map of Shanghai. It was a big map, stolen from the British bank's offices, and they'd had to bring in every table in the place to set it up. He took in the various coins, bottle caps, cigarette butts, baseball cards, and even a couple of toy soldiers, which represented his forces, and the wooden blocks, which represented the Imperium. His own icon was a rock, and it was sitting smack dab in the middle of the Imperium Section, right in the Chairman's face. He figured since their air power was now involved and at risk, he might as well make the best use out of it. Sullivan was going to take the *fast way down.*

"What's an Imperium platoon run at, Toru?" Lance asked.

"It depends on its mission and its operational status. A fully reinforced Imperium weapons platoon would have a maximum of sixty-four men each."

"Japs run their units bigger than the AEF did. That's...four hundred and forty-eight soldiers."

"I did not know Beasties could do multiplication," Toru said flatly. "Keep in mind, these are troops recently brought from the front, so it is only because their unit has demonstrated considerable martial prowess, and many of them will have been summoned in order to receive high commendations. It is an incredible honor to serve as military escorts for a visit from the Chairman. They will all be experienced warriors."

"Oh good. So if any villages full of defenseless Chinamen show up needing to be massacred, they'll be ready," Lance said. Most of the room laughed. It helped break the tension.

Toru scowled, but didn't respond. Which was good, because Lady Origami was quietly standing in the back of the room, and Sullivan knew she was just itching for an excuse to make Toru spontaneously combust. "There are other complications as well. I know that there were two *gakutensuko* stationed at the palace, previously. They may be present."

"Mechanical men?" Diamond asked. His team had fought them at Mason Island.

"Similar to those American...*robots*. But the *gakutensuko* are superior in virtually every way. Speed, durability, decision making..."

"You once said their guns are smaller," Sullivan pointed out.

"Size is not everything," Toru declared. Several of the American knights snickered, and this time Toru didn't seem to have any clue why.

"Those could be a problem, if we get in, but before that I see a few problems with our approach." Diamond was leading one of the three assault elements. As a Mover, he didn't even need to approach the map to move the baseball card which represented his group. Sullivan noticed it was a Ruth card. The Babe simply floated off the paper and down the blue line of the Whangpoo River. "This bridge into the section is wide open. How are we supposed to make it past this checkpoint without being seen?"

"You don't," Sullivan answered. "Wait until I make my move, then hit it hard and push through. Hopefully they'll all be focused on me, so it'll buy you a minute."

Diamond let the baseball card float back down. "You'll probably get killed during that minute."

"Eh." Sullivan shrugged. "I ain't planning on it." He reached over and thumped the map. "Important thing is that both routes out of the neighborhood are cut off. We can't let the Imposter get away."

There was the polite clearing of a throat. Sullivan looked up to see Dr. Wells shouldering his way through the assorted Grimnoir. The way the thin man so easily bumped aside the robust young men suggested he was using just a bit of his Power. "The Imposter will not try to escape. He knows it is vital that he act as the Chairman would during this attack. To do otherwise would invite suspicion."

"The Chairman would never flee from battle," Toru agreed. "Never. In his own writings, he taught retreat is only acceptable when it is from a superior foe in order to save your forces for future conflict. For the Chairman to retreat would suggest that he had a superior foe. That is impossible."

"I reckon Faye would disagree with that," Lance said. Their Beastie was really looking for trouble today, but it was probably because he was distracted with keeping a bird in the air on the look out for incoming trouble.

"Regardless, he's not really the Chairman," Heinrich said. "So what the Chairman would do is irrelevant."

"Quite the contrary." Wells smiled like the broken predator he was. "He is not the Chairman, which means that he will feel insecure and thus go out of his way to act in the manner which he perceives would be correct. You saw how quickly Toru decided that the Chairman would *never* flee. This is an immediate assumption shared by all of the Iron Guard. The Chairman, being himself, would have far more agency in his decision making. Dosan Saito does not. His deceptions have become his own trap. No, he's not going anywhere."

Ian Wright wasn't convinced. "Assuming he isn't the real Chairman, because then he could just Travel right out of there whenever he felt like."

"Travel?" Lance cut the Summoner off. "Hell, that's the least of our worries. If he's still the real deal, you'd better hope he leaves. Otherwise we're all dead as soon as we piss him off."

"Fair point... But whoever he is, he knows we're in Shanghai, or at least he knows our Iron Guard is—"

"I am not *your* Iron Guard," Toru corrected.

"Whatever you are, he knows you're here because you've been murdering secret policemen in public all week! They're going to be on high alert because of your personal blood feud, or whatever the hell it is you've got going on here."

"It is true," Zhao said. "The *Tokubetsu Koto Keisatsu* have stepped up their campaign against us. They are offering a huge amount of gold for information. This meeting was very difficult to arrange. They are watching everything now."

Ian pointed an accusatory finger at Toru. "You didn't even attempt to hide your identity."

Wells seemed rather pleased with himself. "That was my idea."

"What?"

Sullivan stepped in before too many of the knights got worked up. "Toru's famous in the Imperium now. We're using that to our advantage."

"My continued existence is a personal insult to the Imperium," Toru stated without inflection. "Backing down from such an insult would be dishonorable. My presence ensures the Imposter's visit will continue as planned. To do otherwise would be to lose face."

"Absolutely," said Wells. "If it was only you Grimnoir, then Saito could easily make some excuse and avoid the city entirely. He'd simply leave us to be dealt with by his minions. Toru, however, is a slap in the face. He cannot be overlooked. His presence here practically demands a response from Saito. In reality, it is unlikely that anyone would question the Chairman changing his mind, yet Saito's insecurities will not allow him to make the reasonable choice. He will take this risk and come to Shanghai. He will continue on his scheduled business, *because* Toru is present."

The Grimnoir were thinking about it. Sullivan could see the wheels turning. They were a crafty bunch. "It increases our exposure and makes us all more vulnerable. You know he'll try to root us out before then, but this is the only way we can guarantee this son of a bitch shows his mug. He can't back down."

There were some murmurs, but most of the Grimnoir seemed to like the idea. Maybe a frontal assault against a numerically superior foe made up of the most elite military in the world wasn't totally bad. Which was good, because now came the part where Sullivan told them about the *crazy* part of his plan.

After the meeting had broken up, most of the Grimnoir had skulked off back to their own hiding places to brief their men, while the others had found places to sleep amidst the wreckage of the hovel. Toru had gone back to his sacred work. He knelt among the armored bits in a room filled with peeling wallpaper and spreading water stains and concentrated on doing the impossible.

There were only a few days left until his appointment with destiny.

Toru knew he would more than likely die fulfilling the final commandments of his father, but he accepted, even embraced that fate. The discovery of the Nishimura armor was a great blessing, a sure sign that his father was still watching over his mission and providing the tools necessary for success.

Working with his hands was a welcome distraction. He had been feeling ill at ease ever since his conversation with the newspaper man, Xiang. He had spoken of things which he had thought forgotten. Toru did not relish picking at scabs.

The suit was in better shape than expected. It had obviously seen combat, most likely at the front. Judging from the dents left by large, low-velocity bullets and the claw marks of a bear, it had been used in Siberia. Cossacks were worthy adversaries, but nothing like it would be facing shortly. Would the great Cog Nishimura ever have imagined one of his magnificent works would be turned against the Imperium? Toru did not know the answer, so he merely went back to testing each individual kanji.

The fit was tight. Ideally he would have time to adjust the armored chest piece. Normally the Iron Guard using such armor would have a few assistants to help him get into it, but he would not ask the Grimnoir for their help. To them, this was simply a device, a mix of machinery and magic. They would not understand the spiritual nature that came with preparation for war. They were simply incapable of understanding the connection between a true warrior and his tools.

He'd already tested the lower pieces. It took nearly an hour to get his legs and pelvis fully encased in steel and laminate, and then tied into the torso pieces. It was especially difficult to attach the hoses on his back. The floor creaked as he lifted one armored boot, but it seemed like it would hold.

He placed his hand against the design on the suit's shoulder and let his Power free. He could feel the energy collecting in his muscles, and he concentrated and guided it down into the spell. It flared briefly with magical light as the connection was formed. Another kanji was ready. Toru estimated the armor was functioning at about eighty percent effectiveness. He was certainly no Fixer, but he hoped that over the next few days he might be able to get that up to ninety.

Though Toru had heard the stomping of huge boots against the damp wood a floor away, his visitor was polite enough to knock. "Come in, Sullivan."

The Heavy entered, looked over the armor which was spread out across the floor, and then took a seat on an overstuffed and slightly moldy chair. "You getting the hang of this thing?"

"I was trained in its use many years ago, though I never had to privilege of using one in combat..." He realized that did not actually answer Sullivan's question, and he had too much on his mind to be obtuse out of spite. "I am 'getting the hang' of it."

"Will it be ready in time?"

"It is ready now." Toru slid his arm inside the steel sleeve, carefully guiding each finger into the gauntlet. He willed the gauntlet to curl into a fist. "It still requires some adjustment and fine tuning. I would like to test it more, but I believe it to be combat effective."

"You need a hand putting it together?" Sullivan reached down for the *mempo.*

"No! Do not touch that."

Sullivan removed his hand. "Easy there."

The armor made a slight grinding noise as he willed the legs to work. The boards beneath his steel boots popped as he took a step over. Bending at the waist was difficult without all of the parts attached for balance, but Toru managed to scoop up the face mask. "You are not to touch it."

Sullivan seemed more curious than offended. "Why not?"

"It is..." Toru sighed. "It is difficult to explain. This armor is meant only to be used by the greatest amongst my...amongst the Iron Guard. Bearing it is a sacred responsibility."

"Never knew you were the religious type, Toru." Sullivan leaned back in the chair and produced a pack of cigarettes from his coat.

"I do not subscribe to your superstitions, but I know what I believe. Just...just do not touch the armor again."

Sullivan lit the cigarette. "So it's a worthiness thing?"

Toru thought it over for a moment. In normal times, the Iron Guard would ritually prepare himself before donning the armor, cleansing both mind and body. "Yes."

"Fair enough...Did my brother have one of these?"

"He had been promoted to First before his death, so yes. He would have been given one if he had lived."

"If that was considered worthy, then I suppose I wouldn't want one anyway." Sullivan shrugged. "I'll be heading back to the *Traveler* soon with Barns and Lady Origami. Lance will be in charge here. Before that, though, I wanted to talk to you about the plan. You know what we're facing better than anyone, but you were awfully quiet tonight."

"You ordered me earlier not to destroy the hope of your men." Toru turned away and went back to tying in the arm to the shoulder piece. "You are willing to lie, dishonor yourself, and bring eternal shame to your name—"

"I think Wells is right about the man. Whatever Saito's real Power is, or whatever deal he's got with the creature, I think this is the only hope we've got of exposing the Pathfinder. The only thing that matters is beating it."

"So you intend to expose deceit through deceit...Despite the dishonor inherent in this, your plan is bold. Provided your assumptions are correct, your Cog's assumptions are correct, and your alienist is not a madman sending us to our doom in order to amuse himself, there is a small possibility of success..."

"That ain't so bad."

"Success is possible. Survival is not. We will surely die."

"That's what I figured." Sullivan took a long drag off of the cigarette. "Me and you, I figure we're done for no matter what, but I was hoping to get as many of the others out alive as possible."

"That will be entirely dependent upon how well we die."

"If that's what it takes, then I suppose that's what it takes."

Sullivan did not have the true code of the warrior, but he did have a code nonetheless. It was a remarkable achievement for a man raised in a culture with no concept of true strength or honor to follow such a path. Toru looked down at the Nishimura face mask he had set on the floor. Even such a weapon had been carefully carved in the style of their ancestors. It was a perfect melding of art and death. Only a true warrior was worthy of wielding the sacred weapons of the Imperium, but if there had ever been anyone among the Chairman's enemies who might have been worthy, it was Jake Sullivan.

My father was a wise man to choose his champion so well.

"We fought once, Sullivan, and we were unable to decide which of us was the stronger. I have vowed to finish that fight. I am unable to take back that vow ... However, the idea that we will die together now, fighting against my brothers and restoring my father's stolen honor ... It makes me glad that we will be unable to finish our duel." Toru gave Sullivan a small bow of respect. "Let them speak of our deaths with reverence for generations to come."

The two of them stayed there in silence for a time, Toru putting on his armor, and Sullivan thinking about the fate of his volunteers with a heavy heart.

Major Matsuoka of the *Tokubetsu Koto Keisatsu* used his binoculars to scan down the docks. There were no lights visible in the abandoned apartment building indicated by the informant. The patrol boat rocked from a strong wave, and Matsuoka had to lower the binoculars, as the added movement made him a little nauseous. It would not look good to get motion sick in front of his distinguished visitor. "Are you certain this is their hideout?"

The translator conveyed the question to the worthless Grimnoir traitor. They'd said his name was Pang, and that he was supposedly a Brute. He rambled on for far too long with his answer.

"He says this is the place. Toru is here as well as several foreign Grimnoir. He says that Toru insulted him, and that he is a terrible person, and that is why Pang is willing to give him to us. He says that their leader is very young, and he is tired of being bossed around by a kid."

Of course. It had nothing to do with the staggering amounts of gold promised for information. Those who would betray a trust were always the same, and when caught would inevitably try to justify themselves by saying that they'd been somehow wronged, and were thus justified in their actions. Matsuoka had been a police officer for a very long time and had dealt with many such men. "I do not care what his reasons are. His information was reliable last time." He turned toward the slight figure standing to his side, dressed entirely in dark, unassuming colors. "Does this please you, Shadow Guard?"

The terrifying little man simply nodded. He had been introduced as Hayate, a very senior, very experienced warrior, whose reputation for effectiveness preceded him. Hayate's Shadow Guard would be the ones to handle Toru.

"Radio the other units. Summon all of the men and surround the sites. No closer than a block. Avoid being spotted at all costs. If anyone comes or goes, tail them discreetly. Use disembodied spirits if available. I would rather lose one than alert the majority." He checked his watch. Raids always worked the best in the still hours before dawn. "We strike in one hour. We will hit all of the safe houses simultaneously. Standard procedures. Kill any who resist. If possible, take captives for interrogation."

The message was relayed. The operation was in motion.

Pang spoke in Mandarin, asking again for his traitor's blood money. Matsuoka spoke some of the language, but would not lower himself to talking to a dishonorable informant. He snapped his fingers, and two of his men came forward carrying a wooden chest. They placed it in front of Pang, who greedily knelt down and opened the lid. The gold bars had been neatly stacked in straw. Pang's fat face split into a wide smile.

"It is too bad," the Shadow Guard said. "They are normally so loyal. It is rare that a Grimnoir would break his oath."

"True," Matsuoka agreed.

"Nearly as rare as an Imperium warrior breaking his. Not completely unheard of, I am afraid . . . Oh, foolish Toru. What shame you have brought. Were you aware I knew him, Major Matsuoka?"

"No, Shadow Guard. I was unaware."

"We served together during the offensive in Manchuko, and then again during the Thai insurgency. Despite his poor judgment, he is one of the finest combatants I have ever seen. He deserves to be felled by an equal. Is that understood?"

"Of course, Shadow Guard," the major agreed. He had no intentions of stealing the Shadow Guard's glory. Matsuoka was a policeman. Hayate was a legendary killer of men, a ruthless magical assassin who came in the darkness, like a ghost from nightmares, leaving no trace of his passage, other than the corpses. Matsuoka was certainly not an idiot. "My troops are merely here to facilitate your needs against the Grimnoir."

"The Grimnoir are different from us . . . But in some ways, they are similar. They have oaths as well. I have fought them all over the world. They are stubborn and courageous, and seldom will one surrender. They are one of the few foes I truly appreciate fighting. I am thankful for the challenge they present." The Shadow Guard looked over at

Pang as he reached into his voluminous shirt. "Thus, I find this one disappointing." And then he disappeared.

Matsuoka turned when he heard the gurgling noise. Shadow Guard Hayate had reappeared right next to Pang. The hilt of a dagger was protruding from the intersection of Pang's jaw and throat. Blood gushed out of the obviously fatal wound. Pang was surprised and couldn't even make a noise, but the traitor did have some fight in him after all. He surged his Brute magic and took a wild swing at Hayate, who simply Traveled out of the way, appeared on the other side of the Brute, raised one foot, kicked Pang in the ass, and sent him over the side. He fell over the railing with a splash, where he thrashed for a moment before sinking into the dark water.

"Save your gold." Hayate went to the chest and carefully closed the lid. He walked back to Matsuoka and leaned against the rail. "We are fighting Grimnoir tonight, so expect casualties. You may divide this gold between the families of your men who perish."

Matsuoka bowed. "That is very kind of you, Shadow Guard."

Hayate looked at him with heavy-lidded grey eyes that seemed to glow in the dark. "That is because I am a very kind man."

They kept a few boats stashed in the flooded first floor. Crumbling holes where the windows had been made for great hidden docks. Sullivan had been impressed by the Shanghai Grimnoir's creativity.

Zhao was driving their little boat. He was the only one in view, standing in back, steering the small outboard motor. Lady Origami, Barns, and Sullivan were under the lifted tarp which served as a sort of tent-cabin. If they were accosted, Lady Origami was closest to the flap, because hopefully if anybody saw that there was a Nipponese passenger, the rest of them would be left alone.

Their little boat practically disappeared into the shadows of the massive freighters. It would take them a day to make it back to where the *Traveler* was hidden at this rate. It wasn't going to be a fun trip, all crammed up beneath a tarp, especially since Barns had pulled his fedora down over his eyes and gone right to sleep. He hadn't started yet, but Sullivan knew it was only a matter of time before Barns started talking in his sleep. Bunking together in the officers' quarters had taught him that, but the sleep talking would be extra annoying on a tiny boat stuck under a tarp.

"It will be good to get back to the ship," Lady Origami said. "I prefer to be in the air."

"Not me. I'm all about being on the ground."

"You are a Heavy." She smiled. "Of course you like ground. I am a Torch. I am of fire and live in the sky, but now we are on water. However can we cope?" She gave him a wink, and when he returned it, she laughed.

Was she flirting with him again? He really wasn't used to that. What a strange—

There was a thump. Zhao had just stamped on the boards to get their attention. "Quiet."

Lady Origami put her ear next to the tarp. Sullivan did the same. There was a noise growing on the river. *Engines.* Big engines.

"Patrol boats," Zhao hissed. "Many patrol boats."

The Grimnoir had posted guards. They were not sufficient.

Hayate appeared behind the sentry. He was a local man. Young. Strong. Fit. With the build of a farmer or a worker. He had a Mauser rifle, slung over one shoulder, that he would never have the opportunity to use. Hayate struck so quickly that no reaction was possible. One hand over the mouth, other hand driving the blade into the spinal column and twisting until it was severed from the base of the brain. Near-instantaneous death. Hayate had lost track of how many times he had performed such a maneuver.

The Shadow Guard silently lowered the corpse to the floor. He had timed his attack for the exact moment when the sentry was passing through the deepest night. He scanned across the rooftops, noting a few brief flashes of movement as his men took down other sentries. Hayate scowled. He would reprimand the men for such sloppiness. Even though he could see in the dark with his grey eyes, the fact that he'd witnessed their sloppy takedowns meant that the act of seeing them at all had been briefly possible. Such a failure was unacceptable. He would personally reprimand them for such carelessness on such a vital assignment. And a Shadow Guard's reprimand was usually extremely painful.

Waterboarding built character.

Hayate drew his short sword and waited. It was the preferred weapon of the Shadow Guard, small enough for close quarters, but sharp enough to remove a limb. It was not a fighting weapon. It was a killing weapon. Fighting was for the Iron Guard. Victory belonged to the Shadows.

The final rooftop sentry was visible for a moment, silhouetted against the city lights. He walked around a corner and simply did not reappear. There had been no sound. No sign of struggle. That pleased Hayate. That was how it should be done.

With the guards eliminated, now the real test began. They would take their time and search for inscribed spells of warning. The Grimnoir excelled at such things. Then the Shadow Guard would enter the apartment and begin killing. It would be a race to see how many lives they could end before the alarm was raised.

Hayate froze. The sound of a motor began far below, and a small boat appeared from beneath one of the rusting overhangs, leaving a white wake through the muck floating on top of the water. The timing was unfortunate, as that meant someone had just slipped his grasp.

Major Matsuoka would have to pick them up with his patrol boats. The small boat did not matter, as long as it wasn't Toru. The life of Tokugawa Toru belonged to one of his thousand brothers. Tokugawa Hayate intended to take that life tonight.

Lance Talon had been having a hard time going to sleep. He'd taken his boots off, but was still dressed, lying on a shitty mat in a shitty apartment building, wired from too much coffee and too much dwelling on the insurmountable task before them to even begin feeling tired. Maybe it was the excitement of being in a foreign city again. After all, he had been an accomplished world traveler in his youth. Maybe it was the idea of striking such a wild blow against the Imperium, which had murdered his family. Maybe it was because deep back in the recesses of his mind, he knew that this time they'd bitten off more than they could chew, and they probably wouldn't make it out of crashing this particular party. Whatever it was, Lance couldn't sleep.

Neither could Diamond, apparently. The Mover was sitting in a chair on the opposite side of the big room, reading a skinny paperback book. Since they were in the middle of the building and the windows had been covered, it was safe to have a little light, and Diamond had opened the shutters on an oil lamp just a crack.

"Hey, Diamond."

The Mover looked up and pushed his glasses back on his nose. "Am I keeping you up? I can kill the light."

"Naw... Can't sleep. What're you reading?"

Diamond chuckled and held it up. "Believe it or not, it's one of your adventure books."

Lance immediately recognized the cover. It was a hunter about to get run down by an elephant stampede, and even though that had never actually happened to him, and the scene wasn't even in the book at all, that exciting cover sure had helped sell a lot of copies when it had first come out. "No shit? How about that?"

"I found it on the *Traveler*."

Somebody must have brought it along as a joke. That often happened when Lance ended up working with unfamiliar Grimnoir. At some point, usually over dinner, with a big crowd, somebody would make a big deal about getting his autograph, and everybody would have a good laugh. It wasn't like any of the knights ever actually *read* it. "What do you think of it?"

"I'm a bit of a critic. I used to write reviews for the local paper even, but it's pretty good..." Diamond grinned. "Maybe a little far-fetched, though."

"Far-fetched?" Sure, he embellished his life a bit, what writer didn't? But for the most part, that was how it had really happened. He'd always had the wanderlust. Ironically enough, the only thing that had ever got him to settle down was meeting the right woman, and it just so happened she'd turned out to be a member of a magical secret society. "Says a guy who's about to fight the whole Imperium in order to defend the world from a magic-eating outer-space monster."

"Oh, not the adventure parts, or the cattle drive, or the auto racing, or the bare-knuckle boxing, or the logging, or the panning for gold in Alaska, or the big-game hunting on the savannah. Those I can buy. It's the chapter where you went looking for sunken treasure wrecks around the South Pacific that tests my suspension of disbelief."

"Nope. All true." Lance smiled, thinking back, good times. He'd learned how to use an atmospheric diving suit and had walked on the bottom of the sea. He'd even used his Power to play with the sharks. "Every last word of it, completely truthful."

"The ladies really don't wear any clothes there?"

"Hardly a bit. Just little skirts made out of grass."

Diamond went back to the book. "Well, how about that? And all these years I've been working for the society in boring old America, I've been missing out."

Lance rolled over on the hard mat which served as his bed. "You Pittsburgh boys lost a man back at the North Pole, didn't you?"

"Our Healer. Heck of a thing..." Diamond sighed. "You know how it goes."

"Sure do..." Lance muttered. "Damn sure do."

A piece of paper floated up from the ground and landed in the book. Page marked, the book closed itself, and then drifted to the ground. Diamond took off his glasses and rubbed his face. "You know what? You've inspired me, Lance. When this job is done, I'm moving to someplace warm and filled with beautiful, young dancing girls who don't wear hardly any clothes."

"Fiji was pretty nice."

"Fiji? Naw... I'm moving to Las Vegas. They made gambling legal there a couple years back. Just imagine how much money a telekinetic can make playing suckers at the roulette tables. I'll build a casino and social club with the winnings." Diamond waved one hand through the air as if he was taking in the majesty of it all. "I'll call it 'Diamond Steve's.'"

"License to print money," Lance agreed.

"Beats being a book reviewer."

Lance laughed. "Hell, it beats being whatever it is I am now."

And then a ninja appeared in front of Lance and stabbed him in the chest with a sword.

~⚔ Chapter 16 ⚔~

It has long been my philosophy that magic comes with a price.

—Baron Okubo Tokugawa,
Chairman of the Imperial Council,
My Story, 1922

Free City of Shanghai

TORU WAS PLEASED. The armor was coming together nicely.

Tonight was merely a test to see what needed to be fixed, corrected, or adjusted. Before he wore it into battle, he would ritually cleanse himself with bathing, meditation, and prayer. Each piece would be laid out carefully and donned in the order which was most conducive to awakening his warrior spirit. Everything had its place, a mixture of ancient tradition and modern effectiveness, all in a search for unachievable martial perfection. That was the manner in which Toru had lived, so that would be the manner in which he chose to die.

Getting the helmet on without an assistant was the most difficult part. Once the shoulder guards were in place, it was difficult to get his now-cumbersome limbs and thick steel hands into the correct angle. Not to mention that if he was sloppy, and burned his Power too hard while willing his limbs to move, he could potentially rip his own head off.

The world seemed different through the mempo. There were delicate kanji engraved onto the inside of the thick, shatterproof glass. They came to life and began feeding him information. The Nishimura armor did not just make him stronger, faster, and damage resistant, its true force-multiplication abilities came from the integrated system

269

which kept him apprised of the battlefield around him. He had not worn such a device since the academy, but one would never forget such a magical marvel. As the American knights were fond of saying, *it was* "like riding a bicycle."

He needed to replace the helmet padding, because the steel ridges were cutting into his skin. He wrinkled his nose in disgust. Despite cleaning it repeatedly, it still smelled like tobacco smoke. When this was over, Pang was getting a tetsubo to the face.

Toru studied the magical kanji unfolding before his eyes. Sadly, the helmet had taken more damage than he had expected, because it was sensing an impossible amount of magic in the vicinity. The Grimnoir tended to be above average Actives, but the majority of them had gone back to the other safe houses or returned to the *Traveler.* There were less than twenty of them remaining here, but the Nishimura kanji was sensing four times that number. Toru would have to adjust the sensitivity—

No . . .

The helmet had been carved with kanji to pick up outside sounds and amplify them to the user's ear. They were designed to cut out once the noise reached a dangerous level in order to protect the user's hearing, but whereas normal armor made a warrior less aware of his surroundings, the Nishimura had the opposite effect. There was a noise coming from the floor above. The briefest cry, then a sort of sliding. It was the gentle lowering of a body as the life pumped out. A trickle of plaster dust fell from the ceiling.

Toru surged his Power, bent his knees, and leapt. The suit lurched upward with surprising agility. His fist went right through the boards. The kanji bonded directly to his nerves, and he felt the steel as if it was his own skin. He caught hold of something soft, an ankle, as gravity pulled him back down. He pulled a man right through the floor.

He released the leg. The man hit the ground next to Toru, surprised and choking against the spreading cloud of mold and dust. Toru looked him over. Nipponese. Young. Strong. Dressed in greys and dark browns. Knives in his belt. A Nambu pistol with a sound suppressor had fallen on the floor next to him. The Nishimura warned that this man had been branded with three kanji.

The Shadow Guard looked up, and the shocked expression on his face said that he realized he was lying at the feet of a mighty Iron

Guard. Toru could tell that the Shadow Guard was confused and had not been expecting to see one of the ultra-rare suits of Nishimura armor here, and best of all, since he automatically assumed they were on the same side, he did not try to escape. Shadow Guards were usually Fades or Travelers, so they could be slippery.

A single drop of blood fell through the hole in the ceiling, spilled from the neck of the Grimnoir the Shadow Guard had just eliminated. The drop landed on one of Toru's horns and rolled down in a red line.

"What are Iron Guard doing here?" the Shadow Guard hissed. "This is Master Hayate's operatio—"

Hayate?

Toru lifted one metal boot and stomped on the Shadow Guard's chest. He'd forgotten the intensity of the strength-amplifying abilities of the suit, and the Shadow Guard nearly popped as Toru put his foot through the floorboards. Hayate was one of the best assassins in the Imperium. If he had found them, then their entire mission was in jeopardy. He jerked his foot free and moved to the corner where his weapons had been stacked. He took up the spiked steel tetsubo. The mighty war club felt like a pencil in his new steel hand.

The armor would be tested more thoroughly tonight than he'd expected.

Lance saw the sword pierce his ribs before he felt it. The ninja went to shove it in deeper, but Lance grabbed hold of the blade. It sliced through his palm, but he locked down hard. His other hand reached for the holstered revolver resting next to him.

The ninja shoved. The blade slipped through his bloody palm. Now Lance felt it like a fire filling his lungs. He yanked the big revolver from the holster, thumbed back the hammer, and jammed it up into the ninja's armpit. Lance levered it in toward the vitals. The Traveler realized what was happening, but too late, as most Travelers weren't near as quick as Faye had been.

Lance blew the ninja's heart out his side.

There was movement everywhere. Diamond's oil lamp fell on the floor and ignited. Black cloth boots with the weird Imperium toe cuts were landing around him. Lance grimaced as he pulled the sword out and it scraped against his ribs. There was blood everywhere. Blood from his chest. Blood from his hand. Blood from the other knights who were being hacked to pieces in their sleep. A black shape loomed over him, but Lance fanned back the hammer with his injured hand while holding down the trigger and gave the ninja three rounds to the chest.

Before that one was even done falling, Lance had sat up and discovered that Diamond was in a wrestling match with a ninja, so he shot that assassin in the back of the head. There was one more headed his way. Lance aimed and the masked face and fired his last shot. That ninja went grey the instant he pulled the trigger, and the bullet passed harmlessly through the Fade.

"Shit." Lance dropped the empty Colt and went for his other one.

There was a glint of steel. The Fade drew a throwing knife and hurled it, end over end, directly at Lance. It struck him in the arm in a splash of red, and he lost his grip on the other revolver. "Aaaahhh!"

The ninja quickly drew another knife and flung it.

This knife froze inches from Lance's eyes and hung there. Then it flipped around and shot back at the ninja like it had been launched from out of a cannon. The Fade couldn't react in time and the knife hit him right in the forehead. The ninja went limp and hit the floor.

Lance wanted to tell the Mover thanks, but he found that he was panting too hard.

Diamond stood up. Wobbling. He took a halting step, and then collapsed on his face with a moan. He'd been stabbed repeatedly, and there were bright red spots blooming across the back of his white shirt.

There were screams and gunshots coming from all around the apartment building. Shadow Guard were slaughtering everyone, and as the flames spread and Diamond's blood spilled out of his body, it was just like being back at his home in Mar Pacifica all those years ago, on the night the Imperium had murdered his wife and children.

Not again, you sons a bitches. Not again. Such a powerful hatred filled him that he couldn't even feel his wounds.

They'd be coming for the others. Lance activated his ring to send a warning. He was hurt bad. The stab wound in his chest was *deep*. He couldn't hardly breathe. The laceration on his strong arm was making it hard for his bicep to contract, and his other hand had been cut to the bone. He'd gotten a single healing spell carved on him before leaving on this mission, and that would keep him going and slow the blood loss, so if he found a place to hide, he could probably survive.

He looked at the spreading flames and the dead and dying knights. *Fuck that.* These Imperium bastards were going down. Lance threw his gun belt over one shoulder and began reloading his empty Colt.

Then Lance Talon went hunting.

Judging from the engine noises, there were boats all around them. While staying at the hideout over the last few days, Sullivan had seen the Imperium patrol boats from a distance. They were sleek, grey things, heavily armed, and so fast when they were moving that they left a giant plume of water in the air behind them as they skipped across the waves. Their little boat was dead meat if the Jap patrol boats were looking for them.

Sullivan kicked Barns. "What? Huh?" Their pilot automatically reached into his leather jacket for one of the Saive GP32 machine pistols he kept there. Those things had a cyclic rate like a buzzsaw, and Sullivan had a bad feeling they'd be needing them in a moment.

"We've got company."

Lady Origami was sneaking a peek out a hole in the tarp. She gasped as the hole suddenly filled with light.

They were being spotlighted. The patrol boat's engines roared as they closed.

Sullivan's ring began to burn.

The Nishimura armor was many things. Stealthy was not one of them.

Toru did not bother to hide his approach. That would have been impossible. The armor clanged and rattled as he made his way up the stairs. Normally, he was six feet tall and two hundred and forty pounds of muscle. In the suit, he was seven feet tall and over six hundred pounds of muscle, steel, and righteous fury. The tetsubo he was wielding was a five-foot-long, eighty-pound bar of heat-treated steel and spikes. There was simply no way the Shadow Guard could not hear him coming.

Luckily, like the first Shadow Guard he'd eliminated, they were not yet aware that he was not on their side. They were looking for the traitor Toru Tokugawa. Apparently their intelligence had neglected to tell them Toru might look like a walking samurai tank.

Two of the assassins intercepted him on the stairs. A Fade and a Traveler. "Master Hayate did not speak of any Nishimura-equipped—"

Toru swung the club. The armor may have appeared lumbering and slow, but it was *not*. The club whipped through the air so fast that it was a blur. The impact pulverized both of them. The Traveler died instantly, rupturing into a fine red mist. The Fade barely caught the edge and went over the side of the stairs, screaming. He might have been able go grey and survive the landing, but since one of his legs had been torn off and was lying there, twitching, at Toru's feet, he would not be of further concern.

There were so many magical connections moving within the building that Toru could not discern ally from enemy. The building shook as some powerful Active utilized destructive magic. At first he thought that the blasted ashtray smell had somehow grown stronger, but it was smoke. The apartment was on fire.

The next floor was a chaotic dance of knight and Shadow Guard. Most of the Grimnoir had left, and it appeared that the majority of those who had been staying there had been quickly overwhelmed. Sullivan and Koenig had left to ready their respective parts in the mission. Talon was the senior knight here, but Toru did not see him.

The few survivors seemed to be fighting with the ferocity of demons. He surveyed the room and found Mottl the Icebox, Simmons the Torch, Genesse the Mouth, Willis the Reader, and two of the local Shanghai Grimnoir of unknown name and ability futilely trying to fight off the quicker and numerically superior Shadow Guard. The Mouth was shouting commands in the lull between gunfire, trying to confuse or turn the attackers against each other. Fire and ice streaked across the floor to sweep away the Imperium warriors. The Reader was firing an American automatic rifle. One of the Shanghai Grimnoir appeared to be extremely skilled in a martial art the locals called *wing chun*, and had engaged two of the Shadow Guard in hand-to-hand combat.

The knights were using the sparse furniture for cover, moving and shooting, sending out bursts of magic, and trying to watch every impossible angle a Shadow Guard could choose to attack from. They had stacked the bodies deep, which was a testament to their courage, but it would not be enough.

He did not quite fit through the doorway, so he lowered one

shoulder plate and smashed his way through onto the main floor. Toru walked into the melee. Now the Shadow Guard were aware that he was not their ally. Subsonic pistol bullets and thrown knives bounced harmlessly off of his armor.

Iron Guards were trained to think clearly as they fought, to ascertain an opponent's abilities and then understand how they would best counter. A Traveler used his Power to get out of Toru's way, but Toru anticipated where he would move. Most Travelers were not capable of going very far, so it was a simple process to guess where they would consider a safe place to go. The Traveler landed to the side just in time to catch a backhand that nearly tore his jaw off.

Toru clubbed one of the Shadow Guard who was distracted fighting the martial artist. The impact launched him through the wall in a spray of red. The Grimnoir used that distraction to disable another Shadow Guard with a swift blow to the throat. Another Fade went grey to avoid the arc of the tetsubo, reformed, and ran for his life. Toru kicked the disabled Shadow Guard into the fleeing one, knocking them both down, and then Willis finished them off with several rapid shots.

Momentarily surprised, the remaining Shadow Guard retreated, Traveling away or Fading through the floors and side walls. Toru picked up a dropped sword and hurled it through the boards where a Fade had just gone. He was rewarded with a scream of agony.

Toru turned toward the injured Grimnoir and let his voice radiate through the magical kanji. He could see that every one of them had been injured, some worse than others. "Flee, Grimnoir."

"We've got men unaccounted for!" Genesse shouted back at him. In their brief conversation while training aboard the *Traveler,* the Reader had struck Toru as an argumentative, proud man. Those were useful qualities in a barbarian society, but they were hindrances now. "We can't leave them—"

"You can and you will! Sullivan's mission comes first. You must survive in order to complete the mission. These are Shadow Guard. The men you cannot see here are already dead. Get to the water. I will hold them."

They knew he was right. Nobody wanted to debate with the walking tank, so the Grimnoir took up their guns and limped for the stairs.

Toru waited. He knew what was coming next.

His brother, Hayate, appeared first, landing smoothly amidst the spreading fire. His Shadow Guard came next, appearing through the walls or dropping through the ceiling, surrounding Toru with lifted blades that had never been intended for this sort of work.

"Toru..." The First Shadow Guard did not bother to bow. "I was not expecting such armament. This is an intriguing development."

"Our father has seen fit to bless my endeavors by placing this armor in my path." Toru's voice passed through the magical kanji of the mempo. It could be magnified to terrible levels, but for now, he kept it as if they were having a polite conversation.

"I was frankly shocked to see you trying to save the lives of these Grimnoir. Sending them away is interesting...yet ultimately pointless, since my men will pick them off one by one as they attempt to escape...After them!" Hayate barked the command at the Shadow Guard surrounding Toru. "Kill them all!"

The other Shadow Guard disappeared, leaving Toru and his brother alone.

Lance let his mental control of the rat slip. He didn't speak Japanese, but he'd still understood the Shadow Guard leader's meaning clear enough. The ninjas were going after the remaining Grimnoir. Knowing he didn't have much time or much blood left, Lance forced himself onward. One bare foot in front of the other. He had to keep one hand pressed against the wall so as not to fall over. It left a bright red trail along the peeling wallpaper behind him.

There wasn't much he could do with his Power. There weren't many useful animals around here, and most things were running from the spreading fire. He kept on scanning, using his Power to pick out living creatures from the surroundings. There were rodents in the walls, fish in the water below, birds in the sky, and he kept grabbing hold of one, taking a quick look through its eyes to keep track of the bad guys, his fellow knights, and any other hazards.

It was hard work switching between so many different brains, but it was all he could do. Lance reached the stairs, already knowing that there was a ninja waiting in ambush because a mouse had smelled him and sensed the vibrations. Lance pressed the muzzle of the Colt into the wood and let the ninja have it right through the wall.

The door was harder to shove open because of the dying ninja blocking it, but Lance squeezed through. The Imperium man was squirting blood out of his neck, but still trying to raise his sword, so Lance shot him again.

Keeping his mind in multiple places made it hard to be graceful even when he wasn't bleeding to death. He nearly slipped and fell on the stairs. The blood from his chest had run down his jeans and into his socks, and now things were getting slippery. Smoke was coming out of everything and curling its way up the stairwell. He coughed and stained his beard with blood. The Healing spell Sullivan had carved on him felt like it was on fire. Without it, he knew he'd already be dead. Lance hoped it would be enough to get him out of this.

There was a terrible roar as a big chunk of the flaming building's interior collapsed above.

He took a gull past the bank of windows below. They were blacked out, but enough were broken that he caught glimpses of black-clad men preparing to jump the escaping knights. Lance gathered up all of his mind back into his own body so he could concentrate. He'd need it.

Second floor. The bad guys were looking the other way, waiting for his friends. It was going to be hard to aim. One arm didn't want to flex and the other was slippery with blood. Lance lifted the Colt and went to work anyway. He managed to drop a couple of them with bullets before a Traveler reacted and appeared behind him. Lance had been waiting for that, so he let himself drop as soon as he felt the change in the air.

The sword swept by overhead and embedded itself in the door jamb. Lance was at a funny angle, so the .45 only hit the Shadow Guard in the thigh. There was a mighty big artery there, though, and that Shadow Guard let out a terrible holler and dropped. He raised the Colt, but the Shadow Guard smacked it away. Lance crawled up him, grabbed one of the ninja's knives off of his belt and stabbed him in the chest, once, twice, three times, and on the fourth wild swing, the ninja gathered up enough magic to Travel away.

Lance fell on his face. That ninja landed in a bloody heap fifteen feet away, spitting blood.

There was a Grimnoir knight nearby on the floor. A Chinaman. Chen had been his name. Nice fella. Lance had taken a liking to him. He'd found that Chen had a good sense of humor and was always

going on about how funny his kids were. But now Chen was dead
because some Imperium asshole had nearly sawed his head off, so
Lance lurched over and took the sawed-off double-barreled shotgun
from Chen's hands.

The smoke parted. A ninja was coming his way. Lance pulled the
trigger and filled the hall with buckshot. *Fade!* He managed to go grey
just in time and came out of it unfazed. Lance pulled the second
trigger. The Fade barely made it again. Lance broke open the shotgun
and the shells auto-ejected as he knelt down to pick up some of the
buckshot shells scattered around Chen's body.

Lifting his sword, the ninja charged. He opened his mouth and let
out a battle cry. Most Fades never got to Heinrich's level of control.
The ninja would need to be solid well before he could hit Lance with
that sword.

It was a race.

Lance got the shells into the chambers and snapped it shut. The
stubby double-barrel came up as the Fade swung.

Lance won the race.

The ninja got splattered across the hall. He hit the ground with a
gaping hole in his ribs.

The Imperium bastard was still moving, so Lance tried to give him
the other barrel. Lance grunted as he tried to manipulate the shotgun,
but it wouldn't go. He looked down. His right hand wasn't responding
because it was lying on the ground, along with most of the rest of his
arm, and then the unbelievable pain hit. "Aw shit."

He hadn't won after all. It had been a tie.

Lance went to his knees. His right arm had been removed just
above the elbow. Blood was pumping out. He'd better do something
about that. There were still Imperium in need of killing.

With unnerving calm, he pulled off Chen's belt, looped it around
the stump, and pulled it tight. Lance screamed. Now *that* hurt. He bit
down on the leather with his teeth to keep tension on it until he could
get his pocket knife out to poke a new belt hole.

It was a strange feeling, pulling his own severed hand off of the
shotgun, but he did it anyway. There was movement in the smoke as
a ninja ducked across the hall. He fired the last round of buckshot
through the wall but couldn't tell if he'd gotten anything.

There was shooting ahead. The surviving Grimnoir had engaged the Imperium. He grabbed the nearest available weapon—the short sword that had cut his arm off—and used it like a crutch to get to his feet. Lance staggered toward the sound of gunfire, the tip of the sword dragging along the dirty ground behind him. Lance knew he was a goner, no denying that, but he was going to take as many Imperium assholes with him as possible.

The next room was a red haze. He hacked a Shadow Guard in the back, cutting him clear to the spine, and then he shouted for more. The other bastards saw him coming and ran. Lance went after them.

And then he got shot. He knew that feeling well.

Lance lost the little sword. He hadn't even seen that sneaky Shadow Guard who had appeared behind him and shot him in the back. Lance turned around and started limping toward the ninja, who then shot Lance again. It was a funny-looking little pistol with a big sound muffler on the end. Lance barely even heard that one, but he sure felt the impact. The ninja got him with one more round before Lance got ahold of his wrist and pushed the gun aside. Lance tugged him in and headbutted the ninja in the face. It took them both down. *That's what they get for using those pussy little 8mm rounds instead of a real gun.* Lance wrestled the weird little Nambu up, stuck it under the ninja's chin, forced his finger into the trigger guard, and put a bullet hole through the assassin's brain.

He got back up and fired the pistol at the fleeing Shadow Guard. "I'm Lance Talon, you sons a bitches!" He wasn't nearly as good a shot with his left hand, but he still hit at least one of them. "You'd better run!"

And then he was down.

His ears were ringing. He couldn't hardly see. The bastards had shot him in the back again. He started getting up, but they shot him again, and again. He slowly sank to the ground. Lance grimaced and tried to force himself back up, but his legs wouldn't respond. He tried to lift the gun, but a split-toe shoe appeared in his vision and kicked the Nambu away.

Had he bought the others some time? Had they got away? If so, then it was all worth it.

The remaining Shadow Guard gathered around him in a circle, seemingly in awe at the berserker fury of the American. They were warriors. They could appreciate a good death.

He was nearly dead, but Lance wasn't done yet.

There were always stories about Beasties so incredibly powerful that they weren't limited to just controlling animals, ones who could actually take over humans. As far as he knew, those were just stories, but he did think it was possible, just that it required more magic than he'd ever been able to use at once without fear of killing himself in the process. Lance had never been able to pull it off, and even poking around with it had told him that for him to draw that much Power at once would mean certain death.

He reached for his Power. There was absolutely nothing left to lose.

His vision faded. The world was a flat, grey, quickly shrinking circle. The Imperium ninjas were half-a-dozen glowing blobs of life, with minds far greater than any animal. He picked one in particular. The son of a bitch who had finally brought him down was carrying a big Type 70 light machine gun, so at least Lance had been killed by a real gun.

The Imperium men drew closer. A ninja lifted his sword to take Lance's head.

He gathered up *all* his Power, *all* his life, and then reached for more. He concentrated on the man with machine gun and treated him just like he'd treat a rat or a dog or horse. This mind was complicated in comparison, but it didn't matter, Lance just forced his way in and slammed that spirit right out of the way.

Now he was seeing through different eyes. Human eyes. There was his executioner, and there was his body. Lance was wearing socks. He'd died with his boots off, and that struck him as so damn funny he started laughing.

The Shadow Guard with the sword paused, confused, and looked to his laughing compatriot.

"Burn in hell, you Imperium fucks," Lance said in English, with his own voice, through the mouth of the mind-controlled ninja, which surely came as a surprise, and then he opened fire. He worked the machinegun back and forth across the five of them, shredding the ninjas with heavy bullets. He massacred them all.

The real ninja was fighting, struggling, panicking, futilely trying to reclaim his body.

"You want it back?" Lance asked as he dropped the empty, smoking machine gun to the floor. He then forced the ninja to reach down and draw his sword. How was it the Imperium did it with their fancy ritual suicides? Right across the stomach to spill the guts? *Bet that hurt.* The sword arm trembled as the ninja struggled for control, but Lance wasn't done yet. The sword pierced the ninja's belly and Lance forced the ninja to push hard. It was so sharp there was hardly any resistance at all. Lance felt it. Felt it just like it had been his own body, and he relished in the fact that it hurt worse than he'd even imagined. The blade popped out the other side, and the ninja's entrails tumbled out.

"It's all yours."

The Shadow Guard collapsed in a heap.

Lance let go of the hijacked mind and let his consciousness snap back.

His own body felt cold and empty in comparison. His magic was gone. Burned out forever in one final push.

Deep in the burning building, surrounded by a pile of dead Shadow Guard, Lance Talon closed his eyes and drifted off, dreaming about his family that he hadn't seen in a very long time.

The sleek Imperium patrol boat roared toward the small Chinese craft. A teenage boy stood at the rear of the boat, his hands raised in a position of surrender. Surely blinded by the brilliant spotlights, he knew better than to try anything. The first boat had already pulled alongside. The men were preparing to board and search it.

Major Matsuoka spoke into the bullhorn. "You are under arrest. Do not resist or you will be shot." The boy kept his head down, afraid. Matsuoka could not confirm this boat had come from beneath the target building, but it was possible. The boy would be taken in for torture and questioning. Just because he was young did not mean he was not a member of the terrorist resistance, and if he was merely an innocent bystander, then it didn't really matter anyway, because he was only Chinese, and none of those could ever truly be innocent.

His pilot moved them alongside. The Chinese boat was trapped between the two much larger patrol boats. There was a third boat on over watch. There were several bolt-action rifles, submachine guns, and even a mounted machine gun on each patrol boat, all pointed down at the target. Resistance would be stupid, but experience told Matsuoka that just because something was stupid did not mean criminals would not try it anyway, especially the desperate ones. Matsuoka drew his pistol. "Be careful," he ordered the men who were preparing to climb down.

Water droplets began to rise from the river. It was like rain...In reverse...

Suddenly, everything was *wrong*.

It happened too quickly to react. It was so confusing, so unnatural, that it took the major a few seconds to realize just what it was which had changed. *Gravity*. It was as if up and down had somehow changed direction. And in those seconds, he discovered that he was flying through the air.

The men who kept their wits opened fire, but gravity's sudden change had caused the ships to lurch so violently that aiming was impossible. Someone below...above...snarled a curse as they were struck by a stray bullet.

And then it all came crashing back down.

Matsuoka hit the steel railing hard enough to break a rib. The whole patrol boat shuddered as it landed with a *whump*, displacing water in every direction. Many of the men went splashing into the water, and a few unlucky ones hit the metal boats. His Nambu went sliding over the side. The spotlights careened wildly in differing directions.

There was a scream. He looked over to see that one of his men had burst into flames. He was thrashing around, batting at his clothing, but that only seemed to make it worse, and then the man dove overboard. The major turned the other way to shout an order at the radio operator, but he had turned white, *no, blue*, and seemed to be trying to *peel* his hands off of his frosted metal equipment.

The tarp on the tiny boat was ripped aside and a young Caucasian man lifted a machine pistol and ripped off an entire magazine in one burst. The men twitched and jerked as they were struck. Then that entire patrol boat was engulfed in flames.

Wincing at the horrible pain in his side, Matsuoka got up. Since they'd all been lifted and splashed back down a bit off to the side, the patrol boat that was supposed to be covering them did not have a shot at the smaller boat. He waved his hands over head, trying desperately to get their attention. That little boat needed to be strafed *now*.

There was a thud next to him. Matsuoka looked over, and up and *up*, at the very large man who had just landed next to him. A stubby

British revolver was stuck under Matsuoka's nose, and a giant hand grabbed him by the uniform coat and lifted him off his feet.

"You speak English?"

Matsuoka didn't answer. The covering boat gunned its engine. It was coming over to get a better view of what was happening.

"Hang on," said the giant, and then he smashed Matsuoka in the face with the revolver.

He hit the deck, head swimming. The giant went over to the prow, took hold of the mounted machine gun's spade grips and swiveled it in the direction of the approaching patrol boat. The machine gun roared. A line of orange tracers was worked back and forth across the approaching craft. They tried to return fire, but the giant was methodical, quickly walking his bullets directly into the muzzle flashes until they were out, and then back. He continued. On and on. Ripping the other boat apart, making sure that it was no longer a threat. He finally stopped when the other patrol boat's fuel tank ignited and it coasted to a stop.

Matsuoka shook his aching head, spotted a discarded Arisaka rifle, and crawled toward it, but the giant came over and stepped on his hand. "Not so fast." He lifted the revolver and fired a single round. The pilot, who appeared to be frozen to the deck, flopped over with a hole in his head. The giant reached down, picked up one end of a rope and tossed it to the smaller boat. "Barns, grab this. We're taking this boat."

"You will never get away with this," Matsuoka spat.

"Oh, I am." The giant casually pointed the revolver at Matsuoka. "And you do speak English, then. So first you're gonna tell me what's going down."

They did not look like brothers. That was to be expected, since the Chairman had known the affections of so many different concubines over his many decades. Rumor had it that some of the thousand brothers were not even from Japanese mothers, but Toru had never actually met one. Hayate was as small and thin as Toru was tall and broad. He was also twenty years Toru's senior, and had spent every single day of that training, teaching, fighting, or otherwise serving the Imperium. He was First Shadow Guard, singled out as the pinnacle of his secretive order.

It was a great honor to face such an opponent . . .

Yet, his father's mission had to come first. That was all that mattered.

"Hear my words, Hayate. The man you serve is not really our father. He is an imposter. Master Dosan Saito has usurped his place. He is in league with the Enemy."

Hayate smiled. "They had said that all of the bloodshed during the occupation had driven you insane...I can see now that they were correct. Spare me, Toru. I am familiar with your delusions. The report you gave to the newsman was sent to military intelligence for analysis. I read it and I was filled with an incredible sadness. To see one with so much potential fall so very far... You are quite mad."

"It is the truth! Master Saito has corrupted the dreams of Dark Ocean."

The First Shadow Guard looked over the blood dripping from the tetsubo. "You are like a mad dog. You are rabid, Toru. And you know what must be done to rabid dogs."

"Do not do this, Hayate."

"They must be put down...I volunteered for this duty, though I must admit I was not expecting you to be so well armed. I had been hoping to look in your eyes when I took your life with my sword, face to face, man to man, brother to brother...warrior to warrior."

His body was squeezed between steel plates, and bending at the waist was extremely difficult, but Toru managed to will the Nishimura armor to give a respectful bow.

"I doubt that I would be successful in talking you into taking off that armor."

"You would be correct."

"Luckily, I am a firm believer in being prepared for the unexpected." Hayate clapped his hands. A masked Shadow Guard with a huge tube resting over one shoulder stepped around the far corner. A blue glow radiated from the end of the tube. Toru did not recognize the weapon, but it seemed similar to one of the magical anti-tank weapons he'd seen Unit 731 experimenting with. That one had been powered by magic ripped from the flesh of Boomer subjects... Using such a device inside this enclosed space would be suicidal.

But they were Imperium. Suicide was all in a day's work.

"Farewell, Toru." Hayate Traveled away as the remaining Shadow Guard fired the device.

✧✧ ✧✧ ✧✧

"The safe house is burning," Lady Origami shouted to be heard over the engines. "I can feel it."

"Hell," Sullivan muttered, but there was nothing they could do about it yet. She could sense it with her magic, but the rest of them were able to see the growing orange glow against the night sky a moment later. There was nothing they could do. Barns was driving the boat hard, and they were launching over the top of each wave and crashing back down, casting a huge plume of water into the air behind them. The patrol boat was fast, but it wasn't going to be fast enough.

They rounded a bend in the river. The safe house came into view on the other side of the docks. The whole upper half was wreathed in flames, and there were shapes moving along all of the cobbled together walkways surrounding it. Giant shadows created by other patrol boats' spotlights showed that the shadows were cast by soldiers carrying rifles. There were at least three other patrol boats between them and the fire. Barns reached for the throttle to slow their approach.

"Hold on," Sullivan ordered. They were running dark. The spotlights were off. "The Japs will think we're one of them until they get close."

Barns took a deep breath. "If you say so."

Zhao put his hand on Barns' shoulder and pointed through the windscreen. "Head for that freighter."

"The rusty, listing one?"

"Yes. It has been stuck in the mud for years. If any of our friends escaped through the flooded lower floors, the path out will take them under the docks to the side of that freighter."

The other patrol boats hadn't turned the spotlights on them yet. *Come on.* Sullivan could only pray that some of the knights had made it out. As swarming with Imperium as this place was, if they didn't get out fast, they never would. One of the patrol boats must have spotted them because a spotlight swung their way, skipping across the water. Once they were made, there wasn't much they could do against that many riflemen along the shore. They'd have to leave the survivors and make a run for it. *Damn it.*

Suddenly the whole top half of the apartment building exploded in a blue flash.

"What the *hell*?" Barns shouted.

Debris flew in every direction. One particularly large fireball shot out the side of the building with kicking legs and windmilling arms. It was a huge, armored figure, wreathed entirely in blue flames.

"Toru..."

The flaming, armored Iron Guard crashed through another building with a terrible racket. A split second later their apartment building made an even worse noise as the upper floors collapsed into the lower, pancaking the whole thing down in a gigantic inferno. A huge cloud of smoke and dust welled outward across the docks.

At least the other patrol boat wasn't looking at them anymore.

"Head for that freighter," Sullivan said. "This is our only shot." Dozens of Imperium troops were already converging on the spot Toru had landed in. That building had caught fire as well. There wasn't a damn thing they could do for Toru now. If he'd even lived through that explosion, and the fall hadn't finished him off, then the fire or the Imperium troops would.

Barns killed the engine and let them drift toward the freighter.

"They'll be coming out over there," Zhao pointed at a spot in the black muck beneath the crumbling stone.

"Keep your eyes peeled," Sullivan told the others, as he walked toward the back of the patrol boat.

The Imperium copper was there, shackled to the rail with his own handcuffs. Sullivan didn't know how to read the Japanese police rank insignia, but this one had been wearing the fanciest uniform, and that usually meant they were in charge. Sullivan pulled the rag out of his mouth, and the Jap gasped for breath. Sullivan knelt next to him. "I'm gonna make this quick. How many safe houses did you hit?"

"Go to hell, Grimnoir."

Sullivan reached up and broke the cop's pinky finger. "Try again."

The Jap grimaced but did not speak or cry out.

Zhao had joined him. The kid seemed totally unmoved by the Imperium man's plight. Many of his men had been in that safe house. If anything, Zhao would have even less mercy. "Do you want me to freeze him?"

"I got this." Sullivan pried loose the next finger and broke it too.

"Gah." The cop ground his teeth together.

Sullivan broke another.

"Three. We knew of three hideouts."

Shit. Sullivan looked at Zhao. There were only four in total. This was bad.

"Who sold us out?" Zhao demanded.

Sullivan took up the next finger.

"A fat Brute. Pang."

Zhao gasped. "No. You lie."

"It is not the first time. He has been an informant for years."

"I'll kill him," Zhao snarled.

"He is already dead. Master Hayate was disgusted by his disloyalty. Fat Pang is dead, like you soon will be."

Barns gave a sharp, attention-grabbing whistle. "Got somebody swimming." He whistled again. "Hey! Over here. Ori, grab that life preserver."

Sullivan breathed a sigh of relief. At least somebody had made it. The other boats were distracted by the destruction, so they might still be able to get out of here.

"I demand to be released. I am Major Matsuoka of the *Tokubetsu Koto Keisatsu.* My men will—"

"Wait. Your name is *Matsuoka?*" Zhao asked slowly. Sullivan shuddered. It was like all the natural warmth had just been sucked from the air. "Major Matsuoka?"

"Yes. I am the commander of the Second Sector Garrison. You will free me or face terrible consequences."

Sullivan could feel the sudden Power draw in the air. "You're the one who had my mother and father tortured." It dropped ten degrees in an instant. "You're the one who ordered their execution." The air got colder. "You're the one who had their bodies . . ." *colder.* "hung on a bridge for the whole city to see."

So very cold.

Matsuoka began shaking uncontrollably.

There was a sphere of terrible, piercing, life-sucking cold, and it was directed at the secret policeman. Matsuoka's skin was turning blue. "You put up a sign. You called them traitors. Enemies of the people, it said. The sign encouraged everyone to throw rocks at the bodies. And people did, because that is what traitors deserve . . ."

Sullivan was shivering. The policeman's skin was starting to pucker and crystalize. He thought about just pulling the Webley and putting a bullet into the man. It didn't make tactical sense to waste Zhao's valuable Power, simply because they might be needing every bit they could scrape up if they got spotted and had to fight their way out, but then again, sometimes you just had to get your personal business out of the way. He looked to Zhao. "Don't let him start screaming, because I don't want the attention."

"Do not worry." Zhao's brows were knit in concentration. "He won't."

The policeman looked to Sullivan, eyes pleading, but only steam was coming out of his open mouth. Blood turned to slush and froze in his veins. Then the water in his eyes turned to ice and his eyeballs cracked.

"All yours, kid." Sullivan walked away.

The air was considerably warmer at the front of the boat, but Sullivan remained chilled to the bone. He counted four heads bobbing on the water, all of them holding onto a life preserver or each other as Barns hauled them in. Sullivan took hold of the rope too and dragged them in faster. It was three men from the *Traveler* and one of Zhao's men. The first one pulled into the boat was young Mike Willis. He'd been shot and had one hand pressed to his side. Blood was coming from between his fingers.

"Where's everybody else?" Sullivan asked.

"We're it," the knight gasped. "Five of us made it to the bottom. Mottl got stuck in the tunnel and drowned... I couldn't pull him out in time. There wasn't anybody behind us."

"Lance?"

He shook his head. "Just me, Genesse, Simmons, and Yip."

"Hell..." Sullivan looked to the giant funeral pyre, but there was no hope to be found there. The smoke was stinging his eyes.

There was a crack at the back of the boat as Zhao kicked the superchilled handcuffs and the chain snapped in two, then a splash as the frozen policeman rolled into the river.

They'd have to regroup. Figure out how bad they'd been hit... But he feared the answer. *Was there any coming back from this?* "Barns, get us out of here."

Toru
Explosion

⚔ Chapter 17 ⚔

If I only had to fight one enemy, this war would already be won. Instead I have the Kaiser's zombies and wizards on one front and your wife and her blasted devil monk on the other. I do not care how strong his magic or how true his prophecies. He is a malignant growth on the Motherland and if you do not remove him then I will find someone who will. You are aware of what the men with the black rings would do if they learned of his abominable experiments.

—General Aleksei Rybakov,
Personal correspondence to Tsar Nicholas II. 1916

Somewhere in Eastern Europe

ZACHARY had not written the man's name under his picture. He'd only given him a title. *The Black Monk.*

Faye knew nothing about the Black Monk, nothing at all.

Except that she was supposed to kill him.

He hadn't been hard to find. She didn't really know her way around, she didn't even speak the language, but luckily for her, one of the many pictures of this event had showed a road sign with the names of two towns and the distance between them. It had taken a lot of Traveling in constant short hops, and then sleeping overnight like a hobo on a train that was heading east, and then a lot more Traveling the next day too to get there. She hadn't asked Jacques for directions, because frankly, she didn't really want him involved. Did Jacques or the Grimnoir even know who the Black Monk was? Did it matter?

Her magic was burning bright. Her head map was showing her a larger area. She'd been in the building when Zachary had climbed into the furnace, so she suspected that she'd stolen his connection to the Power too. Magically, she was fine, but physically and emotionally, she was a mess. She was tired, hungry, and still smelled like Dead City. Faye knew she probably looked a little crazy, with crazy-person hair that had bits of plants and burlap stuck in it, but that's what she got for sleeping on a train like a hobo.

She was all by herself. And knowing what she knew now, that was probably for the best. Jacques had said the Spellbound couldn't have friends, but even he didn't realize just how dangerous she could become to everyone. There was a job that only she could do, and anyone around her might get consumed in the process.

Faye had spent so much of her life surrounded by people, with a huge family crammed into one tiny shack, but she'd spent most of those years living another life inside her own head. She hadn't minded the idea of being lonely back then so much. Heck, she might have welcomed the idea. It wasn't until finding Grandpa and the years in California, and then the Grimnoir knights after, that Faye had found she didn't like being by herself. She liked people. She liked them a lot. But she didn't want to destroy them even more.

Alone. It was for the best, Faye told herself, even though the idea of maybe never seeing Francis again made her heart ache.

The road sign looked exactly like the one in Zachary's picture. She'd found the name of a town on a map at the train station and had been heading in that direction ever since. She didn't know how much ground she'd covered over several hundred Travels. She wasn't even sure what country she was in. There was a valley past that sign, and there was a village in that valley. She could see the white church steeple from here. The bell was ringing . . . It simply wouldn't do to kill the Black Monk in front of his congregation, so Faye sat down by the road sign and waited.

It could all have been an elaborate plot. Trick the poor naïve Okie girl, make her think all sorts of craziness was afoot, and then give her a picture of a man you wanted murdered and let her do it for you . . . Except Faye knew that wasn't it at all. There were plenty of easier ways to kill a man than to bring a Traveler across the whole world and trick them with zombies to do it for you. That was just stupid.

Plus, Faye could feel *it*. The Enemy was there, just outside of the world, and she could feel it pushing to get in. She'd felt it before, but hardly anybody had believed her. The Enemy was closer now. That was undeniable. And on the other side of *it* was her Power, that seemingly endless river of magic, but beyond that was the Spellbound curse, and the curse wanted to be used. The Power wanted her to do the job that Sivaram had been too weak to do. Somehow the Black Monk was part of that.

Faye got tired of waiting and got tired of smelling like Dead City and tired of knowing she looked like a crazy person, so she found an isolated stream to bathe in. The water was freezing cold, but it was worth it to scrub the dust of Dead City off of her skin. Bathing gave her a chance to shiver, but more importantly, a chance to slow down and think.

She was flying fast and blind, getting into things over her head. She didn't know why the Power wanted her to kill this man, but it did. What about all her promises to remain good? Was she about to prove Jacques right? The Power wanted this to happen. Every one of the Zachary's pictures of the event turned out the same, with her killing the Black Monk.

Regardless of fortune tellers or the wishes of big magical space jellyfish, Faye wasn't a slave to magic and she wasn't a slave to some zombie's pictures. She'd make up her own mind . . .

And as soon as she thought about that, she knew it was a lie. If she really wanted to make a stand, why even come here to begin with? Why confront the Black Monk at all? Why not just keep on Traveling down the road? Shanghai was where she was really needed.

Except deep down inside she knew she wasn't ready to face the Enemy yet.

She dried off in the sun, put on clean clothes, and checked the .45 Mr. Browning had given her and the big knife Lance had made for her, before popping into the village, being extra careful to appear in a place where nobody would see her. It was easy enough to do, since her head map told her almost everybody was inside the church. She picked a house where no one was home, popped inside, and ate some of their thick-crusted bread and strong-flavored cheese. Really, it was more of a hut than a house. Having grown up dirt poor and hungry, she knew how important that bread and cheese might be for humble folks like this. She felt bad for eating their food, but she made sure to leave a bunch of extra money in the pantry she'd taken the food from.

It wasn't Russian money, but she figured it might still do them some good.

Faye ate and thought. She didn't want to do this. She didn't particularly want to kill anybody, unless they were bad, of course, but she had to see this through.

The church was clearing out. The people were going home. Now was her chance.

She found the Black Monk inside the chapel. He was putting out candles under a big statue of Jesus. *Forgive me for this, and I'd do it someplace else if I had the time. Sorry, Lord.*

Zachary had probably given him the title because of his robes. They were big, billowy, dark things. The top of his head was bald, but he had wild, long black hair on the back and sides, and a huge, unkempt, bushy beard. He was very tall, very thin, but with wide shoulders and arms that seemed too long, and hands that seemed too big. He heard her footsteps on the stone, and said a greeting in a language she didn't understand. When she didn't answer, he turned to see who his visitor was. His skin was pale, like he didn't see the sun too much, and when he turned to look at her, his eyes were as black as his robes.

As she looked at his black eyes, he studied her grey ones.

He did not smile. His face showed no emotion at all. Not even a hint of surprise. He spoke again, and this time it was a challenge.

"I'm Sally Faye Vierra."

He looked at her hands and saw her ring. "Grimnoir?"

"Yes."

"English?" His accent was harsh, like gravel.

"American."

The Black Monk nodded. It took him a moment to switch languages in his head. "So, the Grimnoir know I still live?"

"I don't think so. Just me."

"They thought they killed me before, but I am too strong. My countrymen poison me. Stab me. Shoot me. Drown me in river. Bury me, and burn me. But I not die so easy. The Pathfinder showed how to grow new body, copied from others. I have hid, very long time. Hid in this *tiny* place." He gestured around the church dismissively. Faye didn't think it was so bad. The stained-glass windows were very old-fashioned and pretty. "I hide from Grimnoir like all the other magical factions. I hide from Stalin. I hide from the Cult, I hide from Machine

God and the Shaper and the Order, and most of all, I hide from the Chairman. I hide from any who would take mine things, and I *wait*... And I study, and I prepare, but for long time, I *wait*."

Faye had no idea who some of those folks even were. "Who are you?"

He cocked his head to the side, seemingly curious. He was certainly no simple village priest, that was for sure, especially if the Grimnoir knights had gone through all that effort trying to kill him. "You do not know who I am?"

"You're the Black Monk."

"That is one name I called. Man with so many enemies must change bodies every generation. Today I am a simple priest. I took this new body so I could hide. Before that I used another name to rise to greatness, that name Grigori Yefimovich Rasputin..." He waited for a reaction.

Faye shrugged. It wasn't ringing any bells.

"Really? Huh." the Black Monk scowled, now seeming a little less sure what Faye was doing there. "Before I take this body, I was one of very first wizards in world."

She didn't know what he meant by *taking* bodies, but Faye knew he was telling the truth. She could practically feel the magic boiling under this man's skin. He was powerful, more powerful maybe than anyone she'd met since the Chairman. And she wanted nothing more than to *take* that Power away. Faye shook her head and cleared her thoughts.

The Black Monk continued, "I was not the first. That is Okubo Tokugawa."

"Him, I've met."

He tilted his scraggly head the other way. "Yes. I can see it on your soul. Knowing Tokugawa changes you. I fought for his cause once. I was member of the Dark Ocean."

"You were there when they killed the last Pathfinder?"

"Yes. But it not really killed. Body killed, but it never left. It has been here, hiding, whispering, ever since. Tokugawa did not realize this. During the battle, it hurt me. It crawled inside my mind, made a nest, and hid. It did that to a few of us. Those harmed by it... It remains in your head, always a little piece. Always... *chewing*. I think am not alone in this. That is why you come? The Pathfinder?"

"Yeah. I'm off to fight the new one now."

"Ah, yes." He stroked his unkempt beard. "I knew this day would come. I knew it well for so very long. I have spoken to it in my dreams. It talked to me for years after the battle. For a time, I believed it. I listened to the words in my head and did as it asked. It wished me to help build an empire for it to use. It had plans. For a time, I did as it asked. I helped it. It gave me magic to heal the hemophilia of our heir. It helped give my words magic to make influence. Some I swayed, others I seduced. It put me in place to fulfill its wishes. I followed its counsel, and gave that counsel to the rulers and nobles who would heed me. I became great and important."

"You listened to the Pathfinder?" Faye was shocked. "Why would you ever do that? It wants to kill us all!"

"Not all. It will change things. Kill many, yes. Not kill *all* the things. It whispered secrets. Offered me much. You try to resist. You know it speaks in lies, but the lies become comfort. Soon, you bend, then you break, and you do as it says. I see now that it used me, but back then, I could not."

"What did it want you to do?"

"Counsel the Tsar to bring all the wizards together. Make them live in one place . . . Make them easy for harvest."

This was horrible, and then she thought of Zachary's pictures showing the skinless men carrying people away. "So when it finally attacks it can scoop up all of the magic it needs all at one time and nobody will be able to stop it in time!"

"Yes. Before it came boldly, but Okubo won. Now it creeps, ever so slowly." He made a little chittering noise through his teeth. "Battles everywhere . . . The Power must win every fight. The Pathfinder only must win but one."

"Is it still talking to you now?"

"No longer." He touched his thumb to the center of his forehead. "When Grimnoir murder me, the ghost in my mind, gone forever . . . It knew I could no longer serve. My chance at empire, ruined, so it go elsewhere . . . Whisper to others, corrupts them, gives them same counsel . . . I not know who. Does it matter? Look around, child. Every land does this thing now. I was murdered. My empire died, yet the empire which replaced it has gone on to realize the same goals, only bigger . . . Stalin has done more than I ever could have. This time, the harvest, very swift. I knew it would come back."

Now Faye understood. She understood the picture of the old samurai with the shadow in his head. She understood the picture of the skinless man, wearing a suit made out of a person, telling lies in Washington, and she realized that they were all in even greater danger than they'd expected.

She knew how all the pictures ended with the Black Monk, but she refused to believe it had to end that way. He had helped her, given her new information, regardless of what he'd done in the past or how much incredible Power he had for the taking, Faye did not want to kill him. "The time's come to fight the Pathfinder again. You were Dark Ocean before. Will you help us?"

"Help, child? You do not know its promises. You did not hear the whispers." The Black Monk chuckled. "Now you tell me Pathfinder has returned, I will go to it and offer my services. For this, I thank you." He extended one long arm, spread his fingers wide, and the incredible wave of force that issued forth shattered every stained glass window in the church.

Faye saw it coming and had even run all the calculations in her head as the benches were lifted from the floor and the tiles were peeled off the walls and the statues were blown to bits. She stepped through space, just ahead of the wave, and appeared behind the Black Monk. Lance's knife came out of the sheath and she put it square between his shoulder blades.

He turned, snarling, more magical energy building. Faye tore the knife out in a spray of red, and Traveled just as the altar was smashed into splinters. She'd never seen the like of this kind of magic. It simply seemed to make things come *apart*. She appeared on his other side and slashed the knife down one arm. He responded with more crackling energies, but Faye was already on the other side running the razor edge across his wrist.

The Black Monk took a few halting steps away from her. Calm, Faye lifted the dripping knife and followed him. The church was crumbling, hammered to its foundations over the course of a few seconds. She had just given him a couple lethal wounds, but the Black Monk wasn't showing it. Whatever his Power was, he was *tough*.

He ran for it. Faye Traveled after him, but he'd been ready that time. Her head map screamed in warning as a circle of magical energy exploded outward from his body. Her feet hadn't even hit the stone before she Traveled straight up, launching herself at the roof beams. She caught hold, then had to step through space immediately as he blew a ten-foot hole through the ceiling.

The dust blinded her for a moment, but her head map warned her that he was trying to get away. He reached a small door at the back of the church, fumbled with some keys, got it unlocked, and yanked it open.

And Faye was there waiting for him.

She ran the knife across his throat, real quick, and it opened up like a bright new red smile. He stumbled back, surprised, nearly tripping in his clumsy robes. In Faye's other hand was the .45. It came up spitting fire as fast as she could pull the trigger. Bullets him in the stomach, chest, chest, shoulder, then she missed, and again, and then in the teeth, and the last one hit him square in the right eye.

The Black Monk landed flat on his back.

The church groaned. The big brick stacks that held up the center were all broken now. His magic was odd, and she couldn't tell by looking at it with your eyes, but her head map told her it was like the little tiny invisible bits that made up everything—Heinrich called them *molecules* when he Faded between them—were sloughing apart. The statue of Jesus was on the floor, and that offended Faye, because here was a man pretending to be a man of God, but he secretly wanted to help the Pathfinder that wanted to gobble up all of God's green earth, and then she was glad she'd cut his throat and filled him full of holes.

Faye quickly looked around the little room that had been locked. It was some sort of study or laboratory. There were lots of vials and jars and beakers and things cooking over candles. There were magic spells drawn on all the walls and there were human body parts hanging from chains or placed on tables, mostly hands and feet, but there were a few heads and a big box of torsos. There were bits and pieces of guts and internal organs that she could identify from butchering pigs on the farm, because people parts really didn't look that much different on the inside, and all of them were neatly stacked in pails or stretched out on workbenches where he could draw spells on them with needles. The spells written on the walls were keeping everything inside from rotting and stinking. The Black Monk had been experimenting, drawing new kinds of magic on the parts, and from the big, meaty lump of different folks stitched together lying on the table, he had been trying to stick them back together to make new sorts of living things.

It was sick, and gross, and it filled her with rage. These parts were fresh. They weren't dug up from old graves. She wondered just how many poor innocent folks had disappeared from these quiet mountain valleys so the Black Monk could continue his experiments. In one way, though, it did make her really glad. She only liked to kill bad people, and this was one heck of a confirmation that he'd been bad.

And then the Black Monk got up off the floor.

"Killing you is *hard*," Faye complained. It must have been something to do with being from the first ones magic had bonded with, because the Chairman had been the same way. Her head map could see what was going on, though. His magic didn't just take the little bits apart, he could also put things back together, and that included flesh.

He couldn't talk. He tried to, but only blood came through the hole in his teeth, and a bunch of air whistled through the gaping hole in his neck. He lifted one hand, gathering up a terrible burst of his dissolving magic, aimed it at her, and let it fly.

Faye knew what to do.

She Travelled around the magic, laid hands on the Black Monk's robes, and then dragged them both back through space, reappearing right in the path of his magical attack. Faye let go and leapt aside at the last possible second.

The dissolving magic washed over the Black Monk.

His black eyes turned on Faye. Wide. Surprised. A little confused . . .

And then he simply came apart.

She could hear the cries of terror coming from the village and she could see them running around on her head map. They didn't know what was happening. One minute it had been a quiet Sunday afternoon, and a minute later their church was falling down. The bell broke free of the tower, crashed through the beams, and landed on the stone floor with a terrible racket.

Walking over, Faye kicked at the pile of black robes and slowly melting pink sludge that had been a real live person only a few seconds before. He was melting like the candles that had been sitting on the altar. One eyeball turned liquid and ran down his cheek. The last of his air was coming out of his chest as white foam. Even his bones were melting. She'd have to tell Mr. Sullivan about this type of magic, because she didn't think he had anything about it in his notes.

The Black Monk gurgled, spat out some pink fluid, and within a few seconds, melted flat out into a puddle on the floor. This time she was sure he was dead. There weren't no coming back from turning into a blood puddle. And then Faye got her confirmation when she felt the Spellbound curse steal his ancient mighty connection to the Power. She'd not really felt the individual deaths before, but she certainly felt this one. It was a weird sensation, like she was now somehow *more*.

Nervous, she checked her Power. The river had grown deep and fast. Faye closed her eyes and found that her head map stretched for *miles*. It was almost too much information to process, and she began to swoon. Faye didn't have time for that sort of nonsense, as she wasn't the "fainting lady" type, so she wiped her knife on the curtains, put it away, reloaded her .45, picked out the spot where she'd hidden her clothing and Zachary's art two and a half miles away, and Travelled there in a single hop.

Now she was ready to fight the Enemy.

UBF *Traveler*

THE COMMUNICATION spell was severed. The ring of fused salt fell and shattered on the table. Sullivan stared at the fragments, trying to reason his way through the implications of the news. The ready room was totally silent as the last bits of magical energy bound to the mineral slowly dissipated into the air.

He raised his head and looked at the others. The feelings were easy to recognize on their faces; disbelief, anger, sadness, even resignation. They'd been worried that the Imperium might somehow detect the spell, so Heinrich's report had been kept very brief. It hadn't taken him much time to tell them that they'd been sucker-punched. Three of their four hideouts had been hit simultaneously. The only known survivors had been the four knights pulled out by the stolen patrol boat.

The Grimnoir had been gutted.

Sullivan couldn't let his doubts show. They needed him to be the rock. He'd thought he'd left his soldiering days behind, but this was much the same. When you were in charge, you couldn't ever let your doubt show.

Pang must not have known about the small place where Heinrich and a few others were staying. Most of the *Traveler*'s knights were unaccounted for and assumed dead or captured. The local Grimnoir were functionally *gone*, the entirety of their membership consisting now of Zhao, the badly injured man Yip, and a woman who had been serving as a guide for the knights stationed with Heinrich.

It sounded like the Shadow Guard had been effective in quickly removing resistance in two of the three attacks. Ian Wright had been in charge of the last group. Somehow they'd managed to break through the Imperium perimeter. Knowing Ian, he'd probably had a spirit out and about, which had given them some warning. Those knights had made it out into the streets, and that raid had turned into a long, running gun battle down the Nanking Road. There had been no word from any of those knights, but there was still a possibility that some of them had been able to escape. Since they hadn't called in, Sullivan figured that was mighty unlikely, but at times like this, it was best for the troops to cling to whatever hope they had left.

He kept his expression flat. Inside, Sullivan knew this was his fault and he accepted full responsibility. He'd made the call. Dr. Wells' idea had seemed like their best option, so Sullivan had run with it. If he hadn't stuck Toru out there as a personal insult to the whole Imperium, would they have gotten this level of response? Sure, they'd been betrayed by one of their own, but it had been Sullivan's call which had put them all in danger. The Imperium had killed those knights, but they'd only been able to do so because Sullivan had put them there.

It wouldn't do to let the others know his dark thoughts. They might not realize it yet, but the mission still had to go on.

Bob Southunder stepped back from the table and ran one hand across his bald cranium. Even the experienced pirate captain didn't know what to say. Lady Origami and Barns were there, both of them looking pale and scared. Buckminster Fuller and Chris Schirmer had come into the ready room near the end of Heinrich's report. They'd surely heard enough to know how bad things were. The Cog and the Fixer were both stained with grease and stunk of chemicals from their project, which had taken over the cargo hold.

"Is your device ready?" Sullivan asked by way of greeting.

"It is based upon my previous nullification technology, only multireinforced and omnireconfigured to repel a portion of the recently discovered Enemy geometries instead. Despite the scavenged materials being insufficient to complement the tensegrity of the spherical—"

"Yeah, I got it rigged so it'll function," Schirmer said, quickly demonstrating the difference between scientists and engineers by getting right down to how things actually *work*. "The hard part is going to be where we'll have to have to put this dirigible in order to make it effective."

"Where exactly do we need to place my ship?" Pirate Bob asked suspiciously.

At least Fuller was excited that he had a new gizmo to play with. "The magically charged particles' range is functionally unlimited, but they must travel in a straight plane. The further out from the curvature of spaceship Earth, the greater the area of the nullification zone!"

"Real high altitude. Higher we can get this thing, the better." Schirmer explained. "It'll take a minute to move the array back and forth. Think of it like a cone. But the higher we get, the more ground we can sweep."

"Real high altitude, like where the entire Imperium can see us in broad daylight and shoot their line-of-sight Peace Rays at us? That's a hell of a good plan," Barns said sarcastically. "I'm a good pilot, but I'm not dodging-Peace-Rays good."

"Nearest land-based Peace Ray is in Japan. Given the altitude the *Traveler* is theoretically capable of, we would be over the horizon . . . They could be radioed our coordinates and start flinging death rays, but their odds of hitting us are slim to none," Captain Southunder muttered. "The real concern is, how close is that *Kaga* class we saw on the way in? We've been parked for days and there's been no sign of that monster on the teleradar device." Pirate Bob wasn't coming out and saying it; there were supposedly only a few of them built so far, and one had gotten splashed along with the *Tokugawa*, but they all knew that if the Chairman was in Shanghai, then that meant that one of the Imperium's super battleships would be close. "That beast and its ray beams are the only thing I'm scared of. Anything else in this sky we can outrange, ou run, or outclimb. Good thing I can control the weather. I can provide us some cover at least."

"That will not work!" Buckminster Fuller exclaimed. "The refraction of atmospheric moisture will cause a dissolution of the concentrated magical energies—"

"It won't shoot as far in the rain or fog," Schirmer explained. "That'll defeat the purpose. We'll only get maximum power in a clear sky."

"I'm just going to keep you around as Mr. Fuller's translator from now on," Pirate Bob said. "Thank you, Mr. Schirmer."

"You still wish to go through with this?" Lady Origami asked Sullivan quietly.

Sullivan nodded. "Got no choice. This is our only shot. He'll come to Shanghai for sure now that he thinks he's got us on the run."

"He does have us on the run," Barns pointed out.

"Yeah. So he won't expect us. Toru's probably gone, but I'm sticking with Wells' theory of the man. He'd come to the party now just to gloat."

"Is Dr. Wells among the dead?" Buckminster Fuller asked.

"He was with Ian's bunch. They made a run for it." Sullivan shrugged. "So maybe..." *Probably.*

"Too bad. He was an intellectual peer, a charming conversationalist, and I much enjoyed his attempts at describing my childhood based entirely upon my current speech patterns, an absolutely fascinating endeavor indeed." Fuller Said. "I would say that the untimely loss of such a great mind will be a terrible thing for humanity, except for that part where he was absolutely terrifying and completely amoral."

"Yep..." He'd gotten the alienist sprung from jail just to get him killed too. One more failure to throw on the pile. Sullivan turned to Southunder. "I know it's dangerous, Captain, but I'm still asking you to do this."

Southunder mulled it over. He turned and walked to the map on the wall, running one bony finger from their current position up the coast to Shanghai. "Even if we don't attract that *Kaga,* half the Imperium navy will come after us." The captain scowled at the map, as if that would give him any better answers. "I would ask only one thing. Before we depart this village, we explain to the crew exactly what we face, take volunteers, and then we ask every single person without an absolutely vital responsibility to get off. I know some of the local captains. I could call in a favor and arrange their passage home. We will make this attempt, but only with a skeleton crew."

The captain didn't want any extra blood on his hands. Sullivan understood the sentiment, especially today. "Agreed."

"What about the rest of Wells' plan?" Schirmer asked. "We need boots on the ground, but we're down almost everyone. Heinrich's got five men on the other side of the town, and the Shanghai Grimnoir are all dead."

"Not all of us." Zhao had entered the room silently. Sullivan didn't even know how long the kid had been there. Zhao hadn't talked much on the ride back or during the walk through the woods after they'd ditched the patrol boat. Getting betrayed by somebody you believed was a friend, and then executing your parents' killer, was a lot to absorb. The burdens of leadership were tough, even tougher when everyone you were in charge of was gone and somehow you weren't. "I will return to Shanghai and meet with Heinrich. We will still attack when Du's gangsters begin their riot."

"Assuming that big-eared bastard keeps his word," Barns said.

"I will make sure he does." There was ice in the young man's words. "If he does not, he will regret it, and then I will find a way to distract the military myself. This is my fault. Pang was one of my men, and I trusted him, like a fool."

"Naw." Sullivan shook his head. That sort of crushing weight didn't belong on a teenager. It was Sullivan's to bear. If there was anything he was good at, it was not being crushed under a lot of weight, and he'd gathered a lot over the years. Zhao was new at this. Sullivan had lots of practice. "You were lied to by a snake. Happens to the best of us. I brought us here. This was my plan. My responsibility. Got it?"

Zhao didn't respond. It would have to do.

Schirmer returned to his point. Apparently Fixers were compelled to tackle all problems, not just the mechanical ones. "Every last knight you pulled out of the river is injured and in no shape to fight, and our Healer's dead. Even if the new Chairman's one-tenth what the old

Chairman was, you'll need more men to confront him. I can go with you."

"I need you here to make sure Fuller's device runs right. Exposing the Pathfinder is first. Killing its stooge is second. We have to wake the Iron Guard up. That's all that matters."

"All right." Schirmer was a brave knight, but he knew Sullivan was right. Some problems just couldn't be fixed. "I'll shine the light so everybody can watch the roaches scatter."

"I can go, burn many Imperium," Lady Origami offered.

"You're going to keep this ship in the air when it starts getting shot at. I got this myself."

"You hide it, but I see your sadness. You think this is your fault. Being killed will not bring them back! It was too much danger when there were many of you!" Ori was getting upset. "Alone, you'll die!"

"Maybe . . ." There was one other, drastic, final option. He hadn't wanted to use it, because frankly, it scared him. He'd already figured it would come to this, even before they'd heard from Heinrich, so he'd retrieved the sheet he'd hidden in a compartment beneath his bunk. Sullivan reached into his coat and pulled out the folded sheet of paper that he had meticulously copied from the personal spell book of Anand Sivaram, when he had taken it from Bradford Carr. Sullivan carefully unfolded it and placed the paper on the table amidst the fused chunks of salt. "Maybe not."

It would just look like complicated scribbles and lots of weird geometric designs to most folks. Sullivan had succeeded in binding several spells to his body over the last year, but those had all been child's play compared to this thing. He'd thought of those as an intellectual, magical, and physical challenge, an opportunity to even the odds against Iron Guard. And even then each of those had been incredibly risky, with each one taking him right up to death's door before he'd forced himself to come back. This thing was a monster in comparison. It was doomsday. Buckminster Fuller scanned over it and then let out an audible gasp.

"I know of only two men this spell's been carved on. Giuseppe Zangara and the OCI man Crow. Zangara was a no-account weakling, and this turned him into the scariest Boomer anybody's ever seen. And you all know what Crow the Summoner unleashed on D.C."

Fuller swallowed hard. "It drastically magnifies the user's Power, that much is clear, but there is so much there . . . I would think that there could be terrible side effects."

"Don't matter . . ." Of course there would be side effects. You didn't screw around with this level of magic without dire consequences. Bradford Carr had been a fool. Zangara had already been crazy, but this thing had gradually pushed Crow right over the edge. Sullivan had studied Sivaram's book, and though the actual Spellbound curse the Grimnoir elders were so scared of hadn't been in there, this thing had been. He figured it was a sort of early prototype of the Spellbound curse. The elders would surely come apart if they learned what he was about to do, not that it mattered, since this was more than likely a one-way trip. "All I need to know is, can you carve this spell on me?"

Fuller was shaking. The others didn't get it, but Fuller did. The Cog could read magic, simple as most folks could read letters. One slip and Sullivan was dead. He understood exactly what Sullivan was asking, and God bless him for it, he manned up. "Yes. Yes, I believe I can do that."

As Toru had said back when they'd first embarked on this quest: they'd defeat the Pathfinder, or they'd die trying.

Rasputin

⇜ Chapter 18 ⇝

Dear Miss Etiquette,
My boyfriend is a Mover. Is it still considered opening the door for a
lady if he does it with his mind powers instead of with his body? And if
it is not, how should I broach this subject so as to not hurt his feelings?
                                                                    Signed,
                                                    Confused in Cleveland

Dear Confused,
It most definitely is not proper to use magic of any kind around a young
lady, especially telekinesis. It is difficult enough for boys to keep their
hands to themselves, let alone extra invisible hands. If he is a proper
gentleman he will get the door for you with his actual physical hands
and never use his ghost hands in polite society.

                                                    Miss Etiquette,
                                        newspaper column, 1931

Somewhere in Russia

IT HAD TAKEN what seemed like forever to find them and the nice
new airship that Francis had so thoughtfully named after her, but Faye
tracked them down eventually. She'd hoped for a pleasant reunion,
but instead she'd damn near scared the hell out of everybody. They
were jumpy, and it hadn't helped that everybody thought she was
dead.

Her magic was a boundless torrent of energy and limitless
potential, but her body was still human, so after she'd squared off
against the Black Monk, she'd had to get some sleep. Being the most

powerful wizard ever was great and all, but she wasn't stupid. If she got tired and careless, she'd still be every bit as dead as anybody else if she accidentally Traveled and wound up with a bumblebee stuck in her heart or a tree branch in her brain. As marvelous as Traveling was, it still had some limitations, but it sure beat walking like a normal old boring person.

She'd found a Russian fur trapper's cabin with nobody home. Faye figured that sleeping in a bed made out of bearskins was much comfier than sleeping in some hay loft or open field. And she was about to go fight the Pathfinder anyways, and sometimes a girl just had to treat herself to something nice. She'd eaten some old potatoes and a whole bunch of jerky made out of who knew what kind of animal which had been stored there, and left a big handful of money to make up for it. There was a bag of salt there for treating the game they killed, so she'd used that to fashion some communication spells.

Faye knew she was a danger to be around. All the time these poor Grimnoir had the Spellbound around was like keeping a rattlesnake in the living room, and they'd never even realized it. But Sullivan's expedition was surrounded by rattlesnakes, so what was one more? Besides, she knew they'd have no chance at all without her.

She was still rather bad at spellbinding. Sure, she had more magic than anybody else in the world now, but that still didn't mean she could draw it very well. She was still clumsy at making the designs, nothing like Lance or Mr. Sullivan. It took her several tries, but she finally got one to connect. She tried to reach Francis' Grimnoir ring first, but hadn't gotten a response. That worried her to no end, but she figured he was just busy. She had wanted to warn him about what she'd seen in the pictures about the skinless man in disguise who was whispering to the president. She didn't know who that skinless man was pretending to be, but Zachary's pictures told her that back before his body had been taken over he had built lots of fancy buildings.

Jane, Dan, or Mr. Browning would also know what to do there, but she knew that she really needed to get to Shanghai, so then she tried Mr. Sullivan's next, and hadn't been able to raise him either... Maybe he was preoccupied. He was, after all, leading a dangerous mission deep into Imperium territory. Then she tried Lance, and that link was completely dead too. It wasn't just that she didn't get a response from his ring, but like there was nothing to get a response from. Now she was really starting to worry . . . Hours passed as she kept trying to get the communications spells to take, and she cursed her clumsy hands. Heinrich's connected, briefly, but then his was gone too, like he was too busy to stop and make a spell.

This frightened Faye. Something bad was happening to her friends in Shanghai. She was preparing another spell, intending this one for Mr. Browning, when someone contacted her. Before, when the magic would activate her Grimnoir ring, she'd just felt it as a terrible burning sensation. Now, her much finer head map clearly recognized the magic as coming from Mr. Sullivan's ring before the connection had even built up enough energy to make her ring finger tingle. Sullivan's ring still felt like Black Jack Pershing, since he'd worn it for so many years before Mr. Sullivan. Everybody left a little stamp of themselves on everything they touched. Regular folks couldn't hardly see it, but Faye could now.

It took a couple of tries, but Faye got the spell to take, nice and clear. That was good, since she intended to hop right through it and go all the way to Shanghai, just like she'd once gone from Tennessee to Virginia in a single Travel. Only it wasn't Mr. Sullivan on the other side, it was the weathered old face of Captain Bob Southunder, and his brow knit in confusion.

"Where's Mr. Sullivan?" Faye demanded before the Captain could even speak.

"Indisposed. . . . I sensed the summons coming through his ring. Is that . . . *Faye*?" The nice old pirate was a smart man, but like everybody around her, his brain seemed to work infuriatingly slow.

"Of course it's me."

"I'd been told you'd died."

"It's either me, my ghost, or a really clever Imperium trick." She focused her head map down through the spell, like shining a powerful spotlight through a pin hole. This was only the second time she'd tried this trick, but she figured at worst she had like a one percent chance of dying badly. "Hang on. I'll be right there." *Clear.*

Traveling wasn't about distance. When you took two bits of far-apart space and smooshed them together, it really didn't matter how far apart they were on the flat, since the distance you actually Travelled was the same every single time, just the space between the smooshing.

It was just like how she'd solved Jacques' tricky mazes. He'd thought of it as cheating, but to Faye, that was just how the universe really was. It wasn't her fault if nobody else could wrap their slow brains around the truth. She didn't know if she had the technical terms right, especially since *smooshing* didn't sound particularly scientific, but that was pretty much how it really worked. The hard part about Traveling was being able to see in your head map far enough to not get yourself stuck into something when you got there. Most Travelers never even figured out how to work their head maps at all, so they could only go as far as they could see. Not Faye, and right now she could see right into the insides of the airship *Traveler*.

She appeared directly behind Pirate Bob. He jumped in surprise. His communication spell was shining back on an empty cabin. She was in a pretty big room for an airship, with lots of crates and boxes and a gigantic weird-looking magical machine with lots of spinning balls and cones on it, so it had to be the cargo hold, and there were eight other people in the cargo hold, mostly working on the big machine or getting guns ready for some manner of excitement.

"Hey, everybody."

She must've surprised them, because a whole lot of guns got pulled out at one time and pointed at her. To be fair, it wasn't like strangers suddenly popping into existence in the middle of your secret pirate ship was very often a good thing.

"Stop!" Pirate Bob shouted. He wasn't the type of leader who raised his voice a lot, but when he did, it certainly got everybody's attention. "Lower those weapons."

Faye felt a nervous, hot tingling building on her skin. Magic was gathering, hesitating on the border of igniting. She recognized the feeling right away. "Hey, pirate Torch lady. I forgave you for setting me on fire last time because that was all a big misunderstanding and you thought I was a ninja, but if you set me on fire again, I'm likely to get *real* mad."

The Japanese woman stepped out from behind the big machine. She hadn't so much as lifted her hands, but she'd been ready to make Faye combust. Apparently this Torch wasn't as flashy with her magic as Whisper had been, with all the hand waving, but then again, Whisper had always been the dramatic sort.

"It's fine, Ori," Pirate Bob said.

The tingling magic on Faye's skin drifted away. "Thank you. So where's Mr. Sullivan?"

"Recovering," the captain answered. "Now hold on just a second."

"I need to go—"

"I said *hold on*," he said, and the way he did it showed that even though he looked like a kindly old grandpa, he was actually a pirate captain and that she'd better remember it. "You're on my ship—"

"Francis' ship," she corrected.

"He's the financier. I'm the captain. So it's *my* ship, so you'll explain what's going on to *me*, missy. Is that clear?" Captain Southunder knew darn good and well that she'd killed the Chairman, and a small army of Imperium Marines, and he maybe even knew about her blowing up the God of Demons, but he wasn't about to take any guff off anybody on his boat, super powers be darned. "Because otherwise you can get the hell off my ship."

"Ooh, will you make me walk the plank?"

He sighed. "We're not that kind of pirates."

Lance was dead.

Faye couldn't believe it. She just couldn't believe it. Pirate Bob had broke the news nice as he could, but he might as well have stabbed her right in the heart.

Lance Talon was one of her best friends. He'd taught her, helped her, treated her like an equal, saved her life, even given her the Grimnoir oath. It was Lance who had taught her how to drive a car, how to shoot a gun better, how to make spells. The first time they'd met, she'd thought he was a profane squirrel. Lance was family.

She'd wanted to disbelieve. Lance was tough. He'd been everywhere and done everything. He was a thrillseeker and he was too smart to die. But she remembered the feeling when she reached out for his ring, and now she knew it was because that ring had been burned and melted and buried under tons of charred wood and ash.

There was no escaping the truth, and Faye simply cried her eyes out.

Lance's death hadn't been in any of Zachary's pictures, and that made Faye question everything. Were the possibilities spiraling out past what even the Fortune Teller could have seen? What did that mean for everything else?

The *Traveler* had been parked near a little Chinese village on the coast. The whole ship had been covered in ropes with leaves tied to it to make it look like more forest to anybody flying overhead or any ships on the ocean. The fact that the villagers had big camouflage nets ready to go told Faye that this was a village was often visited by smugglers and pirates like the Marauders. There were a bunch of little boats in the cove. Most of the UBF folks and some of the pirates from the *Traveler* were down there, loading their personal belongings. They'd be taken to one of the other Free Cities, which were just a bit freer, and boarding cargo vessels heading to America. Captain Southunder was sending them home so that they wouldn't get killed along with everybody else. That was noble of him.

The rest of the crew were busy pulling off the camouflage nets and fake tree branches and getting ready to take off. Except for Sullivan, who was sleeping off having a huge spell bound to him, and Faye, because she wasn't really part of the crew at all, and she was too sad and angry to be of much help anyways. The crew was muted and solemn as they worked. She wandered around, watching for a bit, but felt even more awkward when they saw how hard she'd been crying. So she'd popped up to the top of the dirigible to sit on one of the two huge gas bags to stay out of the way.

A little later, the Japanese pirate Torch lady climbed up a rope and got on top of the bag, too. She was wearing dirty coveralls, and a dark red sash, and carrying her shoes in her hand so she wouldn't accidentally hurt anything. It was totally unnecessary on the futuristic high-tech skin of the *Traveler,* but it was probably a necessary habit picked up on their old ship.

Now that Faye was paying more attention to the information the Spellbound curse was giving her, she could tell just how strong this Torch was. Her Power was amazingly developed, and that made Faye feel guilty, like she was peeking in on somebody's secrets. A little, greedy voice inside her head said that much Power would be better served with Faye, but Faye just told that stupid greedy voice to shut up. The Torch saw Faye, saw that she was crying, and came over anyway. She sat down cross-legged on the bouncy surface across from her and didn't say anything for a minute.

Faye thought about Traveling away, but something in the Torch lady's expression made it so that Faye didn't.

"I am sorry about Mr. Talon. He was a gentleman."

"Yeah, he really was," Faye sniffed. She hadn't expected to get all emotional and weepy in front of somebody who had once set her on fire, even if it had been by accident. "I'm gonna miss him."

"Of course."

"And I'm gonna avenge him."

Now the Torch gave her a gentle smile. "Spoken like a knight. Mr. Talon would be proud I am sure."

Faye couldn't help it. She really started to blubber. The Torch lady scooted over and gave Faye a hug, and that made Faye completely forgive her for the whole accidentally setting her on fire thing. "I'm sorry. I forgot your name."

"They call me Lady Origami." She had a gentle smile. She wasn't very old, but she smiled like Faye thought a mother was supposed to. "It is fine, sometimes, to cry...Here...This is what I do when I am sad but do not want to be. This is how I got this name." She unbuttoned one of the multitude of pockets on her coveralls and pulled out a sheet of soft paper. She began to fold it, one way, then another, then another, way too fast for Faye to understand. Then she crumpled it a bit to make it seem more natural and more alive, but even that was just another type of folding.

She handed Faye a very lifelike bird. Faye marveled at it. Now that was *magic*. "How'd you do that?"

"It is art. I learned from my father when I was a little girl. The folding changes things. Every sheet starts the same, until you fold it and it becomes new."

Faye studied the bird. It had been a plain, flat old piece of paper, and now it was a bird. That sure was neat... Faye used her head map and focused on the bird. It took her nearly two whole seconds to unfold the entire thing in her mind. It was all just connections on the same piece, but change the connections, smoosh together new ones, and you changed the thing. And then she realized something. "That's what I do. I *fold* stuff."

"Yes. They all may look the same, but every sheet has a destiny. The artist shows that destiny."

This was *intriguing*. Faye focused hard on her head map, studying the bird in her hand. Faye smooshed together bits of space so she could step through them. This art of Lady Origami's moved smooshed bits too, but kept them there, and once you did that, it turned the whole thing into something new and exciting. Faye reached down and began unfolding. Lady Origami just frowned, curious as to why her artwork was being mangled. Faye was clumsy, but she managed not to rip anything. "This is how magic works!"

"I do not understand."

"Magic is all the same. They all talk about geometry and stuff, but magic is all the same at first, until it gets folded! Then it makes a new thing!" Faye's mind was blown. Her magic kept track of the lines as the bird unraveled. She envisioned the flat sheet in her head map, and then viewed it in three dimensions and decided to make something new. She quickly thought through all the necessary connections, and began *smooshing* things back together.

Lady Origami was perplexed, but she didn't say anything as Faye kept folding and twisting things. It took her a whole lot longer to do it with her clumsy hands than with her fast brain. Faye proudly held up the rough thing that had once been a swan.

"I am not sure what—"

"It's a Holstein!" Faye exclaimed.

Lady Origami took it back, obviously confused. Now that she was looking at it in cold reality and not as the majestic animal she conceived in her head map, it was ugly as sin, but at least it was shaped right and had enough legs. "Ah yes. Of course."

"A cow!"

"Oh." She nodded appreciatively. "I can see that . . . That is one of the spotted ones? We crashed the *Bulldog Marauder* on some. Very nice," she lied, trying not to hurt Faye's feelings. "I did not know anyone from the West knew this art."

"Art? No. This is what I do when I Travel. I make connections. I can't believe I never saw this before. Don't you see?" Faye jabbered excitedly. "This is exactly how magic works! The whole world, the universe, that's the sheet. Actives normally get to fold just one part to change the world! Maybe they can grow that bit, make some changes, but they don't ever really unfold the whole sheet and make something new, but it's the folds that decide what each part does! That's how the Chairman could change between different kinds of magic. He unfolded his connection and made new ones."

Faye could tell that she'd completely lost her audience. Lady

Origami just had a look on her face that said Faye had gone crazy. That was okay, Faye was used to that, but this was a *big* deal.

"Do you got any more paper?"

Lady Origami had a lot of pockets.

Magic, a sharp knife, some demon ink, whiskey to dull the pain, and a steady hand . . . That's all it took to turn a man into a weapon.

Who was he kidding? Jake Sullivan had always been a weapon. It was just time to quit pretending he could ever be anything else.

Killing. That's all he'd ever been good for. Even when he'd tried to help, tried to be on the side of the angels, all he'd done was kill.

As a boy, his head had been filled with big ideals about courage and sacrifice and defending the innocent. He'd lied about his age and joined General Roosevelt's First Volunteer Active Brigade. He'd even talked his brothers into it. Think of the adventure . . . *What horseshit.* The Sullivan brothers' grand adventure had turned into years of endless trench warfare, killing with bullets, gravity, and bare hands. He'd survived the biggest battle in history with his body relatively intact, while one brother had lost his life and the other had lost his mind.

He'd come home to a country that didn't understand them. All they'd known was that the First Volunteer had nearly ripped the world apart killing magical Germans at the Second Somme. Some called them heroes, but he could see the fear in their eyes.

Still, he'd tried to help, tried to make a difference. He was stubborn like that. Sullivan had liked puzzles, and what better way to solve puzzles than being a detective? Fixing people's problems, and occasionally using his Power to right wrongs and take care of the dangerous types, and he'd been damn good at it. He'd fallen in love with a girl who had her own kinds of nightmares, and for just a little while, he'd thought he'd build a life for himself.

That had ended in five minutes of blood, because an innocent person had been threatened, and he was just too damned obstinate to let that slide. He'd killed a crooked bastard, but it had been a crooked bastard of an elected lawman, and that life he'd thought he might build with Delilah had all came crashing down.

Rockville. Six years of monotonous rock-breaking hell, and even in chains he couldn't stop killing. The hardest of the hard had tried to prove themselves against his reputation, and he'd broken every single one. He never started anything, but he finished everything. His magic had always been strong, hard as his will, as forceful as gravity, but Rockville had given him time to think, and it turned out that was the most dangerous thing of all.

He'd been freed early to be J. Edgar Hoover's attack dog, and even when he was trying not to kill anybody, they'd left him no choice. Delilah had come back into his life, briefly, until he'd gotten her killed too.

He'd been at war ever since.

The brain of a scholar in the body of a thug with a history so hard it would make an Iron Guard flinch. In another time or other circumstances, he might have accomplished great things with his mind or built great things with his hands. Instead, all he'd done was tear down the world, chipping away, piece by piece, like methodically breaking rocks in a quarry. He could try to hide it in fancy talk, about how he was protecting the innocent from the evil, but those were just words to confuse the issue. Jake Sullivan was good at one thing, and that one thing was killing. Sure, it was always for a good reason, but that didn't change the fact that he was born to fight.

The Grimnoir oath he'd taken was serious business to a man who always kept his word. There were still folks in need of defending, now more than ever before, so he intended to go and do what God had put him on this Earth to do, and that was to kill a whole mess of people.

Jake Sullivan may have been on the side of the angels, but they were some damned bloody angels.

He woke up lying on his stomach. At first he wasn't sure where he was. There was a strange noise vibrating through the floor, and then he remembered that was the sound of turbojet engines, and then he remembered that he was on the *Traveler*, and then he remembered that it was mostly empty since most of its passengers had been murdered in Shanghai. It wasn't until he tried to move that he felt the pain and recalled why he was lying on his stomach. His back had been the only spot big enough to carve the new spell.

The Healing spells he'd carved on his chest were burning hot, repairing the damage to his tissues. Already the cuts and burns that had been inflicted on him had knotted over into rough scar tissue. He'd thought the others had hurt, but they'd been nothing compared to this. It was fading now, but he didn't think he'd ever forget that magical fire.

Madi had held the record. He'd taken thirteen Imperium kanji and lived, and as a result he'd been damned near unkillable. Sullivan now had five, though this new one from Sivaram had to be equivalent to several Imperium kanji designs. Sullivan felt for the Power built up in his chest, but then immediately recoiled. It was *different* than before.

What would happen when he actually used it? Zangara had gone from making firecrackers to artillery shells. Crow had gone from Summoning demons to wearing them like a suit. What would that do to a man who was already a master of gravity? Even as curious as Sullivan was, frankly, he was afraid to experiment with such forces, especially while on board a fragile airship.

He took stock. He was barefoot, wearing pants but no shirt, and he still didn't know where he was. Last he remembered he'd been in sick bay. He lifted his head from the pillow. There was a small mattress on the steel floor. He pretty much covered the whole thing and then some. He'd never been in this room before, and he'd been nearly everywhere he could fit aboard the *Traveler*. She simply wasn't that big of a dirigible.

He realized it wasn't actually a room at all, more of a space between rooms. The ceiling *moved*. And then he realized there was no roof at all. It was rust-colored fabric. It was the bottom of one of the hull cells holding thousands of cubic feet of hydrogen. Light was trickling through the gas bag, and it gave the room a sort of pink tint. Always analytical, Sullivan sat up, wondering how he'd gotten to this forgotten corner of the ship and how long he'd been out.

Other than the mattress, there wasn't much here. A short table had been welded to the floor next to the hatch. There were cushions around it, since it was too small to use a chair. There was a vase bolted to the table, and the vase was filled with flowers. His neck popped as he turned his head. There were lots of little paintings and pictures on the wall, not hung, but screwed, because they would simply fall off the first time the ship banked hard. Then he tensed as he realized there were actually *lit* candles in the room.

He got yelled at for smoking, but somebody had put *candles* directly under one of the hydrogen bags? Sullivan crawled toward the candles to put them out, but then stopped when he realized it was a shrine of some kind. There were two photographs placed between fresh flowers, and several intricately folded paper animals, and then Sullivan knew exactly where he was.

The first picture was of a young Japanese man, stocky, muscular, with a big square face and a wide grin. He was wearing a Western suit and proudly holding some sort of academic award or diploma in his big hands. Sullivan would've bet money that he, too, was a Gravity Spiker. He just had that solid look about him.

The next picture was of a little baby.

Sullivan pulled away from the candles. He realized that though they were emitting heat, they weren't moving at all. It was like the flames had simply frozen in place. Even the light coming off them wasn't flickering. The wicks weren't being consumed and the wax wasn't even soft. Of course, Lady Origami was a Torch, so fire would do whatever she told it to do, and it sure as hell wasn't going to endanger her memorial or her ship.

The hatch opened. Sullivan lurched to his feet on wobbly legs as Lady Origami entered her quarters. She was carrying a pitcher in one hand and a steaming bowl in the other.

"Hey," Sullivan said awkwardly.

She placed the food down on the table, then closed the hatch behind her. "I am surprised you are awake. Do you feel all right? It looked painful."

"I'm okay. Why am I here?"

"Sick bay is very full, with the four knights pulled from river. This is a private place, so I offered. It took three big men to carry you here. Your words were upsetting the others."

"Words?"

"All about killing. Over and over."

Sullivan looked down at his hands. "Uh, yeah..."

"You scared them." She came over, touched him on the chin and lifted his head. He was surprised by the physical contact. Her fingers were callused and surprisingly strong. Her eyes were piercing, and he could see the fire inside. "You scared me."

"I'm sorry for that."

"Oh, Sullivan..." She smiled and shook her head. She stepped away lightly, untying the dark red silk that decorated her coveralls.

She placed it on the pillows. "Do not apologize. You are what you are supposed to be. You are strong, and proud, and smart, and very sad inside. You say very few words, but the words you say are always true. Men such as you are rare in the world."

The jet engines gained in intensity. They were lifting off. "I should be going."

She stepped in front of the hatch, blocking it. "Do not go."

It had been a long time, but he recognized the look. He knew what she wanted, though he could not understand why she would possibly want him. "Lady Origami, I can't—"

"Lady Origami is my marauder name. What they called me when I did not wish to speak after they rescued me from the prison ship. My real name is Akane Yoshizawa."

"Akane." It was a pretty name for a pretty girl. "I—"

"You must think terrible things of me because of the first time we met. You must have thought I was a pirate whore."

"No!" Sullivan shook his head vigorously in the negative. "Never. You just surprised me is all."

"I surprised myself that night too. That was not like me. Many of the marauders have wished to, but they have respect for me when I tell them to go away, and I did not have to burn any of them."

"Hard to get fresh with a Torch."

"True." She smiled. "You were the first man I'd tried to be with since . . . It was just . . . When you told the Marauders your story, you reminded me of someone. A man I once knew." Her eyes flicked unconsciously toward the shrine, and then back to him. "You still do. You are complete, but empty. Never afraid, never false. I can see this in you and I have only ever seen it once before."

He turned away. "I'm sorry for your loss."

"We all lose, Sullivan. We lose our homes, we lose our love, our families, and sometimes we lose ourselves because losing is all we know how to do." She came over slowly, put one hand on his scarred back. It lingered there, her fingers tracing the complex lines of Power, then she gently steered him around to face her. "I see your sadness when others do not, because I share it. You don't want to lose any more. You don't think you have any more to give."

"If you're tired of losing, then you sure as hell don't want to end up with the likes of me."

She ran one hand down the muscles of his chest. This time he didn't try to pull away.

"Then we will not think about it until tomorrow, Heavy Jake Sullivan. Today, we will just be alive." She reached up to her neck and unzipped her coveralls clear to her navel, and she wasn't wearing a damned thing beneath.

"Well..." Sullivan took a deep breath. *Akane.* It really was a beautiful name for a beautiful woman. "All right, then."

ᾱᎋ Chapter 19 ᾱᎋ

I have long felt that great nations are simply the operating fronts of behind-the-scenes, vastly ambitious individuals who had become so effectively powerful because of their ability to remain invisible while operating behind the national scenery. However, I did not expect them to be literally invisible.

—Buckminster Fuller,
personal correspondence, 1933

Drew Town, New Jersey

THE CALL HAD BEEN URGENT. The elders were contacting every single Grimnoir knight in the world. It didn't matter where they were, who they were, if they were old or feeble, on their own or in a group, it was all hands on deck. Not all knights were fighters, but for those that weren't, they needed to go and make sure the local authorities were alert and ready, and they were to do so by any means necessary. If that meant throwing rocks at the Kremlin, do it. Wake up the militia. Load your guns. If you didn't have guns, it was time for torches and pitchforks.

Francis had never gotten a message from the society quite like that before.

The message had been fairly straightforward, mostly because the elders didn't have many details to share. They suspected something very bad was about to happen, especially in places where Actives lived. Any place with a lot of magic collected in one spot was a potential target. Of what, they couldn't particularly say. The threats were of an unknown nature. They didn't say who had set them off, but a knight had brought them a warning that all magicals were in potential danger.

Francis had a sneaking suspicion that this was somehow related to Faye...

John Browning was overseeing all Grimnoir operations in the United States, and he was busily shuffling knights about to cover potential hot spots. Word had been put out discreetly to all of their friends and allies in the military and among the police. Discreet being the key word, since they really didn't want the OCI to think that they were fomenting some sort of Active uprising. They'd already been through that once this year.

As soon as Francis had received the message, he'd known right where to go. If he was some sort of unknown threat looking to target Actives, he'd head right toward the town built for them and advertised as paradise.

Dan Garrett parked their car in the woods on the way into Drew Town. Jane opened the trunk and started removing guns. When you didn't know what kind of trouble to expect, it was best to bring guns and friends with guns. Francis took the P17 Enfield and threw a leather bandolier of shells over his shoulder. They were dressed like they were going hunting, and he supposed, in a way, that's exactly what they were doing.

"We play it quiet. We're just taking a little walk through the forest, picking a spot, and watching the town." Dan removed a backpack from the trunk. "I got the sandwiches."

"You're so clever to bring food," Jane said as she took out a guitar case. "I only brought this Thompson submachine gun."

"Heh... That's my girl."

There were headlights on the road behind them, but instead of passing by and continuing on toward the town, they slowed and pulled off behind them. "You expecting anybody else?" Francis asked.

Dan shook his head. "Everybody else is scoping out other places."

"If it's the cops, we'll just say that we're going coyote hunting."

Dan looked down at the gigantic Browning automatic rifle he was removing from the trunk. "Apparently, they grow some tough coyotes out here... Don't worry. I'll talk our way out of this."

A car door closed. A moment later they saw that somebody was coming through the trees, making their way quietly with no flashlight, but not trying to hide their presence. "Francis? Is that you?"

It was a woman's voice. "Hammer? What are you doing here?"

"Following you!" she called back.

"Oh, good," Dan said. "The one person I'm entirely incapable of charming."

The BI agent got close enough that they could see her clearly in the moonlight. "Hoover ordered me to have you tailed. He said the Grimnoir are up to something." She looked over the open trunk and the growing pile of weapons. "Guess he was right. Look, I know where we are, and considering the timing, I know what you're doing, and I could order my boys to come in and arrest you right now, but I really do like you, so I'm going to try and talk you out of it instead."

"Talk us out of what?"

"Oh, you just happen to show up in Drew Town, a place which stands for everything you're against, right when the architect of the whole scheme is there taking a tour? I don't like that Cog bastard either. He strikes me as a sleaze and an opportunist, and I don't think I've ever heard the man utter a completely true sentence, but messing with him won't accomplish a thing but make you more enemies."

Francis sighed. "Hammer, tune up that lie detector and try this on for size. I don't give a damn about Roosevelt's buddy. We're only here because we got a message saying that places with lots of Actives congregated might be in danger. Don't know what, but from the message I've got a gut feeling it could be really bad." As soon as he said that, he began to develop a splitting headache. "Ow, damn it. Now get out of there. See?"

"You're telling the truth." Hammer breathed a sigh of relief. "Good. I was worried there y'all were about to do something incredibly stupid. It didn't feel right."

Thankfully the headache let up when her Power did. "Great. Now scram back to your boss and tell him we're the good guys. We're going to keep an eye out for . . . *something.*"

"Uh huh . . . Something." Hammer went over to the trunk and pointed at a short-barreled Winchester Model 12. "You using that?" she asked Jane.

"My hands are already full."

."Mind if I borrow that?" Hammer picked up the shotgun, checked it, and pumped a round into the chamber. Then she picked up a box of buckshot and started shoving shells into her coat pockets. "I've seen what you Grimnoir's idea of *something* is. Your last *something* stomped on half of Washington." Agent Pemberly Hammer of the Bureau of Investigation set out into the woods. "Come on. I took the tour with Director Hoover last week. I know a good spot on a rise where we can see most of the town."

The three knights watched her go. Dan hoisted up the backpack and BAR. "I should've packed more sandwiches."

Free City of Shanghai

TORU had not seen this memory before.

Okubo was sitting on the mat in his study. The doors had been slid open, providing him with a better view of the manicured garden. He had been watching flower petals float down the stream and inspired, had called for his servants to bring his writing desk. He had put quill to scroll and was attempting to capture the moment in a poem.

Hattori waited patiently for his Lord to finish writing. It was not good to interrupt the greatest wizard in the world when he was trying to write poetry. Okubo scowled and marked out a line. Sometimes even the best amongst them could be frustrated when he simply could not find the words.

"Small moments of beauty . . . They may seem a trifling thing for warriors to contemplate, especially when compared to the mighty events surrounding us, yet it is still important to take the time to appreciate such things," Okubo explained as he went back to writing. There was no need for someone of his status to make apologies, so he was merely speaking because he felt like it. "A warrior must understand what he fights for in order to strike with a pure heart."

"Of course, my Lord," Hattori said, his voice sounding far too deep.

"What do you fight for?"

The question caught him off guard.

"What brings you here, my son?"

Hattori was gone. Toru was not watching a memory at all. He was sitting across from his father. He froze. His blood turned to ice.

His stomach filled with pained knots. Realizing that he was not even bowing, he quickly placed his forehead to the floor. "Forgive me, Chairman!"

"Rise, Toru. Such deference is not necessary. I no longer hold the office of Chairman because I am dead. I am merely a restless ghost, unable to move on."

Toru lifted his head. Tears filled his eyes. "I have failed you."

"No. It was I who failed. In looking to the future, I tried to shape the world in my image. I was so focused on my great goals that I failed to see the small darkness hidden among my closest followers. I have often warned that the Enemy was not to be underestimated, yet I was guilty of this myself. I prepared to counter its fearsome strength, and did not realize it was capable of subtle trickery."

"Is the world lost, then?"

"No. Though you are close, you are not dead yet, and as long as a warrior's heart beats he may still strike at his foe. There is more to be done." Okubo Tokugawa stood, walked over to Toru, and placed a gentle hand on his shoulder. "You are my son. I can no longer fight in this battle, but you will serve in my stead. I did not choose a successor before I was taken. That was an error caused by my hubris. Fate placed you in the path of these events, and you have valued truth above glory. Honor over tradition. You have proven yourself worthy to be my heir. The survival of the Imperium is your responsibility now. The future of the world will be decided by your actions. The future of our family is in your hands."

Toru was so choked with emotion that he could barely respond. "I will not fail."

"I am humbled by your devotion. I have many regrets from my life. One of them is that I did not realize the greatness inherent in some of my descendants. I am pleased with you, Toru… When you call upon me in your greatest time of need, I will grant you strength."

"I will not fail!" Toru bellowed again.

"Awake."

"Awake!"

A hand slapped him in the face. Toru groaned and cracked his eyes open.

He was upright, being held in place by chains wrapped around his arms, legs, and torso. It took him a moment to realize that he was still wearing the Nishimura armor, everything but the helmet. He tried to move, but it had somehow been depowered, and his limbs were sluggish and did not respond. Some form of stifling magical effect had been placed upon him.

The Iron Guard who had struck him stepped aside. Once again, he was staring into the face of Okubo Tokugawa, only this was the imposter. This was the villain. This was the pawn of the Enemy. How could the others not see? He would have spit in that face if his mouth hadn't been so dry.

He was dressed for ceremony, wearing his military uniform, chest covered in medals and ribbons. "Well, if it isn't the traitor," the imposter sneered. "How pathetic. Once a fearsome Iron Guard, the finest possible example of an Imperium warrior, and now you are chained to a dungeon wall like a common criminal."

"I am not *common*." Toru gritted his teeth and concentrated. He couldn't even curl his fingers into a fist. It was like he'd been paralyzed from the neck down. "You are a traitor, Dosan Saito, and I will kill you."

The guard did not need to be prompted. He backhanded Toru in the mouth.

The imposter smiled. "Save your energy, Toru. This man is of my personal guard. They have already been . . . augmented."

Toru's eyes grated in their sockets as he studied the Iron Guard. He looked completely human, only with dead, unfeeling eyes. This warrior had been a man once, but now he was a puppet made of flesh. Toru was disgusted.

"You have been trying to plant seeds of doubt into their heads, like Hattori did to you. I know that was what you were attempting with your brazen entrance into Shanghai. You hoped to scare me away. You wanted to make the warriors doubt their Chairman with your wild rumors. Sadly, some of the seeds which you have been spreading have taken root among the men. I cannot allow that. I must crush all doubt. That is the only reason you are still alive."

Toru wanted to choke the life from this man, but he was helpless, and that was infuriating. "Why do you serve the Pathfinder? You were a friend of Okubo Tokugawa!"

"I was his friend, his confidant, and his advisor. I knew him far better than you ever did. You are a foolish boy who thinks he is serving the will of his father, while I am the one who will realize his dream. I serve the Imperium. I do not serve the Pathfinder. The Pathfinder serves me."

"Then you are an imbecile."

WHACK. The Iron Guard hit him even harder. This one had to have been a Massive to have knuckles that dense.

The imposter looked to the Iron Guard. It was as if they communicated without speaking, and the soldier stepped away, leaving Toru hanging there, blood running out of his nose and down his lips.

"Okubo hated the Enemy. He was correct to do so. It came here as a mighty predator. His mistake, however, was in thinking it could not be tamed. Like any beast, like magic even, it can be broken and made to serve. For many years I kept a fragment of the defeated Pathfinder secret. I studied it, learned its ways, as was Okubo's command to me, and I took its strength for myself. It is simply another form of being, not so different from the Power."

They had thought it was merely bad luck which had brought the Pathfinder to Asia twice in a row, but in truth, it had never actually left. "You are being deceived."

"You are incorrect. Like all living things, the Enemy merely wishes to continue its existence. Once I spoke with it, I came to understand its needs. It came to consume all of the Power, as it had done before on other worlds, but only because the intelligences there which the Power had been bonded to were not rational. The Enemy merely asks for enough sustenance to support itself, and in exchange, it is prepared to give us so much in return . . . Access to abilities far beyond anything the Power has ever granted."

"What did my father say when you suggested this to him?"

Saito chuckled. "I am not a fool. I never spoke to Okubo about this. He truly believed that the Pathfinder had been completely destroyed. I did not wish to upset his view, so I waited."

"It had you wait. It made you hold your tongue."

"Not at all. Did Okubo himself not once teach that it was the inevitable duty of the strong to control the weak? I am merely following his philosophy. The Predator is strong. The Power is the weaker of the two, and thus must be controlled. The Power is nothing more than a very useful farm animal. It is livestock, to be managed. There is no reason that both cannot exist simultaneously in this world."

"Magic is not chickens, and we are not peasants collecting eggs to present to our lords! It has clouded your thoughts, Saito. It is using you."

"You have not seen what I have seen. You will never understand. When the evil Grimnoir took Okubo from us, I saw my opportunity. Over the years I had been secretly collecting other forms of magic. I oversaw Unit 731, and when the discreet opportunity would present itself, I would have the Power wrung out of another Active and I would take it as my own. Oh, the look on your face . . . Surprised? You think Okubo was the only one who could do such a thing? No, Toru. The Pathfinder offers that to all of its allies. It enabled me to conceal this development from Okubo, and once the unthinkable happened, I stepped in to take his place."

"How do you—"

"Mimic him so perfectly? The Pathfinder is an artist whose medium is flesh. It did not simply give me a new face. Using nothing but a lock of Okubo's hair, it grew me a new body. It has been observing his every word and action for decades, and it recorded them all with perfect clarity for my use. I am not an actor pretending to be Okubo, I *am* Okubo."

Toru did not know if the dream he'd been having earlier had been real or not, but he chose to believe. *Father, grant me the strength to break these chains so that I may snap this bastard's neck.* Nothing happened. "Damn you, Saito."

"I am Okubo Tokugawa, and you are standing in the way of my great vision of unification. Now you may be wondering why I did not simply have you killed when they pulled your nearly lifeless body from the rubble. It is the same reason you still wear this magnificent armor. Your death must be most impressive. I mentioned your seeds of doubt taking root, and I simply cannot allow that to happen. For the good of the Imperium, there can be no doubt in my divinity."

Divinity? The Chairman had never claimed to be a god! "What manner of blasphemous madness do you speak of?"

Saito waved his hand dismissively. "I tire of the Emperor. The time has come to remove all pretenses, but first, you have insulted my rule, and for that I must publicly destroy you. I must defeat you in a manner which leaves no doubt that I am Okubo Tokugawa."

It was as Dr. Wells had predicted. The imposter was *insecure*. Toru's eyes narrowed. "A trial of combat?"

"We will conduct our ceremony, traditions will be kept, and then afterwards, I will face the infamous traitor, Toru, an exceedingly powerful Brute, in personal combat, and not only will I duel such a fearsome opponent, I will even allow him to wear one of the most powerful magical weapons in our entire arsenal. I will make it *sporting*. Surely, only Okubo Tokugawa would be capable of such a feat."

It did not matter how many forms of magic Saito had absorbed, or how much extra magic the Pathfinder was granting him, Toru would find a way to kill him. "I accept your challenge."

Saito laughed. "Of course you do. You were always a fine example of the Iron Guard's fighting spirit. I am certain that you would do your best to defeat me. In fact, you might even be able to somehow achieve this goal, or at least put up a good enough showing that you could perhaps injure me, and it would simply not do to let the people see their *god bleed*."

The other Iron Guard returned, holding something in his hand. Toru's eyes widened when he saw what it was. The tiny metal cup was filled with a thick, black liquid. He recognized it from Hattori's memories of Dark Ocean. It was the corrupted blood which spilled from the skinless abominations created by the Pathfinder's dark magic. It was moving, hissing, and smoking. It was *alive*. It was this foul substance which the Pathfinder had used to spread its malicious corruption through the villagers to build its army.

"Wretched coward!" Toru bellowed.

"This is for the best. When next we meet, you will do what is expected of you, no more, no less. I look forward to our duel. I am sure you will put on an excellent show."

The Iron Guard smashed the metal cup against Toru's mouth. He clamped his lips shut, but the corruption crawled up and out, pressing against his lips. It followed the trail of dripping blood and forced its way into his nose. It pulsed and rolled up his face and into his ear. He closed his eyes as hard as he could, but it began crawling through his lids.

It would enter his brain and corrupt his soul and Toru would be no more.

And for one of the few times in his entire life, Toru knew fear.

UBF *Traveler*

THE AIRSHIP'S CREW had been pared down to an absolute minimum. The corridors of the once-crowded dirigible seemed empty. The engine room was busy, the command deck was busy, and the cargo bay was bustling with activity, but that was it. Fuller, Schirmer, and a couple of brave UBF volunteers were still working on the big, confusing, slap-dash invention which was taking up the majority of the hold. It looked like a mess, but they swore up and down that it would work. *More than likely.*

Sullivan had come down from Akane's room and gone right to work. Southunder had arrived a little later to check on his preparations. "Zhao and a few of my Marauders are on the way back to the city. It seems a few of my boarding-party regulars did not wish to sit this one out. Heinrich will be awaiting our signal."

"You made the right call sending away the rest of the crew, Captain."

Southunder chuckled. "Well, Mr. Sullivan. We'll find out if that's the case should we crash due to lack of sufficient damage-control teams."

"Still . . . Good call." Sullivan unlatched the big metal buckles from the box containing the Gravity-Spiker armor John Browning had designed for him. "Francis' UBF boys did their part. No need to make any more widows."

"Is that what you think?" Southunder grinned. "I'll have you know I sent them on so we'd have a bigger supply of extra oxygen tanks. I didn't want all of those eggheads sucking up my precious breathable air."

"Smart." They would be going pretty damn high, after all. The remaining crew were already donning the same heavy winter clothing the knights had used near the North Pole. It was only going to get colder, and the air was only going to get thinner. Within an hour or so they'd be in the death zone, where, unassisted, a body would just run out of oxygen and croak, and that wasn't even close to what Fuller needed. "How high do you intend to go?"

"According to UBF, this is the most advanced airship ever made. Theoretically, thanks to the Cog-designed hydrogen-compression systems in the bags, to borrow a phrase, the sky is the limit. The main deck will be pressurized, better than a submarine Francis claims, though you should never trust a salesman. Still, we should be safe... Theoretically... The volunteers remaining in the hold and engine room will be wearing the special pressure suits and breathing apparatus, and—"

"I can pressurize myself."

"Yes, lucky, that. Mr. Schirmer said the higher, the better for their—to use Mr. Fuller's term—*magicanical* oddity. Altitude achievable is entirely dependent upon the expansion of our lifting gases, dynamic volume, and pressure."

"Finally, some science around here I can actually understand."

"And this wondrous vessel was designed to break records, so..." The captain went to the side, picked up a phone, and cranked the charge handle a few times. "Bridge... Yes, Mr. Barns. What's the current world altitude record? Yes... Seventy-two thousand feet? A *Soviet* airship? Well, then, Mr. Barns. Maintain heading and take us to seventy-five." Southunder put the phone back in the cradle. "I simply cannot abide a record being set by a Communist... Will that do for your plans, Mr. Sullivan?"

"For what we're trying to do? Hell if I know. It'll work, or it won't, but either way, it should end up memorable. I don't know if that'll bug Faye too much, but she should be able to get us both down in one piece... I was happy to hear she's alive and kicking. That girl is full of surprises."

"Last I saw, she was in the ready room. She sent word to our American compatriots, and now she is folding little paper animals. Apparently Lady Origami has influenced her." Southunder smirked. "And I've been led to believe that is not the only new friend Ori has made recently."

Sullivan just grunted and kept lacing up the big ties on the side of the steel boots. "Come out and say it, Captain."

"You know what I mean, Mr. Sullivan. My crew is my family, so I think of her as a daughter."

"This the part where you bring out a shotgun and a preacher?"

"I shouldn't need to. Besides, buckshot might threaten the integrity of my nice new airship, and a man of the cloth would only suck up precious oxygen. You'll treat her with the respect she's due."

"Of course, sir."

"Excellent, because if you don't, she'd just burn you to a crisp." Southunder patted him on the back. "So come back in one piece then and make that poor girl happy. I really don't want her moping around my ship again. Got it, son?"

They both knew him coming back wasn't likely. "Yes, Captain."

"Very well. You're a good man, Sullivan. I'd be honored to have you on my crew anytime. Good luck down there."

"Good luck up here." Sullivan held out his hand, and they shook on it. Southunder's hand nearly disappeared in Sullivan's big mitt. "The whole world's gonna be watching."

"They'd better. Well, I've got a ship to run. I'll tell Faye you are awake." The Captain left without any further ceremony.

Sullivan went back to putting on the suit. It wasn't nearly as fancy as Toru's nifty gear. If he'd had more time, he would've loved to study that thing in depth. The Spiker Armor was conceptually based on the Heavy Suits they'd worn back in the First Volunteer. Heat-treated, interlocking steel plates covered most of the body to protect from bullets and shrapnel, and beneath that was thick, fire-resistant canvas to protect the skin from Torches' flames or Iceboxes' cold. The whole thing had been spray painted olive drab and tan, not for any particular reason, but it did fit with the traditional colors of the First. The suit weighed a ton, but it was a whole lot nicer than the rusty heap he'd worn while running across no man's land back during the war. Not to mention that this thing was enchanted to hell and back with every spell that John Browning could fit onto it.

Sullivan pulled the helmet out of the box. "What the . . ." He turned it over in his hands. Somebody had sprayed the nearly featureless face mask a stark white, and then painted square black lines for teeth. The eyes were black holes anyway, so now the whole thing looked like a skull. "That's ominous." *Who'd been screwing with his gear?* He flipped it over. The artist had used a paint brush to put a small signature and a note on the base.

Now it has got class. A Lance Talon original, 1933.

"That joker."

Faye popped into existence a second later. "Mr. Sullivan!" She rushed over and threw her arms around his neck.

Straw-colored hair hit him in the eyes. "Hey, Faye." Careful not to squish her, he returned the hug. Then he pushed her away and held her carefully at arm's length. "How in the hell are you alive? And where have you been?"

"Just now? Figuring out how all of magic really works so I can be stronger than the Chairman ever was. It's all about folding the world into little chunks to make designs that do what you want. Before that, I had to kill somebody called the Black Monk, he acted all high and mighty like I'd know him as something something Rasputin, but he was evil so I killed him and got all his magic. But before that I was in Dead City talking to a zombie Fortune Teller who showed me how I'm probably gonna end the world, and before that I was hanging out with one of the elders so I could learn how to be the Spellbound without ending the world. I pretended to get blown up when I blew up the God of Demons so I could do that and not get murdered by the elders for being all cursed and whatnot. How about you? How've you been?"

"Not as good as you, apparently." As usual, when talking to Faye, you sometimes had to take a minute to let all of the information sort of settle into a groove. "If I'm still alive later, you'll have to explain all that to me nice and clear, like you have to with the real slow-witted folks."

"Oh, Mr. Sullivan. Your brain ain't slow. You just like taking your time before you open your mouth."

"You heard about Lance?" Faye nodded. The skin around her grey eyes was puffy from crying. Even saying his name made those eyes get a little shiny before Faye blinked it away. "Well, I'm sure he did us all proud. You been told the plan?"

She nodded again. "I think it's a bad plan, but I see why you're doing it. They already say we're the bad guys anyways. Might as well make it true."

"That's the idea. Dr. Wells called it preconceived notions. Can you Travel me down there? I'll need a few minutes to do what I've got to do before you start killing anybody."

"I promise. I don't like leaving Iron Guards alive on principle, but I know what you want to happen." Faye turned her head quizzically to the side. "Your magic is different now. Not like mine, but different. Bigger."

Sullivan studied her back. He'd never been able to see it before, but he could sort of, now, if he squinted just right. Faye had so much extra Power hanging around her it was like a fuzzy halo of raw magic. She'd always been strong, but this was downright scary. They had both changed a lot since that fateful day they'd met and she'd put some bullets in his back. "Girl, I don't think anybody is close to you anymore."

"That's what I need to talk to you about before we do this." Faye pulled out a piece of paper and handed it to him.

Sullivan studied it. It was a horrible picture, full of death and carnage, and Faye was some sort of monster ripping out people's souls. "What's this nonsense?"

"A possible future. You know about the Spellbound curse?"

"Not much. I learned more about it from Bradford Carr's testimony than anything. The elders were mighty tight-lipped on that subject."

"That's because they like it secret, hoping nobody else was dumb enough to mess with it." Faye spent the next few minutes explaining what she'd learned. When she outlined Sivaram's genius schemes, Sullivan felt his jaw drop open. It was crazy, but it made a sick sort of sense, and as Faye spoke, Sullivan thought of Fuller and his stolen shoelaces. The Spellbound was one step removed from the Enemy, if not in overall strength, in potential for chaos.

Poor Faye.

"I can beat the Pathfinder, but it might change me. I need you to live, Mr. Sullivan. Please, do everything you can to live through this, because if this goes wrong, and I'm not strong enough, and I get corrupted and turn evil, you're the only one who may be tough enough or smart enough to kill me. Promise me, if I start to change, if I'm not in control, you'll put me out of my misery."

Sullivan swallowed hard. Faye was deadly earnest. "Faye... That's..."

"Please, Mr. Sullivan."

"Don't you worry. I swear that I'll do whatever I have to. But this?" Sullivan reached into his shirt and fumbled around until he found a book of matches. He took it out and struck one. He lit the picture on fire. Faye tried to snatch the drawing back from him, but Sullivan gently blocked her hand. "No, Faye. This is bullshit. This is *not* you. This isn't set in stone. This isn't real. You decide your future. No person, no magic, not Power or Enemy, God or the Devil, they just offer you paths. Only *you* choose which one you take. Got it?"

Faye folded her arms, like she was hugging herself, but she did manage to nod in the affirmative, and then she started crying again.

"Fire is serious a safety violation in this area!" Buckminster Fuller shouted from the other side of the cargo bay.

Sullivan put the burning paper on the floor and smashed it flat with a steel boot. "Come here." And he hugged Faye again and gave her a minute to sob. The poor girl had been through far too much in her short life, and now they were going to go fight the toughest army in the world. If he could talk to the Power, he'd tell it just what he thought of it picking such a gentle soul to put through this kind of hell. "You okay?"

She sniffed and wiped her nose on the back of her hand. "Yeah."

"Good. Now go over to that locker and pick yourself out something nice. John filled it with guns for us."

Faye was still rubbing her eyes when she opened the locker. Her face split into a wide, malicious grin. Maybe *gentle soul* was the wrong choice of words after all. "Can I take the bazooka?"

"Knock yourself out, kid."

Free City of Shanghai

FIRST SHADOW GUARD HAYATE could not resist the temptation to see his brother one last time. It had been decreed by the Chairman's personal guard that no one should speak to the traitor before the duel. They were calling it a duel, but that was a misnomer. Challenging the Chairman was an execution.

It was a violation of an order, but Hayate was Shadow Guard. He had learned long ago that orders were often given by those who lacked imagination. Certainly, a chained Brute was no physical threat, and Toru's poisonous words would be meaningless to a man of honor and conviction such as himself. Hayate justified his disobedience by telling himself that there were still Grimnoir out there. They had cost him two full teams' worth of young Shadow Guard. Perhaps Toru would tell him their locations as a form of death-bed repentance.

But in truth, Hayate was simply curious. How could a son of Okubo Tokugawa fall so very far?

Reaching Toru without being seen was a simple enough matter. Hayate was, after all, the greatest living assassin in the Imperium. The torture chamber beneath the palace was warded with all manner of clever spells, but nothing that he could not easily circumvent. There were many guards, but Hayate was nearly invisible when he wished to be, and these guards seemed oddly content and still.

His brother was chained to a wall. A temporary kanji of paralysis had been scrawled on his forehead with blood and ash. Toru's head was lowered. His chin resting against the armored neckpiece of the Nishimura, yet he did not sleep. Hayate drew closer. Toru's eyes were closed, but he was not sleeping. He could see the rapid eye movement beneath the closed lids. Toru was panting, occasionally grimacing in pain.

Something was off. It was enough to raise the hair on the back of his neck. A Shadow Guard learned to trust his instincts, and Hayate's instincts demanded that he flee, but he had come too far to be timid now. "Toru?" Hayate whispered.

His brother's eyes snapped open. They were crazed. Wild. The eyes of a lunatic.

"It is in my head," Toru growled. "Kill me before it wins."

"What manner of torture is this?" Hayate asked, genuinely curious. Unit 731 was always coming up with vile new methods.

"The Pathfinder lives! The imposter has exposed me to it. It seeks to possess my body and claim my soul. You must kill me before he can use me."

Hayate stroked his chin thoughtfully. Toru truly had gone insane. His mother must have been of particularly weak stock, as he was aware of no other of the thousand sons having such a frail mind. "I would like nothing better than to take your life, but that is not my place. Our father has claimed this right for himself."

"I can hear their plans. The schools..." Toru's face contorted as he ground his teeth together. "This corruption is in the schools. Concentrated... So the Actives there can be harvested. You must find and eliminate the infiltrators quickly. Or else when they receive the signal, they will feed, and the Enemy will come."

Hayate was saddened by the piteous display. Brutes were so strong, but Toru's madness was overcoming his own body. It was as if he was at war within himself. Veins stood out on his forehead. Sweat rolled down his face in fat beads. Toru was fighting *something*. He screamed in agony, and then his head flopped forward, limp and unconscious. Blood came trickling from his ear.

That was not blood.

The First Shadow Guard leaned in closer. Close enough to feel Toru's breath. The substance coming out of Toru's ear looked more like demon's ink than blood. *Curious.*

And then the substance defied gravity and crawled back up to disappear inside his brother's ear.

Hayate swore like a *burakumin* dung shoveler and leapt back across the prison cell. What new Unit 731 butchery was this?

Curiosity satisfied, and completely unnerved, Hayate decided he had seen enough, so he Traveled from the dungeons.

Like most Imperium military affairs, the ceremony had begun with a great deal of flourish. It was a rare treat for the local officials to be visited by any members of the high command, let alone the greatest luminary in all of the Imperium short of the Emperor.

The Imperium Section of Shanghai had been scrubbed and polished until the whole neighborhood gleamed. This was the richest, most prosperous, most advanced part of the city anyway. An example to the other cultures gathered in the city of the inherent superiority of the Imperium way of life. It was normally beautiful, but it had been taken to a new level for the Chairman's visit. Every tree, bush, and flower had been carefully tended. Servants had cut the lawns with scissors. There wasn't so much as an errant leaf or cigarette butt cluttering the ground within six blocks.

Flags and banners were strung between the buildings and hung from every light pole. The buildings surrounding the Imperium compound were all new, between twenty and forty stories each, and every sparkling window on them had been cleaned until there wasn't so much as a fingerprint. If a pigeon shit on a ledge, Hayate was certain that there would be a servant out there scrubbing it with a toothbrush a moment later or somebody was getting beheaded. The center of the Imperium Section was the ambassador's palace. It was only a few years old, but it had been built to look like a castle. Hayate found it a bit ostentatious, but that just meant it fit Shanghai. The parade would end on the palace grounds.

The Chairman's parade was impressive, five hundred soldiers, all marching in perfect unison. The only reason there weren't any tanks was because their tracks might damage the pavement and make things ugly, and it was felt that the loud engines might disrupt the natural tranquility of the area. Instead, a pair of *Gakutensuko* marched, awing the crowd with their gleaming metal bodies and Cog superscience. After that came one hundred fearsome Iron Guard, and in the middle of all those perfectly pressed uniforms was the Chairman himself, riding on a magnificent white stallion.

Every Imperium citizen in Shanghai had turned out for the event, and they packed the sidewalks. Most of the lesser people and non-people had been banished from the Section for the day. The only foreign eyes that would be allowed to behold the Chairman's magnificence were the very highest ranking of the Chinese, French, British, Russian, and American diplomats in the city. Thousands bowed and stayed bowed as the Chairman rode past.

Hayate watched all of this finery from the windows of the military command center on the fourth floor of the palace. He was still distracted, troubled by his brother's words...No...Not his words, because to say that would be to imply doubt.

Several Iron Guards and Imperium military officers were also watching, taking reports from functionaries, and giving orders. The lieutenant governor of the Imperium Section was in charge of the events. "First the Chairman will present the medals. He wishes to give a speech. As soon as he is done, then the traitor and the Grimnoir prisoners will be brought into the courtyard for all of the crowd to witness. Are the executioners ready? Excellent. I don't care if their blades are dull. The more squealing and begging the better...Good, good. Then the Chairman will duel the traitor, and once he is dispatched, behead the prisoners, and then we will serve dinner. Have all the mats been changed? Splendid."

Hayate, who had no patience for courtly matters, went back to scanning the crowd. His men were among them, mingling, ready to strike down enemies should the need arise. Nobody paid much attention to the Shadow Guard. They were not flashy like their Iron

Guard brethren. He went back to being a unremarkable part of the command center, like a particularly dangerous chair.

And while he stood there, being unremarkable, he could not help but wonder about what he had seen in Toru's ear . . .

A soldier rushed into the room and saluted the leader of the Iron Guard. "Forgive my interruption, Master Goto, we have an aerial contact along the coast."

"What is it?"

"Unidentified dirigible. Multihulled and extremely fast, climbing to a high altitude. Thirty miles to the south and heading this way. The Navy has moved to intercept."

The Iron Guard grunted. "They'll handle it. Keep me apprised."

A few minutes later, another obviously flustered functionary came into the command room. This one went right to the head of the secret police and gave a whispered report. The fact that it was whispered probably meant that it was something embarrassing enough to cause the *Tokubetsu Koto Keisatsu* to lose face. Hayate had magically augmented hearing, so eavesdropping was no struggle.

"I am sorry, sir. A riot has broken out."

"Are you certain?"

"Yes, sir."

"Where?"

"It began in the old Chinese district, but has already spread across three other sections. We are not sure of the cause of the disturbance, but they are attacking our officers, and the Chinese police have fared no better. Some of the looters have been shot, but that only seemed to awake more anger."

"Ah. Damn it." The police chief pinched the bridge of his nose. "Dispatch every military unit that is on ready status. I want this quashed. This will not cloud the Chairman's visit."

"Should I order the naval vessels to shell the affected neighborhoods?"

"Do you wish to mar the Chairman's journey with the rumble of artillery? Do you wish to wrinkle his nostrils with the smell of smoke?" The police chief hissed. "Get out of here, fool."

Hayate suppressed a smile. Ah, the Grimnoir. They were such clever foes. He was curious to see what manner of mischief they had planned this time.

Chapter 20

Like most self-proclaimed grand visionaries, Bradford Carr was an imbecile. He filled this office with toadies, flunkies, and bullies. One minute after you put my name on that door I am firing the lot of them. The stated mission of the OCI is to keep America safe in all matters pertaining to magic. That's noble. That's something I can stand behind. But Actives are Americans too, and they'll be treated like Americans. There will be no more flouting the law under my watch, so help me God. The OCI man should respect the Constitution, understand magic for good or ill, and be tough enough to get the job done no matter what. You want to know how I'd run the OCI? The ideal OCI agent is a PhD who can win a bar fight. Bradford Carr made an enemy out of Jake Sullivan. I would have offered that man a job.

—William Donovan,
Closed door confirmation hearings for the
office of the coordinator of information, 1933

UBF *Traveler*

THE CLEAR BLUE SKY had gotten darker and darker until it had turned to night.

"Seventy thousand feet," Barns stated as he carefully adjusted a knob. "And still climbing..."

People had never been meant to go this high. Faye stood at the rail, staring out the armored window, marveling at how clearly she could see the curve of the blue world from here. For once, Faye could actually admit she'd found another interesting way to get somewhere other than Traveling.

"Mr. Black, how many contacts?" Captain Southunder asked the man sitting behind the fancy teleradar machine.

"More returns than I can count. They've scrambled the entire navy."

Faye hooked her legs around the rail so she could lean *way* over. The glass went clear past the catwalk and on down so she could see directly below. Even though she was mostly all bundled up, she really didn't want to get her forehead stuck to the freezing glass. That would have been embarrassing.

She couldn't even see the Imperium ships below, but when she checked with her head map, she could pick them out. Engines pumping, magic surging, thousands of soldiers looking for a chance to shoot them down. She knew that they'd already tried, and she could sense the friction and the hot bits of matter as projectiles were futilely lobbed in their direction. There was no use distressing the Marauders with this information, she figured, since the odds of them actually getting hit were about two thousand, five hundred to one. They were a tiny, nearly invisible spot in the sky to the Imperium airships and fighters. Of course, those odds would change the higher the bad guys climbed and the more lead they threw.

Captain Southunder was biting one knuckle. "Engines?"

"Still functioning," answered one of the crew. The board in front of him had nothing but green lights on it.

"Pressure compensators?"

Faye looked over. That board had several lights flashing yellow and one that was red. "Fifty percent, Captain." The pirate thumped the panel with his fist a few times and the red one turned yellow. Now that was engineering that Faye could understand. "Back up to seventy." The light went red. "Hell. Fifty."

She didn't know what was going on, except there wasn't any air up here at all, it was freezing, stuff was starting to break, and if certain specific things broke on the machine that was pumping in heated air, they'd all pass out and choke to death or have their blood boil off before they even had a chance to fall to their deaths. Her head map was feeding her information that even the Captain didn't know. Barns was Lucky, and he was using his Power hard. The tremble in his hands and the sweat on his face wasn't from flying the ship, it was from the physical stress of unconsciously burning his Power to manipulate probability in their favor. He was better at it than he knew, and Faye got a little mad at herself when she realized how jealous she was of that particular Power, and just how much better she would be able to put it to use. Meanwhile, a few things had snapped from the cold and the stress deep inside the ship. There had been a spark, and it had immediately ignited the fuel in a machine, but Lady Origami had forced the fire out from here merely by getting stern with the unruly fire.

Faye was impressed. She wondered if the Captain realized just how many times those two Actives had saved his ship. Probably not, since he was so distracted. The man who could control weather was probably feeling extra uncomfortable, since for the first time in his long life, he was in a place that didn't have weather as he knew it. He was trying not to show it, but Faye could tell. The energy and currents that existed up here for him to manipulate were too alien for him to understand. *Poor Captain Southunder.*

In the hold, the genius Cogs were using their magic to make sure Buckminster Fuller's contraption was going to work, and she could see how they were folding and unfolding bits of the Power to grant themselves flashes of extra wisdom. That type of magic was starting to make more sense to her, and, in fact, it even seemed familiar for some reason. Not too far away from them was Mr. Sullivan, all suited up in steel, his body made extra dense to keep out the cold. He was impervious as stone, waiting, thinking . . . About what, she didn't know, but heaven help anybody who got in Mr. Sullivan's way after he'd had a chance to think through how to get them.

Now the Captain was addressing her, so Faye had to pull out of her head map and snap back to reality. "Faye, can you reach the Imperium target from here?"

"Yes, Captain," she answered with what surely seemed like no hesitation to everyone else. In reality, she'd had to think it over hard, for nearly one-eighth of a second. She'd be falling through the air, carrying a thousand pounds of steel and Mr. Sullivan, but even then she'd be able to Travel up to forty times to correct her trajectory and get them in the right place before she built up too much speed and hit the ground and went splat. Once again, it wasn't the distance, but the view, and if you were going four hundred miles an hour, it sure made landing challenging. "No problem."

"Seventy thousand, five hundred feet," Barns said.

"Grab Mr. Sullivan and get down there. The hold will depressurize the second we open the doors, and it won't do to have you two get sucked outside."

"That's mighty thoughtful of you, Captain."

Something was wrong. Faye tilted her head to the side, like her head map had just made her inner ear feel off balance. Barns had stiffened too, as his Power had just recoiled against something that even he couldn't help shift the odds on. She checked her head map. One of the Imperium navy ships far below them felt different from the others swarming around it. It was bigger, faster. Moving quickly across the ocean, and the magic that was gathering inside of it was deadly and familiar. "Peace Ray charging up!" Faye warned. Now that was something that would be a whole lot more effective than the explosive shells the Imperium had been lobbing up at them. A Tesla beam could shoot clear out into space if it felt like it.

"Barns, evasive maneuvers." Southunder ordered.

But Faye knew that would be next to useless. The ray would travel in a perfectly straight line seemingly as fast as the light from the sun. Their altitude was protecting them from everything else in the sky, but that same altitude would just make them a better target for the Peace Ray. They might miss a few times, maybe, but that was it. The Imperium certainly weren't stupid. Faye had already done the math. "Keep going, Captain. I got this." She didn't wait for the inevitable response.

There was a scary white skull face looking down at her with big black eyes in the cargo hold. Mr. Sullivan's voice seemed odd coming through all that steel plate. "It time?"

She reached down and picked up the bundle of guns and bombs she'd left here. There were a bunch of pistols already holstered on her body. Behind her, the Cogs had fired up their new machine, and it was crackling with magical energy. "Can't. Peace Ray incoming. Gotta stop it."

Sullivan may have seemed slow to most folks, but he was anything but, especially when it came down to matters pertaining to them not getting dead. "I'll catch up."

Faye checked her head map, picked a spot nearly sixteen miles away, and set off to absolutely wreck a battleship all by herself.

Imperium Warship K3 *Auspicious Dragon*

FAYE QUICKLY REALIZED that the main reason the massive airship hadn't fired its Peace Ray at the *Traveler* yet was because the designers hadn't ever thought they'd ever have to fire it nearly straight up.

She had to hand it to whoever the captain of the Japanese battleship was, because he'd pumped hydrogen forward and swiveled the engines so that the front end of the ship was rising hard and fast. She'd never set foot in an airship which was pointed at this steep of an angle before—well, except for the *Tempest* while it was crashing, but she'd been in a coma for that. Normally when an airship climbed it was a sort of floating with just a bit of an upward angle inside. They were actually pretty gentle. This, on the other hand, felt rather extreme, and if she'd been anybody other than Sally Faye Vierra, landing on a catwalk at such a sharp angle would have been disconcerting.

To Faye, it merely threw her aim off a bit. Her first bullet hit the Japanese soldier in the shoulder, but that was the beauty of the Suomi Gun. She'd only picked the Finnish gun out of the locker because it had had the prettiest wooden stock, but it was really easy to shoot, so she just adjusted her aim and put the next few in the center of his chest. In her defense, she'd been holding the heavy gun in one hand, and her other hand had been holding the handles on her big sack of guns, which weighed a ton. She dropped the sack with a clatter and used her other hand to grab the magazine.

Of course her gunshots had gotten the attention of everyone else in the room. They looked up in surprise. She wasn't even sure what this room did, but it had a lot of energy flowing through it, so she figured it must be important, and everybody inside looked like mechanics, so killing them might help.

Mashing the trigger, Faye worked the muzzle back and forth. The compensator on the end kept the gun from rising too much. The rest of the thirty rounds was gone in one long, angry burst. Most of the men had been struck. Bodies hit the deck. Some still shouting, a few crawling, others still. Steam was squirting from a pipe. A few had run for it, and a couple of them had even escaped, not yet aware that there were bullets stuck in them. She'd deal with them later, but right now she could still feel the energy building in the Peace Ray. She dropped the Suomi and reached for the sack of guns. Last time she'd done this she'd realized that stopping to reload took up precious seconds which could be better spent murdering Imperium. The ship was at such a crazy angle that the bag had slid down the floor until it hit a wall.

That reminded her that the captain had to be pretty clever to steer his battleship like this, so she'd deal with him next. Her hand landed on a Browning Auto Five shotgun. It was one of her all-time favorites.

It was easy to pick out the bridge. It had lots of equipment, big chairs, and electricity flowing up to the various devices and displays. Faye landed on top of one of those banks of instruments. The man operating it looked up at her in confusion. She kicked him in the teeth and he spilled from his chair.

There were lots of Imperium in this room, but the Captain had to be the one with the fanciest hat, so she blew his head clean off.

There was an Iron Guard on the bridge. If she hadn't been able to tell by all the extra magic bonded to him through the ritual kanji scars, she would have been tipped off by the way he quickly drew a sidearm and started shooting at her. She disappeared as the bullets perforated the console.

Iron Guards were tricky, and she'd found that they sometimes they could get lucky and predict where a Traveler might reappear, so Faye played it smart. There was a big air-conditioning conduit that ran under the floor. She put herself in it, right under the grating beneath the Iron Guard's feet. She couldn't lift the shotgun, but she got one of her .45s out and popped eight rounds up through the grate, shredding the Iron Guard's feet and legs. The way he just grimaced and stayed standing told Faye he was a Brute.

The Imperium Marines were pretty sharp, and they figured out where she was shooting from right quick, but it didn't matter, since she was on the opposite end of the ship before their first bullets punctured the grate in response. She'd pulled the pin on a grenade and left it under the bridge for them as a present. She was far enough away she didn't hear the explosion, but she clearly felt the Spellbound curse stealing the magical connection of the Iron Guard and several of the marines after the grenade shrapnel killed them.

The Peace Ray fired.

It didn't make much noise. There wasn't much outward show as the particles were magically accelerated and hurled into the distance. Just a sort of snap and a flickering of the lights.

No!

She checked. The *Traveler* was still there. They'd missed. If they'd been hit then the *Traveler* would have simply been swept away. They would adjust and fire again. She scanned her head map. This ship was over a thousand feet long and packed with life. Who looked busiest?

That room was busy! Surely somebody in there was involved in shooting the Peace Ray. She arrived unseen. Since nobody even noticed little old her, she stuffed another mag into her pistol, stuck it back in the holster and lifted the shotgun, but then thought better of it. A man in coveralls was working next to a big machine with giant gears grinding together. That machine looked super important and worth stopping, so she walked over, thumped the man over the head with the shotgun butt, and knocked him into the gears. Sadly, he didn't so much as slow the big gears as they mulched him to pieces, but he sure did scream a lot, which got everybody's attention.

So she lifted the shotgun and went to work, dropping Imperium left and right. The Auto Five kicked really hard, but it ran *fast*. Like her. Everyone scrambled. Some rushed her, screaming, brave, not even armed, while others ran for help, but to the Imperium's credit, nobody stood there stupidly. They all did *something*. Not that it did them any good, since ten seconds later the entire engine room had been depopulated.

Faye went back to the slowly turning gears. They looked too important not to break, so she jammed the empty Auto Five between them. The big machine shrieked and ground to a halt. The whole airship shuddered, so that was more like it. That had broken something, and fire came shooting out a pipe in the wall. Faye couldn't read the weird Japanese letters, but luckily a nearby drum had a flame drawn on it. She hoped that meant it was flammable, so she lifted her .45 and poked a hole in the tank before Traveling away.

Sure enough, the contents of that tank weren't just flammable. They were *explosive*. She sure heard that one, even felt it through the soles of her feet as the floor vibrated, but she was already four hundred feet away and three floors up, to pick up something new from her big sack of guns. Two of the crew had approached the abandoned bag cautiously, poking at it with their toes, so she simply shot each one once in the back of the head. The airship was still pointing up drastically, so that told Faye she needed to hurry up and use one of the biggest guns. She picked the bazooka. It had gotten brains on it. *Icky*.

Lance had told her *bazooka* wasn't its real name, just something they called it for short. It was really the something-something-mark-something-or-other launcher, but she preferred the slang term *bazooka*, and she figured it would do a real number to the delicate membranes inside the giant hydrogen cells. Lance had been fond of the bazooka, so she figured this was for him.

There was a great spot on the swaying platform suspended between the hulls. This place wasn't so armored as the outside, because, come on, how was a bomb going to end up in here? There were ten men on the platform, one of whom was an armed Imperium marine, so she made sure to land right behind him. He had his back to her. Faye took a knee and shouldered the big tube. Lance had always warned her about the dangerous hot gases that came shooting out the back of the bazooka when you fired, but she figured it wouldn't hurt if she hit an Imperium man with it. She didn't even really have to aim, since pretty much everything in the wide-open red space was vulnerable. She pulled the trigger and was rewarded with a terrific BOOM.

It made all of the Imperium men jump or hit the deck, except for the marine who had been standing behind her, of course. He never knew what hit him. The bazooka's back blast had knocked him right over the railing. He was falling toward the lower hull, burning and screaming. Faye found that amusing for some reason. She turned back in time to see the explosive shell's impact. There was a great shower of sparks and smoke as the big round tore through multiple cell walls. There was a blue flash as gas ignited.

The Torches on the damage-control team were easy to pick out. They were the ones not coming to kill her. They were concentrating on the explosion, trying to keep the fire in check while the other armored cells sealed themselves off. Everybody else was charging at her, but you can't hardly tackle a Traveler. Faye simply dropped the empty bazooka, stepped through space, and let all those tough guys dogpile each other. Then she lifted her .45, shot one Torch in the throat, turned and shot the other right between the shoulder blades. Then she Traveled back to her bag of guns, because the oncoming wall of fire would take care of the rest.

An alarm began to sound. Why had it taken them so darn long? But then she realized that she'd only been aboard for one minute and fifteen seconds. She could sense the Peace Ray recharging, but the ship was listing a bit to the side. She'd certainly upset their aim, but they could still get themselves corrected, and that simply wouldn't do. She had to take this big battleship *down*. There would be other Torches on a ship this big, and they'd all be concentrating on controlling the fires she had started, which meant it was time to switch tactics. She had to find other things to blow up.

She went back to her bag and pulled out the two really big Russian stick grenades. She could barely lift them and couldn't imagine how some poor sucker was expected to throw these further than the blast radius. Lance had said these things could blow up a tank!

Her boots landed on a narrow catwalk. She was out in the open. The blue ocean was visible through the grating. The hangar was filled with biplanes. They were suspended by hooks and chains, dangling over the open floor. Airplanes were filled with gas, but more importantly, they could be loaded with bombs, and if she was a bomb, where would she be kept?

There.

There was a big armored door in the side of the hangar. The bombs were fed down a mechanized chute. She followed the chute up with her head map . . . And landed in an armored room absolutely filled with deadly steel ovals, thousands of them, each one weighing hundreds of pounds. Faye grinned. This was perfect. The armor was supposed to keep explosions out, but it was going to have a heck of a time holding this one in . . . She struggled to pull the massive cotter pin out of the Russian grenade, but she managed. Then she dropped it and hurried out of there. She didn't want to be anywhere near that thing when it went off.

She landed on the far end of the ship, and good thing she did, because the bottom middle section came apart five seconds later. Not counting Tesla devices, it was the biggest explosion Faye had ever seen. Debris, people, even whole airplanes got launched out by the blast and went spinning toward the ocean. Her head map told her it was actually hundreds of smaller blasts all piled on top of each other, but nobody else would be able to tell that.

The bottom hull's hydrogen was burning. The explosion must have killed several of their damage-control Torches, because they weren't doing nearly as good a job stopping this fire.

Somebody must have had the good sense to try to steer this thing. Faye had to hand it to the Imperium Navy, they were very steady under pressure. They'd realized they were crashing, and they were going to try and put it down soft. Faye didn't think so. Her head map told her which engines were being used to power the compressors on the remaining bags which would enable them to control their descent, and she still had one of the big stick grenades left.

This room was filled with roaring turbines, big as trucks, and pumping pistons as big around as trees. The alarm was blaring. The lights were flashing. Men were scrambling. They'd all been rocked by the big explosion and they were scared.

Faye grabbed hold of the pin, but it didn't want to budge. She pulled, straining, hard as she could. The darn thing was stuck.

There was an Iron Guard in this room. A big, terrifying man, and Faye could sense the magic roiling off of him. He was moving quickly, bounding between the machines. She could tell what he was because he had made himself so very light. He was a Heavy, like Mr. Sullivan. And he'd been pursuing her futilely through the ship. She could respect the effort, but she wasn't planning on sticking around.

The grenade's pin wouldn't come out. As long as this *Kaga* was in the air, then the *Traveler* was in danger. Faye tugged and pulled, but the pin was stuck, and she had cow-milking hands, so it wasn't like she was weak. *Stupid Soviet junk!*

Gravity intensified. She could feel it building on top of her. The Heavy was hurling Imperium engineers out of his way. He drew his sword. Her head map screamed as the weight of ten worlds tried to squish her flat.

This stupid bomb was stuck and she wasn't strong enough to free it. Her body wasn't strong enough to shrug off all the extra gravity, and in a couple of seconds, some of her internal organs were going to pop. She needed to be stronger.

The Heavy roared a battle cry and threw himself at her.

She'd met the Chairman briefly. She'd seen how he'd changed his

Powers back and forth, tapping whatever part of the Power he needed to. Faye hadn't understood it then, heck, she barely understood it now, but the Power wasn't that much different than Lady Origami's folded animals. Every type of magic had a shape, and that shape touched other shapes, and all those shapes together made up the world. Your type of magic just determined which part of the world you could tweak. If you reshaped your own connection, you could steer it to a different part of the Power and call on a whole new form of magic.

She'd changed this before, instinctually calling on Whisper's fire magic while inside the belly of the God of Demons. Faye felt for the connection to the Power she'd just stolen from the Brute on the bridge, found it, studied the complex geometry . . .

And in the half a second it took for the Heavy to cover the distance, Faye figured out how to make herself *strong*.

Faye easily shrugged off all of the extra gravity like it wasn't even there. The pin came right out of the grenade. The Heavy's sword was coming right for her head, but it seemed *so slow*. Faye simply moved her body out of the way.

The grenade and the Heavy hit the floor at the same time. *So this must be how Delilah felt.* The Heavy swung the sword at her ankles, but she just hopped over it like she was playing jump rope. She kicked him in the ribs, and the big man flew back and crashed hard into a pylon. *That big old razor sword could come in handy.* She crossed the distance in a blur, reached down, grabbed him by the arm, not even that hard, mind you, and his bones snapped like brittle twigs. Faye had surprised herself. The Heavy bellowed.

Fun as that was, that big Russian grenade was about to go off, so Faye focused, realized that she couldn't Travel because she was currently a Brute, let her Power spring back to its comfortable state, and stepped outside.

She was whistling through the sky. The Pacific Ocean was bright blue and pretty. It was a beautiful day.

Faye realized she still had the Heavy by the arm. He began screaming his head off as he realized where they were, so Faye just let go of him and he went flailing off to the side. That fancy Iron Guard sword of his was flipping through the air, so Faye timed it just right, reached out, and snagged it by the handle. From what she'd seen, those things were so darned sharp that if she'd missed she probably would've left fingers behind.

As she fell toward Earth, another giant explosion rocked the battleship. Her grenade had ignited something else vital. The entire left side of the ship came apart. The bags were consumed in three rapid fireballs, and then the entire sky above her was one big spreading cloud of red and black as one of the most advanced warships in history was blown to kingdom come. Hundreds died instantly and a thousand more would ride the flaming wreckage into the ocean.

Faye had been on board the Imperium battleship a grand total of three minutes and forty-seven seconds.

UBF *Traveler*

"CAPTAIN SAYS we're almost ready to open the cargo bay!" Chris Schirmer shouted from across the hold. The Cogs were still scrambling, banging away on the delicate machine with desperation achievable only by men who knew they only had one shot at getting something right and lives were on the line.

Sullivan waited next to the ramp, still as a statue, every inch of him clad in bulletproof steel. Browning's enchanted BAR was lashed to his back, and there were magazine pouches all over his body. The magical .45 was on his hip. He had grenades, knives, and no doubt that his metal fist to the mouth would ruin just about anybody's day. The weight on his shoulders and the narrowed field of view through the helmet felt familiar. Trade the fancy new suit for a rusted-out pot-metal piece of shit and the bullpup BAR for an old Lewis and it would almost feel like being back in the Great War, waiting for the whistle to sound so he could launch himself out of the trenches.

Almost... He flexed his Power, testing it ever so gently. It felt like there was enough filling his chest to crush the whole world flat.

Yeah. This was just like the trenches. Take the ground. Hold that ground. Kill anybody who gets in your fucking way. That's what Faye was probably doing right now. He'd be doing the same in a few minutes. The only added complication this time was that he was going to *talk* to the enemy first. Then he'd kill them.

Schirmer was the most practical of the geniuses in the hold. "Get those helmets on and make sure the seals are tight." It was a good thing he did, because it wouldn't have been surprising if a few of them had been too distracted working on their machine and ended up forgetting. "Check your hoses and make sure the oxygen flow is good. Then everyone check your buddy. Fuller, go make sure Sullivan's sealed up."

He'd stayed out of the Cog's way. The plan depended on the device doing what it was supposed to. Sullivan was a distraction. He was the sideshow. This device was the key. But he was still glad when Buckminster Fuller came over to check his oxygen tank.

The pressure suits had come from United Blimp and Freight's testing division. The Cog was wearing a big, clear glass bubble on his head. The neck of the leather and rubber suit he was wearing was threaded for the fishbowl to screw on. Fuller's voice came out funny, emanating from a brass box with holes in it mounted on his neck. He took a moment to check Sullivan's air tank. "Considering your protective system's respiration mechanisms were designed in anticipation of surviving poison gas rather than high altitude operations—"

"Is it good?"

"Yes. It's good . . . I must say, Mr. Sullivan, I am worried about you and the young Ms. Vierra."

"Faye will be fine," he assured Fuller. She'd better be, or else they'd all be getting vaporized by a Peace Ray any second now, so no use dwelling on it.

"Of course. She is very forceful for a Cog. I would say—"

"Hold on . . ." For a second Sullivan thought that Fuller's voice box machine had malfunctioned. "Faye's not a Cog."

Fuller tried to shake his head, but it turned out that was impossible inside the neck gasket of the bubble helmet. He gave up. "No. I could see it rather clearly. As you are aware, my own Power enables me to see magical connections. She is perhaps the most complicated and capable specimen I've yet encountered, and I so wish I had not been so occupied with this current project, because I simply must speak with her. Ms. Vierra is very clearly a Cog, and a potent one at that."

"Faye's a Traveler. You sure you're not seeing that Spellbound curse that's on her?"

"Oh no, of course not. I can make that out rather clearly. It is vast, terrible, and thus completely unmistakable. She was clearly born a Cog. That connection was there first. The exceedingly complex magical construct which is bound to her is in addition to that."

The idea clicked. Sullivan whistled and it made an odd echo inside the helmet. "Can you tell what kind of Cog somebody is by looking at their Power? Like Browning makes weapons, or Ira's medical stuff, or you and your...domes."

"Partly. I hesitate to form a hypothesis, but my considerable instinct in this manner would point toward her adaptive magical genius being related to physics, spatial matters, and relativity."

"So she's a genius about how stuff works? How the world fits together?"

"Fundamentally, yes...I was not aware that this was a new fact to you. I would have assumed that anyone could very clearly see that Ms. Vierra is a Cog."

And all this time they'd just thought she was odd because she was a Traveler...

That was why the Power had picked Faye to be the Spellbound when Sivaram died! She'd been born brilliant, all Cogs were, and her specific genius just happened to fall into the area most useful for battling the Enemy. She became a Traveler because Sivaram had been a Traveler. It had dragged his magic along with the curse. Of course, she was absurdly capable as a Traveler, but it wasn't because of how much Power she had, but rather because of how damned scary *fast* her brain worked.

"Holy shit, the Power is smarter than we gave it credit for." Sullivan patted Fuller on the shoulder, and the steel gauntlet nearly knocked the man over. "Thanks, Doc. You better get back to your gizmo. It's almost show time."

"We will make it work, Mr. Sullivan. No matter what."

"You're starting to sound like a Grimnoir knight there, Fuller."

The bubble helmet bobbed back and forth as Fuller tried to nod. "I would not have thought that was such a compliment before embarking on this journey. Now, however? Thank you." Then the Cog scurried back to his device.

Schirmer was watching the instrumentation on the machine. "Congratulations, we have now achieved a greater altitude than any other men in history." The UBF Cogs cheered. "Now, make sure your suit is tethered to the safety line." Good idea. It wouldn't do to suck their Cogs out the door.

Sullivan didn't strap in. He couldn't afford to wait for Faye. He was so engrossed in thinking about this new revelation into the world's most powerful wizard and staring at the waiting ramp that he hadn't heard her approach. There was a hard metallic thump on his arm. He wouldn't have felt anything less. He turned the helmet to see Lady Origami there, wearing one of the UBF suits and clear fishbowl helmets. Safety ropes had been run through the harness she was wearing. She put the wrench she'd used to hit him back into a pouch on her belt.

"Akane? What're you doing here?" And he immediately regretted that, because it sounded accusatory. "I'm glad to see you."

"Captain said I could see you off. I can put out fires anywhere." She reached up and tapped the helmet. "I would give a kiss for luck, but..."

"Yeah, I wouldn't want you to get your lips ripped off... In case you can't tell, I was smiling when I said that. That was a joke... I like your lips just fine."

"I am aware, Sullivan. You talk more when you are nervous. It is funny talking to a woman makes you more nervous than war."

The huge armored shoulders could still manage a shrug. "I'm good at war."

She opened one glove and revealed another delicate paper animal. This one was a duck. "For luck again." She shoved it into one of the magazine pouches on his chest. "Probably it will not make it. So you better come back so I can make you another."

"Deal." He put one gauntlet alongside her bubble helmet, gently as possible. She put her hand on top of his.

"We're on in sixty seconds!" Schirmer shouted. "Sullivan? How come you aren't strapped in?"

Sullivan just waved. "I'm taking the quick way down." After all, that had been the plan before they'd known Faye was alive. He went back to Akane. "You'd best stand back."

She took up the rope so she wouldn't trip over it and made her way back to the interior. When she reached one of the pylons next to the machine, she tied another safety line to that with an expert sailor's knot.

The red lights started blinking. The buzzer sounded. The hydraulics activated.

Sullivan took a deep breath. He turned the skull-faced helmet toward Akane. She was watching him. She seemed a little afraid, maybe excited, but mostly she seemed proud, defiant. "Beat them, Sullivan. Every last one!"

"Every last one."

The door began opening. The air screamed past.

It was dark as night. The grey and white patch of straight lines so incredibly far below was Shanghai. The Cogs were already wrestling their machine along the tracks and chains toward the opening.

He took one last look at Akane. "Show me a smile on that pretty face."

She did.

Sullivan stepped off the ramp into space.

Sullivan in Armor

⚔ Chapter 21 ⚔

In my campaigns I've found there are two types of effective soldier, the gazelles and the grunts. The gazelle is capable of incredible bursts of speed but can be flighty, distracted, and useless, but in those moments of brilliance, nothing can catch a gazelle. The grunt, on the other hand, will never blind you with his grace or swiftness, but will simply plug along until the job is finished. Now after watching the Imperium in combat action, I must add a third type. I'd thought I'd seen warrior fanaticism amongst the Moro, but I was unprepared for the total devotion of the Imperium warrior. Say what you will about their methods, but a true believer is not to be trifled with.

—Captain John J. Pershing,
Army Observation Report on the taking of Vladivostok, 1905

Free City of Shanghai

IT WAS A NIGHTMARE wrapped in a poem. It was a dream shrouded in fog.

Toru struggled against the beast rampaging through his very thoughts. He knew how to fight with his hands, but he did not know how to fight on the battlefield of his mind. The creature was there, in the background, whispering, speaking in lies and secrets.

Time passed in incoherent fits and starts. He was in the present. Then in the past. He was back at the Iron Guard academy, a young boy, standing proud while his sensei beat him with sticks to test his resolve. He was in the present, screaming in agony as the pain like a drill bit bore through his eyes. He was in the past, collecting heads in Manchuko. Then he was in a dream, listening to the words of his father, or perhaps that was Hattori's past. He could not tell. And then the present, except that had to be a hallucination as well, since Hayate had been there.

Hours passed, days maybe. He could not tell. But he relived every single moment of his life against his will as if the invader inside his head were flipping randomly through the pages of a book. Exhausted, he drifted into an unconscious haze.

His Iron Guard brothers came to unchain him, but they were not his brothers. He could see that now. They were wearing the skin of men, but their insides were foul corruption, an extension of the Pathfinder's malicious will. They had been Iron Guard once, until Dosan Saito had exposed them to the cancerous sludge and it had slowly dissolved them into these mindless shells. That would be Toru's eventual fate as well, only mercifully his life would end long before that process could be completed.

The kanji of paralysis was roughly scrubbed from his forehead and he could feel life returning to his limbs. The chains were unlocked and he fell to this hands and knees. The Nishimura armor clanged when it hit the floor.

The false Iron Guard were on each side. Toru would die fighting. He reached for one, but nothing happened. He willed his arms to work, but it was as if his spirit was a helpless prisoner inside his own body. He was no longer magically paralyzed, but it did not matter. Hands were placed on his shoulder, and against his will, he rose. *No!* He tried to shout, but his mouth would not work.

The Pathfinder's puppets did not have to speak in order to communicate with each other. They brought over the Nishimura helmet, and his body obediently bent so it could be placed over his head. Magical kanji began scrolling across the interior glass but Toru couldn't even steer his eyes to follow.

His feet were moving, one in front of the other. His hands opened and the steel tetsubo was placed into them. He wanted to kill them, to strike them all down with it, but no matter how hard he strained, nothing happened. His body was an obedient slave.

Toru was furious, far angrier than he'd ever been, angrier than he'd ever thought humanly possible. This was offensive. Insulting. He would die as a pawn, used as an example of the imposter's greatness. This was *unacceptable*. He would have flown into a berserker rage if his damned limbs would just respond.

They stopped and waited at the end of a darkened tunnel. Two hundred yards away, the imposter stood upon a dais, speaking to a proud troop of Imperium warriors. The soldiers were standing in perfect formation, awestruck by the Chairman's presence. One by one their names were called, and they walked up to stand before him to be presented their medals. Merely being near the Chairman was the greatest moment of any of those soldiers' lives, and that made Toru even madder. These noble warriors, their entire empire, they were all being lied to.

The ceremony was over.

The puppets let him into bright sunlight. The helmet's glass automatically darkened to shield his eyes from glare. The Nishimura armor lumbered into view of the crowd, obviously towering over the muscular Iron Guards' flanking it, and they all turned to gawk. There were thousands of people in the courtyard. Stands had been erected around the parade ground. They began to shout and jeer him. He was heckled, booed, insulted, and mocked by his inferiors.

More Iron Guard came from under the palace, leading a line of prisoners. The captives were chained together, shackled at the wrists and ankles, and the short chains forced them into the indignity of shuffling. Grimnoir knights. Survivors of the raids. Most were from the *Traveler*. A few were from Shanghai. All of them had been severely beaten so badly they could barely stand, and then marked with kanji so they could not call upon their magic.

Ian Wright was in the lead. The proud young man was shoved so that he would kneel. The knight spit in the Iron Guard's face, so the Iron Guard shattered Wright's kneecap with a swift kick. Wright fell to the ground, writhing in pain. His chains snapped tight, and that pulled the others to their knees. Dr. Wells was at the end of the line. The alienist seemed mildly amused by all of the activity.

The Iron Guards walked away from the prisoners and left them there. The audience immediately began throwing things at them, garbage, rotting fruit, rocks, bottles. Allowing such items into the presence of the Chairman was inconceivable, so they had more than likely been supplied to the nearest spectators for just this moment. Hard objects bounced harmlessly off of Toru's armored shell, but the Grimnoir flinched and cringed as they were bashed, cut, and further injured. A scalp was split open by a bottle. Blood flew and the crowd screamed at the traitor and his conspirators to hurry and die.

The imposter appeared in the center of the parade ground.

Toru bowed. He did not wish to. He would never willingly have bowed to this wretched thief, but the Pathfinder was controlling his body. Even as he was still being struck by rocks and insults, the greatest indignity of all was that he was forced to offer respect to the real traitor.

The rocks stopped falling. The crowd grew still, awed by the presence of their leader and hero. They spoke in hushed whispers or not at all. This was a day that none of them would ever forget.

Okubo Tokugawa's face displayed a stern look. He raised his voice so that all could hear. Magic carried his words to the outer edges of the crowd. "Behold Toru, once of the Iron Guard, who has committed the crime of treason. He has been subverted and led astray. He betrayed many of his brothers so that they could be assassinated by the foul Grimnoir. He has been plotting with the Grimnoir in order to murder the son of heaven and the entire council. They would overthrow your lawful rulers. Their organization is evil, and exists only to plunge the world into chaos... What do you have to say for yourself, traitor?"

Toru's hands moved up to his helmet, opened the seals, and carefully removed it. Of course the imposter would force him to show his face. There could be no doubt of the identity of the man in the armor. Toru wanted to shout the truth, but only lies came out of his mouth. "Your judgment is correct, Lord Tokugawa. The Grimnoir wish to end our civilization. They intend to crush the Imperium. I have been sent by them to murder you."

"Let it be known by all that Toru is a capable warrior who fought in many righteous conflicts before his fall. He is a Brute, recipient of six war medals, six campaign medals, and fourteen separate commendations for exemplary service. Today he wears the legendary Nishimura armor, granting him even greater strength..."

The masses were frightened. They had faith in their Chairman, but Toru's legend had grown.

"It will not be sufficient." The Chairman placed one hand on the hilt of his sword. "I, Baron Okubo Tokugawa, Chairman of the Imperial Council, accept your challenge."

There were hundreds of gasps from the crowd. Truly, the imposter intended to give the masses the display of heroism they'd hoped for. Toru's hands lifted the helmet back into place. The forces controlling his limbs were careful not to twist his head off, because an accidental beheading would be an underwhelming finale. Kanji flashed before his eyes as the tetsubo was hoisted from the ground.

Toru charged.

He was so angry he could taste it. The charge was clumsy, full of Power and show, but useless. It was an embarrassment to his skills. The blustering fury would look intimidating to the onlookers, though, which was all Dosan Saito cared about. The imposter easily dodged the tetsubo, again and again, then he reached up, channeling Brute strength and slammed Toru across fifty feet of grass.

He hit the earth and dug a divot. Toru willed himself to spring right back up, but his body took its time, making a great display of how terribly hard the Chairman had struck him. *LIES!*

They circled. Toru saw half a dozen different angles of attack, but his body would not listen. He attacked wildly, spinning, swinging, with big flashy movements and overhead blows that blasted showers of dirt high into the air.

The Chairman's face was expressionless, nearly bored as he moved far faster than was humanly possible. He was demonstrating to those harboring doubts that he truly was the greatest wizard of all time. *Behold as I toy with the terrifying Toru.* Then the Brute magic switched to that of a Massive, and the imposter froze in place, willing his body as hard as steel.

The tetsubo impacted with a hit that radiated down the shaft, through the armored gauntlets, and through Toru's bones. The crowd came to their feet.

But when the dust cleared, the Chairman was still standing there, completely unharmed. He lifted one hand and a gout of fire leapt from his hands, engulfing Toru. The Nishimura suit sounded an alarm. Toru wanted to fight through it, but his body flailed back wildly instead. He was struck with ice, then lightning. Gravity changed, and Toru was falling into the sky.

The imposter leapt, intercepted Toru in mid-air, and slammed a golden, glowing fistful of magical energy into his chest. Toru hit the ground so hard that everything went black.

⁂

If he hadn't been a master of gravity, density, and mass, Sullivan was pretty darn sure he would've passed out seconds after jumping off the *Traveler*.

Jake Sullivan had done some dangerous shit in his life, but surely this took the cake.

He began spinning, harder and harder. Blood rushed through his system. Sullivan just concentrated and willed himself dense. *Blood goes where I tell it to go.* It was a good thing he was so analytical under pressure... *I'm going clockwise.* He adjusted gravity's direction slightly, pulling himself gradually out of the spin. *That's better.*

He could've made himself light as a feather and slowed himself down, but spending extra time in a place with no warmth or atmosphere wasn't a particularly inviting idea. The runes Browning had carved into the Spiker armor were glowing, keeping him from freezing, but he didn't have a whole lot of faith in the fragile oxygen tank. *What the hell? Let's see what this thing can do.* He tucked his arms into his sides, put his feet together, pointed his helmet at Shanghai, and *increased* gravity's pull.

It was like being launched from a cannon.

Sullivan streaked through the upper atmosphere. The sky went from black to dark blue. It felt like he could see half the Chinese coast from here. He picked out the blue line of the river and followed it with his eyes. Shanghai was the cluster of grey and black lines in all that organic green, brown, and blue. The city covered a big area, but he had plenty of time to pick out landmarks and tug himself toward the correct destination.

His Power was burning hot, analyzing all of the forces, pulls, and friction, but his new magic seemed to be keeping up. Earth was pulling him in, so he reached out, took hold, and willed it to pull even harder. This was what a speeding bullet felt like. Sullivan's body was moving faster than sound waves.

He'd have to check the record books, but he was pretty sure he was the first man to go faster than sound. He'd read a *Popular Mechanics* once saying that was impossible, because a man's innards would blow up if he went that fast, but Sullivan figured he was about as pliable as a bar of iron right about then, so there really wasn't much that could hurt him.

Except for hitting Shanghai at six hundred miles an hour. That would probably do it.

He had to admit, it was scary as hell, but it was kind of exhilarating.

The Spiker armor was holding up, because John Browning was the greatest inventor in the history of the whole wide world. It wasn't just on his body, but the magical connection made it practically an extension of his body, and when he went dense, so did it, and steel was a whole lot tougher than flesh to start with.

But then the oxygen bottle ruptured with a *pop*. That was a bad sign. Sullivan held his breath and pulled even harder. By the time he needed to take a breath, he'd damn well better be someplace where there was actually air to fill his lungs.

Once he'd gotten the ocean on the right, he oriented himself toward his target. He'd memorized a map of the city, and all it took was a bit of concentration to shift gravity's pull every few seconds to correct his course. He used the river as his compass and shifted gravity's center toward the correct end of the town.

There was a horrible whistling noise screaming past his helmet. Sweet, sweet air. Cold enough to hurt his teeth and so thin it was barely there, but it was still air.

There were small shadows beneath him, and they quickly grew into Imperium airships. There were black puffs of smoke as they fired upward at the *Traveler*. Surely he was too small of a target to have been noticed, but that didn't make him any less comfortable flying between the shells. He went through the smoke. It was tempting to steer himself right *through* one of those warships, but a man had to know his limitations, and he didn't know if he could go *that* dense.

He was past the screen of ships so fast that they'd probably never even known he'd been there at all. Shanghai was close enough he could pick out individual neighborhoods. Gravity's center changed to the Imperium Section. A few seconds later and he picked out the rectangle of the main compound, then the green square of the parade ground in front of their palace.

The speed was so great that he was worried if he lifted his arms away from his torso they might get ripped off. He let go of three or four extra gravities of pull and immediately began bleeding speed. He got his arms up, one armored finger running across the back of his other hand. The rune was already prepared. If this worked, Captain

Southunder would receive his voice loud and clear. It came from his mind more than his vocal cords. "I'm almost there. Turn Fuller's machine on!" He hoped that would go through, but there wasn't time to mess around if it didn't. Sullivan switched hands and went to the rune on the other side. Now this one had to work, or he was screwed.

The ground was rushing up to meet him and he had just set the world air-speed record. It was time to throw the brakes on. Sure, folks jumped out of airplanes using parachutes, but he was a Gravity Spiker. What did he need with a parachute? Sullivan was positive his trajectory would take him directly into the Imperial courtyard. The moving sea of colors down around the green square was people. The place was packed with bodies. Good. The more witnesses the better.

He changed gravity's direction. Now instead of pulling him toward Shanghai, it was coming from above. He imagined that the *Traveler* was the new center of the world, but he was gentle, just one gravity at first, and then another, and another. Timing was everything. As his momentum died off, he slowed. Not too slow, though, because he really didn't want the Imperium army to take up skeet shooting, and if they hadn't seen him yet, they were bound to soon.

He was still going a couple hundred miles an hour when he felt he was in range to activate the second spell. There was a matching rune engraved into the inside of his helmet, right in front of his mouth. Fuller had come up with this one, basing it on the magic of a Babel he had once met. It had worked fine when they'd tested it, but he hadn't been flying through the air at the time.

Dr. Wells had simply pointed out what they'd always known. To the Imperium, the Grimnoir were the bad guys. They were the Imperium's boogeyman. In every piece of propaganda, the Grimnoir were evil incarnate. It seemed so obvious, but then Wells had asked, why would you ever take a villain at his word? In what possible way would the Iron Guard ever believe a warning from the Grimnoir about the real Enemy?

By telling them something so easy to believe that they wouldn't even stop to question it.

It was time to play the villain.

Please, dear God, let this work.

Sullivan ran his finger across the rune and activated the spell.

First Shadow Guard Hayate watched the duel with increasing unease.

Iron Guard Commander Goto stood next to him at the window. "Hah! This is excellent. The Chairman is taking that traitor apart."

Hayate tended to stroke his chin while thinking, a habit he'd picked up long ago. "Have you ever seen Iron Guard Toru in a fight before?"

"He is no Iron Guard!" the commander roared. "How dare you?"

"Yes, yes, of course," Hayate said soothingly. It would not do to have to get himself into a duel because he'd hurt some blustery Iron Guard's tender feelings, not that he would have been in any danger of losing, because Hayate would simply cheat and have the man poisoned first. "My apologies . . . I have seen the traitor in combat before. In comparison, he seems *off* today."

"He is probably just overwhelmed with shame, as he should be, there in the magnificent presence of his father!"

He was not sure, and Toru's words kept running through his mind. The Grimnoir were capable adversaries, but they were few in number. Why would they throw away so very many of their warriors in an assassination attempt against a man they had repeatedly been shown was immortal? Such a waste of resources was not like them. He had enough respect for his longtime opponents to know they had to have logical reasons. Had Toru somehow convinced them of this delusions, and if so, how?

Hayate was surprised at himself. Truly, the Chairman was correct. Toru's words were poison.

A soldier ran into the room to give a report to the Iron Guard. "Sir, we just lost contact with *Zuiryu*. Other ships report seeing a large explosion at its last position."

"What!" The control room sprang to life. This was dire news indeed. There had only been four of the death-ray-equipped *Kaga*-class vessels built so far, and they'd already lost one last year. The *Auspicious Dragon* was the most capable vessel in the entire region. "Was it attacked by that unidentified dirigible?"

"We do not know, sir. Telescopes confirm that the dirigible is still up there at an extreme altitude. The Navy has launched one of their experimental demon interceptors to deal with it."

Curious. Hayate glanced back out the window. The Chairman was still whipping Toru like the Brute was a disobedient puppy. He noticed a flash of reflected light in the air high above the grounds. There was an object falling. "There is something up in the sky." He pointed.

The chief of the *Tokubetsu Koto Keisatsu* squinted. "Is it an aircraft?"

The Iron Guard, fuming about the potential loss of such a valuable vessel, turned to look. "It's a bird."

"No..." Hayate leaned forward. "I believe that is a man."

Suddenly there was a great noise, a boom like thunder, so hard it rattled the windows. The crowd shifted, thousands looking upward as one. Even the Chairman paused in the administration of his beating and looked to the heavens.

A terrible voice came after the thunder.

"Attention Imperium. This is Jake Sullivan, knight of the Grimnoir."

It was a fascinating magical effect. Hayate had clearly heard the words in Japanese, but since he could also speak Mandarin, Cantonese, English, French, Dutch, German, and Russian, it was as if he had heard it in all of those simultaneously. If he had spoken other languages, he had no doubt he would have understood it in those as well. Truly, that was a masterwork of spellbinding.

"Shoot him down!" Iron Guard Goto commanded. His men were scrambling. "Go! Movers prepare to deflect incoming!"

"I've got a message for the warriors of Dark Ocean. The Pathfinder has returned."

That was such an unexpected message that many of the Iron Guards temporarily froze in place, shocked. It was not often they heard those names invoked.

The shape in the sky was getting closer, gleaming metallic in the sun. It was clearly man shaped. *"Your Imperium schools have been infiltrated. Its monsters are hiding among you right now!"*

Then there was another voice, just as loud as the first. Okubo Tokugawa shouted back at the new challenger. "Do not listen to him! The Grimnoir are evil!"

"The Chairman says we're evil... Well, he's right. We are evil. I know the Pathfinder's here because I AM THE PATHFINDER! I answer to the Enemy. I'm bringing it here right now. You hear that, Dark Ocean? I am your worst nightmare."

"No!" The Chairman's voice shook the world. "Destroy him! Kill him!"

"Go look to your Imperium schools and see. We're already there. We're all over the Imperium. You want a fight? Come get some!"

The Chairman extended his hands and lightning blasted upward into the sky.

There was another horrendous boom, much closer and stronger now. The windows cracked. It was as if the man falling through the air had suddenly accelerated. He fell quicker than any bomb, streaking downward impossibly fast. No amount of concentrated magic from the Movers could turn that aside. He hit the ground so hard it caused a massive explosion of earth. It obliterated a huge circle of the parade grounds. The Chairman disappeared beneath a rolling cloud of dust.

"In the name of Dark Ocean, protect the Chairman! Go!" The Iron Guard were running for the exits, trying to get to their Chairman's side. One leapt through the cracked window, launching himself into the crowd four stories below because it was the most direct route.

Hayate scowled. "Fascinating."

"Are you mad?" the leader of the Iron Guard shouted. "That is how they destroyed the *Auspicious Dragon*! We are being attacked. The Enemy has returned! We must protect the Chairman!"

"Indeed." Hayate stroked his chin as he thought it through. Perhaps Toru had not been mad after all. It was either a brilliant deception by the Grimnoir for some unknown tactical reason, or something much, much worse. Either way, the truth would be discovered and justice would be satisfied. "And the Chairman is an immortal super wizard. Do not dishonor him by thinking you can protect him when he cannot protect himself."

"But—"

"Remember your training, Iron Guard! Preventing the arrival of the Enemy is our greatest single mission. You heard the invader. We have been infiltrated. Send word to the schools." Hayate turned to his own aide, who had been trying to appear even more innocuous than his master. "Dispatch shadow strike teams to every Imperium school. Investigate everyone. If anyone tries to stop you, kill them. If we are turned away, firebomb the schools to ash."

And with those words, the sacred eradication mission of Dark Ocean began anew.

UBF *Traveler*

"IT ISN'T WORKING."

"Damn it!" Schirmer hit Fuller's infernal device with a wrench. "How about now?"

"Nothing," Fuller said. He was so excited that the inside of his bubble helmet had fogged over, so he was having to put his head at a really weird angle to see the instruments.

Schirmer whacked it again. "Damn it!"

Lady Origami found it fascinating that the greatest magical mind in the world and a man who could build any mechanical device out of junk and spare parts were reduced to beating on their invention like chimps with rocks. "What is wrong with it?"

"I failed to take the current lack of thermoenergy available in the omnilocators into—"

"It's frozen," Schirmer translated.

"Oh? Is that all?" She placed her gloved hands on the machine's housing. She'd never understood the science behind how magic worked. She had grown up in a home where her extremely pious father had believed magic was the interaction between the spirits which dwelled in all things. So his talented daughter was simply gifted in talking to the fire spirits, and that was how she had thought of her Power ever since. It seemed to work well enough for her. "Yes... The fire inside is very dim. Should I wake it up?"

"Uh... Yes, please, but gently," Fuller answered.

"Sure." She concentrated. Fire dwelled inside everything. Sometimes it just needed to be *agitated*. Within seconds, the interior of the device began to glow with a warm yellow light. The electrical lights began blinking on Schirmer's instrument panel. The ball on top of the device started spinning. "How is that?"

"It's working! It's working!" Fuller exclaimed as the device began to emit an ominous hum. "Thank you!"

"Begin sweeping," Schirmer ordered the two UBF men. "Aim it at Shanghai first, then work it up and down the coast, then inward. I want to hit every school in China!"

She was disappointed. She had hoped the magical beams it released would be visible. But nonetheless, it was a good thing that she had come down to see off her Heavy. Whatever would these people do without her?

BANG!

Everyone lurched and nearly fell as the *Traveler* shook from the impact. Lady Origami fell and slid across the floor, but her safety line kept her from falling out the open door. One of the UBF men was not so lucky, and he went rolling over the side. His line snapped taut, so he did not fall the seventy-five-thousand feet to his doom, but instead he was dangling, flapping in space, ten feet past the ramp. Schirmer grabbed that rope and began tugging the screaming man back from the abyss.

She sensed the intrusion into her ship. Demons made their own sort of fire, deep within. This one was tiny, but it was inside the *Traveler* now, and it was growing. When the Imperium vessels could not climb high enough to shoot them with bullets, they'd started launching demons at them instead.

Warning buzzers began to sound. They were losing altitude. The demon was attacking the interior of their ship. It was inside the third cell of the port bag. It sensed her and shrieked in frustration. She concentrated hard on its internal fire and made the demon explode. It took even more magic to keep that fire from spreading, but there wasn't anything she could do about the original damage.

The suit was clumsy, making it difficult to stand, but she did. She rushed over and took hold of Fuller's device and helped the other UBF man struggling to aim it. Sullivan needed this to work. She would not let him die in vain.

BANG! BANG!

More demons. They were tracking in on the ship, punching holes, and ripping the *Traveler* from the sky.

BANG!

Free City of Shanghai

FATHER . . . Please help me. I need your strength. Banish this ghost from my soul. Free my limbs so that they may work. Do not let me die a failure. Help me achieve the dreams of your Dark Ocean.

Toru opened his eyes. There were black clots in front of his vision, and then he realized that they were merely dirt clods resting on the glass of his helmet's visor. He was lying on the grass of the parade ground.

The imposter stood above him, his sword drawn. Apparently the show was over and the time of his execution was at hand. Yet, the imposter was looking to the sky.

And then there was a terrible crash.

They were blasted with a rushing wind and then a wall of dust, dirt, and grass.

Now was his chance.

Father! Grant me your will!

And then Toru was filled with light.

The light scalded him. It burned like the sun. The invading ghost inside his mind screeched, wilted, and died.

The imposter was silhouetted above him. A shadow in front of a searing second sun. The invader in Saito's mind was older, stronger, and far more entrenched. It did not shrivel and die before the onslaught, but it hissed and thrashed as it was scorched by the light of truth.

Thank you, father.

He could no longer see the imposter through the cascade of dirt. Toru willed the Nishimura armor to move, and this time it did. The tetsubo erupted from the ground and swept through the air in a blur of steel, and he felt it hit the imposter, sweeping him aside like a rowboat before a tsunami.

The impact sent the imposter flying. Toru forced himself up and out of the hole his body had dug. He took a halting step, awkward to be in control of his muscles again, and then stumbled and went to his knees as a terrible agony ripped through is head. He was barely able to get one hand up to pull open his mempo. Flying grit struck him in the face, but he had to. He leaned forward and retched.

The vile black liquid he'd been exposed to had been alive. Now that it was dead, his body was forcefully expelling it. Toru coughed and hacked, spitting up chunks of the foul stuff. It tasted like lethal chemicals. It poured out of his nose like snot, fell from his eyes like tears, and dripped from his ears. It burned, but he was glad for the burn, because that meant he was *free*.

He spit, wiped his face with the back of one gauntlet hard enough to split his lip, and then closed the mempo back up. He was thankful for the smell of stale cigarettes, because anything was better than the stench of the Pathfinder's mind-controlling ooze.

The dust was settling. Iron Guard were rushing onto the parade grounds to intercept him. Most of them were human, but as the second sun flickered over them, several were clearly revealed for what they were, sacks of human skin filled with pulsating corruption. The human Iron Guard recoiled in horror as their brothers' true nature was laid bare before them.

The imposter was rising. Dosan Saito was not the Chairman, but the Pathfinder had built him a strong body, and he'd absorbed the magical essence of hundreds of powerful Actives. He was a deadly foe, and he was already rising, channeling the Power of a Shard in order to quickly warp his splintered bones back into place, and the Power of the Healer to knit together his ruined flesh. Toru could see the Pathfinder's alien presence resting upon Saito. It engulfed him, it rode upon his shoulders, its invisible tentacles stuck into Saito's ears to whisper its secrets. Other tentacles crisscrossed Saito's head, embedding themselves into his eye sockets so that he could only see what the Pathfinder wished him to see.

And then the scalding second sun was pointed elsewhere, the Pathfinder disappeared, and Dosan Saito once again appeared to be the Chairman.

The explosion had dug a crater in the field. Something moved, lifting itself from the center of the hole. A gleaming white skull appeared, followed by a steel body.

Very nice, Heavy.

"Destroy them!" Dosan Saito ordered with the Chairman's voice. "Destroy them!"

But the world had plunged into chaos. Thousands of Imperium citizens were trying to escape the grounds. Some of the Iron Guard rushed toward Sullivan or Toru, while others hesitated, confused. A few had witnessed the truth from the second sun, and they turned against the infiltrators. Brother against brother, as Iron Guards attacked the corrupted. Other Iron Guards who had not seen the truth were baffled by their brothers' seeming treachery.

A brave Iron Guard tried to strike down an infiltrator wearing the uniform of the Chairman's personal bodyguard, but was tackled by some of his brothers. "Did you not see! It is as we've been taught!" He fought off those holding him and lurched toward the infiltrator. The false Iron Guard turned and stabbed the human in the stomach with his katana. Undeterred, he crawled up the blade, grabbed the infiltrator by the face, and *ripped* the mask away. "Behold!" He spit blood as the infiltrator tore the sword free. The sword flashed, and the courageous Iron Guard's head rolled away.

The infiltrator's true nature was revealed. The torn skin lay across his uniform like a scarf. It had a face beneath a face, bare muscle pulsing red and black under a translucent shell.

The Iron Guard had been taught about such beings since they were inducted into the academy as children. Their worst fears had just been realized.

There were gasps and shouts from the assembled Iron Guard as they pushed their way through the crowd. Bodies were hurled aside as the infiltrator tried to hide its corruption, lifting the torn skin like a mask. The infiltrator was struck by crackling lightning, burst into flames, and was then ripped in half by an Iron Guard who had forced himself to grow claws of bone. Flaming black corruption sprayed across the grass.

"The Grimnoir are in league with the Pathfinder!"

"Alert the high command!"

"Protect the Chairman! Slay the Enemy! Slay the Grimnoir!"

Toru lifted the tetsubo and strode toward Saito. The imposter's guise had slipped. "There is no Pathfinder here! They seek to trick you!" Saito was panicking, realizing that the Grimnoir had twisted his own words against him to reveal his lies. The real Chairman would never panic, and that offended Toru even more. Saito was focused on using his magic to heal himself, so he wasn't even broadcasting his voice so that all could hear. "It is a Grimnoir trick!"

Sullivan had done well. Word would spread, faster than the imposter could stop it. All that remained was to destroy the imposter before he could rein in the righteous mission of Dark Ocean.

Jake Sullivan crawled out of the crater he'd dug with his face. When the lightning had come streaking his way, he'd called on all the gravity and density he could to get the hell out of the way. He'd fallen through a train car once, even survived being stomped on by a demon god, and that hadn't been anything compared to this. The amount of earth he'd moved with just his body was rather awe-inspiring. That was one damn fine spell on his back.

The goal had been to alert the Iron Guard, and as he poked his head over the side, he'd seen Fuller's device do its job, revealing the monsters inside. Between that and his words, the Iron Guard had immediately started hacking each other to pieces, so *mission accomplished*. They knew the Pathfinder was on Earth, and once that hunt started, those merciless bastards wouldn't let up until they'd exterminated ever single infiltrator.

Only problem was, now they thought he was the Pathfinder.

If he'd flat out said that the Chairman was the bad guy, nobody would have believed him. He needed to give them something plausible to latch onto, and a man's preconceived notions were a powerful thing.

Toru was gunning for Saito, but much as he'd like to help, a whole mess of Iron Guard were heading for Sullivan. He called on his Power, and gravity bent outward in a wave. The amount used was unexpected, and a wall of pure force crashed out across the lawn, flattening Iron Guard and Imperium citizens. The sudden shift in gravity caused the recently constructed stand's supports to buckle and snap. The seats came crashing down. Those who had still been inside were tossed aside or crushed beneath.

Sullivan made himself weigh nothing, and he launched himself out of the crater in a spray of rocks. Reaching over his shoulder, he found the BAR and ripped it from the straps. He returned to his normal weight as he hit the ground. The bullpup came up spitting .30-06 rounds.

There were Iron Guards everywhere, they all thought he was the devil incarnate, and they were doing their level best to kill him. Bullets struck his armor. Burning heat and freezing cold washed over him, but Browning's runes kept them from reaching his skin. The insulation kept the electricity from burrowing through his skin. The BAR came sweeping around, and he pumped bullet after methodical bullet into charging soldiers.

He had to reach Saito. Sullivan could die here, and probably would, but he needed to take that son of a bitch down first.

A Spiker nailed him with extra gravities. Sullivan laughed, gathered it up, and flung it right back tenfold. That Spiker exploded into a pink mist. A Shard came up on the side, magically hardened claws spread wide, and remarkably enough, they managed to shear through a chunk of armor. Sullivan swiveled, jammed the muzzle of the BAR against the Shard's ribs and blew him away.

A big rifle bullet hit him in the forehead. It didn't penetrate the steel plate, but it rocked Sullivan's head back so hard his neck popped. He kept moving, changing magazines, pulling a new one from his chest while he scanned for where that came from. The sniper fired again, and had to be shooting an elephant gun because it hit so damned hard. One of Sullivan's legs went out from under him and he fell on his chest and slid, but he'd seen the flash and the smoke from the top of the palace. He worked the BAR back and forth, shredding those windows and whoever was behind them.

Before he could get up, there was a Brute on his back. Sullivan slammed a steel elbow into teeth, but the Brute wouldn't shake loose. He hardened his body for the impact, and the Brute kidney-punched rock. Even then, the Brute managed to dent the suit. Sullivan made himself weigh four thousand pounds and then simply rolled over, smashing the Brute flat beneath.

He tore gravity apart and flung it out, throwing the attacking Iron Guard off and buying himself some time. He was breathing hard. Every magical scar on his body was burning hot. Even his augmented Power couldn't keep up with this kind of draw. *Come on!* Sullivan returned to his normal weight and struggled back up. Regular soldiers were rushing in, trying to put their bodies between him and Saito.

There was a flash of light and a ring of steel on steel. Sparks flew from his chest and he was stumbling back. An Iron Guard had seemingly come out of nowhere and cleaved him in the chest with a sword. *That ain't gonna pierce this—oh hell...* And then Sullivan realized he felt far heavier. The swordsman hadn't been trying to pierce the armor, he'd been trying to disrupt the runes carved on it.

He must have seen a vulnerability. The Swordsman blocked the rising BAR, stepped inside, carefully aiming his sword point at Sullivan's eye, and then his skull opened up in a spray of red.

Faye was standing there, holding a dripping Iron Guard sword. She'd just clumsily hacked the swordsman's face like she was chopping wood. The swordsman started to sit up, so Faye casually leaned over, jabbed her blade between his ribs, and twisted. "Hey, Mr. Sullivan. Are you ready for me yet?"

"Don't let the Chairman get away," he shouted. "Nothing else matters!"

She nodded once and then disappeared.

Sullivan looked around, realized Saito was retreating for the mansion with Toru right behind him, what seemed like half the Japanese army was heading Sullivan's way, and he was standing in the middle of a field with absolutely no cover. He turned and ran for it.

Chapter 22

Do you wish me to give them my word? It is said that a warrior does not make promises, for everything we speak is a promise. If a warrior says he will do something, then it will be done. If a warrior speaks, it is a vow. I have already said why I am here. We will fulfill the duty of the Dark Ocean. Tell your men the entirety of the Imperium would not stand in the way of fulfilling the final command of Okubo Tokugawa. The Imperium will come to understand the coming danger or they will perish. I will make them understand the truth of this.

—Toru Tokugawa, May 1933

Free City of Shanghai

IAN WRIGHT was incoherent with pain. His leg had been destroyed by the Iron Guard. Everything below his knee was flopping uselessly at an odd angle, a bone was sticking through the skin, and there was blood everywhere. He couldn't even put his hands on it to stop the bleeding because they were shackled, and those same chains were being used by the others to drag the lot of them back toward the tunnel and the torture chambers beneath the mansion. It wasn't a safe place, but it sure as hell had to be a safer place than out in the open.

He was in so much agony that he had a hard time wrapping his brain around what was going on. It was like the Iron Guard were throwing a civil war. He'd never imagined Iron Guard slaughtering each other before, but then he realized what was happening.

Some of the Iron Guard weren't Iron Guard at all. They weren't even human... Everything Sullivan had said was true. *Absolutely true.*

These were soldiers of the Pathfinder, and now they were *eating* people. He'd been a fool to doubt, and now it was too late.

"They're consuming magic!" Doctor Wells shouted from the far end of the chain. "Now that they've been found out, they will go on the offensive. They must consume as much Power as possible so they can summon their master!" And there were five powerful Actives here chained together, wounded and nearly defenseless. "Summon a demon. Hurry!"

That was a good idea, but they'd been marked with some sort of spell to keep them from using their Powers. Ian reached for his forehead and started scrubbing hard. It had been put on with some sort of thick demon grease, so he'd probably have to rub all his skin off to cancel it out . . .

An Iron Guard was coming their way. His skin had been burned off, and beneath it was a mass of bulging purple muscles. He looked hungry.

Ian started scratching wildly at the mark.

Suddenly the skinless man turned grey like a fade, sank into the ground, flailing, and disappeared. A moment later, another grey figure crawled out of the grass and became solid. Heinrich Koenig gasped for breath as he rushed over. "Hello, my friends. Busy day, no?"

"You're a master of fucking understatement!"

Heinrich grabbed Ian, and suddenly he felt insubstantial. When he reformed, his shackles were lying on the ground. Heinrich repeated that with the next knight in line. "You must flee while they are paying attention to Sullivan. Carry those who cannot walk. Cross the south wall. Zhao is by the river waiting for you in a patrol boat."

An Imperium soldier rushed them, long rifle and bayonet aimed at Heinrich's back, but he was knocked aside at the last instant by Wells. The alienist was still shackled, but he threw the chains over the soldier's head and twisted until his neck snapped. Wells didn't have access to his magic, either, but he seemed to be enjoying himself. "Just like a Rockville prison riot," he explained after Heinrich freed him.

"Herr Doctor, get these men out. *Schnell!* Hurry!" Once the last of the knights had lost their shackles, Heinrich turned toward the mansion.

"What're you doing?"

Heinrich bent over, picked up the dropped Arisaka rifle, and kept walking. "Making a difference, I hope." He worked the bolt action. "Go!"

The Chairman, or the guy that looked exactly like the Chairman but really wasn't, tried to escape by Traveling.

Faye didn't find that very sportsmanlike at all.

The real Chairman could Travel too, but what Faye had learned was that there was Traveling, and then there was really *Traveling*. Any Active could pick a nice safe spot in clear view and hop on over there, but it took an artistic touch and a whole lot of practice to do better than that. The Chairman could do darned near everything, but he wasn't a specialist like Faye, and he'd paid for that sloppiness with his hands.

This Chairman wasn't even nearly as clever as the old one. Sure, he had buckets of Power and a horrible little monster helping him, but he'd never really worked for it, he'd never had to struggle and figure it out on his own. It had been given to him by the invisible octopus riding on his shoulders with its tentacles stuck in his eyes and ears. Faye simply could not abide that.

That critter was the Pathfinder everybody had been talking about, but they couldn't see what it really was. They had been expecting a giant, indestructible beast because that was what it had grown into last time. This thing was just a tiny little part of a great big whole spread all over the place. There was what was in our world, but the great big dangerous rest of it was still in another world, right next to this one, where it couldn't help. The little part had to figure out how to open the door to let it in, and it had been letting humans do all the hard work for it, gathering up all the magical folks into one easy bucket to dump into its mouth hole.

Now that its plans were all messed up, all those little bits were on the move. The rest of the folks didn't realize it yet, but a war had just started. There were going to be battles now in every single part of the world the skinless men were hiding in, but Faye couldn't worry about that right now. She had to stop this big part of the monster from getting away.

The new Chairman Traveled away just as Toru swung his big club. The club whistled through the air where the Chairman had been and a big lion statue got turned into gravel instead. Even though Faye's head map was filled with thousands and thousands of moving people she easily picked out the spot where the new Chairman moved to. He thought he was quick, jumping seven times in just over eight seconds, but she was right behind him.

She intercepted him on the roof of the castle.

He saw her the same time she saw him. The invisible monster that was steering him opened its parrot beak and hissed at her. The new Chairman's mouth opened in surprise. He could see magic as clear as she could, and she knew he'd never seen anything close to her before. "What are you?"

"I'm the Spellbound. The Power picked me. So now your time has come."

He raised his hands and a sickening wave of destruction came at her.

Even as the energy surged through the air faster than a bullet, Faye was processing the information. It was the same type of magic as the Black Monk's. She quickly changed her link, folding and refolding it until it connected to a new section of the Power. The destroying magic washed harmlessly past her as the roof began to disintegrate. He changed tactics, and the air around her began shedding energy, trying to freeze her solid and make the water in her body turn to ice to rip her cells apart. Faye merely switched to Whisper's magic and heated everything back up.

They went back and forth, he'd try to hit her with magic, but she'd change things and hit him right back. He tried to electrocute her, but she thought of George Bolander's magic and deflected it. Lightning bolts shot into the sky. A current of fire formed between them, which rapidly spun into a tornado, and when they let go of it, the fire crawled down the castle wall and drifted across the panicking crowd. He tried to command her, like a Mouth, but she just laughed at him while their fire tornado crashed into the high-rise next door and the whole thing exploded.

Demons sprang into existence beside her. She slugged one in the face and it exploded, took control of the other one, and ordered it to go eat the Chairman. He blasted it into chunks of black ink, which Faye then gathered up with her mind, hardened the droplets into bullets, and launched them into the Chairman's flesh. He hardened his body and absorbed the impacts, started to Heal himself, but then Faye appeared before him and drove the stolen sword through his heart. He used Mover magic to knock her away, and he grimaced and yanked the sword free. It hit the roof with a clatter, and she immediately focused on it, made it spring into the air, and impaled it into his leg.

He roared, gathering the energy from the air, focusing it for a mighty destructive release, but Faye snagged it from him and shoved it aside. The Boomer magic was diverted and another of the high-rise building's lower floors was hit instead. The explosion rocked the entire city. The forty-story building fell, slowly thundering its way down into the escaping masses. Instead of soaking up that freed magic like it was used to, the Pathfinder was shocked as Faye took it all instead.

Faye was fueled by death and Power.

In all of its millions of years chasing the Power, the Enemy had never met anything quite like her.

Hopelessly damaged, the roof collapsed. He tried to Travel away, but she was much faster at that, so she reached the part of space he was trying to smoosh together and *smacked* his hand away.

"How—"

The roof came apart around them. The Chairman simply turned himself into a Brute to take the fall. Faye went back to what came natural and Traveled off to the side.

They fell inside the mansion. Mr. Sullivan and Toru were there, on the ground floor, completely surrounded by Iron Guard. The two of them were moving from room to room, shooting, bludgeoning, stabbing, kicking, smashing their way through enemy after enemy, leaving a pile of broken bodies behind them.

The Chairman landed with a crash in the middle of a group of Iron Guard, scattering them.

Faye landed perched, on the balcony railing high above on the third floor.

The Chairman got to his feet and spoke to her, only she quickly realized it wasn't the Chairman speaking at all, but rather the monster which had been hiding inside of the imposter for so very long.

"You may beat me here, but the spores have settled across the entirety of your world. All you have done here today is speed up the inevitable harvest. I am everywhere."

Faye felt a sudden alarm. Her pulse quickened. Her head map was spinning. It was as if the Power itself was trying to warn Faye of something.

She opened her head map, couldn't find the problem, then used up more Power, and more, burning the energy of some of the hundreds who had just been killed around her. It was further than she'd ever dared push before, but she fueled it with a battleship worth of dead connections. Her head map expanded outward until it seemed to cover the whole world. The information was too much, it screeched against the wall of her sanity, but Faye could see everything, every connection to the Power, natural and unnatural.

The unnatural was easy to spot. The monster was not lying. It really was *everywhere*. It had been planning for this moment since long before Faye was born, even before Sivaram had shown the Power how it could defend itself, and now that it had been exposed, it was making its move. There were thousands of infiltrators spread across the world, and all it would take would be one bunch of them consuming enough magic in one place to anchor the big Enemy to this world forever.

There were patches of death in the world as the skinless men began their harvest. Faye watched her head map with horror as the blackness began to spread.

"*I am everywhere.*"

"Well so am I!" Faye shouted back. She picked a location, threw caution to the wind, and stepped through reality.

UBF *Traveler*

"WE'RE GOING DOWN!" Barns shouted. "We've lost half our major systems."

"Keep us in one piece, Mr. Barns," Captain Southunder responded.

There was a terrible clatter, a tearing of metal, and another one of the small demons came crawling up out of the instrumentation. "Gremlin!" the teleradar operator shouted.

Captain Southunder calmly drew his .45 auto, centered the front sight on the screeching beast, and blew its head off. The operator was splashed with sizzling ink, but better that than being rent by their razor claws. The creatures were only the size of small dogs, but they had certainly made a mess of his fine new airship.

"Losing altitude fast," Barns said, having ignored the gunshot. "I'll do what I can."

"Very well, Mr. Barns." Southunder went over to the nearest phone, spun the charger a few times, and picked it up. "Cargo hold. Mr. Schirmer, are you there?"

"Schirmer was attacked by a demon. He cannot come to the phone right now."

"Ori. Listen, we're in trouble. I need you to keep us from going up in a ball of fire. We'll be in range of the entire Imperium navy in a few minutes."

"Yes, Captain. I will not let us burn."

Southunder glanced out the front window. They were out of the unnatural night and back in the blue skies he knew so well, and that meant he could fiddle with the weather. "I might be able to get us out of this, but it's going to get choppy. Have the eggheads aim that device back at Shanghai. Let's give Mr. Sullivan our full support. I have a sneaky feeling he needs it."

"Covering," Sullivan shouted as he fired the BAR through the doorway.

"Moving!" Toru charged forward through a wall, plowing into the soldiers on the other side. The war club rose and fell, and two more died. Toru picked up a submachine gun in the other hand. "Covering." And he opened fire into the next room.

Sullivan rushed past Toru and took up a position behind a marble pillar. "Reloading." He dropped the spent mag and pulled another from his chest. His magic was overheated and exhausted. He hadn't pushed this hard since the Second Somme.

Hundreds of troops had converged on the mansion. It was falling apart around them. Bullets were competing to fill every free bit of air space. Iron Guards were everywhere. Sullivan had been shot so damned many times he couldn't even keep track. The Spiker armor was being pulverized and picked apart by the sheer volume of impacts. He was bleeding from an unknown number of cuts, punctures, and burns, and his Healing spells were barely keeping up.

Toru wasn't faring much better. His fancy samurai armor was missing a horn, and one big impact from a recoilless rifle had nearly put him through the foundations. He was limping and leaving a blood trail behind them. "Where is Saito?"

Sullivan pulled the bolt back on the BAR. "Lost him."

"The coward has fled!" Furious, Toru kicked a couch across the room.

The wall next to Toru exploded and a gleaming metal man appeared. It slammed a fist into Toru's side and launched him into a marble pillar so hard it cracked. Sullivan shot it, but the bullets bounced off the *gakutensuko*. It was far sleeker and more humanoid than the American versions. It raised an arm, and bullets ricocheted off Sullivan. The two kept firing into each other, and then stopped when they fell empty at the same time. They charged and collided, and the metal man knocked Sullivan through the ceiling.

He was in a bathroom. "Son of a bitch." He rolled over, saw the machine man walking beneath him through the hole in the floor, and swore again. His Power was already rebuilding in his chest. Sullivan got up, found the cast-iron bathtub, made it weigh nothing, ripped it out of the floor, took it back to the hole, aimed it, and then quadrupled its weight. The tub fell, smashing the mechanical man in the head. Sparks flew. Then Toru appeared and hit the *gakutensuko* with the tetsubo so hard that gears flew like confetti.

Sullivan jumped through the hole and landed next to Toru. He lurched when he hit the ground, realizing that at least one of the mechanical man's bullets had made it through the armor and embedded itself in his stomach. "Reloading," he said again.

There was a huge crowd of Iron Guard coming up the front entrance. They were moving cautiously now, covering each other with firearms and magic. Sullivan moved to the opposite side of the room to see if there was any potential escape, but as soon as he neared the window he started taking machine gun fire. Something big and silver moved in the yard. The second robot tracked him through the wall, and much like Toru had said earlier, it really was accurate, as more bullets struck his armor.

He moved behind a shelf, and for the first time Sullivan realized they'd been pinned down in a library. He marveled at the stacks, which stretched to the ceiling. It was a rather nice collection.

Well, that was certainly an appropriate place for him to die.

He came around the corner shooting, dropping another two soldiers and injuring a third. A Fade came through the wall, grabbed onto his arm, and tried to sink them both into the floor. Sullivan surged his Power hard, making himself as dense as when he'd fallen from the sky, and the Fade was simply unable to muster enough Power to drag them into the ground. The second he reformed, Toru smote the ninja's head from his shoulders with the club.

It felt like the entire Iron Guard collectively opened fire. Bullets tore through everything. Books ignited under the intense heat. Lightning arced through the doorways and tracked up the electrical outlets, and the overhead lighting exploded in a shower of sparks. Sullivan was hit at least another dozen times. Another bullet pierced his side, and he winced as breathing filled his lungs with fire. "Son of a bitch." Another pierced the armor of his leg and ripped through his calf. He crashed into a shelf and fell to the floor.

Toru lurched to the side as a heavy round struck him in the helmet. It was an incendiary, and it was still glowing like a coal. It sizzled as it burned his forehead. Toru wrenched the damaged helmet off and threw it away. "Curse you dogs!" And then he had to rub the fire out of his hair.

The noise tapered off as the Iron Guard reloaded or let their Power recollect.

He didn't know what was going on around them, but there was a terrible racket outside. Entire buildings were falling down and there was Power humming through the air like he'd never felt before. But he knew hundreds of troops were converging on the mansion.

"We are surrounded," Toru stated with grim finality.

Sullivan pulled another mag for the BAR. The origami duck fell from the mag pouch and landed on the floor in a puddle of blood. Sullivan studied it for a moment, picked it up, and then went back to reloading his rifle. "I'm not the surrendering type."

"Agreed. I would rather die looking a fellow warrior in the eye than wait in here and be executed like a fish in a bucket."

"It's like shooting fish in a barrel. You don't execute fish."

"Very well, Sullivan. We will die with honor. I leave this world with only two regrets. First, that we did not manage to kill the traitor, but we can die knowing that his infiltrators have been exposed."

"I'm sure your father would be proud," Sullivan said, and he wasn't mocking Toru in the least when he said that. "What's the other?"

Toru turned and looked him in the eye. "Now I really am curious to see who would have proven the better warrior between us..." He lurched over and offered his bloody hand to Sullivan. "Come, we finish this... *brother*."

Hell, why not? He'd already had one Iron Guard for a brother. Sullivan took the bloody hand. He winced in pain as Toru helped him stand.

There was a commotion among the Iron Guard. Something was going on at the mansion's entrance. Sullivan risked a look around the corner.

It was the imposter.

He was torn, battered, burned, bleeding. His uniform hung in tatters, but he was not running. Somehow, Sullivan understood. Saito was no longer in charge. This was the Pathfinder, and it was done running. It had been exposed, and its war had begun. It was coming to kill them, and then it would kill every Iron Guard, and then it would consume the whole city.

Toru had seen it as well. They exchanged a glance. "Fortune smiles upon us."

"Let's end this fucker."

They went through the door. Sullivan put the sights on the Chairman and opened fire. Bullets stitched him through the torso in bright red splashes. Toru was right behind, and he fired his Power, leaping over Sullivan, screaming his battle cry.

"TOKUGAWA!"

There were Iron Guard all around. They reacted immediately and Sullivan was hit with more bullets than he could count and more forms of magic than he knew what to do with. The BAR was torn from his grasp, but without pause Sullivan drew his pistol and kept shooting as he pushed forward.

The Chairman didn't so much as flinch as the bullets tore through him, he simply turned, his lips curling up in a snarl as he prepared to Travel out of Toru's way.

Sullivan hit him with every bit of gravity he could muster. Every ounce of magic he could wring from his body, his spells, or drag from the Power itself was thrown into that burst. Any lesser being would have been flattened like a tin can being stamped by a heavy boot. The excess magic which bled off instantly killed three other Iron Guard.

But the Pathfinder had made Saito's new body incredibly tough. Fifty extra earths' worth of gravity hit flesh, but Saito didn't die, even as a circle of cracks spread around his feet and marble was churned to dust. He tried to Travel away, but even somebody with that much magic couldn't teleport weight equivalent to a fully loaded freight train.

Sullivan bellowed as the magic threatened to rip him apart, but he was not letting that bastard get away. Even with the new spell on his back, there was only so much one body could channel. The new spell began to smoke and his flesh sizzled like bacon hitting a hot pan.

The Chairman raised his hands as if he was pushing back against the gravity. Sullivan felt the magic recoil back against him. He roared.

Toru was struck in mid-air by another Brute, and the two crashed at the Chairman's feet. Toru rolled over, slamming the other Iron Guard in the face with his fist. Blood flew. A powerful Mover blasted Toru away. He hit a pillar hard enough to shatter it and came right back up. An Iron Guard got in the way of Toru's tetsubo and died, and then another, blood flew as a ninja appeared and drove his sword through a gaping hole in Toru's armor.

Dosan Saito's eyes narrowed as he pushed back against the gravity. They both knew, one second after that pull let up, he would escape, and the harvest would continue.

You ain't getting away. Sullivan concentrated. He had nothing left to give. He couldn't push any harder. Keeping this up was taking inhuman focus. An Iron Guard slammed a rifle butt over Sullivan's head and the wood stock shattered. Another came from behind and hamstrung him with a sword. Sullivan went to his knees in a shower of blood.

Constant as gravity... *Fuck you, Jake Sullivan don't quit that easy.*

Toru flung off the other Iron Guards and swung right over Sullivan's head, and the ninja who'd nearly cut Sullivan's leg off was torn in half.

Something changed. The light seemed to brighten. Beams showed between the floating dust and blood and gunsmoke, cutting as clean as the sword which had just pierced his flesh. It was like the light was coming from heaven, and it brought truth with it as the *Traveler* aimed Fuller's ray beam at the city.

There was a horrific thing bonded to the fake Chairman. It could be seen clear as day, hanging there. It screeched as the light scorched through it. That was the real Pathfinder, and it knew that it was done for.

The Iron Guards stopped struggling. They cried out in shocked disbelief as they saw the reality of what they'd been fighting and dying for. There were other monsters there too, pretending to be Iron Guards, and they were revealed for what they really were. They were just sponges, collecting up the magical energy as the real Iron Guards died around them.

Exposed, the monsters fell on the Iron Guards, ripping them apart with terrible savagery. Every inch of the vast marble room was quickly covered in blood.

But the Iron Guards were no longer trying to kill Toru. The unstoppable force came off the floor, the tetsubo was rising. Sullivan saw it coming. Dosan Saito and the Pathfinder didn't.

"*TOKUGAWA!*"

Sullivan cut his Power and collapsed.

Toru smashed the club down onto Saito's shoulder. Half the bones in Saito's body exploded. He struck again. Defined by the light, the Pathfinder was vulnerable. The Pathfinder shrieked as it was compressed into pulp. Tentacles ripped from Saito's eyes and ears in bright sprays of red. Toru smashed the legs out from under Saito and he hit the floor, totally pulverized.

The Pathfinder was crawling away, leaving a trail of black ooze. Sullivan dragged himself forward, leaving a trail of red blood. He reached the monster and lifted one steel arm. It screeched in frustration. Sullivan channeled everything he had left into a single pinpoint of terrible gravity and brought his fist down like the *finger of God* and he smashed it through the Earth.

The center of the Pathfinder collapsed. The outer edges of the creature blew up like a balloon before it burst beneath the terrible pressure.

The Pathfinder was dead.

Sullivan lay there, bleeding. The spell on his back had been burned out, forever extinguished, pushed too far. His body wasn't far behind. Toru took a few halting steps, and then fell, blood drizzling down his arms from several deep wounds.

Saito was still breathing, barely. Blood was coming out of his mouth with every breath. Toru had utterly destroyed the man, and Sullivan had destroyed the Pathfinder.

The Iron Guard were occupied battling the monsters. It was as if the three dying men were alone.

"That was for my father," Toru spat. "I reclaim my honor, traitor."

Saito went first. He rattled out one last gurgling breath, and was gone.

But the Pathfinder had been a spiteful beast, and it had prepared one final spell of revenge. A glowing line appeared in the air over the splattered creature, and it quickly drew itself into an elaborate kanji floating in the air. Sullivan could not read it, but he could feel chaotic energy building.

"Boomer," Toru said with tired resignation.

Sullivan opened his hand and examined the bloody paper duck.

A few seconds later the mansion exploded.

Sullivan & Toru Armored

Chapter 23

Take the case of courage. No quality has ever so much addled the brains and tangled the definitions of merely rational sages. Courage is almost a contradiction in terms. It means a strong desire to live taking the form of a readiness to die. "He that will lose his life, the same shall save it," is not a piece of mysticism for saints and heroes. It is a piece of everyday advice for sailors or mountaineers. It might be printed in an Alpine guide or a drill book. This paradox is the whole principle of courage; even of quite earthly or quite brutal courage. A man cut off by the sea may save his life if he will risk it on the precipice. He can only get away from death by continually stepping within an inch of it. A soldier surrounded by enemies, if he is to cut his way out, needs to combine a strong desire for living with a strange carelessness about dying. He must not merely cling to life, for then he will be a coward, and will not escape. He must not merely wait for death, for then he will be a suicide, and will not escape. He must seek his life in a spirit of furious indifference to it; he must desire life like water and yet drink death like wine.

—G.K. Chesterton,
Orthodoxy, 1908

Drew Town, New Jersey

"**WELL,** this has certainly been an exciting way to pass the evening," Hammer said.

"Palling around with us last time must have spoiled you," Jane answered. "It can't all be Iron Guards and superdemons, now can it?"

Hammer got comfy. "Wake me when your *something* happens."

They were taking turns watching the orderly streets of Drew Town through a pair of binoculars. The large number of electric lamps and their position on a rise above the populated part of town made the watching easy. Monotonous, but easy. Francis felt like they were well hidden, but since nobody was looking for them, it didn't particularly matter.

The town was growing fast. The construction crews were working around the clock. They could clearly hear the machinery running from their current position. More families had moved in since their last visit, so there were probably several hundred people living there now. Francis moved the binoculars across the streets, but it was quiet. Hopefully the elder's warning had been a false alarm. So then tomorrow he'd just be exhausted as he went about his day's business of being raked over Roosevelt's malicious coals.

"I see something moving on the first street," Dan said. "Glass them, Francis."

Francis turned the binoculars toward the entrance of the town. Six men were walking down the sidewalk. They had come from the administration building. "I've got a fellow in a suit and what looks like some construction workers and some security guards. Hang on . . . That's the architect. Mr. Drew himself. They're walking up to a house."

"Little late for an inspection, isn't it?" Hammer asked as she got up.

All four of them were looking over the edge now. It was the first activity they'd had in hours. "Hey, check out Fourth and C streets," Jane said.

The binoculars shifted. The orderly grid of streets made picking targets easy. This was much farther away, so he had to adjust the focus. A car had parked and four men had gotten out. They broke into pairs and began walking up the driveways to two different houses. Francis shifted back to the architect's group. They'd also broken into pairs, and were moving to three separate homes. It seemed rather coordinated and downright eerie. "What the hell is going on down there?" They didn't knock. Didn't need to. They had master keys. Of course they did. They'd built the place. Simultaneously, like they were communicating somehow, even though they didn't appear to be saying a word, they entered the homes. "They're breaking into people's houses."

"Those are all occupied," Dan said. "That's our Heavy's street."

Jane came up alongside him, so he handed her the binoculars. Francis was getting a really bad feeling about this.

A few seconds later the men began leaving, still in pairs. They moved quicker now, running across the lawns and jumping fences. Jane gasped as she tracked them through the magnification. "Those are not men!"

"What?"

"I can see people's insides. Those are not people. Everything is wrong. Their skin is a shell!"

"Shit!" Francis pulled his rifle around. *So much for this being a false alarm.* "Get down there!"

The front door of one of the invaded houses flew open. A child in a pink nightgown ran outside. He couldn't hear her from here, but he could tell she was screaming. She made it out into the street before one of the men appeared highlighted in the doorway. He came down the steps, wearing a white security-guard shirt splattered red. He lifted his head, like he was testing the air. He caught the scent and took off after the girl, *running on all fours.*

It was too far to use his Power. The safety was off. The butt of the Enfield met his shoulder and Francis welded his cheek to the stock. The scope picked up what little light there was, but there wasn't much. The wire crosshairs were grey blurs. His finger went to the trigger as he exhaled.

The little girl fell in the road. The man, thing, whatever, was on her in an instant.

The scope filled with pink. Francis lifted it. Found white. And pulled the trigger.

"Got him!" Dan shouted.

Francis worked the bolt. The little girl got up and ran again. The security guard had fallen, but he was already getting back up. As soon as the little girl was clear, Dan lit him up with the BAR. *Thud Thud Thud Thud.* It almost felt slow and rhythmic as Dan ripped the man apart.

That should wake everybody up.

Other men were coming out of the homes, dripping Active blood. Some of them had lost bits of their skin in various altercations with the residents, but they didn't seem to care. They methodically turned toward the next house in line. Francis had four more shots, and he cranked them off, hitting every time, but only managing to drop one of the men. They simply seemed to shrug off the impacts, focused entirely on their next target.

The people of Drew Town were being slaughtered.

Francis was up and running down the hill without even realizing it. Jane and Hammer were already halfway down.

The elders had warned every knight in the world... And Francis realized that meant this was happening *everywhere*.

Stuttgart, Germany

FIRES COULD BE SEEN through the office window and police sirens could be heard in the distance. Jacques Montand hung his head in shame. "I have failed you, the society, and all of mankind. My willful blindness allowed this crisis to come about. I accept full responsibility for my failures."

The other elders were quiet. Two of them were present in the darkened room, and the other four were attending through communications spells. Their last member was missing in action. It was dire news which had brought them together. The secret Enemy seemed to be attacking all across the world simultaneously.

"Jacques..." began the British elder. "How could you have known?"

"That the girl was picked to save mankind? That Sivaram was merely a trial run for our ultimate weapon of self defense? I could not have known. I could only assume the worst, but I should have not let that blind me to the true evil. Faye and Sullivan tried to warn us. By hiding what I did know, and by keeping Faye's continued existence a secret, I have placed us all into terrible jeopardy. As I have said, I accept full responsibility for my failures, and accept any punishments which the society deems fit. If I am to die to atone for this, so be it."

"That will have to wait," said the American. "We need everyone we can get. Hang yourself later for all I care, but right now we've got a crisis of unknown proportions brewing in every corner of the world. These creatures are killing innocent men, women, and children."

"We've been dispatching our knights as we hear of outbreaks, and trying to alert the local authorities wherever possible," said the

German elder. "As soon as we are done here I will be joining my men in the street fighting."

"My boss is a stubborn man," the American said. "But I think I've convinced Roosevelt to see the light. The military has been called up. We've responded as best we can to each outbreak of violence, but we don't even know where or how many there are."

"I do."

Jacques and Klaus turned in surprise.

Faye Vierra walked into the light. She was covered in blood, her eyes were wild, and she held a pistol in one hand. It was locked open empty, but she casually dropped the spent magazine on the carpet, pulled a new one from her clothing, slammed it home, and dropped the slide. She smelled of smoke and death.

They were scared of her. Nobody spoke.

"I've been fighting them all over the world for the last hour, picking whichever spot is the closest to opening the door. I stopped a bunch. I don't know how many I've killed . . ." Faye rubbed her face with her free hand, but all that did was smear the blood around. "I came here because I've got a minute before the next door is built. I can't fight a war by myself. I need help."

Jacques spoke for all of them. "Whatever the society can do, we are here."

"One of y'all is a Reader. I can taste it." Faye glanced across them. The German elder raised his hand. "Okay, pay attention. I'm gonna show you a map of the world in your head." Faye spied something in the corner. A decorative globe floated over and landed on the table between the elders. *She was using more than one kind of Power!* "Then you're going to mark down all the places that need help, then you're going to do your best to make sure help gets sent to all those places. Russia was real bad off, what with Stalin's gulags, but that's where I just came from." She shivered. "It's still bad, but they'll hold for a bit. I felt it when the main Pathfinder died, and that'll slow it some, but its babies are still working. The Imperium's up in arms, killing everybody, and they're even using their secret agents to help in countries they ain't even supposed to be in. But there's places we can get that they can't. Ready?"

Klaus nodded. Then he screamed and clutched his temples. "*Mein Gott!*"

"Yeah...Sorry about that." Faye apologized. "No time to be gentle. Now get help to those folks that need it. This is the most important thing the Society has ever done."

Klaus took the globe, removed a pen from his pocket, and began making X marks around the world.

Suddenly, the Spellbound jerked in surprise. She closed her eyes for a moment, as if concentrating. "Oh no...Didn't see that coming... Nobody saw that one coming."

"What is wrong, Faye?" Jacques asked.

"The Pathfinder's been steering leaders and important people toward sticking Actives all in one place to make its job easy, but it's had one out-of-the-way place all ready for a real long time, and it just got there and ate everybody. I've got to go. I'm the only thing left in its way."

"Good luck, Faye," Jacques said. "And I am sorry."

"Don't worry, Jacques. I keep my promises."

Billings, Montana

THE SPECIAL PRISONERS WING of Rockville State Penitentiary was where they put the most dangerous criminal Actives in America. This was the place Jake Sullivan had served six years of hard time. There had been nearly a thousand Active prisoners housed in this one facility.

Faye arrived just as the last of those prisoners was dragged from their cells to have their magic devoured. The whole thing had happened so fast. There had only been a few skinless men hidden there among the guards, but they had overwhelmed and replaced all of the others in a matter of minutes, and then the prisoners had been easy pickings.

That was more than enough magic to open the door.

Faye landed in the middle of the depopulated prison.

Part of the Pathfinder was waiting for her. It was wearing the body of the warden, whom it had just killed a few minutes before. That made Faye sad, since Mr. Sullivan had spoken of the warden as a kindly man who had let him read books.

"I told you I was everywhere." The biggest, smartest part of the

Pathfinder had just been destroyed in Shanghai, but the Pathfinder was like a weed, and pulling up part of it wouldn't kill it all, and the roots would just keep on growing. *"You are too late. The rest of us have been called. We are coming."*

"It don't matter," Faye answered. "I intend to kill you all."

"Other intelligences have said that before you, but all have failed. You are not special. You do not comprehend how long this cycle has gone on. The prey chooses new intelligences and we consume them. The cycle repeats. The prey chooses new intelligences and we consume them. The cycle is eternal. The prey chooses new intelligences and we consume them. You will not be the last."

"You're wrong." Tens of thousands had died around her tonight, and their connections to the Power now temporarily belonged to her. She could no longer describe her Power in terms like a river, or a stream, or any other sort of quantifiable thing. Faye's Power simply was *the* Power. It was trusting her not to fail. It was tired of running. "I am the last one."

The Pathfinder's puppet looked toward the night sky. It had been daytime in Shanghai. There was a blank spot where there weren't any stars at all. The circle was growing. It was an opening to someplace else.

"The prey will run as it always has. It will abandon you. You will become weak and you will be consumed. That is the cycle. You are an abomination. You are an intelligence which has copied our methods. You consume the prey as well. You have taken that which is rightfully ours. You will not be allowed to become us."

She was tired of listening to it, so Faye lifted the .45 and shot the Pathfinder in the face. The night was quiet. That was more like it.

The big Enemy was on the way. It was being drawn here, to Rockville, and once it landed, there wasn't a thing that anybody in the world would be able to do about it.

Faye ran through all of the possible uses of the Power she'd seen so far. She could pick any one of the connections she'd stolen, and then refold hers to utilize that section of the Power, but as she thought through them, she couldn't think of any which would actually make a dent in the Enemy. She could think of maybe one type of magic she knew of which maybe could work, but she had no idea how to use it. The Power was a complicated critter all right, and there were tons of parts, some of which rarely managed to connect to a human being, and maybe some of those might work, but Faye had no idea how to connect to those sections herself. She couldn't fold herself a new connection to a specific part of the Power if she hadn't seen it before.

The hole in the stars was growing. The universe on the other side was a different color which human eyes had never seen before and which human brains didn't have a word for. It was far out in space, but everybody in the northern hemisphere could see it now. She didn't have much time.

One of the Iron Guards who had died around her in Shanghai had been a Reader, so she'd stolen his Power. She hadn't tried it yet, but it was worth a shot. Faye knew of only two people who had ever seen this particular spell's geometry. One of them had a brain that was a constant weird jumble of information, faster maybe than anybody else's brain except for hers, so Faye didn't know if she'd be able to pull anything out of that head at all, especially since she'd never practiced Reading. The other brain wasn't nearly as fast, but she liked it a whole lot better, plus intruding on it didn't seem nearly as offensive as intruding on a stranger's brain. Faye opened up her head map, burning through several lifetimes' worth of Power to reach all the way to New Jersey.

Francis was busy beating a skinless man over the head with the butt of his rifle. They were in a construction site of some kind, and there were lots of people running around fighting the monsters. She was pleased to see that Francis had managed to kill a bunch of the Pathfinder's puppets all by himself by throwing bricks and rocks at them with his Power. She shot that skinless man in the brain, not that she didn't think Francis could handle it himself, but rather because she was in a hurry.

"Thanks." He flicked the slime off the end of his rifle and then looked to see who'd helped him. "Faye?" He only gawked at her disheveled and bloodstained appearance for a second before rushing over and sweeping her into his arms. He kissed her on the lips, and wonderful as that was, she really had to get back to saving the world.

She was going to shove him, but she decided the world could wait a few more seconds after all . . . *Okay, back to business.* She pulled her face away. "Francis, I need you to listen."

"What're you doing here? I haven't heard from you in months! I thought you might be dead!"

"Francis, concentrate," Faye ordered. She snapped her fingers for emphasis.

"Okay." A skinless man was running at them, but Francis floated a pipe up from the ground and hurled it like a spear with his Power. It impaled the creature through the ribs and sent it flying back. "Okay, I'm listening. What's up?" She pointed at the sky. Francis looked up and noticed the expanding hole in the universe. "Sweet merciful Jesus! What is that?"

"The Enemy's coming. I need you to think real hard and remember that spell you made that ate Mason Island."

"The black hole? Browning said that came from a Power called a Nixie. But what—"

"Don't matter. Just think of the shape in your head. I've never done this before, so remember as hard as you can."

Francis closed his eyes and his brow furrowed.

Faye had never read minds before, so she figured she'd throw a few extra Actives' worth of Power onto this one just in case.

And then she nearly knocked herself cold. It was like a sucker punch to the head.

Faye didn't just read that spell clear as day, she read all of the memories attached to it, the frustration and anger at trying to make it work, the brutal fight for freedom, the near-death experience, and then the overwhelming feelings as he was reunited with her, and then the incredible sadness while reading her letter because he really did love her. She couldn't help herself, she read the surface, and the layer beneath, and the layer beneath, all of the hopes, and strengths, and weaknesses, and frailties, and insecurities, and screw ups, and moments of greatness, and everything in between. She learned every single thing there was to know about who Francis Cornelius Stuyvesant really was and the man that he could hope to be, and most of all, she learned that he truly wanted to spend the rest of his life with her.

She snapped back to reality. Francis swooned and nearly lost it. She had to catch him by the arm to hold him up. She'd Read him so hard it had made his nose bleed. "What did you just do?"

"Oh, Francis." Faye held him tight. "If I didn't have a reason not to turn evil and destroy the world before, I surely do now."

"What?"

"I'll try to come back, I promise." Hesitantly, she let go, and stepped back into Montana.

The prison yard was still quiet. The spotlights cast ghostly shadows. She'd only have once chance. The Enemy was coming from one reality and heading straight for this one, only she never intended to let it land. Instead, she'd send it someplace *else*. Nobody knew where the black hole went. She'd only gotten the barest glimpses as she'd tossed Crow inside. It was a terrible realm of endless darkness and cold.

Yet, the god of demons had been strong enough to crawl out of it. Even though it didn't have a body, the Enemy was infinitely stronger, which told Faye she needed to make this spell that much *bigger*. That last hole had been big enough to suck in Mason Island. This one would be big enough to swallow Montana. But if she set that off here at the surface, it would kill hundreds of thousands, maybe millions if the calculations in her head map were even the tiniest bit off . . .

Did that matter? Kill a million, save billions. That was easy math. Plus she'd just absorb all those millions' Power. It wasn't like it would go to waste, and she'd still save everybody else in the world from the Enemy. She'd be a hero. The whole world would love her.

Faye shook her head. Those thoughts were dangerous. She needed to get up there where the world could be safe from the dangerous spell. She had to get up in the Enemy's *face*. And that meant she probably wasn't coming back.

So be it. Sometimes heroes didn't get to come back.

Her head map helped her with the calculations. She was going to have to channel multiple forms of Power at the same time, something not even the Chairman had done before. She could switch between them really quick, but that wouldn't be good enough. It needed to be several at once or nothing. Failure meant instantaneous death.

She concentrated on the magic of a Fade, imagining herself to be as insubstantial as Heinrich. That would help keep her from being pulled in by the hole's gravity. Then she channeled the opposite type of magic, that of the Heavy, and imagined that she had as much control over those forces as Mr. Sullivan. Between those two types of magic, she might have a chance to get out. Then she gathered up the vitality of a Brute like Delilah, and knowing that her body would begin taking damage immediately, she asked for the Healing Power of a mighty Healer like Jane. She'd need to keep her body from freezing instantly, so she thought of the energetic magic of the Torch, like Whisper or Lady Origami, and the Crackler magic of Mr. Bolander. And for one last touch, she thought of Barns' magic, because a little Luck never hurt.

Faye was so scared she couldn't hardly breathe. So first she folded her connection to be like the Mouth's Power, imagined she was clever like Mr. Garrett, and said out loud. "I'm gonna be fine. I'm really good at this. The Power picked me for a reason." And then she immediately felt better.

She said a little prayer in her head, looked up at the monster eating the sky, and Traveled like she never had before.

Nothingness.

And then a billion stars.

It was terrifying. The world was thousands of miles below. The Enemy was before her.

Faye's head map was screaming in confusion, so she shoved it aside. Her physical magic flared, stronger than any Brute. Her tissues hardened into an impenetrable shield, but even then her skin began to die and the fluids in her body wanted to boil into nothing. She became denser than any Massive. The Healer's magic went to work. The molecules of her own body which were burning off were energized by the magic of the Torch to form a sort of barrier between her and the nothing.

The Enemy was coming closer, incomprehensible and hungry. It knew the Power had been found, and it had been waiting a very long time for this moment. It wasn't clever at all, at least not in any way Faye could ever understand. The Pathfinder had been clever because it had been living with humans for so long that it had grown smart. All the Enemy understood was the cycle of eating and chasing. It had been anchored to a point in Montana and nothing would turn it away. The cycle was everything.

Faye was about to break it.

She folded her connection to the Power, over and over, in all manner of convoluted designs. Her mind was working faster than any other living being was capable of, and she knew that was why the

Power had picked this poor Okie girl from a dirt-floored shack to be its champion. It was all for this one perfect moment.

Faye created the spell. A hole appeared in space. The other side of the hole was the real nothing. This side was paradise in comparison. The rift grew.

Not fast enough. The Enemy was too big. She needed to block it off entirely. She needed to make a new door, just as big as the hole the Enemy had made, big enough to completely shield the world. She needed the Enemy to be absolutely consumed by the nothing place, and it could *never* be allowed to escape. Faye gathered up *all* of her stolen magic, the composite Power of tens of thousands of dead souls, and she shoved it hard against the new spell.

It tore a mighty rift in the universe.

The tear opened with a flash that could be seen from Earth. It expanded fast. Too fast. It tried to pull her in, so hard that she couldn't even Travel out of it. Faye called upon the gravitational mastery of the Heavy to pull herself away and when that didn't work, the Fade ability to make herself insubstantial. But this rift was so terrible that it was sucking in *light*.

The Enemy continued onward, oblivious, toward its feast.

Only the trail it was following went through Faye's rift. The black hole which had consumed Mason Island had been tiny in comparison. This one was hundreds of miles across.

Too late, the Enemy realized it was a trap. The portal from its reality fed directly into the infinite nothing. Faye understood where the black hole went now. This was where the Power would go if it died.

It was Hell.

Faye knew she was about to die too, but it was all worth it to feel the great Enemy's surprise before it was sucked into the eternal void.

So long, sucker.

She managed to stay just ahead of the rift. It reached its maximum size, which was good, because if it had gotten any bigger it probably would've eaten the whole world, and then she would've felt really stupid, and then it went snapping back.

It dragged her along on the ragged edge of nothing, and the smaller it got, the harsher the pull became. Faye was burning every form of magic she could think of, but her Power was spent, all of the

Spellbound curse's stolen magic had been used. She would not be able to Travel out of this one.

It sure had been an adventure.

And then the Power spoke to her. Not with words, but it was there, watching, feeling her pain and her anguish and her sadness and her hope and it truly marveled at this bizarre species it had bonded itself to.

It was thankful, for the great cycle had been broken. Mankind had accomplished what no other species had ever done before.

So the Power offered her a choice.

It was an easy decision.

Drew Town, New Jersey

FRANCIS WAS PRONE on top of the water tank as he took careful aim. The skinless men were incredibly fast when they were sprinting, so he led this one like he was shooting a jack rabbit. Francis pulled the trigger, and the Enfield barked. The skinless man spilled forward and crashed into the hole that had been dug for a foundation. "Got it!" He worked the bolt and watched for more targets, but that seemed to be all of them. Since these things seemed so damned hard to kill, Francis noticed that there was a cement mixer still running next to the hole, so he focused his Power, pulled the lever, and caused the liquid cement to run down and bury the creature. *That ought to do it.*

"We okay?" Pemberly Hammer called out.

Jane came out from behind the car she'd been using for cover, still holding her favorite Tommy gun. "I think so."

Dan joined his wife. "I believe that's the last of them."

They'd been fighting for an hour. The town had come alive. Most had run. Many had fought. A whole lot had died. And then the dead had gotten back up, shed their skin, and joined in. He'd burned through most of his ammo and nearly all his Power, but for now, it was quiet.

Francis climbed down the water tank's ladder, made it three-quarters of the way, slipped on a rung, and fell the rest of the way. He landed on his ass in a mud puddle. Francis got up, cursing, and quickly inspected his rifle to make sure he hadn't plugged the muzzle. "I didn't see anything else, but keep your eyes peeled."

"There are so many wounded. I can feel them all around us," Jane said. "I've got to help them."

"I'll go with you," Dan said. "The police are here now, but I'm not letting you out of my sight."

"Oh, Dan, you are so chivalrous."

There were lights and sirens coming up the road toward the "planned community." Francis walked over and leaned on the hood of a car. "Hell of a night, Hammer. Just promise me you're going to go back and tell your boss he's an idiot."

"Not a problem." Hammer joined him. "Did you see that weird light in the sky? What do you think that was?"

He studied the night. It looked like an aurora borealis. "Faye... doing Faye stuff."

"How do you know?"

"Just a hunch." And when she'd read his mind so hard it felt like he'd woken up from a three-day bender, a little bit of her thoughts had jumped lanes, and as the thoughts had settled down, he'd come to understand what was really at stake. Lots of men liked to say their girl was the most important girl in the world... his really was.

"Do you think she's okay?"

"I know she is."

Hammer nodded. She could tell Francis was telling the truth. "I've got to go fill in the law. There might be more of those things out there." She held out her hand, not in any sissy ladylike fashion either, but like she meant business. Francis shook it. "Thanks for being such a paranoid jerk."

"And thank you for being such an obstinate nag."

"Anytime." She grinned at him and then went down to meet the arriving cars.

Francis looked back up at the weirdly lit sky. "Come on, Faye..."

There was a sudden *CRACK*. The noise was deafening. It was like lightning had just struck next to him. Something hit the ground hard and he flinched away.

He spun, raising the rifle, but stopped when he saw who it was. "Faye!" She was standing there, surrounded by a brilliant halo of pure, crackling Power. It burned his eyes like looking at a welder. He had to raise his hands to shield his face. "Faye!"

The magic flickered and then disappeared. The light was gone. His ears were ringing.

She gave him a weak little smile. "It offered me a choice..." And then she fell to her knees.

Francis rushed to her side. She looked like she was about to topple over. He caught her just in time. "What's wrong? What choice?"

Her eyes were closed, her head was rolling weakly on her neck. "The Power. It offered me everything. I could have the whole world. I could control it, run it, all to keep the Power safe for forever."

He held her tight. She was shaking so hard. "Okay, Faye. I've got you. It'll be okay."

"All mine. Whatever I wanted. So no more bad guys, no more wars, or hate, because I said so. No more Chairmen or Madis or Crows. Never again." She was nearly incoherent with exhaustion. "All of them. Stopped. But to do that, I'd always need to be so strong...I'd always need more. So I'd take what I wanted, because I'd need to. That's how I'd tell myself it was okay. But that's how the evil always starts. Nobody would be safe, not even you."

She wasn't making any sense. Francis realized they were kneeling in the puddle. He pulled her to dry ground and carefully laid her down with her back against the car tire. He brushed the matted, bloody hair from her face. The blood didn't seem to be hers, but he couldn't really tell, there was so much of it. "Jane! Jane, I need a Healer!"

"I could have done that. I would have done it before. But Zachary showed me what would have happened eventually if I had. It would always be too tempting. It said I could be a god here, Francis. That ain't right. Not like that. No one person should have that much Power. If only it was just the curse, but I had to choose between what I love and who I love." Faye opened her eyes. "So I gave it up. All that extra magic, I just gave it up. I chose to be me."

He was staring into Faye's *blue* eyes.

War Faye

⨯Epilogue⨯

But down these mean streets must go a man who is not himself mean, who is neither tarnished nor afraid. The detective in this kind of story must be such a man. He is the hero; he is everything. He must be a complete man and a common man and yet an unusual man. He must be, to use a rather weathered phrase, a man of honor—by instinct, by inevitability, without thought of it and certainly without saying it...I think he might seduce a duchess and I am quite sure he would never spoil a virgin; if he is a man of honor in one thing, he is that in all things.

He is a relatively poor man, or he would not be a detective at all. He is a common man or he could not go among common people. He has a sense of character or he would not know his job. He will take no man's money dishonestly and no man's insolence without a due and dispassionate revenge. He is a lonely man and his pride is that you will treat him as a proud man or be very sorry you ever saw him. He talks as a man of his age talks—that is, with rude wit, a lively sense of the grotesque, a disgust for sham. And a contempt for pettiness.

The story is this man's adventure in search of a hidden truth, and it would be no adventure if it did not happen to a man fit for adventure...If there were enough like him, the world would be a very safe place to live in, without becoming too dull to be worth living in.

—Raymond Chandler,
The Simple Art of Murder

ONE YEAR LATER

HE HAD WOKEN UP long before sunrise, kissed his still sleeping wife on the cheek, peeked in on their newborn son in his crib, and then left quietly. He'd heard the call. The time had come for them to go back to the world, which meant that it was going to be a busy day, but right now he just needed time to think.

The ocean wasn't very far from the house, so he just walked. He had a bit of a limp now, probably would for the rest of his life. The Healing spells carved on his body had kept him alive and repaired most of the damage. The rest would be left to time.

The pre-dawn mist brought a bit of a chill with it. The ocean was close enough to sometimes hear the waves at night. Other than the water and the wind, this was a quiet place, a good place to heal, study, and prepare, a safe home, an isolated place. He liked it that way.

But apparently it hadn't been isolated enough.

Toru Tokugawa was waiting for him on the beach with a sword in his hands. It looked like he'd been there for quite some time.

"Can't say I'm surprised to see you." Jake Sullivan stopped twenty feet away, hands in his pockets. "I figured this day would come."

Toru had aged since they'd last met, but if the rumors were true, he'd been a very busy man. He was wearing traditional Japanese clothing, a dark kimono and hakama, with a daisho through the obi at his waist and another, longer no-dachi resting in his hands. Sullivan actually knew the terms now, but that was because he'd gotten a lot of practice speaking Japanese over the last year. They'd wanted their boy to grow up knowing both languages.

Toru bowed in greeting. It was a rather respectful gesture, all things considered. "You are a difficult man to find when you choose to be, Sullivan."

"I told the whole Imperium that I was their devil..." Sullivan shrugged. "Then they went on a crusade killing every single thing they could get their hands on that might have been touched by the devil. Didn't seem wise to go waving a big flag saying I survived."

"I am curious. How did you survive? Saito's death spell obliterated the palace."

"Heinrich. He showed up, grabbed me, and Faded us through the bedrock when it blew." It had been a hell of an exciting few days after that, hardly able to walk, full of holes, beaten half to death, and trying to get out as the city of Shanghai melted down around them. "You?"

"One of my brothers, Hayate—so a literal brother in this case— Traveled me away the instant before Saito's spell triggered... but you were already aware that I still lived."

"I've been laying low, don't mean I haven't been paying attention." Sullivan said. "Your story went all over. The Imperium found out they'd been snookered, and then you cleaned out that nest of vipers. They even named you First Iron Guard."

"I offered my *seppuku*. The Emperor disagreed."

"How does it feel to go from traitor to national hero?"

"I would not know. I was never a traitor." Toru chuckled.

Sullivan just smiled and shook his head.

The two men stood there silently for a time. Toru turned and studied the sea. "This war was brief, but costly. The last of the infiltrators have fled and are hiding in sewers, high mountains, or desolate swamps. They are nothing more than a dangerous, carnivorous nuisance now. I have been led to understand that this is the case in other lands as well, and where the Iron Guard cannot go, the Grimnoir have hunted these creatures nearly to extinction."

"Rumor I heard was that they're making you Chairman."

"No. That office has been forever retired. I will merely serve as a humble advisor to the Emperor and the council on strategic matters. It is a posting of minor importance."

Sullivan knew that was either false modesty or an outright lie. "I bet. And what do you plan on advising?"

"The nature of Okubo Tokugawa's grand vision must adapt. With the Enemy imprisoned, we can look to a better future. The Imperium schools are no more. Unit 731 has been disbanded. I ordered an end to the experiments, and for now, our borders will stabilize and consolidate rather than grow... But already I have said too much... Did you know that the Imperium has decided to remove our military presence from Shanghai?"

"I'd heard something to that effect."

"While our military was occupied dealing with the infiltrators, a charismatic young man managed to unite the city's various feuding factions into a coherent resistance. With the Imperium Section in ruins, the council felt it was no longer economically viable to help manage the city."

"So now it's not just a Free City in name only." Sullivan tried not to smile. *Good work, Zhao.*

"He is lucky he gave up my ashtray..." Toru shook his head ruefully. "But were you aware that Big Eared Du was murdered? There were many turf wars between the gangs after we pulled out. The new mastermind of the Yuesheng Greens is a mysterious figure known only as the Alienist."

Now that was news. Nobody had seen Wells after the battle. "That I did not know. Guess he didn't want to go back to Rockville...Not that there is a Rockville anymore."

"And what of you, Sullivan? How have you passed the time?"

"You know me. Reading books, playing with spells. Nothing important."

"Ah, of course... *Elder.*"

The Imperium's spy network was better than expected. It wasn't like he'd known about the society's job offer for very long himself. "I was never much for titles."

"And what do you 'plan on advising'?"

"I'm more a hands on type, but if the Imperium torture schools are shut down and the eugenic madmen really are done, then I'd advise...restraint."

Toru nodded thoughtfully. "There is wisdom in this."

They'd lost a couple of the elders during the war against the infiltrator. Browning had filled one spot, and they'd figured who better for the seventh and final position than the man who they should have been listening to from the beginning? Montand had given Sullivan his vote before stepping down. Churchill had voted for him too. The deciding vote in Sullivan's favor had come from the already serving American elder, and Sullivan had been surprised to learn that was William Donovan, newly appointed head of the OCI. And now that a long time knight had ensconced himself into the government job of watching Actives, they'd managed to completely sabotage Roosevelt's control and registration schemes, all without the president being wise to it at all. Sullivan had to give them credit. The Grimnoir knew how to take the long view.

"One other thing I must know before we conclude our business, what has become of the Spellbound?"

Of course the Imperium spies would want to know about *her.*

Faye had saved the world after all. "She's not the Spellbound anymore."

"There have been rumors."

"They're true. Faye's not a Traveler anymore. That magic was connected to her curse, and she burned that up trapping the Enemy."

"No longer a Traveler . . . I was not aware of this. Someday the Enemy may escape, but for now the entire world owes her a debt."

"She's fine," Sullivan assured him, because even if she was no longer the most powerful wizard in the world, she was probably still the sharpest. The Imperium didn't need to know that she was actually a Cog genius who was taking magic into all sorts of exciting new directions, especially now that she'd taught herself how to connect her magic to different parts of the Power, with all of that talk of *folding*. Last time he'd talked to Francis, the kid had sworn up and down that Faye was dead set on figuring out how to Travel again. He had no doubt that she would. Faye might have lost some of her abilities, but that girl was only getting started. She'd saved the world, and now she intended to change it into something better.

Surprisingly enough, Toru actually seemed a little moved by her sacrifice, but that was just because to some of them, magic was more precious than life. "How is Faye dealing with the loss?"

"Faye is tougher than any of us . . . But come on, Toru. You're not here to reminisce about old friends, not that she ever particularly took a liking to you."

"No, that she did not . . ." Toru kept on watching the waves crash against the rocks. "I am here to finish what we started. It must be decided who is the better warrior once and for all."

Sullivan took his hands out of his pockets. His Power was ready. "It really doesn't have to end like this."

Toru lifted the still sheathed long sword. "Do you know how I knew you were still alive, Sullivan? No?" Toru had the blade in both hands, like he was balancing it carefully. "This is the no-dachi of Sasaki Kojiro, a sword which once belonged to my father. At the time, I took its discovery at Mason Island as a sign of my father's approval. Finding this sword at that particular time was very *important* to me."

"I didn't recognize it." The only thing Sullivan had noticed about it up until then was that Toru was probably going to try and kill him with it.

"When I was captured in Shanghai, this sword was still aboard the *Traveler*. As was this…" Toru placed one hand on the katana at his waist and slowly drew it. It was three feet of killing steel. "Only then it was in two pieces. I have since had it repaired after my office was restored. Both of these things should have been lost to me forever. So how was it that these items came into my possession?"

Southunder had gotten the *Traveler* down in one piece and hidden it until the chaos on the mainland blew over. Luckily the Imperium had plenty of other things to worry about just then, so Sullivan and the others had rendezvoused with them and then gotten the hell out. "By the time we got home, I'd heard you were back with the Iron Guard. I called in some favors, and got your kit sent back with some diplomats."

"Why did you do this?"

"I was there when you broke that sword. You said you were going to put it back together when your honor was put back together…" Sullivan shrugged. "Why would I stand in the way of a man trying to put things right?"

"When I received them, I knew only you would have done this. That was how I knew you still lived." Toru tossed the bigger, sheathed sword to Sullivan.

He caught it with one hand. It was a lot lighter than it looked. "No offense to all your traditional bullshit, but I'm not big on the whole dueling thing. Last time I tried to use one of these things, turned out I was bad at it. You want to fight, I intend to just Spike you half way to hell."

"It is a gift." Toru sheathed his katana. "Keep it to remember our battle against the Enemy."

"I wasn't in danger of forgetting."

"I wished to know which of us is the better warrior… I believe the question has been answered sufficiently." Toru bowed deeply.

Sullivan returned the bow.

"Eventually, there will be a war between our nations, or the Grimnoir and the Iron Guard may again become foes. When this happens, the two of us may meet in battle and reexamine this answer… but until that time, fare well, Sullivan."

First Iron Guard Toru Tokugawa turned and walked away.

Jake Sullivan, elder of the Grimnoir Society, kept the sword and watched the sunrise.

Someday he would pass it to his son.

⚔ END ⚔

⊰Glossary⊱ of Magical Terms

From the notes of Jake Sullivan, 1932

⊰A⊱

Active—The catch-all term for people with magical abilities. Specifically those who have strong enough connections to the Power to utilize their ability at will and with a greater degree of control than a Passive. Actives vary in the amount of Power available to them, with some being more naturally gifted than others. The conventional wisdom has always been that Actives are only able to use one type of Power.

Actively Magical—Old fashioned term for Active.

Angel of Death—(see Pale Horse)

⊰B⊱

Babel—Rare type of Active capable of understanding, deciphering, and communicating in any language.

Burner—(see Torch)

Beastie—Similar to Dolittle, but stronger, with the added ability to control animals telepathically. Extreme cases can actually put part of their consciousness into the creature and fully control it, including broadcasting the Beastie's speech, etc. There have been some rumors of Beasties capable of controlling human beings, but that may be anti-magic propaganda.

Beastman—(see Beastie)

Boomer—An extremely rare form of Active capable of creating explosive effects out of thin air. Unknown type of Active. The Special Prisoners' Wing guards at Rockville mentioned holding one of these in solitary confinement in a special lead-lined chamber.

Brute—One of the most common of all Magicals. Brutes channel Power through their bodies, increasing their physical strength and toughness. They must work up to greater feats of strength. If too much Power is used too quickly, severe injuries or death can occur. They have been banned from professional sports in most countries, but there is always work available for a Brute.

C

Cog—The second most popular of all Actives. Cogs are able to tap their Power to fuel their intelligence and to receive strokes of magical brilliance. They usually only have one area that they are gifted in; for example, Ferdinand von Zeppelin was a Cog when it came to airships. If it weren't for his bursts of magical ideas, who knows what we would be riding. I do not know if all Cogs are already intelligent, but I've never heard of a dumb one.

Crackler—Capable of channeling, harnessing, and controlling electrical current. They are a relatively common type, and most make their living as electricians or in industry. The more powerful Cracklers can draw energy from the air and generate their own lightning.

D

Demon—(see Summoned)

Dymaxion Nullifier—A device invented by Buckminster Fuller, capable of blocking magic from a small area. Some magic effects, if already established, can enter a Nullifer's area and not be dismissed, like a Summoned or a Healer's vision. Dymaxion Nullifiers detonate violently if they come into contact with Nixie magic.

Beastie

Boomer

Brute

Cog

Crackler

Dolittle—Active with the ability to communicate with animals. Extreme cases who can actually take control of the animal's body are usually referred to as Beastmen or Beasties. A series of popular children's books have been written about a fictional veterinarian with this ability, so it has become one of the more socially acceptable types of magic.

E

Edison—(see Crackler) I have been told this is considered the polite term now.

Elder—Member of the Grimnoir Society leadership.

Enemy—A predatory creature which pursues the Power. I believe it has been doing this for a very long time. Unknown predatory creature that is pursuing the Power, according to Chairman Okubo Tokugawa.

F

Fade—Capable of walking through solid objects. Perhaps they do this through modifying their density so that other matter fits between their molecules. They are the opposite of the Massive, yet both of them originate from the same density-related section of the Power. Fades are universally loathed for their reputation as thieves, cutthroats, and peeping toms.

Finder—Related to the Summoner, but dealing more with disembodied spirits rather than physical beings. Finders are primarily used as scouts, and their sensitivity varies greatly. It is possible that Finders and Summoners are using the same region of the Power, with Summoners simply being more powerful.

Fixer—(see Cog) Usually a term reserved for lower-level Cogs, who are better at repairing than inventing.

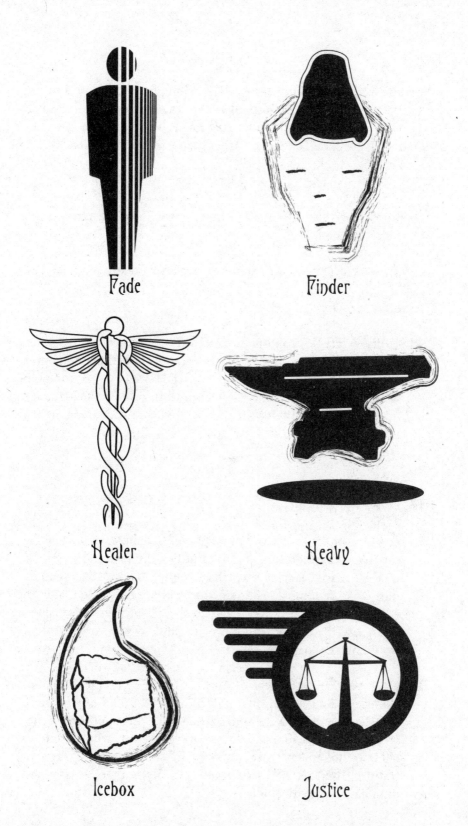

Fade

Finder

Healer

Heavy

Icebox

Justice

Fortune Teller—An odd sort of Active, long believed to be a myth, Fortune Tellers are capable of glimpsing possible futures. Charlatans who pretend to have magic and know the future to rip off suckers. There is no proof of any precognitive Active.

⚖ G ⚖

Gravity Spiker—(see Heavy) The much more dignified term for an Active Heavy.

Grey Eye—(see Traveler) All known Travelers have strange grey eyes.

Grim Reaper—(see Pale Horse)

Grimnoir Society—A combination of the French words *grimoire*, for book of spells, and *noir*, for black, because at the time the origins of magic were shrouded in mystery. The Society was founded to protect Actives from the Normals and to protect the Normals from the Actives. Their primary operatives are known as knights, and their leaders are referred to as elders. They work in secrecy.

⚖ H ⚖

Head Case—(see Reader)

Healer—One of the rarest and most popular of all Actives. They are capable of accelerating the natural healing process. Even the weakest Passive Healer is worth a fortune. Strong Healers can fix most wounds almost instantaneously. I have been told that even without using their Power, they can always see a person's insides. I suppose it's a good thing they're paid so well, because that would make me ill.

Heavy—A very common type of Active. Most Heavies are limited to changing the gravitational pull in a very limited area. Strong Heavies can change the pull and also the direction in a larger area. Heavies are one of the few types of Actives who all tend to fall into the same physical category; most of them being large of stature. There is an undeserved stereotype that Heavies are dumb. (see Gravity Spiker)

≈ I ≈

Icebox—Always handy to have around when you want some ice in your drink, the Icebox is able to lower temperatures. Stronger Actives can freeze water or even blood and tissue instantly. There have been stories of Iceboxes who could produce ice walls or spikes out of thin air, but these may be the result of a popular radio program, the Adventures of Captain Johnny Freeze. As a physical benefit, Iceboxes cannot be harmed by frostbite or extreme cold.

≈ J ≈

Justice—A type of Active capable of discerning truth from lies. I know one, but haven't had the opportunity to interview her about the specifics of how her Power works. This is a rumored type of Active. Supposedly, they can always tell truth from lies. Personally, I'll believe it when I meet one.

≈ K ≈

Kanji—(see Spells) The Japanese term for physical spells. Their Kanji tend to be more stylized and artistic than the western-European-style markings of the Grimnoir, but are very effective at channeling Power.

Knight—An operative of the Grimnoir Society.

≈ L ≈

Lazarus—An Active capable to chaining the spirits of the recently dead to their bodies, creating tortured undead. This is the worst of all, sheer magic scum, and the only good Lazarus is a dead Lazarus.

Lightning Bug—(see Crackler)

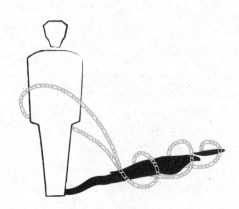

Lazarus

Lucky

Massive

Mouth

Mover

Lucky—I had heard about these for years, and thought they were a fairytale to explain people who cheated at cards. They use their magical ability to alter probability. The term used by Dr. Fort to explain this ability to influence chance was psychokinesis.

⚐ M ⚑

Machine Head—(see Cog) Usually a Cog who is in tune with physical machines rather than theory or science.

Magicals—A common term for people with Power, which can include both Actives and Passives.

Massive—An extremely rare type of Active, capable of increasing their physical density until they are almost invulnerable. I believe they are related to Gravity Spikers, and are the opposite of the Fade, but at the opposite end of the spectrum.

Mender—(see Healer)

Mover—The scientific term is *telekinetic*, which means moving things with your mind. They are very rare, and very few are capable of moving more than a small number of small objects at a time. As a Mover's Power increases they are able to lift more weight, lift more individual items at once, move them to higher velocities, and, most difficult of all, exercise a finer degree of control over the controlled objects.

Mouth—The most hated or most loved Actives, depending on if they are in charge or not. Mouths are able to influence anyone listening to their voice. Passive Mouths can alter moods and emotions, while a powerful Active can directly control your thoughts and feelings. The smarter you are, the harder it is for a Mouth to steer you. Mouths tend to gravitate toward politics.

N

Nixie—One whose ability creates a continuously growing sphere that annihilates everything in its path. The area of effect seems to be set at a fixed distance, but because of the rarity of this type, I can't confirm. There have only been a few known cases. The Mason Island Incident was caused by a spellbinding of the Nixie's Power.

Normals—Term used mostly by Actives to describe people without any magic. Depending on who is using it, it can be a derogatory term.

O

Opener—(see Lazarus) short for Grave Opener.

P

Pale Horse—The opposite of the Healer, the touch of the Pale Horse causes disease and sickness. No Active is more hated than these. Luckily for us, most Normals think that they are a story used to scare children.

Passive—A Magical who does not have active control over their Power. They usually have one small trick that they can do, but are unable for whatever reason to grow their ability. For example, Passive Heavies are instinctively able to pick up heavy things. Passive Healers can accelerate the natural healing process just by their presence but cannot target specific areas or wounds. Passive Readers can pick up snatches of other people's thoughts but often go insane from being unable to control the input.

Pipes—Unknown type of Active. Intelligence reports during the Great War showed that the Germans held one of these in reserve, but it is uncertain if we ever encountered him.

Power—A. The energy that all Magicals possess. As the energy is used, our reserves are depleted. The rate at which it recharges and the total amount that can be stored depend on the individual's natural gifts and practice. It is currently unknown if a Magical is born connected to the Power, or if the connection forms at some point during their early life.

Power—B. The living being that all magical energy originates from. Its origin is a mystery. I believe it to be a symbiotic parasite. It grants magical abilities to some humans, and as we develop those abilities, the magical energy that we carry grows. When we die, the Power 'digests' this energy and feeds. The process is then repeated. The growth of the being explains the increase in our numbers over time.

R

Reader—Someone possessing the magical ability to read another's mind, sometimes called telepathy. Weak Readers can get general feelings from their target, while a strong Reader can crack your head open and watch your memories like a motion picture. Readers can also broadcast thoughts and memories. The stronger their target's will or intelligence, the more difficult they are to Read, and the more likely they are to sense the intrusion.

Ringer—An extremely rare type of Active who can change their appearance and voice to perfectly mimic another. It is unknown if they actually physically change, or if they just create the illusion in other people's minds. I met one once in Rockville but he escaped within 24 hours of arrival.

Rune Arcanium—A book of spells collected by the Grimnoir Society.

S

Scales—(see Justice)

Slinger (see Lucky)

Pale Horse

Reader

Ringer

Shard

Shadow Walker (see Fade)

Shard—A rare type of Active who can modify their bone structure at will. I had one start a fight with me in Rockville. They still squish just like everyone else.

Shifter—(see Ringer) It is believed in some circles that there is a type of Active who can actually change their physical form, but my personal belief is that these are just talented Ringers.

Spellbound—A. A term used for when you've connected a person or thing to some area of the Power through the use of a spell.

Spellbound—B. The title for the bearer of the parasitic spell created by Anand Sivaram, and first held by him, and later by Sally Faye Vierra.

Spells—Through creating a representation of one of the coordinate sections of the Power, specific magical energies can be channeled into, and connected to, those markings. Grimnoir-designed spells tend to look like old-European-style writing, while Imperium Kanji are more artistic.

Summoned—A being brought into our reality by a Summoner. The strength of the creature is dependent upon the Summoner's skill. Summoned only communicate at a rudimentary level, though they do have some language. They originate on the world or possibly worlds previously abandoned by the Power and consumed by the Enemy. It is unknown where they originate from, and they will never communicate on that subject except in the vaguest terms. Summoned remain in this world until destroyed or dismissed.

Summoner—An Active who can bring in creatures from another world to serve their bidding. It is unknown where these beings come from. The personal beliefs of the Summoner seem to affect what the Summoned looks like. Extremely powerful Summoners can bring in drastically strong creatures. The more forceful the creature, the more Power and attention it takes to keep it under control.

⚜ T ⚜

Teleporter (see Traveler)—A scientific term that has recently come into common usage.

Torch—The single most common type of magical ability. Torches control fire. Passives are usually limited to very small flames, while a powerful Active can put out a flaming hydrogen dirigible. Unlike the Icebox, who can't be harmed by cold, Torches can still be burned just like any other human. I happen to be very fond of Torches.

Trap—(see Mouth) Usually used with a dual meaning, as in "That politician is a Trap."

Traveler—One of the only Actives that can be spotted by a physical trait. All known Travelers have grey eyes. They are one of the rarest types, but not by birth, but rather because so few of them live long enough to control their ability. Travelers are able to move instantly between two places. The stronger the Traveler, the further they can go and the more they can carry.

⚜ U ⚜

Undead—A being created by a Lazarus. Physical death has occurred, but the body remains animated. Consciousness and intelligence remains, but so does the pain of whatever killed them. Undead possess no natural healing abilities and only continue to deteriorate. They cannot be magically Mended. Very few undead remain sane for any length of time and they tend to grow increasingly violent and erratic. They do not truly die until their body is utterly destroyed. There is a special place in hell for anyone who would curse someone to being undead.

Summoner

Tinker

Torch

Traveler

Weatherman

W

Weatherman—A Magical with the ability to influence the weather. Strong Actives can actually stop or start storms and change wind patterns, sometimes even up to hurricane force. Too-harsh use of this skill can cause severe side effects, such as the great dustbowl of 1927.

Words (see Mouth)

Y

Yap (see Mouth)

Z

Zombies—(see Undead). The first known Lazarus originated in Haiti. It is believed that is where the term *zombie* originated from.

100

THINGS TO DO IN
MONTGOMERY
ALABAMA
BEFORE YOU
DIE

• •

MARY JOHNS WILSON

REEDY PRESS

Copyright © 2024 by Reedy Press, LLC
Reedy Press
PO Box 5131
St. Louis, MO 63139, USA
www.reedypress.com

No part of this publication may be reproduced or transmitted in any form or by any means, electronic or mechanical, including photocopy, recording, or any information storage and retrieval system, without permission in writing from the publisher.

Permissions may be sought directly from Reedy Press at the above mailing address or via our website at www.reedypress.com.

Library of Congress Control Number: 2023951763

ISBN: 9781681064666

Design by Jill Halpin

All photos provided by the author unless otherwise noted.

Printed in the United States of America
24 25 26 27 28 5 4 3 2 1

We (the publisher and the author) have done our best to provide the most accurate information available when this book was completed. However, we make no warranty, guarantee, or promise about the accuracy, completeness, or currency of the information provided, and we expressly disclaim all warranties, express or implied. Please note that attractions, company names, addresses, websites, and phone numbers are subject to change or closure, and this is outside of our control. We are not responsible for any loss, damage, injury, or inconvenience that may occur due to the use of this book. When exploring new destinations, please do your homework before you go. You are responsible for your own safety and health when using this book.

DEDICATION

To Mom and Dad—thank you for teaching me to work hard
and to appreciate the hard work of others.

To fellow author Fr. Francis Sofie—thank you for your endless
encouragement and your childlike joy throughout life.

CONTENTS

• •

Music and Entertainment

• •

Sports and Recreation

• •

• •

ACKNOWLEDGMENTS

You know the old adage, "It takes a village to raise a child." Well, I'm convinced it also takes a village to accomplish a dream, like writing a book.

First and foremost, I am grateful for the support of my husband, Matt. He is the source of so much good in our lives, and I never would have believed I had the ability to do something like this if it weren't for him.

When it came to narrowing down this list of 100 things to do in Montgomery and the surrounding River Region, I turned to my friends through the forum of Facebook. Countless people answered questions, offered suggestions, and even brought my attention to undiscovered gems in the River Region. I'm thankful I know people who also love this area and are willing to help.

My immediate family members all live back up in Kentucky, but I've checked a lot of the items in this book off my own bucket list thanks to their visits to this area. They're always supportive, as are all my in-laws, those who live here and those in Georgia.

And finally, I have to take things back to second and third grades at Wilmore Elementary School. I have a box full of things my mom kept from my school days, and in it, there are all kinds of short stories I wrote during those years, and that's thanks to the encouragement of my teacher, Mrs. Jan Thornton. Whenever I was getting antsy in class because I'd already finished another

• •

project, she would tell me to write. She may not know it, but she's a big reason I've discovered this passion in my life. Her support and direction laid the foundation for my writing career. It's a blessing in my life that I was assigned to her primary class. Thanks, Mrs. Thornton!

PREFACE

I was born and raised in the small town of Wilmore, Kentucky. During my time in the Bluegrass State, I also lived in Bowling Green and Lexington, and I enjoyed a year in Starkville, Mississippi, before moving to what we locals call the River Region in 2010.

No matter which small town or (relatively) big city I've called home, I'm always surprised when out-of-towners ask, "But what is there to do there?" I suppose these folks yearn for the "City That Never Sleeps" vibes of New York City or Los Angeles. I don't know about you, but I enjoy rest, especially when I get to rest in a peaceful park beside a babbling creek. I enjoy walking into a restaurant where I know the owners and can strike up conversations with acquaintances who happen to also be dining there. I enjoy going to a play or concert and applauding friends and relatives who have put their all into their performance.

I am convinced, no matter where you live, as long as there is a community of people, there will always be something to do. And that's because where there are people, there are talents. And to be talented means to have passion. And passions must be shared with others, because unshared passions are merely passing trends.

All you have to do is look, and you'll find passionate people eager to share their talents—whether that's cooking, acting, dancing, singing, storytelling, decorating, or just good ol'

• •

Southern hospitality. In this book, you'll find 100 things to do in Montgomery and the surrounding River Region, which includes Autauga, Elmore, and Montgomery counties. But it's more than that. The entries that follow represent the passions of hundreds of people who call the River Region home. I urge you to eat at these restaurants, visit these museums, watch these performances, and shop at these stores. Engage with the people who have been brave and vulnerable enough to share their passions, and enjoy every minute of it.

My passion has been putting a spotlight on all the good there is in the River Region through writing this book. Thank you for allowing me to share with you.

FOOD
AND DRINK

DEVOUR A DOG
AT CHRIS' FAMOUS HOTDOGS

In 1917, Greek immigrant Chris Katechis opened a restaurant in Montgomery that spoke to his love for this country, because what's more American than a hot dog? Chris' Famous Hotdogs has been owned and operated by the same family in the same location since opening day, and they've captured the secret sauce for success. Chris' famous chili sauce is legendary, and it brings people back time and again.

Look for the iconic green-and-white awning, step inside, and be greeted by an atmosphere and decor that celebrate times gone by. Photographs of famous patrons, including Martin Luther King Jr. and Hank Williams, hang above rows of booths. Counter seating is also available. While the menu includes hamburgers, chicken fingers, and chicken salad, you must order a hot dog with a side of fries or onion rings.

138 Dexter Ave., 334-265-6850
chrishotdogs.com

SAMPLE EVERY DISH
AT UNCLE MICK'S CAJUN MARKET & CAFÉ

If jambalaya, étouffée, or sauce piquante are foreign terms to you, fear not because Uncle Mick is here to help. Named for its gregarious owner, staff at the charming cafeteria-style restaurant encourage hungry customers to sample dishes until they find their favorite. To make the most of a trip, order a split regular plate, which comes with two entrees and two sides. Fan favorites include shrimp à la crème served over dirty rice and crawfish étouffée, but you can't go wrong when you fill your belly with a meal from Uncle Mick.

Family-owned-and-operated, Uncle Mick's closes on weekends, serves only lunch on Mondays, and closes between lunch and dinner service the rest of the week. Check the website for specifics.

136 W Main St., Prattville, 334-361-1020
unclemickscajun.com

HOP TO EVERY RESTAURANT
IN THE VINTAGE HOSPITALITY GROUP

No matter the taste or atmosphere you're looking for, Vintage Hospitality Group has an establishment to fit the need. Owned by Jud Blount, a Montgomery native, the group's host of restaurants and bars in the historic districts of downtown and Old Cloverdale offer delicious menus created by renowned chef Eric Rivera.

Want a casual vibe with great draft beer plus small plates and outdoor activities? Red Bluff Bar at the Silos overlooking the Alabama River is just the place. Need something upscale for a fancy anniversary dinner? Ravello Ristorante is sure to please with its Italian menu and Roman-inspired decor. Just need lunch? Head to Vintage Cafe, located in a renovated bank, and order tomato bisque as your side. Looking for a good burger or steak? Find it at Vintage Year Restaurant & Bar.

TIP
Vintage Hospitality Group also owns MGM Greens, an urban farm inside a two-story storage container. Greens and herbs from MGM Greens are served in the group's restaurants.

Red Bluff Bar at the Silos

Put on your walking shoes. Patrons must enter through the railroad tunnel behind the Hank Williams statue, walk to the riverfront, and then head up the hill. Dogs are welcome.

335 Coosa St., 334-223-9625

redbluffmgm.com

Ravello Ristorante

Get reservations. Enjoy a drink before or after dinner in the adjoining rooftop Bar Attico, which is also part of Vintage Hospitality Group.

36 Commerce St., 334-356-2852

ravellomgm.com

Vintage Cafe

Appreciate the food and the repurposed bank pieces, including old safety deposit boxes serving as the counter and the old vault converted into an office.

416 Cloverdale Rd., 334-356-1944

vintagecafemgm.com

Vintage Year Restaurant & Bar

Tuesday night is burger night. Get the VY Classic featuring Alabama Wagyu beef. Brunch is served Sundays.

405 Cloverdale Rd., 334-819-7215

vymgm.com

SHARE SMALL PLATES
AT TASTE

Who says a flight has to be reserved for beer? Not Chef Ginger Hahn. She and her husband, Clint, co-own Taste, a community restaurant. The atmosphere is casual, while the food and wine are upscale. Speaking of wine, don't feel restricted. Order a flight. It's the best way to ensure you have the right wines for each of the tapas, or small plates, your party orders. Share orders of Spanish meatballs, baked brie, and stuffed mushrooms.

At the original location in the planned community of Hampstead, brunch is served Saturdays and Sundays. Get a sugar rush from the cookie butter French toast or make a healthier decision with the spinach and artichoke Benedict. During regular hours, this location offers entrées for those who don't want to share. Taste Too! in downtown Montgomery has a modest menu of tapas, wine, beer, cocktails, and desserts.

Taste
5251 Hampstead High St., Ste. 100, 334-676-4333

Taste Too!
79 Commerce St., Ste. E, 334-523-8703

tastemgm.com

KICK BACK WITH A BREW
AT A CRAFT HOUSE

Owned by John and Paige Stewart, Autauga Creek Craft House epitomizes the traditional neighborhood pub in historic downtown Prattville. Sit at the bar or a handmade, high-top table inside, or head outside to the patio. The 15 beers on tap change regularly. Order a flight of local favorites, or mix it up with a glass of wine. Thursdays are Open Jam nights. Musicians and vocalists of all skill levels are welcome, and the resulting rhythms are a true celebration of community.

Music is also a main draw at the Stewarts' second location, Coosa River Craft House in Wetumpka. They host local musicians for concerts. Try your hand at performing during an open mic or on karaoke nights. The slightly larger of the two, Coosa River Craft House also offers a larger selection with 28 beers on tap. Both locations encourage patrons to support other businesses and bring in outside food.

Autauga Creek Craft House
140 W Main St., Prattville, 334-356-5840
facebook.com/autaugacreekcrafthouse

Coosa River Craft House
191 Spring St., Wetumpka, 334-569-9779
facebook.com/coosarivercrafthouse

NOSH
AT A FRIDAY-OWNED RESTAURANT

Cork & Cleaver Gastropub in the Zelda Place Shopping Center was the first River Region restaurant for experienced restaurateurs Ryan and Danyalle Friday. They added Coosa Cleaver Casual Cuisine in 2018, long before HGTV made downtown Wetumpka trendy.

While the flavor-packed Cowboy Burger and the super-southern Fried Green Tomato BLT are available at both locations, that's where similarities stop. Coosa Cleaver is laid-back with down-home flavors like portabella meatloaf or grilled porterhouse pork chops. Cork & Cleaver is sophisticated fun with a can't-miss weekend brunch. Enjoy an open-faced bialy bacon sandwich or the chicken and waffles. Wash it all down with a mimosa or Bloody Mary.

Speaking of brunch, it's all brunch, all the time at the Fridays' third restaurant, the Bubbly Hen. Spice it up by ordering shakshuka or keep it tame with prosciutto and fig flatbread. But definitely order the featured monkey bread for dessert.

Cork & Cleaver Gastropub
2960A Zelda Rd., 334-676-2260
thecorkcleaver.com

Coosa Cleaver Casual Cuisine
106 Company St., Wetumpka, 334-731-1190
coosacleaver.com

The Bubbly Hen
7915 Vaughn Rd., 334-649-1111
bubblyhen.com

FILL A PLATE
AT DAVIS CAFE

Back in 1988, Davis Cafe opened to the public. Now run by Sheila Davis, granddaughter of the original owners, it's the epitome of soul food excellence. A true meat-and-three located in a simple and humble building on the north side of town, the lunch menu changes daily. Choose one from a few entrées and three from a handful of vegetables. The fried chicken and cornbread muffins are the best in Montgomery. Ox tails over rice pairs well with collard greens, macaroni and cheese, and purple hull peas, or try the pot roast with fried okra, mashed potatoes and gravy, and sliced tomatoes.

Don't miss out on breakfast, either. Order the scrambled eggs with salmon patties and grits, served swimming in butter. For a sweeter breakfast, enjoy hotcakes with sausage. Davis Cafe is open weekdays from 7 a.m. to 3 p.m.

518 N Decatur St., 334-264-6015

TAKE ON TACO TUESDAY
AT SOL RESTAURANTE
MEXICANO & TAQUERIA

When an irresistible craving for tacos is the problem, Sol Restaurante Mexicano & Taqueria is the only solution. When it first opened, Sol occupied a small space in a strip mall, and consistent long waits proved the family-owned-and-operated eatery's extreme popularity. Since, the original location has expanded to more than double its seating capacity, and a second location opened east of Montgomery in the growing town of Pike Road.

There is no better value on any menu in the River Region than Sol's street tacos. Order guacamole and enjoy the entertainment of the dip made tableside. Add a side of elote, corn on the cob smothered in mayonnaise and queso cotija with a lime-chili powder. Wash it all down with a margarita or stay sober with an agua fresca.

3962 Atlanta Hwy., 334-593-8250
9539 Vaughn Rd., Pike Road, 334-593-7984
solrestaurante.com

HEAD TO OUR PLACE CAFÉ
FOR COZY FINE DINING

Outside of Wetumpka's main business district and driving distance from the city's walkable downtown, Our Place Café is definitely off the beaten path. It's fitting because the restaurant is unlike any other in town and fills Elmore County's need for fine dining.

Exposed brick walls and reclaimed corrugated tin ceiling tiles create a cozy atmosphere inside the two-story building, but the white tablecloths nod to the establishment's upscale offerings. Owner David Funderburk's menu is seafood-centric and Cajun-inspired, a nod to childhood days visiting his aunts in New Orleans. The crab cakes are legendary. Catfish has never tasted better than their New Orleans–style catfish filets. If you prefer turf rather than surf, try the filet mignon or lemon herb chicken.

While the food is first-class, the dress code is "come as you are," whether that's jeans and a T-shirt or a tux.

809 Company St., Wetumpka, 334-567-8778
Search Facebook for "Our Place Café"

LET THE GOOD TIMES ROLL
AT WISHBONE CAFE

Located at the end of a busy strip mall, Wishbone Cafe may be easy to overlook, but that would be a travesty. Your taste buds deserve to enjoy this food. Montgomery native and owner Paul Dallas learned all about Cajun cooking while living in Houma, Louisiana, and he brought those flavors back home when he opened Wishbone Cafe in 2008.

The Pasta Mardi Gras is a celebration of proteins with crawfish, shrimp, chicken, and sausage. John Ed's Po Boy is a tasty take on Louisiana's trademark sandwich. With an addictive Jamaican relish, Mr. Blount's Cuban is a tip of the hat to Houma's Caribbean-influenced cuisine. Whatever dish you try, order soup as your side. With rotating daily specials, you can try gumbo on Mondays, veggie on Tuesdays, Mexican corn on Wednesdays, and purple hull on Thursdays. The collard green soup is a must-try. It's such a fan favorite, it claims the special spot on Fridays and Saturdays.

6667 Atlanta Hwy., 334-244-7270
wishbone-cafe.com

DELIGHT AT THE COLLISION OF CULTURES
AT D'ROAD CAFÉ

When Janett Malpartida came to Montgomery, she wanted to share her Venezuelan and Italian heritage. For her D'Road Café, she transformed a portion of the old legendary Elite (pronounced E-light) Cafe in downtown, painting the walls a rich, royal purple and adding a hot bar.

Tuesdays through Fridays, that hot bar is filled with dishes that demonstrate a collision of cultures. Expect to see items like pork ribs and honey ginger chicken alongside black beans and plantains. Pick one entrée and three sides.

D'Road Café serves breakfast Tuesdays through Fridays along with an all-day breakfast on Saturdays. Arepas and empanadas are solid choices, but don't skip out on the crazy Benedict or the French toast sandwich.

121 Montgomery St., 334-328-2938
droadcafe.com

TIP
On Thursday evenings, Janett offers a special Latin/Spanish dinner menu. Start with the fish ceviche, order a paella or the Venezuelan parrilla for your entrée, and finish with flan. Be sure to follow D'Road Café on Facebook, because Janett often plans Friday night dinners, too.

HANG OUT
AT MIDTOWN PIZZA KITCHEN

When a pizza craving strikes, Midtown Pizza Kitchen has what you need. The dough, made in-house daily, creates a thin, crispy crust that's flavorful and addictive. House specialties range from a simple margherita to more complex flavors of the VY, which is topped with red sauce, provolone, spinach, fennel sausage, artichokes, and cherry tomatoes.

The neighborhood joint opened in Montgomery in 2011 and added a second location in Prattville in 2015. Both provide a cozy atmosphere with a big bar where a good selection of Alabama and regional brews are on tap. And the menu doesn't stop with pizza. MPK, as the locals say, offers excellent sandwiches, salads, and pastas. Pair the pasta genovese con pollo with a glass of wine, or try the balljacker—a meatball sub.

2940 Zelda Rd., 334-395-0080
mpkmontgomery.com

584 Pinnacle Pl., Prattville, 334-285-6128
mpkprattville.com

TIP
At lunch, order the special. It's not on the menu, but it's a smaller serving of any specialty salad plus a huge slice of a specialty pizza, a smaller serving of lasagna, or a lunch portion of the pasta of the day.

EAT
AT RED'S LITTLE SCHOOL HOUSE

It was almost the end for Red's Little School House back in 2022. Owner Debbie Deese announced its closing so she could care for her dad, the restaurant's namesake. In what would have been the eatery's final days, customers lined up and waited hours for one final meal. That tremendous community support convinced Debbie's children they needed to take over operations and save the community landmark. One taste of their fried corn bread cakes will convince you they made the right decision.

Housed in the old Hills Chapel Community School, there are two dining rooms. Sit down to order drinks, and then grab and fill a plate from the buffet. Try the fried chicken and the butter beans. Other staples include fried livers, pulled pork BBQ, green beans, and cream corn, while other buffet items rotate based on the day. Don't get up from the table till you've tried a piece of one of their homemade pies.

20 Gardner Rd., Grady, 334-584-7955
facebook.com/redslittleschoolhouse

SAY "DAS IST GUT"
AT PLANTATION HOUSE
RESTAURANT'S GERMAN NIGHT

The Plantation House Restaurant is deceiving. It doesn't look or feel like a restaurant. It feels like walking into someone's home. That's exactly what chef-owner Renate Lindsey wanted. Every Wednesday and Sunday, the restaurant opens from 11 a.m. to 2 p.m. with a hot buffet of chef's excellent down-home cooking.

Friday evenings are the real attraction, though, when Chef Renate shares her home country's cuisine on German night. Since it's a buffet, it's OK to try everything, from the jägerschnitzel and sauerbraten to Hungarian goulash and bratwursts. Potatoes, cabbage, and brussels sprouts are side dish stars. Don't fill up on pretzels and brötchen! You have to save room for desserts such as apple strudel, Black Forest cake, bread pudding, and German chocolate cake. Wash it all down with a German beer.

3240 Grandview Rd., Millbrook, 334-285-1466
plantationhouserc.com

TIP

Park in the gravel lot in front of the building, up the stairs, and around the porch to the back door to enter.

ENJOY AN EVENING
OF FINE DINING

For an anniversary dinner, book a reservation at one of Montgomery's upscale options with rotating menu items, craft cocktails, and delectable desserts.

Don't let the strip mall location of La Jolla fool you. Massive black curtains draped over the windows transforms the space into a romantic, intimate atmosphere. Start with the tuna nachos, then move to the sautéed red snapper for dinner, or the 10-ounce rib eye filet.

In nearby Hampstead, City Grill's appetizers are a cheese lover's dream with a triple-cream brie, baked feta, and fig turnover with Gorgonzola. Stay on the lighter side with a grilled Halloumi cheese salad or beef up your order with the surf and turf.

For downtown finery, check out Central. While the massive chandeliers, exposed brick walls, and lively open kitchen strike you first, you'll quickly be bowled over by flavors. Share a charcuterie board before enjoying the roasted half chicken or the pork osso buco.

La Jolla Restaurant & Bar
8147 Vaughn Rd., 334-356-2600
lajollamontgomery.com

City Grill
5251 Hampstead High St., 334-244-0960
Search Facebook for "City Grill"

Central
129 Coosa St., 334-517-1155
central129coosa.com

STUFF YOUR FACE
AT FAT BOY'S BAR-B-QUE RANCH

Danny Loftin was a trucker and farmer before he became a restaurant owner. His old CB handle, "Alabama Fat Boy," inspired the name of his barbecue joint, which opened on the banks of Autauga Creek in 1998. Two months later, it was destroyed by a fire, but Loftin stayed dedicated and rebuilt.

With Greg Bennett as pitmaster, Fat Boy's Bar-B-Que Ranch smokes up some of the tastiest meats in the River Region. They use a proprietary rub on their pork butts, ribs, chicken, beef, and turkey, which is smoked over hickory and mesquite woods. Order the pulled pork or rib plate with baked beans and coleslaw, or try a tater. It's a baked potato filled with smoked meat, butter, sour cream, cheese, and onion. Dine inside or outside on the porch overlooking Autauga Creek.

Finish the meal with a bowl of banana puddin' or a fried blackberry pie.

154 1st St., Prattville, 334-358-4227
fatboysbbqranch.com

TRY BIBIMBAP
AT SO GONG DONG TOFU & BBQ

Thanks to Hyundai Motor Manufacturing Alabama, the city of Montgomery boasts a large Korean population. To everyone's benefit, that means it's easy to find authentic Korean cuisine, including So Gong Dong Tofu & BBQ.

For those unfamiliar with Korean food, there's a learning curve for menu items and preparation styles, but the payoff is worth it. Start with Bibimbap, a simple rice dish served in a bowl or on a hot-stone plate. Select beef, pork, chicken, seafood, kimchi, or vegetables, which are segmented with vegetables and served over steamed rice with a fried egg. Mix it all together before eating.

Or choose Korean BBQ. Select your meat and sides and enjoy cooking it at your table. Hot pot is similar, though instead of a grill you cook meat and sides in a hot pot of your choice of broth. Other menu items include variations of tofu soup, noodles, and stir fry. Ask your server questions, and enjoy a unique dining experience.

1633 Eastern Blvd., 334-593-8400
sgdalabama.com

SIP HOT OR
COLD BREW COFFEE
AT LOCAL COFFEE SHOPS

In the River Region, it's easy to find a good cup of joe served in unique, community-minded spaces. Prevail Union MGM was one of the first businesses to open in the award-winning renovated Kress & Co. department store building. Caffeine fiends will love the Alabama Stinger with four shots of espresso. Plus, they offer cold brew and pour-over coffees. Hilltop Public House is leading the charge in rejuvenating the business district of the historic Cottage Hill neighborhood. They offer a full menu of espresso drinks along with beer, wine, cocktails, and food, courtesy of the Funky Forte Food Truck out back.

In downtown Prattville, find cozy spaces to relax inside West Main Coffeehouse and Creamery. Come for the coffee, stay for the ice cream, which comes from Old Dutch Creamery in Mobile. A new attraction to Wetumpka, Restoration Coffee House is in a restored old bank, and the coffee and tea lattes will restore your soul. Grab a cinnamon roll or scone, too.

Prevail Union MGM
39 Dexter Ave., Ste. 102, 334-416-8399
prevailcoffee.co

Hilltop Public House
3 Goldthwaite St., 334-239-7752
publichouse.hilltopmgm.com

West Main Coffeehouse and Creamery
167 W Main St., Prattville, 334-568-2100
facebook.com/westmaincoffeehouse

Restoration Coffee House
110 E Bridge St., Wetumpka
Search Facebook for "Restoration Coffee House"

CONQUER THE B.O.B.
AT 5 POINTS DELI & GRILL

Exploding onto Montgomery's food scene in 2018, 5 Points Deli & Grill filled the city's need for massive, flavorful burgers made with high-quality ingredients served in a casual atmosphere. Their burgers are tasty and award-winning. In its first year competing, 5 Points won the Max Burger Bash in 2019 and claimed second place when the event was revived in 2022.

One of their custom offerings, the big ole burger, or B.O.B., is a massive beef patty run through the garden and topped with provolone and cheddar cheeses, ham, roast beef, turkey, and homemade horseradish sauce. Ravenous patrons might also want to tackle the grilled cheese cheeseburger. Instead of buns, the burger is sandwiched between grilled cheese sandwiches. Traditionalists can stick with a regular hamburger or select an option from the sandwich menu such as the Mighty Casey, which features roast beef and grilled red onion and bell pepper on a marble rye.

1010 E Fairview Ave., 334-354-5309
5pointsdeliandgrill.com

SOOTHE YOUR SWEET TOOTH
AT JOZETTIE'S CUPCAKES

Cupcakes were all the rage in the 2010s. During the cupcake craze, Ida McCrary opened a cupcake shop using recipes she'd honed through decades of baking at home. While other bakeries closed down as the trend waned, Ida's baking skills and superb flavors proved her cupcakes were here to stay. In fact, they're so popular, she had to open a second bakery.

She called the place JoZettie's, a combination of her parents' names. Ida has created recipes for more than 35 flavors of cupcakes and cakes, including pecan pie, German white chocolate, peanut butter banana, and sweet potato. Select flavors are sold daily as jumbo cupcakes and cake slices. Special orders for whole cakes or cupcakes by the dozen must be made 48 hours in advance.

Original Location
1404 S Decatur St., 334-239-9289

JoZettie's #2 with a drive-through
2229 E South Blvd., 334-676-1598

jzcupcakes.wixsite.com/jozettiescupcakes

SWIRL A GLASS OF WINE
AT LAKE POINT VINEYARD & WINERY

When Daniel and Rita Lewis retired from the military, they tried their hand at growing fruit and making jellies. The Lewises succeeded and ended up with more muscadine grapes, berries, and tree fruits than they could use themselves, so they decided to try making wine. They've succeeded in that endeavor, too, opening Lake Point Vineyard & Winery on their 10 acres in Mathews in 2018. Their Honey Love, a mead, is a gold-medal winner, and their pear fruit wine is a bronze-medal winner.

Their facility includes a tasting room and covered patio for special events. On Saturdays and Sundays, they host wine tastings. Fridays are reserved for date nights with overflowing charcuterie boards and generous wine tastings. Along with the award winners, be sure to try Tonea's Chocolate Cherry port and the Desert Rose red. Reservations are required and can be made online.

674 Lake Point Dr., Mathews, 334-517-8334
lakepointvineyard.org

ORDER A FLIGHT
AT COMMON BOND BREWERS

Montgomery's craft brewery scene was completely dry until Common Bond Brewers came to town in 2018. The only production brewery in the River Region, Common Bond is a community favorite, especially on trivia night.

The taproom is quaint and comfortable with additional seating out front and in a back terrace. Order a flight of the brewery's Flagship Four: Rambler, Cream Stout, Zelda Blonde, and Single Bond IPA. The seasonal King Cole Holiday Barleywine is a December favorite, and at 11.6 percent alcohol by volume, it'll make you the hit of every holiday party. Grab a growler or crowler to take beer home.

If the small parking lot is full, there's ample street parking along Maxwell Boulevard. The entrance is slightly hidden. Follow the path past the picnic tables and enter through the side door behind Bibb Street Pizza Company. Common Bond doesn't sell food but bringing outside food is encouraged.

424 Bibb St., Ste. 150, 334-676-2287
commonbondbrewers.com

PULL A TAP
AT TOWER TAPROOM
AND LOWER LOUNGE

On any given day, you'll find nearly 60 beers on tap between the upstairs Tower Taproom and downstairs Lower Lounge. Both owned by Montgomery restaurateur Jake Kyser, the unique establishments are Alabama's first pour-it-yourself taprooms. Pick up a tap card, place it in the slot above a tap, and choose your brew. Patrons can even pour a sample size to taste-test before committing to a new selection.

Accessed on street level, exposed brick, high ceilings, and restaurant-style seating create a trendy yet casual atmosphere inside Tower Taproom. Menu item names are inspired by pop culture. Try the Phoebe Buffay, a vegetarian sandwich. Or man up and try the John Wayne, a burger featuring Duke's brand mayonnaise, cheddar cheese, bacon, and grilled onions.

Downstairs from street level, the Lower Lounge is more laid back with couches and cushioned chairs. It's a great spot to meet friends, and it can be rented for private events.

101-A Tallapoosa St., 334-356-5929
towertaproom.com; facebook.com/lowerloungemgm

TIP
Enjoy trivia nights on Tuesday at Tower Taproom. Register your trivia team online through the taproom's Facebook page.

GET THE BLUES
AT CAPITOL OYSTER BAR

Everything about Capitol Oyster Bar is cool, even the address: Shady Street. Owner Lewis Mashburn is usually on-site, behind the bar, shucking oysters and greeting guests. The menu is simple: appetizers, seafood, sandwiches, and sides. It's printed on paper that serves as place mats. Orders come out as they're ready. The covered patio doubles the place's seating and overlooks the Alabama River.

The real cool cats come out on Sundays to listen to the blues. Mashburn lines up the biggest and best names in the genre. There is a cover charge, but it's always worth it. Capitol Oyster Bar is open Wednesdays through Sundays, and they stop seating at 7 p.m. Plan accordingly. Arrive early, stay late, and make a ton of new friends.

617 Shady St., 334-239-8958
capitoloysterbar.com

TIP
The Montgomery Marina adjoins the bar, where boaters can dock or pick up a pontoon rental from Mashburn. He also owns the Montgomery Marina RV Resort beside the bar and rents two Airstream trailers. Contact Mashburn at 334-558-5202.

VEG OUT
AT EL REY BURRITO LOUNGE

El Rey Burrito Lounge is a quirky joint. Think upscale Tex-Mex mixed with hipster sensibilities, low-lighting, and a touch of slacker college-kid style. Transparency about sourcing US ingredients is important to the owners, evident by explanations on the menu. All the shrimp and fish are from Alabama or Mississippi while the goat cheese comes from Belle Chevre in Elkmont, Alabama, and the Duroc pork comes from Comfrey Farms in Minnesota.

For an appetizer, try Malditos. They're roasted jalapeños stuffed with cheese and pumpkin seeds. Chips and salsa fiends will agonize over selecting only three options from the robust salsa and dip menu. For entrées, the menu offers a variety of street tacos, enchilada, fajitas, burritos, and bowls, with vegetarian and vegan options. Try the cocktail of the week or enjoy a frozen margarita. The watermelon margarita is a perennial favorite.

1031 E Fairview Ave., 334-832-9688
burritolounge.wpengine.com

CHOOSE YOUR DINNER
AT DESTIN CONNECTION
SEAFOOD MARKET

There's something fishy going on at Destin Connection Seafood Market, and that's a good thing. This market offers the freshest seafood in the River Region with shipments of fish, shrimp, crab, and oysters arriving daily straight from the Gulf of Mexico. Make a selection, request special preparations, and take it home raw to prepare how you see fit.

When in season, it's impossible to beat the flavors of red snapper, yellowfin tuna, and amberjack. Buy crawfish for a low country boil. In January, run, don't walk, to Destin Connection to pick up a Rouses King Cake in celebration of Mardi Gras season.

Don't feel like cooking yourself? Destin Connection staff also serves sandwiches, po'boys, and seafood dinners. However, the market takes precedence, so patience is paramount. Place your order, and enjoy visiting with other patrons as you wait in the dining room.

3750 Norman Bridge Rd., 334-288-4272
facebook.com/destinconnectionseafood

BRING THE FAMILY
TO CHAPPY'S DELI

Remember when it was commonplace for kids to eat free at restaurants? That's still the case at Chappy's Deli, and that's because family is of utmost importance to owner David Barranco and director of operations Mike Castanza. These men, and their families, are staples within the Montgomery community, and when you enter their restaurants, they treat you like family, too.

At four locations across the River Region, Chappy's serves breakfast, lunch, and dinner. Blueberry pancakes are the star of the breakfast menu, although there's plenty of options including omelets and lighter fare. For lunch or dinner, get Dolly's best, named for David's mom. Or try the NY pastrami and Swiss paired with a cup of magic elixir also known as Mrs. Dolly's chicken and rice soup. End the meal with a free cup or cone of soft-serve ice cream.

1611 Perry Hill Rd., 334-279-7477

8141 Vaughn Rd., 334-279-1226

2055 E South Blvd. (inside Baptist South Hospital)
334-286-9200

585 Pinnacle Pl., Prattville, 334-290-3313

chappysdeli.com

BRUNCH
AT CAHAWBA HOUSE

At Cahawba House, staff wear "Bama Bona Fide Brunch" T-shirts, and it only takes one glance at the menu to know that statement is true. Brunch foods synonymous with the South are prominent.

Take the Southern biscuit. It's piled with bacon and topped with a fried green tomato and pimento cheese. The shrimp and grits brunch bowl features Conecuh sausage, which is the pride of Evergreen, Alabama. Never heard of tomato gravy? Then you must order Uncle D's biscuit and tomato gravy. Those who like a sweeter start to the day will enjoy chicken and waffles or the very berry toast.

Take the "br" out of brunch, and order from the more traditional meat-and-three lunch menu. Along with the usual nonalcoholic drink options, patrons can order beer, wine, or mimosas.

31 S Court St., 334-356-1877
cahawbahouse.com

TIP

On select nights, Cahawba House is home to the Ginger Daddies Late Night Pop-Up. It's a completely different menu with tacos, sliders, quesadillas, wing baskets, and catfish bites. Try it Mondays and Tuesdays from 6 p.m. to 11 p.m. or Fridays and Saturdays from 10 p.m. to 2 a.m.

DINE AT THE MARKET
AT THE JOHN E. HALL STORE

As Montgomery has grown eastward, the town of Pike Road has benefitted. Even with record development in the area, one Pike Road landmark, the John E. Hall Store, sat dilapidated. But finally, Grib Anderson decided to do something about it. He bought and renovated the place into a restaurant serving breakfast, lunch, and dinner Monday through Saturday with live music Thursday, Friday, and Saturday nights.

For breakfast, try a loaded link, egg, and cheese biscuit. At lunch, enjoy the meat-and-three offerings, or try a Conecuh dog made with regional favorite Conecuh sausage from the county of the same name. For dinner, an appetizer of boiled peanuts will make your Southern soul smile. Thursdays are wing nights, and rib eyes are grilled Fridays and Saturdays. When the weather cooperates, head outside and claim a picnic table for your entire crew.

15668 Vaughn Rd., Cecil, 334-300-2844
themarketatjohnhall.com

HANK WILLIAMS

1923   1953

MUSIC AND ENTERTAINMENT

TAME A SHREW
AT THE ALABAMA
SHAKESPEARE FESTIVAL

The Alabama Shakespeare Festival (ASF) offers a professional-level theater experience. Annually, timeless Shakespeare plays are performed, but there's plenty more to love. As Alabama's only member of the League of Resident Theatres, performers at ASF test their chops in Broadway classics, seasonal favorites, and cutting-edge, culturally relevant conceptions from regional playwrights.

Designated the State Theater of Alabama in 1977, ASF moved from Anniston to Montgomery in 1985. For decades, it's been the prime location for theatrical performances as well as a hub of theater education. Nearly 35,000 students experience a matinee theatrical performance thanks to SchoolFest, and hundreds more enjoy summer programming.

Buy season tickets to enjoy at least six plays hosted in the 792-seat Festival Stage, the 225-seat Octagon Stage, or on the outdoor stage.

1 Festival Dr., 334-271-5353
asf.net

SWAY TO THE TUNES
AT MONTGOMERY
PERFORMING ARTS CENTRE

The Montgomery Performing Arts Centre (MPAC) is a hub of downtown. The 1,800-seat auditorium draws household names as well as emerging artists from every musical genre under the sun. Rockers like Joe Bonamassa and Bret Michaels have graced the stage, and country stars from Tracy Lawrence to Clay Walker have strummed a note or two before adoring fans.

The MPAC draws more than musicians. It's the best place in the River Region to enjoy a night of laughs courtesy of comedians such as Leanne Morgan, Rodney Carrington, and Nate Bargatze. Plus, the venue features seasonal favorites like Cirque du Soleil and family-friendly entertainment extravaganzas with paloozas of cartoon characters and superheroes.

The attached deck offers plenty of parking along with metered and free street parking nearby. Make it an overnight stay by booking at the attached Renaissance Montgomery Hotel & Spa, and enjoy numerous restaurants and bars within walking distance.

201 Tallapoosa St., 334-481-5100
mpaconline.org

GAZE AT GRAZING WILDLIFE
IN THE MONTGOMERY ZOO

On the north side of town, the Montgomery Zoo transports visitors to exotic locations. Over 500 animals are divided into exhibits representing five continents. Begin with the macaws and squirrel monkeys of South America, and take a leisurely stroll around to the sloths and capybaras of the Australia exhibit. For North America, watch river otters from above—or below—water vantage points as they twirl and swirl in a day of play.

While walk-through exhibits bring close-up animal experiences, a ride on the Zoofari Skylift over the Africa and Asia exhibits provides safari-style views of giraffes, zebras, and hoofstock. Hop a ride on the McMonty Express, a train that travels the zoo perimeter. Grab lunch at the Overlook Cafe before sharing the wealth and feeding everyone's favorite long-necked mammal at the Giraffe Encounter. Don't forget to walk through the Mann Wildlife Learning Museum and grab a souvenir at the gift shop.

2301 Coliseum Pkwy., 334-625-4900
montgomeryzoo.com

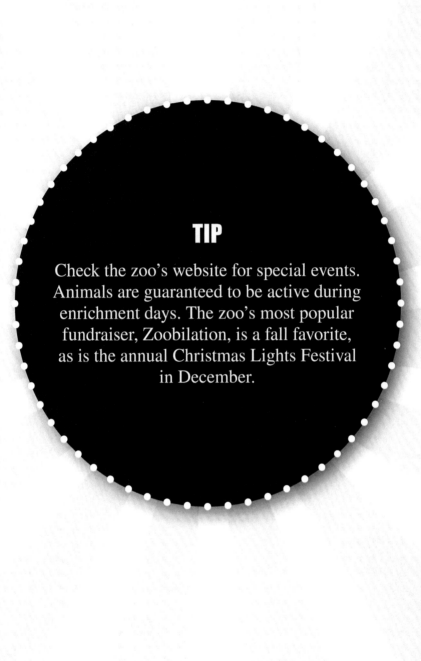

TIP

Check the zoo's website for special events. Animals are guaranteed to be active during enrichment days. The zoo's most popular fundraiser, Zoobilation, is a fall favorite, as is the annual Christmas Lights Festival in December.

TAP YOUR FEET TO THE SOUNDS
OF THE MONTGOMERY SYMPHONY ORCHESTRA

During a performance of the Montgomery Symphony Orchestra, soothing reverberations of violins and cellos mix with the lilting sounds of flutes and piccolos joining harmoniously with rattling timpani drums and breathy rhythms of clarinets and trumpets. With more than 50 expert, volunteer musicians, the orchestra covers all four orchestral sections: strings, brass, percussion, and woodwinds.

After hours of practice, the prowess of the Montgomery Symphony Orchestra is displayed for audiophiles and casual listeners alike during annual events, including a classical concert series. A Memorial Day in Montgomery is incomplete without attending the Pops Concert, a celebration of patriotic music held in sight of the Alabama State Capitol. In December, the symphony joins the Montgomery Chorale for the Holiday Pops Concert featuring Christmas carols and other sounds of the season.

507 Columbus St., 334-240-4004
montgomerysymphony.org

WATCH A CULT CLASSIC
AT THE CAPRI THEATRE

The Capri Theatre in Montgomery's historic Cloverdale neighborhood was an indie theater long before indie was cool. First opened as the Clover in 1941, the Capri has a cheeky history. It was shut down by the district attorney in 1982 for showing films of ill repute, to put it kindly. At that time, the Capri Community Film Society took charge of operating the run-down, one-screen theater. Since, it has maintained a quirky yet family-friendly reputation.

With viewings on Fridays through Mondays at 4 p.m. and 7 p.m., the Capri features multiple showings of independent films. One-night-only viewings are reserved for holiday favorites; true classics such as *Rear Window* or *Singin' in the Rain*; and cult classics such as *The Big Lebowski* and *Repo Man*. Located in a commercial strip with notable restaurants and bars, it's easy to enjoy a meal, movie, and nightcap all within walking distance.

1045 E Fairview Ave., 334-262-4858
capritheatre.org

SING ALONG WITH PERFORMERS
IN THE MONTGOMERY CHORALE

Nearly 100 voices flawlessly hitting all the right notes, whispering each pianissimo and building anticipation toward a boisterous fortissimo—that encapsulates each performance of the Montgomery Chorale. The volunteer choir has been around for more than 45 years. Now under the tutelage of Artistic Director James Seay, the group practices August through May with a handful of performances hosted in excellent concert venues and the most beautiful churches in Montgomery and the River Region.

Fall and spring concert themes cover the spectrum from Broadway to bluegrass. Come December, tradition dictates two performances—joining the Montgomery Symphony Orchestra for the Holiday Pops Concert and leading the Messiah Sing Along. Both are worthy seasonal favorites and are guaranteed to put you in the holiday spirit.

It's easy to purchase tickets online. Military and student discounts are available.

315 Clanton Ave., 334-314-9072
montgomerychorale.org

PACK A PICNIC
FOR THE CLOVERDALE-IDLEWILD
ASSOCIATION SPRING CONCERT SERIES

As the cold of winter fades, the fun ramps up in Montgomery's historic neighborhoods of Cloverdale and Idlewild. The joint neighborhood association hosts an eight-week Spring Concert Series at Cloverdale Bottom Park, where towering live oaks provide plenty of shade. Admission is free. It's smart to arrive early to find a good parking spot, and bring a picnic blanket and lawn chairs to claim your spot around the gazebo. During the concert, neighborly chatter and children's squeals mix with the musical stylings of favorite local and regional acts, creating a cordial, laid-back atmosphere.

The lineup is usually announced in March with concerts hosted in April and May. Acts cross genres from rock and roll and country to zydeco and blues. To be one of the first with the information, follow the Cloverdale-Idlewild Association on Facebook.

3124 Cloverdale Rd.
facebook.com/cloverdaleidlewild
montgomerycia.com

SUPPORT THE ARTS
AT LOCAL THEATERS

The River Region is ripe with theatrical talent. With the area's four major cities boasting their own volunteer theater companies, there are new performances debuting monthly. Plus, the Cloverdale Playhouse features musical acts and offers educational programming for children and adults covering topics such as lighting, improvisation, and stage makeup.

Each company has a heart for historic preservation as they've converted old buildings (including churches, a school, and a train depot) into intimate performance venues. Selected plays run the gamut from modern comedies to seasonal classics and timeless dramas. In a short time, it's possible to see a performance from an emerging, regional playwright as well as others written by Tony Award winners.

Cloverdale Playhouse
960 Cloverdale Rd., 334-262-1530
cloverdaleplayhouse.org

Wetumpka Depot Players
300 S Main St., Wetumpka, 334-868-1440
wetumpkadepot.com

Way Off Broadway Theatre
203 W 4th St., Prattville, 334-595-0854
facebook.com/prattvillewobt

Millbrook Community Players
5720 Main St., Millbrook, 334-782-7317
millbrooktheater.com

WALK THROUGH
THE FICTIONAL TOWN OF SPECTRE

At Jackson Lake Island, a herd of goats runs the show. But it wasn't that long ago that Tim Burton was here, calling all the shots for his film *Big Fish*. The island provided the perfect scenery for the fictional, idyllic town of Spectre. In the movie, it was a Utopia of sorts, and its citizens would force visitors to stay by stealing their shoes, tying the laces together, and throwing them over a high rope.

A city street of the fictional town remains. The buildings have taken on a ghostly feel. Plus, that high rope still exists, and it's always covered with shoes left by tourists. If you prefer to keep your shoes on your feet, simply enjoy taking photos of the dilapidated set or fish from the banks of the Alabama River. Be sure to make friends with the goats, though. They're the prized possessions of the island's owners.

Cypress Ln., Millbrook, 334-430-7963
facebook.com/jacksonlakeisland

FEED ANIMALS FROM ANTELOPE TO ZEBRAS
AT ALABAMA SAFARI PARK

If you took a catnap on a ride through Montgomery and woke up during a trip through the Alabama Safari Park, you'd have a hard time believing you were still in a Southern state. Llamas, emus, zebras, and plenty of hoofed and horned animals have free rein of the 350-acre park, where visitors experience up-close encounters with creatures we don't see every day.

For the drive-through safari, buy a couple feed buckets and feed animals through vehicle windows or from the safety of a truck bed with the tailgate up. Check out the free visitors guide to identify each of the more than 45 species on the grounds, including the park's numerous endangered species.

After the drive, walk through the bird aviary, meet a sloth or a kangaroo, watch lemurs play on their island, and feed giraffes at the tower.

1664 Venable Rd., Hope Hull, 334-288-2105
alabamasafaripark.com

RIDE
THE *HARRIOTT II* RIVERBOAT

Before interstates and tractor trailers, rivers and rails were the main forms of interstate commerce. Riverboats were a common sight, carrying passengers as well as raw materials and manufactured goods from one river town to another. Celebrate this industrial history with a ride on the *Harriott II* riverboat, docked at the riverfront in downtown Montgomery. Named in honor of the original *Harriott*, the first riverboat to haul cotton from Mobile to Montgomery in 1821, the *Harriott II* sailed its way to Montgomery in 2008.

Dinner cruises are offered on Fridays. Saturdays are reserved for the Getaway Cruise featuring lively entertainment and perfect sunset views. Blues musicians get in on the fun on Sundays. A full bar and concessions are available during each two-hour cruise. Tickets must be purchased 48 hours in advance.

255 Commerce St., 334-625-2100
funinmontgomery.com/riverboat/harriott-ii-riverboat

TIP
Pick up your tickets at least 30 minutes before your departure time. The ticket office is a small booth. You'll notice it near the tunnel entrance to Riverfront Park, adjacent to the parking lot in front of the Embassy Suites and located near the corner of Tallapoosa and Commerce Streets.

LISTEN FOR THE GHOST
OF HANK WILLIAMS

Legendary country music artist Hank Williams lived in Montgomery when he got his big break on WSFA radio, hosting and performing during a 15-minute program. He went on to rack up more than 35 top 10 singles, including "Your Cheatin' Heart," "Hey Good Lookin'," and "I'm So Lonesome I Could Cry."

Williams's life was tragically cut short. At age 29, he died of a heart attack brought on by addiction problems. More than 20,000 people attended his funeral at the Municipal Auditorium inside Montgomery's City Hall. His memory is kept alive with numerous tributes. Every year, thousands of people visit his grave at Oakwood Annex Cemetery. A statue of Williams welcomes pedestrians to Riverfront Park, and the Hank Williams Museum is a short, one-block walk from the statue. Visit each spot, and listen closely to hear if Hank's ghost starts singing "Your Cheatin' Heart" again.

Hank Williams Grave at Oakwood Annex Cemetery
1304 Upper Wetumpka Rd.

Hank Williams Statue at Riverfront Park
355 Commerce St.

Hank Williams Museum
118 Commerce St., 334-262-3600
thehankwilliamsmuseum.net

PRACTICE YOUR DRIVE AND JAM
AT RANGE 231 N

It's a driving range. No, it's a bar. No, it's a music venue. No, it's Range 231 N, where a combination of all three creates an exciting experience unlike any other in the River Region. When you drive up, you might be surprised to see trailers, but don't let that fool you. The real party is out back where there's green space, a concert stage, and driving ranges. To practice your golf swing, reserve space online. Or just show up and join the crowd to watch the big game of the weekend.

Range 231 N is a night owl's dream, especially in an area where most of the nightlife shuts down around midnight. They stay open till 2 a.m. on Thursdays and Saturdays, and on Friday nights, you can almost see the sunrise if you stay till closing time of 4 a.m. All three late nights feature live music acts, ranging from country and blues to rap and rock.

3250 Wetumpka Hwy., 334-523-1833
range231.com

FEEL THE SPIRIT OF THE HOLIDAYS
IN DOWNTOWN PRATTVILLE

In the River Region, no other town celebrates the holidays quite like Prattville. With the rustic old cotton gin mill, green spaces galore, and the picturesque Autauga Creek, downtown Prattville is more magical than any Hallmark movie.

February brings the Mardi Gras parade and winter market. Come July, the city is decked in red, white, and blue to celebrate Independence Day. The Prattville Pops kicks things off with a weekend patriotic concert. On the big day, the Lions Club hosts a barbecue sale and market at Pratt Park, and serious competitors try to stay afloat in the Cardboard Boat Races. Of course, fireworks close out the day.

In fall, downtown is transformed into a wonderland of hay bales, mums, and decorative pumpkins. The creekwalk is lined with neon, glowing decorations, and carved bourbon barrels. For Christmas, an entirely new set of decorations goes up, providing plenty of selfie-worthy backdrops. Local businesses decorate trees that are placed along the creekwalk, and children squeal with delight as they slip and slide at the outdoor skating rink.

facebook.com/prattvillealgov

SPORTS
AND RECREATION

KAYAK
WITH COOSA RIVER ADVENTURES

The iconic Bibb Graves Bridge in downtown Wetumpka spans the Coosa River. While it offers a beautiful view of the waterway, a kayak trip with Coosa River Adventures is the best option to experience all the river's sights and sounds.

Trips begin at Coosa River Adventures. Select a single or double sit-on-top kayak, and grab a life jacket. Listen intently to the safety presentation before boarding the bus for a ride to the put-in spot near Jordan Dam. It's a seven-mile trip back to Coosa River Adventures, and the river's speed is dependent on dam water releases. Halfway through, the small island of Moccasin Gap is a fun spot to picnic and wade in the water. It's bordered by rapids—Class II on river left and Class III on river right. Novices can skip the rapids by carrying their boat over the island.

415 Company St., Wetumpka, 334-514-0279
coosariveradventures.com

TIP

Prepare to be on the water for about four hours. Check the river flow rate by calling 800-LAKES11 and entering options for Jordan Dam on the Coosa River. For reference, 2,000 cubic feet per second (cfs) is slow, while 10,000 cfs is too fast for novice paddlers. Also, you will get wet. Bring a change of clothes, and protect your smartphone.

FLOAT DOWN
AUTAUGA CREEK CANOE TRAIL

Autauga Creek is the reason industrialist Daniel Pratt settled the area in the 1830s. Cutting behind the downtown commercial district, the creek remains a major draw as its shallow waters are perfect for wading or floating in your own canoe or kayak.

Enter the lower Autauga Creek trail behind City Hall. While this area is tree-free, it doesn't take long before the creek twists and turns into shadier spots, making it a wonderful, family-friendly respite from hot summer days. It takes two to three hours to reach Canoe Trail Park four miles downstream. This is the safest spot for novices to end their day of water fun. More experienced paddlers may enjoy floating another two miles to the Alabama River.

An important reminder: whenever enjoying water sports, always use the buddy system and wear a life jacket. On weekends, Prattville Paddle Sports rents kayaks and life jackets.

Prattville Paddle Sports
1200 Reuben Rd., Prattville, 334-354-2317
facebook.com/p/prattville-paddlesports-100063588522564

TIP
Creek access: behind Prattville City Hall at 101 W Main St., Prattville; public parking is available.

DRINK FROM
AN ARTESIAN WELL

Prattville is nicknamed the "Fountain City" thanks to spring-fed artesian wells around the city. Enjoy a cool, refreshing drink from these wells at three locations, which offer interesting perspectives on the industrial city.

A favorite spot for budding photographers, Heritage Park is located at the intersection of Main and Court Streets with views of the Autauga Creek dam and the old Pratt Cotton Gin Factory, which now houses high-end apartments. Here, a drinking fountain is fed by the well. A second artesian well is located on the other side of downtown behind the Prattaugan Museum.

The third, and perhaps most visited, is on Doster Road. Covered by a gazebo, benches invite thirsty visitors to sit a spell and enjoy the sounds of ever-flowing water along with views of the tree-covered Autauga Creek.

Heritage Park
183 W Main St., Prattville

Prattaugan Museum
102 E Main St., Prattville, 334-361-0961

Doster Road Artesian Well House
608 Doster Rd., Prattville

CHEER ON THE BISCUITS
AND TAKE HOME A HAT

It's rare to find a sports venue where the team mascot is also a menu item at concessions, but that's the case for Montgomery's minor league baseball team, the Biscuits. At Montgomery Riverwalk Stadium, biscuits are served with fried chicken smothered in Alaga syrup, a local favorite that's bottled at Whitfield Foods just down the street from the stadium. You have to stop by the "Biscuit Basket" for a souvenir featuring "Monty," a smiling buttermilk biscuit with a pat of butter for a tongue. All the gear matches the team's official colors of butter and blue.

As you root for the home team, don't be surprised if you see a train chugga-chugging behind left field. Half of the stadium is a renovated train station originally built in 1898. Make the most of your night at the ballfield by buying tickets on a MAX Fireworks night and hang around for the show.

200 Coosa St., 334-323-2255
milb.com/montgomery

PICK A BOUQUET
AT THE SUNFLOWER FIELD

Imagine millions of golden petals stretching high toward the sun as buzzing bees and delicate butterflies flit from one flower to another. It's a striking sight, sure to bring a smile to the face of even the grumpiest curmudgeon.

First planted by Todd and Kim Sheridan in 2016, the Sunflower Field in Autaugaville quickly became a favorite summertime attraction for locals and out-of-towners. Every July, the farm becomes the happiest spot in the state as millions of sunflowers bloom for about three weeks. Admission is free, but there is a fee to take flowers home. While they do accept credit cards, cash is preferred. Pets are not allowed, and there are no restrooms on-site. Remember to dress appropriately for Alabama summer weather, and bring your own clippers if you plan to take sunflowers home.

Located at the intersection of Highway 14 and County Road 33
For GPS, use either 101 Co. Rd. 33, Autaugaville,
or 3301 Hwy. 14 W, Autaugaville
thesunflowerfield.net or facebook.com/thesunflowerfield

STROLL THROUGH A BAMBOO FOREST
IN WILDERNESS PARK

From the gravel parking lot, the surroundings of Wilderness Park look like typical Alabama, but it only takes a few steps inside to feel like you've been transported 7,000 miles to the bamboo forests of China's Sichuan Province. Countless bamboo shoots tower toward the sky, standing up to 60 feet tall.

The 26-acre park was first planted with bamboo in the 1940s when it was privately owned. In the 1960s, the land was used for military training, as it resembled conditions troops might experience during the Vietnam War. It opened to the public as a park in the 1980s. The city of Prattville maintains a half-mile gravel trail cut through the bamboo and surrounding a small pond. Just off the trail, but still on park grounds, adventurers will find a small, babbling creek. The park is open daily from dawn until dusk, and it's a great spot to snap a selfie with an interesting backdrop.

800 Upper Kingston Rd., Prattville
alabamarecreationtrails.org/trail/wilderness-park-and-bamboo-forrest

TAILGATE WITH FOOTBALL FANS
FOR THE CAMELLIA BOWL

For over a decade, Montgomery has proudly hosted the Camellia Bowl in December. The college football bowl game traditionally pits a Sun Belt Conference team against another from the Mid-American Conference. Drawing an average of 20,000 spectators, the nail-biter matchup is often decided by less than a touchdown, a fitting and exciting end to the college football season.

Owned and operated by ESPN Events, the Camellia Bowl includes the full ESPN Zone experience for pregame tailgating. Hotels, restaurants, and historic attractions are within walking distance of the stadium at Cramton Bowl. A historic destination on its own, Cramton Bowl was the site of the first nighttime football game in the South played under lights. That was on September 23, 1927, when Cloverdale took on Pike Road High School before a crowd of 7,200.

1022 Madison Ave.
camelliabowl.com

DID YOU KNOW?

The Camellia Bowl is named in honor of Alabama's state flower. Camellias grow as evergreen shrubs and bloom in winter during dormancy. Camellia shrubs grace the grounds of the Alabama State Capitol, a few blocks from Cramton Bowl.

ROOT FOR THE HORNETS
AT AN ASU FOOTBALL GAME

Alabama State University (ASU) dates back to July 18, 1867, when nine freed slaves established the institution as Lincoln Normal School in the nearby town of Marion. Today, ASU is the River Region's largest university with a football team, and cheering alongside 26,500 fans inside Hornet Stadium is an exhilarating way to spend a Saturday—or Thursday.

The Hornets' Labor Day Classic is their home opener against a notable opponent, and the season wraps up on Thanksgiving Thursday with the Turkey Day Classic against rival Tuskegee University. Before every home game, fans line the streets near the stadium to cheer on the team during the Hornet Walk. The renowned Mighty Marching Hornets Band provides the soundtrack. In 2019, the band became the first from an HBCU (Historically Black College or University) to lead the Rose Bowl Parade.

ASU Stadium on Harris Way, 334-229-4551
bamastatesports.com/sports/football

GO WILD
AT THE ALABAMA NATURE CENTER

From Tadpole Pond and Cypress Grove Viewing Deck to the Tree Top Loop and Beech Bottom Crossing, hiking trails at the Alabama Nature Center offer terrific perspectives of wildlife in Alabama. But those five miles of trails lined with educational displays aren't the only attractions at the Alabama Nature Center.

In the state-of-the-art NaturePlex, Discovery Hall's wildlife and nature-based exhibits are always a hit. The 120-seat theater is a cool place to watch wildlife films, and the gift shop offers wildly fun souvenirs. The Lanark Pavilion hosts annual events, including the Critter Crawl 5K Trail Run and the state finals for the Alabama Wildlife Federation's Wild Game Cook-Off every August.

Admission is $5 per person, $20 maximum per family. Season passes are available. Plus, special rates are available for those interested in walking, birding, fishing, photography, or naturalist clubs.

3050 Lanark Rd., Millbrook, 334-285-4550
alabamawildlife.org/anc

HIKE OR BIKE
SWAYBACK BRIDGE TRAIL

Located along picturesque Lake Jordan, the trails at Swayback Bridge offer something for everyone and are especially beautiful during spring, when wild azaleas bloom, and fall, as leaves change colors.

The one-mile blue trail is perfect for a family outing. For a longer hike, try the 2.5-mile green trail or 4-mile yellow trail. Longer trails are popular among mountain bikers, and they're the only ways to see the title attraction. The 7-mile red trail or 11.2-mile black trail take hikers and bikers over the historic Swayback Bridge, which was built in 1931 and spans nearly 300 feet across Lake Jordan. Keep a keen eye out for markers. All the hikes twist and turn, and those not familiar with the terrain can easily end up on a different trail.

Back at the parking lot, enjoy a picnic on the covered picnic table. There's also a privacy fence area for changing clothes.

Jordan Dam Rd., Wetumpka, 334-567-9090

TIP

Jordan's Journey is another nearby trail, built in 2020. Off Jordan Dam Road, take the left fork for Boat Ramp Road and continue to its end. The area includes a fishing pier, bank fishing, bathrooms, and a boat ramp. Jordan's Journey offers three miles of trails and connects to Swayback Bridge trails.

PLAY THE DAY AWAY
AT LAGOON PARK

What's the best way to spend a weekend? Is it golf, tennis, hiking, or sharing a meal with friends and family? At city-owned Lagoon Park, you don't have to choose.

The park's 18-hole public golf course and driving range are the perfect place to teach Junior the ropes. Kids play free after 3 p.m. when accompanied by a paying adult. Book a round during spring to see azaleas and flowering trees along the course.

Next, take a swing at the batting cages or catch a softball game at one of six fields. Enjoy a match on the 17-court tennis complex, home to the annual Blue Gray National Tennis Classic for collegiate athletes. When hunger strikes, visit the golf course's bar and grill, or bring your own picnic. Finish the day with a hike and snap photos of birds wading in the adjacent creek and lagoon.

2855 Lagoon Park Dr.

Golf Course: 334-240-4050
playmontgomerygolf.com

Park: 334-625-3095
funinmontgomery.com

SMASH OPPONENTS IN PICKLEBALL
AT 17 SPRINGS

Pickleball is all the rage, and the best spot to enjoy this low-impact sport is at the River Region's newest athletic facility—the Fields at 17 Springs in Millbrook. The facility is so new, in fact, portions of the park along the city's busiest highway are still being developed, and it's all thanks to private and public partnerships.

In 2022, the first phase of the project opened with 12 pickleball courts and 12 tennis courts. Thanks to push-button lighting, die-hard pickleball fans can play daily, 7:30 a.m. to 9 p.m. However, a one-hour time limit is encouraged when others are waiting. For the most part, courts are first come, first served, but they can be reserved 24 hours in advance by emailing your name and phone number to 17springs@elmoreco.org.

2021 Alabama Hwy. 14, Millbrook
17springs.org

PASS TIME AND EAT ICE CREAM
AT BLUE RIBBON DAIRY

Once, Alabama boasted multiple family-run dairies in every county. Nowadays, it takes a rare breed to keep the family dairy running—someone like Michaela Sanders Wilson. The fourth generation of dairymen on her family's Elmore County farm, she's developed a different business model. Rather than delivering milk to customers, as in the days of old, she's inviting folks to the farm.

Around 3:30 p.m. daily for just $5 per person, you can watch them run about 30 cows through the milking parlor. After the milking, head to the next barn for a chance to bottle-feed a calf. In the farm market, you'll find whole milk and whole chocolate milk that's been pasteurized on the farm but not homogenized. Plus, 15 flavors of ice cream ensure every dairy-loving visitor can find a favorite.

5290 Chana Creek Rd., Tallassee, 334-207-5979
blueribbondairyal.com

TIP

Bring a cooler with you to the farm, because you'll want to take milk home. Because it's not homogenized, the cream rises to the top, so you should shake the jug before pouring. Available ice cream flavors change seasonally, but be sure to try the dark chocolate and the cookies and cream.

EXAMINE
THE WETUMPKA IMPACT CRATER

Astute visitors to Wetumpka may notice the topography is a little different. It's hilly with shimmering natural stones and rocks in the Coosa River that don't point the direction they should. Geologists have proven this was caused by a meteor strike around 85 million years ago, making the town one of about 30 confirmed impact craters in the United States.

Natives play this up with a mural and merchandise featuring a concerned T. rex staring down the meteor. But they also educate visitors on identifying the crater's characteristics. Head to the Wetumpka Impact Crater Commission website to download a self-guided tour, and drive to eight areas with educational signage about geological connections to the crater.

Most of the crater area is privately owned. For a more in-depth overview of the crater, the city offers tours in late February or early March.

wetumpkacraterart.org

DRIVE, CHIP, AND PUTT
AT CAPITOL HILL

The Robert Trent Jones Golf Trail provides challenging, professional-level golf with breathtaking backdrops at 11 sites across the state. The only one in the River Region—Capitol Hill in Prattville—includes the trail's most iconic spot on Hole No. 1 of the Judge course. The tee box sits atop a plateau as the fairway slopes drastically downward to a dramatic view of Gun Island Shute, part of the Alabama River. The stunning scenery is sure to ease the pain of chalking up a double bogey on the tough par 4 hole.

Capitol Hill's other courses include the Senator, a links-style course that often hosts LPGA tournaments, and the Legislator, where countless pine trees play defense against getting your ball on the greens. After a round, rest and relax at the Montgomery Marriott Prattville Hotel & Conference Center overlooking the Senator. Hotel grounds include a restaurant, tennis court, and outdoor pool.

2600 Constitution Ave., Prattville, 334-285-1114
rtjgolf.com

PEDAL THE ALABAMA RIVER
ON A SIP-N-CYCLE CRUISE

Start with water, add a pontoon boat equipped with booming surround sound plus countertop coolers stocked with libations, and you've got yourself a grand party aboard the Sip-n-Cycle Pedal Cruise. Moored on the Alabama River in Montgomery, it's the state's first and only cycleboat. Don't worry. The boat's motor still handles the majority of the work.

Choose either a private cruise or a mixer cruise where you'll be grouped with strangers. The master captain and first mate provide entertainment for up to 20 passengers during a 90-minute trip down the Alabama River. The modified-pontoon boat offers 12-cycle stations and is equipped with multicolored LED lighting for night cruises, which offer spectacular sunset views. In order to push off, seven passengers are required. Alcohol is allowed, but it's BYOB. Restroom facilities are available on board.

355 S Commerce St., 334-399-2387
sipncyclepedalcruise.com

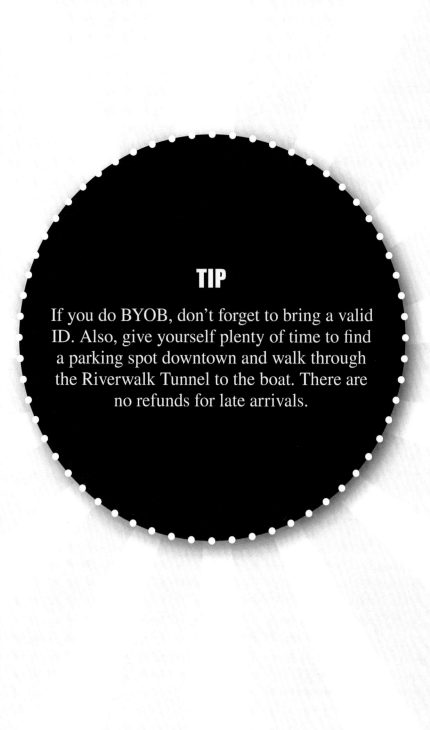

TIP

If you do BYOB, don't forget to bring a valid ID. Also, give yourself plenty of time to find a parking spot downtown and walk through the Riverwalk Tunnel to the boat. There are no refunds for late arrivals.

DON A COWBOY HAT
FOR THE SLE RODEO

Every March, Garrett Coliseum on the north side of Montgomery comes alive in a flurry of bucking bulls, boots, chaps, and more cowboy hats and pickup trucks than you can shake a stick at. With four NFR Playoff Series competitions over three days, the Southeastern Livestock Exposition (SLE) Rodeo was named one of the top 60 rodeos in the nation.

Watching professional riders, expert barrelmen, and entertaining rodeo clowns certainly makes for memorable moments, but there are plenty of additional draws within the rodeo's weeklong host of events. Youngsters can test their rodeo chops in a round of mutton bustin'. The Miracle Rodeo allows children with special needs to experience the fun of ropin' and ridin'. At the facility's Ed Teague Arena, youth demonstrate their skills in showmanship and raising champion livestock during the Jr. Livestock Show. The SLE Rodeo truly offers something for everyone, from country bumpkins to city slickers and everyone in between.

Garrett Coliseum
1555 Federal Dr., 334-265-1867
slerodeo.com

SET YOUR SIGHTS
ON LAKE MARTIN MACHINE GUN

Former US Marine David McGirt's second career was as a purchaser for gun collectors. Himself a collector, he got a bit tired of seeing historic guns placed in storage and decided to open a business that would share the stories of these firearms while giving people a chance to experience each piece's power. The result is Lake Martin Machine Gun.

Each shooting experience starts with a brief history on the guns in David's stock of weaponry, some dating as far back as pre–World War II. Then, it's time to learn safety protocols before heading to the shooting range to fire a historic weapon under the guidance of highly trained staff. There are tommy guns from the gangster days and M60s, which were issued to soldiers during the Vietnam War. Often, visitors gain a better appreciation for their veteran ancestors who had to use these weapons in the theater of war.

2520 Red Hill Rd., Eclectic, 888-660-6462
lakemartinmachinegun.com

HIT THE WAVES
AT MONTGOMERY WHITEWATER

After two and a half years of planning and development, Montgomery Whitewater opened in summer 2023. Arguably the city's largest undertaking in over a decade, this closed-water course marks the beginning of revitalization efforts in the area connecting Maxwell Air Force Base with downtown.

Outdoor enthusiasts will love whitewater rafting and kayaking through the Class IV waves on the 1,600-foot Competition Channel, while the Class II waves of the 2,200-foot Creek Channel are more appropriate for less-seasoned paddlers. A large flatwater pool is a peaceful spot for a morning session of stand-up paddleboarding.

Passes include equipment rental, one scheduled ride, and additional rides as long as there's space. Access to the on-site restaurant, retail outfitter store, and walking trails is free.

1100 Maxwell Blvd., 334-746-6530
montgomerywhitewater.com

CULTURE
AND HISTORY

JOURNEY TO THE RIVERS
AT FORT TOULOUSE–FORT JACKSON PARK

The Coosa and Tallapoosa Rivers converge to form the Alabama River in Wetumpka. With the historical importance of water access, this area was central to numerous civilizations. Native peoples left notable marks, including the Mississippian Mound dated to AD 1100.

The French, who lived alongside the local Creek tribe, built Fort Toulouse in 1717, but they lost the land in 1763 at the end of the French and Indian War. Famed naturalist William Bartram visited the abandoned fort a little over a decade later. After his victory at Horseshoe Bend, General Andrew Jackson arrived, and American forces built Fort Jackson, where he signed the treaty ending the Creek War.

Tourists can walk through replicas of Creek Indian houses and Fort Toulouse as well as a partial reconstruction of Fort Jackson. Well-managed trails lead past the Mississippian Mound and end at the best view of three rivers.

2521 W Fort Toulouse Rd., Wetumpka, 334-567-3002
fttoulousejackson.org

TIP

Visit in November during Frontier Days when the park is teeming with reenactors who bring the area's history to life. Check the park's website and Facebook page for more details, including additional living history events throughout the year.

WITNESS ENDURANCE
AT THE ROSA PARKS MUSEUM

On December 1, 1955, Rosa Parks was arrested on a bus in downtown Montgomery. The next day, leaders vowed to support a one-day bus boycott on December 5. Their stand against segregation on public buses would end up lasting 13 months.

Located on the corner of her arrest in downtown, the Rosa Parks Museum is the only such museum dedicated to her memory. Emotional multimedia representations will help you appreciate the courage and determination of Parks, the city's Black community, and other civil rights leaders. The exhibit ends with the US Supreme Court decision that struck down segregation on public buses and hints at the decades of work that remain in the fight for civil rights.

Major technology upgrades are planned for the museum starting in November 2023. Check the website to ensure exhibits you want to see are open.

252 Montgomery St.
Tour Reservations: 334-241-8661
Museum Information: 334-241-8615
troy.edu/student-life-resources/arts-culture/rosa-parks-museum

STEP INSIDE
THE ALABAMA GOVERNOR'S MANSION

While Alabama's governor works downtown at the Capitol, the top state official resides a few miles away in the Garden District. Originally built by the prominent Ligon family in 1907, the stately, neoclassical home with its grand staircase and ornate columns didn't become the Governor's Mansion until 1950. Governor-elect Gordon Persons was the first to call the house on Perry Street home, moving in before he took office. He set a precedent of regularly opening the home to the public.

Today, guided tours remain available. Buy a ticket, and visit during Holiday Candlelight Tours in December to see the mansion decked with decor. Otherwise, free guided tours are offered on Tuesdays and Thursdays, although advanced reservations are required. Groups must provide a list of attendees' first and last names for security purposes.

1142 S Perry St., 334-834-3022
governor.alabama.gov/governor/mansion/tours

STAND AMONG THE CONGREGATION
AT DEXTER AVENUE KING MEMORIAL BAPTIST CHURCH

Named, in part, for its 20th pastor, Dexter Avenue King Memorial Baptist Church was the first pastoral placement for a young Dr. Martin Luther King Jr. He made history here, leading the 1956 bus boycott from his office. From 1955 to 1960, King and his family lived nearby in the parsonage, which was bombed multiple times during the Civil Rights Movement.

The church was founded in 1877 in a slave trader's pen. A decade later, it hosted the first registration for students at the Normal School for Colored Students, which is now Alabama State University. The church's congregation still worships every Sunday at 10:30 a.m.

The parsonage is open Fridays and Saturdays from 10 a.m. to 4 p.m. for tours, but appointments can be made for other days or times. Appointments are necessary to tour the church.

Dexter Avenue King Memorial Baptist Church
454 Dexter Ave., 334-263-3970
dexterkingmemorial.org

Dexter Parsonage Museum
309 S Jackson St., 334-261-3270
civilrightstrail.com/attraction/dexter-parsonage-museum

DISCOVER
HISTORY PRESERVED
AT OLD ALABAMA TOWN

Downtown Montgomery has its fair share of modern buildings, but the six blocks of Old Alabama Town are dedicated to 19th-century structures. Here, the Landmarks Foundation of Montgomery has authentically restored 50 buildings and homes from the 1800s. While many were moved here, the antebellum Ordeman-Shaw House sits in its original location. On guided tours, you'll see the townhome, the original enslaved quarters and kitchen, laundry facilities, storage rooms, and stable.

Visitors can also tour an old-time grocery store, one-room schoolhouse, church, cotton gin, and print shop, among other buildings. Lucas Tavern, where the Marquis de Lafayette once stayed, is the oldest building in the collection. Buy tickets for self-guided tours offered Thursdays, Fridays, and Saturdays from 10 a.m. to 4 p.m. Guided tours of the Ordeman complex are only offered 11 a.m. to 1 p.m. on the same days.

301 Columbus St., 334-240-4500
landmarksfoundation.com

MEANDER THROUGH
THE MUSEUM OF ALABAMA

Archives can be a bore, and museums a yawn. But don't use those words to describe the Museum of Alabama, covering the second floor of the Alabama Department of Archives & History. Interactive multimedia and audiovisual recordings in the Alabama Voices exhibit engage visitors and make the learning process fun. This state-of-the-art exhibit opened in 2014 and houses more than 800 artifacts dating from 1700 to the present day. The audio recordings include words of former slaves and soldiers from the Civil War and two world wars.

Three other permanent exhibits tell the history of the Union's 22nd state. The Land of Alabama exhibition focuses on the state's unique and plentiful natural resources, and the Alabamians in the Great War exhibition powerfully portrays stories from world wars. The First Alabamians exhibit, which focuses on Native American history, is undergoing a renovation with 2026 as the expected reopening date.

624 Washington Ave., 334-242-4435
museum.alabama.gov

CONFRONT THE PAINFUL HISTORY
OF LYNCHINGS IN AMERICA

History is filled with acts fueled by pure hatred—acts we wish we didn't have to remember because we truly wish they'd never happened—and they remind us that humanity is capable of terrible atrocities. But in remembering these acts, we honor the guiltless victims, and hopefully, we learn to never allow repeat atrocities.

In 2018, the National Memorial for Peace and Justice opened in Montgomery. It's the nation's first memorial dedicated to more than 4,400 African American men, women, and children who were known to be killed by angry White mobs between 1877 and 1950. Eight hundred steel monuments hang from the rafters of the memorial, one for each county where a lynching occurred, inscribed with the names of the lynching victims.

It's a sobering experience on somber grounds. Give yourself time to reflect and soak in all the lessons the memorial teaches.

417 Caroline St., 334-386-9100
museumandmemorial.eji.org

TIP

A ticket to the National Memorial for Peace and Justice includes admission to the Legacy Museum. Shuttles run between the two regularly. Enjoy lunch at the museum from Pannie-George's Kitchen, an excellent, cafeteria-style meat-and-three restaurant.

FLAP YOUR WAY
THROUGH THE FITZGERALD MUSEUM

Montgomery native Zelda Sayre met F. Scott Fitzgerald in 1918 when he was stationed in town at Camp Sheridan. Married by 1920, the Fitzgeralds became the most iconic couple of the Roaring Twenties. Zelda is credited with creating the flapper fashion, and F. Scott captured the Jazz Age perfectly in his novel *The Great Gatsby*. By 1931, the literary couple resided in a home on Felder Avenue in Montgomery, where they both worked on novels.

That home is now the only museum dedicated to the Fitzgeralds. Exhibits display mementos from Zelda's childhood along with F. Scott's Princeton days before World War I and move through their fanciful courtship to their tumultuous marriage. Of note, handwritten letters between the two provide a unique glimpse into their lives. Special times to visit include April for the Fitz Spring Gala and October for a murder mystery event.

919 Felder Ave.
thefitzgeraldmuseum.org

TIP
Museum hours are limited to 10 a.m. to 3 p.m., Thursday through Sunday. If you want more access, book a stay at the museum through Airbnb. The Zelda Suite offers two bedrooms and one bathroom while the F. Scott Suite is one bedroom with one bathroom. Find links to the Airbnb listings at thefitzgeraldmuseum.org.

CONSIDER THE COUNTRY'S RACIAL HISTORY
AT THE LEGACY MUSEUM

The Declaration of Independence states "all men are created equal . . . they are endowed by their Creator with certain unalienable Rights, that among these are Life, Liberty and the pursuit of Happiness." However, our country's history is ripe with horrific examples of racial inequality.

The Legacy Museum brings to light the reality for Blacks in America. On the hour, tours begin with an immersive video of the transatlantic slave trade. Museum exhibits use the latest technology to walk visitors through details of the domestic slave trade, the Civil War, Reconstruction, segregation, lynchings, civil rights, and wrongful incarcerations.

Particularly powerful are the lists of Supreme Court decisions that codified racism, and a US map showing the year each state abolished laws against interracial marriages. It's a gut-wrenching experience that ends on a hopeful note in the bright Reflection Room honoring people who have worked to right racial injustices.

400 N Court St., 334-386-9100
museumandmemorial.eji.org

TIP

A ticket to the National Memorial for Peace and Justice includes admission to the Legacy Museum. Shuttles run between the two regularly. Enjoy lunch at the museum from Pannie-George's Kitchen, an excellent, cafeteria-style meat-and-three restaurant.

SEE
THE STATE CAPITOL

Pivotal moments in US history that every schoolchild learns about occurred at the Alabama State Capitol. Here, in the old Senate Chamber, delegates from Southern states created the Confederacy as they voted to secede from the Union. Before the start of the Civil War, Jefferson Davis was inaugurated president of the Confederacy on the steps outside. Over 100 years later in that exact spot, Rev. Martin Luther King Jr. addressed more than 25,000 people as the culmination of the Selma to Montgomery march for voting rights.

Built in 1851 on "Goat Hill," the capitol is an architectural delight. Former slave and African American master carpenter Horace King is responsible for the interior woodwork including, most likely, the impressive spiral staircase. Tours are free and feature an explanation of murals inside the rotunda along with visits to the old house, senate, and supreme court chambers.

600 Dexter Ave., 334-242-3935
ahc.alabama.gov/alabama-state-capitol.aspx

TIP

After a tour, stop at the Goat Hill Museum Store on the east side of the capitol building. The store stocks goods from local makers, a wide selection of local history books, and fun souvenirs.

ACKNOWLEDGE BRAVERY
AT THE FREEDOM RIDES MUSEUM

In 1961, groups of Black and White college students, called Freedom Riders, were determined to end the unfair and inhumane segregation of interstate travel in the South. They practiced peaceful protests, disregarding segregation signs on buses and in waiting rooms and bus stop restaurants as they traveled through the South.

On May 20, 1961, a group arrived at the Greyhound station in Montgomery. They were met with hostility. Three of the men, including future US Senator John Lewis of Georgia, were beaten unconscious. Following the attacks, President John F. Kennedy ordered 400 federal marshals to Montgomery. Freedom Rides resumed on May 24. Nearly six months later, Freedom Riders celebrated as the Interstate Commerce Commission adopted regulations against segregation.

That Greyhound station has been preserved and renovated to house the Freedom Rides Museum, which tells the story of the Freedom Riders and how their experiences steeled them for the following fight for voting rights.

210 S Court St., 334-414-8647
ahc.alabama.gov/properties/freedomrides/freedomrides.aspx

CELEBRATE CULTURAL TRADITIONS
DURING FOOD FESTIVALS

Jewish and Greek Orthodox represent a small percentage of Montgomery's population, but those who live and worship here graciously share their cultural traditions during annual food festivals.

Gyros, spanakopita, and baklava are menu favorites during the Montgomery Greek Festival, held in June. Time it right to tour the Byzantine-style church and enjoy traditional Greek music and dancing. If you crave more Greek food, also plan a visit for the church's annual Labor Day BBQ.

The Jewish congregation of Temple Beth Or hosts its food festival every February. Patrons line up for latkes and challah bread along with kugel, a sweet noodle casserole with eggs and raisins, and rugelach, a buttery pastry filled with pecans and cinnamon sugar. Meals can be taken to go or enjoyed in the outdoor courtyard. Plus, the rabbi offers short educational sessions about Jewish culture.

**Annunciation of the Theotokos
Greek Orthodox Church**
1721 Mt. Meigs Rd., 334-263-1366
mgmoc.com

Temple Beth Or Jewish Food Festival
2246 Narrow Lane Rd., 334-262-3314
templebethor.net

VIEW ALL THE MURALS
IN MONTGOMERY

Montgomery is a city with a complicated past but it also has potential for a bright, vibrant future, which is echoed in the more than 20 bright, vibrant murals across town.

Most of the murals are in or near downtown. Outside Prevail Coffee, there's the homage to activist Valda Harris Montgomery and her ancestors, which includes a Reconstruction-era state senator, business owners, and a Tuskegee Airman. *A Mighty Walk from Selma* at the corner of Lee and Montgomery Streets honors those who participated in the Selma to Montgomery March, and *Unforgettable* pays tribute to Montgomery native and music legend Nat King Cole.

In Midtown, a painted wall of flowers beckons folks to walk through the Cloverdale Community Gardens, and on the West Side, a mural by Winfred Hawkins, Nathaniel Allen, and Kevin King welcomes visitors.

Experience Montgomery's website provides a catalog of murals with background details and addresses.

experiencemontgomeryal.org/things-to-do/arts-culture/murals

STUDY PAINTINGS
AT THE KELLY

Wetumpka is definitely the River Region's artsiest town, and with the new Kelly Fitzpatrick Center for the Arts, it finally has a space worthy of the city's talents. The Kelly was incorporated in 2013 and recently moved into a nearly 5,000-square-foot space on the banks of the Coosa River. The breathtaking natural scenery is a perfect complement to the works of art from 66 artists scattered throughout the building.

The Kelly is part gallery and part museum. Works of member artists are promoted and sold, but it also houses permanent collections. Budding artists of all ages will enjoy a full range of educational workshops, art walks, receptions, and competitions.

Admission is free, and galleries are open to the public Tuesday through Saturday. Check the website for details on special events, including the Arti Gras Gala in spring and the Wetumpka Wildlife Arts Festival in fall.

301 Hill St., Wetumpka, 334-478-3366
thekelly.org

VISIT SITES
WITH CIVIL WAR SIGNIFICANCE

From its founding, the union of the United States was tenuous. In 1861, the Civil War tore those delicate connections asunder. Montgomery and surrounding areas played significant roles in the Civil War and Reconstruction.

After Jefferson Davis was sworn in as president of the Confederacy, he and his family lived, for a short time, in what's now known as the First White House of the Confederacy. The home was originally built in 1834 by William Sayre and is considered one of Montgomery's most historic residences. Self-guided tours are free.

Long after the war, Confederate veterans' war wounds grew worse with age. The Confederate Soldiers' Home in Marbury was the only facility in Alabama that cared for these men and their wives and widows from 1902 to 1939. The site is now home of the Confederate Memorial Park, which includes two cemeteries, a nature trail, and a museum.

Both sites are reminders of the blessing it is to live in a united country.

First White House of the Confederacy
644 Washington Ave., 334-242-1861
thefirstwhitehouse.com

Confederate Memorial Park
437 Co. Rd. 63, Marbury, 205-755-1990
ahc.alabama.gov/properties/confederate/confederate.aspx

PAY RESPECT TO US MILITARY
AT THE AIR FORCE ENLISTED HERITAGE HALL

What do Morgan Freeman, Jimmy Stewart, and Chuck Norris have in common? Aside from Hollywood fame, all three served in the US Air Force as enlisted airmen. Their pictures hang among hundreds of others on the Wall of Achievers inside the Air Force Enlisted Heritage Hall located on Maxwell Air Force Base Gunter Annex.

It's the only museum of its kind dedicated to the Air Force Enlisted Corps, which makes up 80 percent of the force. More than 3,000 artifacts tell the story of the force, from early days when hot air balloons provided aerial surveillance through World War II and the Korean War to current conflicts. Special exhibits honor the Air Force's eight enlisted Medal of Honor recipients.

Military and civilian visitors are welcome. The museum is located on an active military base, so calling ahead to schedule a tour is required.

550 McDonald St., 334-416-3202
facebook.com/airforceenlistedheritageresearchinstitute

TOUR
HYUNDAI MOTOR
MANUFACTURING ALABAMA

Automobile manufacturing is big business in Alabama. More than one million vehicles are manufactured annually in five plants, which includes Hyundai Motor Manufacturing Alabama (HMMA). Built in 2005 on the south side of Montgomery, HMMA employs more than 3,000 people who build more than 300,000 vehicles every year.

Free tours are offered Mondays, Wednesdays, and Fridays. They begin in the showroom where visitors experience all the bells and whistles of current model vehicles. After a multimedia presentation, tour-goers hop aboard the tram for a drive through the pristine facility where a guide highlights the latest in automotive manufacturing technology and enthusiastic employees welcome visitors. Tour reservations are required and can be made online up to six months in advance.

700 Hyundai Blvd., 334-387-8000
hmmausa.com/tours

ROPE AN AFTERNOON OF FUN
AT THE MOOSEUM

Rounding up a few hours of fun and education is simple at the Mooseum, run by the Alabama Cattlemen's Association. Occupying the ground floor of the association's downtown building, the Mooseum tells the history of the beef industry dating back to the 1400s along with the current life cycle of a beef animal, from pasture to plate.

Young'ns are guaranteed to enjoy the Cowboy Arena exhibit as they don cowboy hats, chaps, and other farm garb before saddling-up and riding a rodeo dummy. Inside Slim's Kitchen and at the grilling deck, even parents can learn a thing or two about proper beef handling, prep, and cooking. With a newfound respect for cattle and the farmers who raise them, be sure to snag a family photo with Dusty, a longhorn with permanent residence in the building's lobby.

201 S Bainbridge St., 334-265-1867
bamabeef.org/p/about/the-mooseum

APPRECIATE
THE ARTISTRY OF BALLET

Little compares to the exhilaration and emotion evoked as ballet dancers pirouette and *pas de chat* across a stage. Montgomery is lucky to boast of two renowned ballet groups.

First created in 1987, the Montgomery Ballet is the city's professional company with numerous company dancers as well as trainees. Varying spring and fall performances display the performers' talents, while the annual *Nutcracker* ballet in December is the company's most anticipated performance.

For girls and boys who dream of joining a professional company, Alabama Dance Theatre (ADT) is where they get their start. Founded by Montgomery legend Kitty Seale, ADT employs more than a dozen talented staff who train students in ballet, jazz, modern, hip-hop, Broadway, tap, and contemporary dance. Every June, dancers delight their audience during Stars on the Riverfront, while November's Mistletoe performances kick off the holiday season.

Montgomery Ballet
1044 E Fairview Ave., 334-409-0522
montgomeryballet.org

Alabama Dance Theatre
1018 Madison Ave., 334-625-2590
alabamadancetheatre.com

SPEND A DAY
AT THE MONTGOMERY
MUSEUM OF FINE ARTS

Trappist monk Thomas Merton once said, "Art enables us to find ourselves and lose ourselves at the same time." With a collection of more than 4,000 pieces, you can find and lose yourself over and over again at the Montgomery Museum of Fine Arts (MMFA). Paintings, glasswork, ceramics, photographs, prints, and textiles show the diversity of American artists from the 18th century till now.

Spend a few hours with the family in the massive ArtWorks Interactive Gallery. It's the perfect place to introduce children to aspects of art from painting and molding to puppetry and multimedia. A recent addition, the beautiful Caddell Sculpture Garden lures visitors outdoors to see permanent and temporary installations. Grab lunch from the Verde Cafe and enjoy on the outdoor patio while watching birds on the surrounding ponds.

Parking and admission are free, unless you prefer a guided tour. Call ahead for pricing and scheduling guided tours.

1 Museum Dr., 334-625-4333
mmfa.org

TIP

The MMFA is also home to the Montgomery Chamber Music Organization concert series. To enjoy one of the concerts, featuring acclaimed classical musicians, plan your trip to MMFA accordingly. Find the concert schedule and purchase tickets online at montgomery-chamber-music.org.

SHOPPING
AND FASHION

SEEK TREASURES
AT ANTIQUE MALLS AND FLEA MARKETS

The River Region has no shortage of flea markets and antique malls full of vendors plying their wares. A tour of the best will take you to each of the area's four largest cities.

Start in Montgomery with Eastbrook Flea Market and Antique Mall, which covers two and a half floors. With hundreds of booths, specialty vendors offer the city's largest collection of vintage clothing and music records. There's even a lounge near the register so shoppers can grab a moment's rest. At Amy's Antique & Flea Mall, nearly 100 vendors cover the store's 20,000 square feet.

Find more than 300 vendors in the massive Prattville Pickers, including Sweet Hart Coffee Co. and one of the area's largest selections of farmhouse-style furniture. In neighboring Elmore County, Millbrook's Main Street Vintage Market and Wetumpka Flea Market & Antiques offer high-quality goods, whether they're secondhand or handmade.

Eastbrook Flea Market and Antique Mall
425 Coliseum Blvd., 334-277-4027
eastbrookfleamarket.com

Amy's Antique & Flea Mall
849 N Eastern Blvd., 334-239-8086
amysantiquemallshop.com

Prattville Pickers
616 Hwy. 82 Bypass W, Prattville, 334-730-0266
shopprattvillepickers.com

Main Street Vintage Market
2910 Main St., Millbrook, 334-517-6943
facebook.com/MainStreetVintageMarketMillbrook

Wetumpka Flea Market & Antiques
5266 US Hwy. 231, Wetumpka, 334-567-2666
wetumpkafleamarket.com

BROWSE FOR A SOUTHERN SOUVENIR
AT EVERYTHING ALABAMA

Everything Alabama is true to its name. Every single item in the two-room store comes from an Alabama maker, and there's always something new to see—from Zkano socks and the South candles to pottery, jewelry, books, linens, and glassware. It's the only place in Prattville that stocks Alabama Clay, pottery figurines featuring unique swirls of white and terra-cotta. Continue into the back room to find T-shirts and edible items including Alabama peanuts, Hornsby Farms jams, and various mixes.

A queen of Southern hospitality, owner Tillie Jones personally curates store offerings. She happily offers customers her best suggestions for gifts and souvenirs and can answer questions about each featured maker. With a prime location along picturesque Autauga Creek in downtown Prattville, the shopping and scenery are delightful.

183 W Main St., Prattville, 334-301-0191
facebook.com/everythingalabama

PERUSE THE SHOP AND GREENHOUSES
OF SOUTHERN HOMES & GARDENS

Whether you're looking for timeless home goods, a new flowering shrub for the landscape, or a unique gift, chances are good you'll find it at Southern Homes & Gardens. It's easy to pass a few hours' time perusing the massive gift shop and two accompanying greenhouses.

In the store, expertly designed vignettes provide inspiration for the interior designer inside you. Interspersed among the wide selection of indoor and outdoor furniture, shoppers find serving ware, linens, artwork, jewelry, candles, and more.

While the greenhouses are always filled with seasonal indoor and outdoor plants, including trees, spring offerings are especially mesmerizing. Your eyes are treated to a repetitive rainbow of colors thanks to thousands of flowering annuals and perennials. Experts on staff can provide advice to budding gardeners, and they lead seasonal workshops. Come November, Southern Homes & Gardens offers the area's largest selection of beautiful, artificial Christmas trees. Shop seasonal sales to snag great deals.

8820 Vaughn Rd., 334-387-0440
southernhomesandgardens.com

GRAB A GIFT FOR EVERYONE
AT THE SHOPPES DOWNTOWN

Thanks to the first ever *Home Town Takeover* episode on HGTV, millions of viewers learned Wetu is local slang for the city of Wetumpka. Though Wetumpka is no stranger to big-city productions as it was a main shooting location for Tim Burton's 2003 film *Big Fish*, *Home Town Takeover* reintroduced the world to this artsy town. In 2021, when the cable network shot the series, a visiting HGTV star donned a Wetu trucker hat from the Shoppes Downtown, and it quickly became the store's best-selling item.

Borrowing from a business model often used in antique malls, the Shoppes Downtown is a conglomeration of vendor spaces, each carrying boutique items. There's plenty of clothing, shoes, and accessories for women and children, but men shouldn't feel left out. There's a smattering of masculine merchandise, too, including those Wetu hats. Plus, it's a great spot to find gifts for that special someone in your life.

211 Hill St., Wetumpka, 334-478-7056
theshoppesdowntown.com

TIP

Enjoy the newest offering at the Shoppes Downtown—a tea service. Owners have converted the back room into a shabby chic tea room that accommodates up to 16 guests. To book an event in the tea room, email thetearoomwetumpka@gmail.com.

SIT A SPELL
IN FINE FURNITURE BOUTIQUES

When you're ready to trade in the assemble-it-yourself side tables and that lumpy, uncomfortable couch, it's time to head to the area's fine furniture boutiques for specialty items that make a redesign truly refreshing.

Located inside the quaint, remodeled, red brick McLemore Plantation building, Quite the Pair is jam-packed with every furniture item needed to outfit a swanky home. Plus, they have all the accessories, including lamps of every shape and size, pillows, mirrors, artwork, rugs, and picture frames. Quite the Pair is open Tuesday through Friday.

Across the Alabama River in downtown Prattville, Featherwhite is the place to shop for trendy living room and dining room sets along with lighting and dinnerware. The shop also offers children's items and spa-worthy women's and bath items from pajamas and robes to candles and lotions.

Quite the Pair
15 Mitylene Park Ln., 334-356-8745
facebook.com/quitethepairboutique

Featherwhite
127 W Main St., Prattville, 334-491-0197
facebook.com/featherwhite.hom

BUY FROM LOCAL FARMERS AND MAKERS
AT THE MONTGOMERY CURB MARKET

From late spring through the end of summer, numerous farmers markets operate throughout the River Region, but the Montgomery Curb Market is the area's only one that's open year-round. A covered market, vendors and patrons are protected from the elements. Every Tuesday, Thursday, and Saturday, the market opens bright and early at 5:30 a.m. and closes at 2 p.m.

Along with the best fruits, vegetables, and meats the area's farmers have to offer, the Curb Market is a great place to find homemade desserts and breakfast pastries as well as handcrafted soaps and lotions. Among the seven rows of vendors, you'll find FDL Gourmet to Go, which won Bama's Best Tomato Dish contest with a tomato pie as well as Ukrainian baker Yuliya Childers of Wild Yeast Kitchen who bakes wildly popular breads.

Grab your favorite prepared items and enjoy them on the picnic tables on the north side of the market along Madison Avenue.

1004 Madison Ave., 334-263-6445
facebook.com/montgomerycurbmarket

SHOP TILL YOU DROP
IN OLD CLOVERDALE

One of two business districts in Old Cloverdale, the shops along Cloverdale Road provide a vast array of wares.

Stonehenge Gallery and Stonehenge Lighting offer custom framing and lighting along with works from local artists. Nestled between those two storefronts, there's the adorable gift shop Apropos. Head to the end of the block for fine foods, wines, and local brews at Filet & Vine. Across Graham Street, Buckelew's Clothing for Men is a great stop for the guys, while Welle Studio offers women's clothing and accessories.

Cross over Cloverdale Road for custom-made jewelry from Ex Voto Vintage. Back across the street, behind Filet & Vine, you'll find stunning candles and housewares inside the new Melissa Warnke Candles. Finish off the trip with a stop at Hob Nob. With a wide range of women's wear, it's the best spot to find a hat or fascinator for Kentucky Derby parties.

Stonehenge Inc.
401 Cloverdale Rd., 334-263-3190 for framing and art gallery
334-264-3190 for lighting
stonehengeinc.com

Apropos
411 Cloverdale Rd., 334-265-9100

Filet & Vine
431 Cloverdale Rd., 334-262-8463
filetandvine.com

Buckelew's Clothing for Men
501 Cloverdale Rd., Ste. 101, 334-279-5147
Search Facebook for "Buckelew's"

Welle Studio
501 Cloverdale Rd., Ste. 102, 334-239-8884
wearitwelle.com

Ex Voto Vintage
514 Cloverdale Rd., Ste. B1, 334-647-1080
exvotovintage.com

Melissa Warnke Candles
1620 Graham St., 334-625-1023
melissawarnke.com

Hob Nob
1603 S Decatur St., 334-263-2254
Search Facebook for "the New Hob Nob"

DESIGN YOUR PERFECT ROOM
AT CAPITOL'S ROSEMONT GARDENS

In operation since 1892, Capitol's Rosemont Gardens is entering a new era. While the florist shop closed in November 2023, the gift and home store has expanded to fill the old floral space, and it's now even more delightful to shop. The front room includes jewelry, candles, and items every beachgoer needs. The recent expansion has allowed Rosemont to increase its selection of lamps, furniture, and housewares as well as sections of kitchenwares and cookbooks, children's items, and gardening and outdoors. You're sure to find something for every room and outdoor space in your home.

In November, the decked halls of Rosemont's Christmas Open House are a must-see. The store is one of many locations where you can view the Christmas tree decorating skills of Rosemont's Jerry Thrash. He's responsible for creating breathtaking Christmas trees full of sparkly, glittering ornaments and decorations at the store, and his trees have been displayed at the State Capitol, the Governor's Mansion, and the Montgomery Zoo.

2210 Rosemont Pl., 334-834-7731
facebook.com/capitolsrosemontgardens

FIND LOCAL ART
AT SOUTHERN ART & MAKERS COLLECTIVE

A quirky teal and orange robot-esque statue welcomes visitors to the Southern Art & Makers Collective. It's foreshadowing of the unique and sometimes unconventional artwork that lies inside. The collective is breathing new life into the old green brick shopping center with a recent expansion to give its members more space.

More than 75 artists offer their works for sale in the collective. There's no one preferred medium. Paint, woodworking, paper crafts, pottery, jewelry, and mixed media are all on display. It's a great spot to find books from local authors as well as teas and honeys from local producers. Ample seating allows visitors to sit and chat with the artists, when they're on-site. Visit during special sales or on a day when artists offer classes to up the chances of meeting one of the collective's makers.

1228 Madison Ave., 334-303-2558
southernartmakers.com

TIP
The store is open Tuesday through Saturday. Park along Madison Avenue or down Edgar Street.

SNAG GIFTS AND FINE MEATS
IN PEPPERTREE

The Shoppes at Peppertree offers something for everyone: the budding sommelier, the foodie, the workout fanatic, the monogram queen, the fashionista, and the home designer.

Candle Cabin & Gifts carries the popular lines of Nora Fleming kitchenware and microwaveable Warmies, among a slew of candles, jewelry, clothing, and gifts for four-legged friends. Rooster and the Rose Boutique carries the latest women's fashions, featuring bright colors and available in sizes from small to 3X. Monogrammable merchandise is the name of the game at Embellish, which also stocks Scout bags and Happy Everything! by Laura Johnson home decor.

Montgomery Multisport is a happy place for the area's running community. Specializing in running shoes, the store also carries gear for working out and cycling. Finish a day of shopping by picking up a bottle of premium olive oil from the Vintage Olive, and selecting steaks and a bottle of wine from Pepper Tree Steaks N' Wine. Get the Pepper Tree "Black" seasoning to create a super flavorful steak.

Candle Cabin & Gifts
334-244-2201
facebook.com/candlecabin

Rooster and the Rose Boutique
334-593-2137
roosterandtherose.commentsold.com

Embellish
334-649-2022
preppymonogrammedgifts.com

Montgomery Multisport
334-356-7271
montgomerymultisport.com

The Vintage Olive
334-260-3700
thevintageolive.com

Pepper Tree Steaks N' Wines
334-271-6328
steaksnwine.com

Use the address 8135 Vaughn Rd.
to get to this shopping center.

EXPERIENCE FINER THINGS
IN THE MULBERRY SHOPPING DISTRICT

When you have to look your best or need to impress a hostess with a fine gift, head to the Mulberry Shopping District. There are often new shops to explore, but the area also boasts some of Montgomery's longest-run, locally owned businesses.

For decades, the Locker Room has been clothing men in the highest-quality frocks. Of course, that means suits and ties, but they offer sophisticated casualwear, too, with name-brand denim, collared shirts, shoes, and coats. Painted Pink has the ladies covered with more than 60 clothing lines for juniors and women. Find a dress for a special occasion or a casual outfit for tailgating. Al's Flowers and Gifts specializes in gorgeous floral arrangements, while the gift store stock is stunning and includes stationery, glassware, home decor, planters, and dinnerware. To round out the trip, schedule a painting experience with Barb's on Mulberry, or simply walk in to peruse the infant clothing, toys, and artwork.

The Locker Room
1717 Carter Hill Rd., 334-262-1788
tlrclothiers.com

Painted Pink
1941 Mulberry St., 334-834-2220
shoppaintedpink.com

Al's Flowers and Gifts
1926 Mulberry St., 334-265-1125
alsflowersmontgomery.com

Barb's on Mulberry
1923 Mulberry St., 334-544-0303
facebook.com/barbsonmulberry

READ LOCAL AUTHORS
AT THE NEWSOUTH BOOKSTORE

The NewSouth Bookstore has served as Montgomery's independent, community-minded bookstore for more than two decades. The owners take pride in supporting local and state authors by stocking their books and hosting special events. Sections you might not find in other bookstores include Alabama history, Black history, civil rights, and the ever-popular banned books area. While NewSouth specializes in indie publications, shoppers can find books from well-known authors, too.

After selling off their publishing company in 2022, owners Suzanne La Rosa and Randall Williams expanded the bookstore to include a large kids corner with children's books and plenty of space for young readers to sit as they flip through pages. That's not the last of their planned expansions, either, so bibliophiles should check back often to witness the store's growth.

105 S Court St., 334-834-3556
facebook.com/newsouthbookstore

SELECT A GOOD VINTAGE
AT TED THE WINE GUY & CO.

It can be overwhelming to select a good bottle of wine to serve during a special dinner or to take to a party as a hostess gift. Enter Ted, the Wine Guy, and his business partner, Scotty Scott. They're the owners of Ted the Wine Guy & Co., which offers the most comprehensive wine selection in the River Region. For truly special wines, head to their climate-controlled wine cellar.

Along with providing friendly, expert advice, the guys enjoy teaching customers to become more confident in their own wine knowledge. They host bimonthly tastings on the first and third Fridays, and they organize the annual Big Wine Bash where more than 100 varieties are offered for tasting. Become a Cellar Club member to receive discounts on every purchase along with bigger savings on rotating club member selections.

3062 Zelda Rd., 334-395-9911
tedthewineguy.com

FROLIC AMONG THE FROCKS
AT LOCAL BOUTIQUES

With bright colors, affordable prices, and selections sure to fit any body style, you'll feel like frolicking from the fitting room to the register at these local boutiques.

In Prattville, Harvey & Hill specializes in women's clothing and accessories, including a large selection of game day items for University of Alabama and Auburn University fans. Just down the road, the Southern Refinery's owner started her boutique with hand-painted signs. Now, she's expanded to offer a full range of women's clothing and gifts.

On the way out of Montgomery toward Wetumpka, the 9,000-square-foot Vivian O'Nay is the River Region's largest boutique. Rocking chairs on the front porch are a clue to the Southern hospitality customers experience inside as they browse women's clothing, bath and body products, shoes, accessories, giftware, home goods, and children's items. Bring the fellas along, too. In the Man Cave, there's comfy seating, a big-screen TV, and free food and drink.

Harvey & Hill
696A Commerce Ct., Prattville, 334-300-7283
harveyandhill.com

The Southern Refinery Boutique
1336 S Memorial Dr., Prattville, 334-730-1995
thesouthernrefinery.com

Vivian O'Nay
3500 Wetumpka Hwy., 334-290-5268
vivianonay.com

EXPLORE
MOSLEY'S STORE

Passersby may get a kick out of the marquee sign that reads "Hot dogs, wine, chainsaws, jewelry, all in one stop," but Mosley's Store is a community favorite for a reason. It truly does have everything you might need all in one place. Like the country stores of days gone by, Mosley's is a gas station, mechanic, gift shop, restaurant, and hardware store all wrapped into a must-see attraction.

Located just south of Montgomery, Mosley's has been a staple in the area for more than 45 years. With packed shelves, the store offers even more than the sign claims, with clothing, holiday decor, children's items, Auburn and Alabama team gear, and accessories. Fuel up, fill your belly, and don't forget to buy a T-shirt featuring the words of their regionally famous sign.

13718 US Hwy. 31, Hope Hull, 334-281-9573
Search Facebook for "Mosley's Store"

TIP

To enjoy a drive through rural Montgomery County and check a few items off your list, sandwich a visit to Mosley's Store in between stops at the Alabama Safari Park in Hope Hull and a meal at Red's Little School House in Grady.

PARTICIPATE IN ARTISTRY
AT JULIANNE HANSEN
FINE ART & POTTERY

Pottery was not Julianne Hansen's first career, but it's become her passion. With a decade of experience under her belt, Julianne's fine creations are a delightful display to stroll through in her storefront along Main Street in historic downtown Prattville. Heart-shaped bowls, cookware, mugs, and statues fill the shelves. An artist of many mediums, Julianne's paintings adorn the walls. During holidays, shoppers can find whimsical pieces including pumpkins, witches, ghosts, Christmas trees, angels, and santa figurines.

Julianne often demonstrates her work at the pottery wheel inside, but you can do more than just watch. She also offers pottery lessons. Call to book a class for a private group. Public offerings are listed on her website.

173 W Main St., Prattville, 334-301-0336
juliannehansen.com

TIP

In the weeks leading up to Memorial Day, Julianne displays handmade poppies on the downtown green, just steps away from her store. Anyone can sponsor a poppy in honor of military men and women who sacrificed their lives for our freedom. It's a beautiful and touching tribute.

TASTE-TEST TREATS
AT TUCKER PECAN COMPANY

Pecans are Alabama's official state nut, and Tucker Pecan Company is the best spot in the River Region to taste-test confections where pecans are the star. Some are simple, such as pecans dipped in chocolate—dark, milk, and white. Others take considerably more work, including pecan logs, pecan pies, and chocolate pecan fudge.

Tucker Pecan Company's nutty creations are shipped to customers across the country, and all their offerings are available from the gift shop located in their headquarters in downtown Montgomery. It's a fun place to shop for spunky accessories, clothing, kitchenwares, and holiday decor. Hometown pride merchandise is available for the city of Montgomery and those who live at Lake Martin. Grab your favorite items and candies, and they'll create a gift basket for you.

In November and December, Tucker Pecan Company opens 9 a.m. to 1 p.m. on Saturdays. Others times of the year, they're only open Monday through Friday from 8 a.m. to 4 p.m.

350 N McDonough St., 334-262-4470
tuckerpecan.com

STRETCH YOUR LEGS
AT SWEETCREEK FARM MARKET

In business, location is everything. Located south of Montgomery and visible from a major US highway that leads to the Florida coastline, SweetCreek Farm Market has quickly become a favorite pit stop for beachgoers. Regional farmers deliver fresh fruits and vegetables daily. Coolers and freezers stay stocked with farm-to-table eggs, meat, and milk along with homemade desserts and casseroles. Plus, there's plenty of canned goods and gift items scattered throughout the market.

Before shopping, enjoy a salad or sandwich from the café. Walk around the grounds to meet the resident peacocks, chickens, and goats. Let the kids run off some energy in the play area. Then, head back to the market to make final purchases, and swing through the café again to pick up an ice cream cone and a few swamp cookies for the road.

85 Meriwether Rd., Pike Road, 334-280-3276
sweetcreekfarmmarket.com

SUGGESTED
ITINERARIES

DOWNTOWN

Discover History Preserved at Old Alabama Town, 88

Taste-Test Treats at Tucker Pecan Company, 132

Fill a Plate at Davis Cafe, 10

Meander through the Museum of Alabama, 89

Find Local Art at Southern Art & Makers Collective, 121

Delight at the Collision of Cultures at D'Road Café, 14

Sway to the Tunes at Montgomery Performing Arts Centre, 39

Listen for the Ghost of Hank Williams, 51

Buy from Local Farmers and Makers at the Montgomery Curb Market, 117

Brunch at Cahawba House, 34

MIDTOWN

Hang Out at Midtown Pizza Kitchen, 15

Design Your Perfect Room at Capitol's Rosemont Gardens, 120

Select a Good Vintage at Ted the Wine Guy & Co., 127

EAST MONTGOMERY/PIKE ROAD

Take on Taco Tuesday at Sol Restaurante Mexicano & Taqueria, 11

Stretch Your Legs at SweetCreek Farm Market, 133

• •

CLOVERDALE

RURAL LIFE

CIVIL RIGHTS

FAMILY FRIENDLY

GIRLS' WEEKEND/BACHELORETTE PARTY

• •

Nosh at a Friday-Owned Restaurant, 8

Shop Till You Drop in Old Cloverdale, 118

Brunch at Cahawba House, 34

Pedal the Alabama River on a Sip-n-Cycle Cruise, 74

Share Small Plates at Taste, 6

Flap Your Way through the Fitzgerald Museum, 91

GUYS' WEEKEND/BACHELOR PARTY

Kayak with Coosa River Adventures, 56

Get the Blues at Capitol Oyster Bar, 29

Stuff Your Face at Fat Boy's Bar-B-Que Ranch, 20

Conquer the B.O.B. at 5 Points Deli & Grill, 24

Order a Flight at Common Bond Brewers, 27

Drive, Chip, and Putt at Capitol Hill, 73

Set Your Sights on Lake Martin Machine Gun, 77

Hit the Waves at Montgomery Whitewater, 78

Practice Your Drive and Jam at Range 231 N, 52

48 HOURS IN PRATTVILLE

Float down Autauga Creek Canoe Trail, 57

Drink from an Artesian Well, 58

Sample Every Dish at Uncle Mick's Cajun Market & Café, 3

Browse for a Southern Souvenir at Everything Alabama, 112

Feel the Spirit of the Holidays in Downtown Prattville, 53

Stuff Your Face at Fat Boy's Bar-B-Que Ranch, 20

ACTIVITIES
BY SEASON

SPRING

Peruse the Shop and Greenhouses of Southern Homes & Gardens, 113

Don a Cowboy Hat for the SLE Rodeo, 76

Participate in Artistry at Julianne Hansen Fine Art & Pottery, 131

Flap Your Way through the Fitzgerald Museum, 91

Pack a Picnic for the Cloverdale-Idlewild Association Spring Concert Series, 45

Hike or Bike Swayback Bridge Trail, 66

Play the Day Away at Lagoon Park, 68

Study Paintings at the Kelly, 99

SUMMER

Tap Your Feet to the Sounds of the Montgomery Symphony Orchestra, 42

Buy from Local Farmers and Makers at the Montgomery Curb Market, 117

Float down Autauga Creek Canoe Trail, 57

Pick a Bouquet at the Sunflower Field, 60

Hit the Waves at Montgomery Whitewater, 78

Celebrate Cultural Traditions during Food Festivals, 96

Appreciate the Artistry of Ballet, 105

Feel the Spirit of the Holidays in Downtown Prattville, 53

Go Wild at the Alabama Nature Center, 65

Cheer On the Biscuits and Take Home a Hat, 59

• •

FALL

WINTER

• •

INDEX